KEEPER OF KEYS
THE WITNESS TREE CHRONICLES, BOOK 2

HALEY WALDEN

MORAVON PRESS

Keeper of Keys is an epic fantasy set in a medieval-reminiscent world. Learn more about its themes and tropes at authorhaleywalden.com.

ISBN: 978-1-7353431-4-3
(Paperback Edition)

Published by Moravon Press

Developmental Editor: Allison Martin
Copy Editor: Jolene Perry

Cover Illustration: Saint Jupiter
instagram.com/saintjupit3rgr4phic

Additional Illustrations: Danaye Shiplett
danaye.com

Map Artist: Cartographybird Maps
cartographybird.com

Author Headshot by Jessica McIntosh Photography
jessicamcintosh.net

BOOKS BY HALEY WALDEN

The Witness Tree Chronicles
    1- *Defender of Histories*
    1.5- *Ballad of Stallions*
    2- *Keeper of Keys*
    3- *Vow of Magic*
    4- *Sovereign of Clans* (Coming Soon)

Tales of Rodhlan
    1- *Ruse of Heirs*

~

Stay up-to-date on bookish news and happenings:
www.authorhaleywalden.com

Follow the author on Instagram, TikTok, and Facebook:
@authorhaleywalden

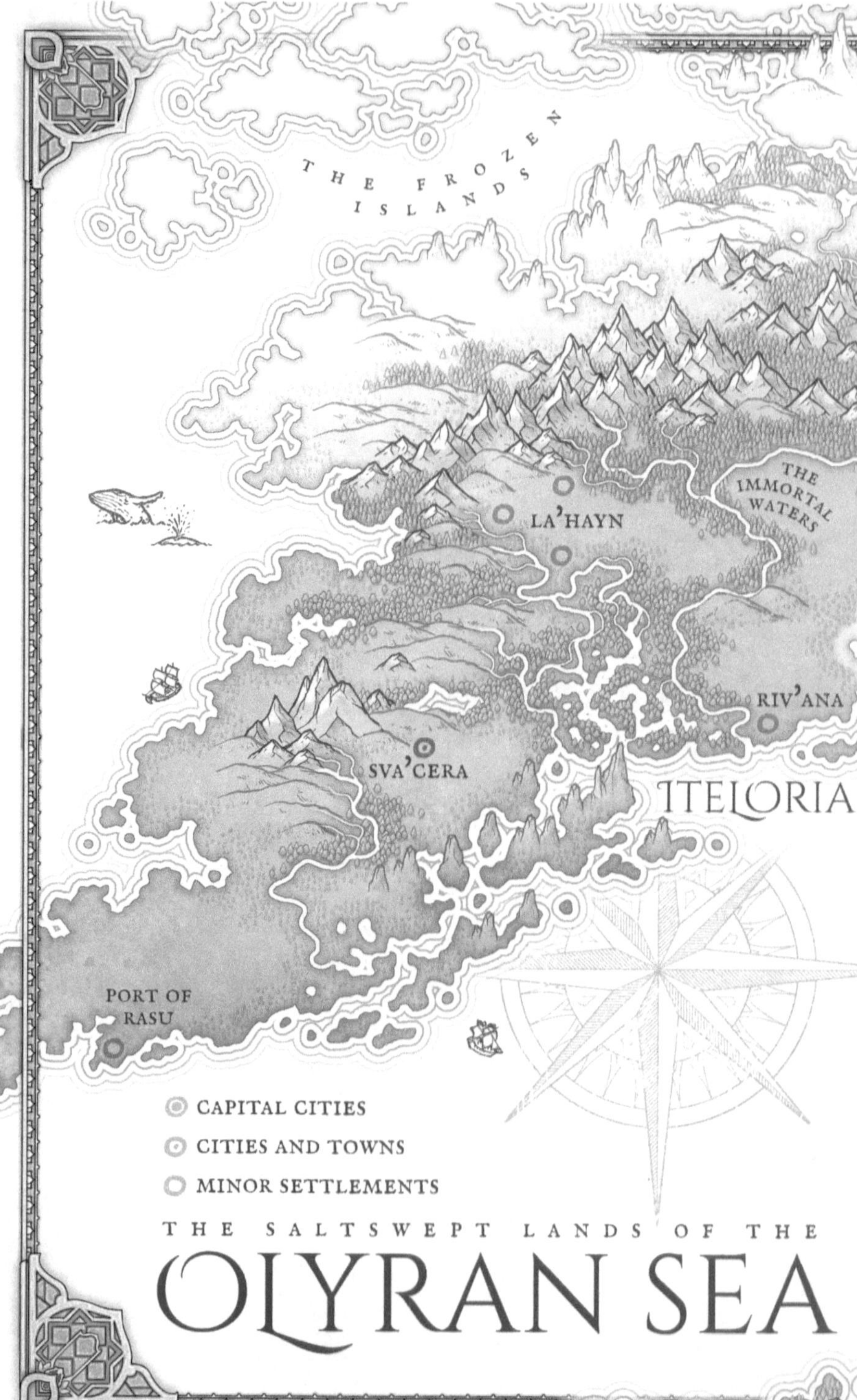

THE FROZEN ISLANDS
THE IMMORTAL WATERS
LA'HAYN
RIV'ANA
SVA'CERA
ITELORIA
PORT OF RASU
CAPITAL CITIES
CITIES AND TOWNS
MINOR SETTLEMENTS
THE SALTSWEPT LANDS OF THE
OLYRAN SEA

AI'KARA
RIKU'S BORDERLANDS
KINGDOM OF SOV'IS
FREYAN'S WILDS
LORJYN
PORT OF NAJYN
THE STRAIT OF ULAN
WHERE THE MUDFLATS EMERGE
RODHLAN
IATHIUM
FORTRESS HALGEIR
CATACOMBS
MORAVON RIVER
THE MEADOWLANDS
VA'HESK
ÉNNA CARAVAN
ACTON'S COVE
RODHLAN RIDGE

For Allie & Jo.
Thank you for believing in my stories. This series would not be what it is without you.

To Elisabeth, Tim, Christa, & Mika:
Thank you for cheering me on and immersing yourselves in this story through what has proven to be the strangest year of our collective existence.

CHAPTER I
AIDRYN TARLACH

Rodhlan Ridge

A cyclone of leaves filled the clearing in the mountain forest, spinning out until it died in the wake of Silira Mór's magic. Lira was gone now, stolen away in a burst of her grandmother's power, as Aidryn had intended. Still, the ache of her absence sent a pang of longing through him.

Protecting Lira had always been the plan—the one Aidryn Tarlach had hatched with Rí Eremon, supreme ruler of Iathium, and their mentor, Lord Irem Énna, over two long years.

No matter what, keep Lira safe. Protect her.

Defend her. That's what Eremon had begged him to do.

As if he'd needed to ask.

The smell of the rich, moist earth overwhelmed Aidryn's senses as he took in the scene around him. Leaves settled on the bodies of Clan Mór's archers, who lay where they had fallen after Lira brought her wrath down upon them—in the form of thousands of leaves fashioned into razor-sharp daggers. Blood soaked through the scattered leaves, sticking them fast to the fallen young men and women as it clotted.

Lira was creative, that was certain—and brutal when the occasion called for it. Aidryn regretted that he hadn't had the time to enjoy her impressive display.

Instead, he had given up his own freedom so she could escape.

Now, Aidryn stood before Artagán Mór, who had inexplicably survived his cousin's maelstrom and was aiming a poisoned arrow at Aidryn's heart.

He kept his breathing shallow and steady, careful not to move as he met the young archer's gaze. Artagán didn't appear to be much older than Aidryn's twenty-one years. His auburn hair peeked from beneath his green hood, hazel eyes enraged.

"What did you do with them?" Artagán demanded, tightening the bowstring.

"Nothing. They used magic to escape," Aidryn answered, keeping his voice as level as he could.

Aila Mór stepped in then, her movements graceful and smooth as she reached for Artagán's arrow, pressing it downward. She looked surprisingly unruffled, with her glossy black hair, pristine skin, and dark green gown.

"He's worthless to us dead, archer," Aila said, her voice soothing.

"Lira said we couldn't kill him," Caitir, Aidryn's half-sister, cut in.

"Well, she isn't here now to protect him with that ring, is she?" Aila snapped.

Caitir flinched and took a step back, wrapping her arms around her middle, golden hair falling over her shoulders in torrents. Blood still seeped from a jagged gash one of Lira's dagger-leaves had slashed across her cheek. It had stained the white fabric of her wedding gown; an offense that would surely warrant punishment later.

Aila and Caitir had carried the Clan Tarlach moniker until yesterday, when they had both married Lira's uncle Gerallt, Master of Clan Mór and Artagán's father. Taking more than one wife was frowned upon in Rodhlan, though Aidryn recalled sparse accounts of it in the histories. Perhaps Aila had brought the idea from her childhood in Iteloria, where it wasn't unusual for a man to have more than one wife—or a woman to have more than one husband.

He wasn't sure what made him sicker: the fact that Aila had pawned Caitir off on Gerallt, or that Caitir had gone along with it. The three had drummed up a wild delusion that they could somehow take the throne in Iathium, the sprawling city-state on the other side of Rodhlan. Judging by the scowl on Caitir's face as she stood between her mother and new husband, she wasn't entirely thrilled with the situation.

Rí Eremon, the supreme ruler, was dead. His mother, Raní Macha, had assumed Eremon's full political power. At best, Aila's idea was a sloppy effort to gain power when she'd failed to get Caitir married to Eremon.

After Caitir's attack on Macha, the Raní had executed Aidryn's father, and the two women had fled the city. Aila must have decided that marrying a clan leader was the next best thing to the throne.

Artagán knitted his brow, forcing the arrow back into position and glaring at Aila.

"Ellwyn's missing," he said, his gaze flicking around the clearing. "That wasn't part of the agreement. So if you can tell me where to find my sister, then I won't harm your precious son."

"Stepson—and certainly not precious," Aidryn cut in. A flash of curiosity crossed the archer's face as he added, "Looks like we share an unfortunate commonality, Artagán."

"Silence," Aila barked.

"Six of my archers are dead, Mistress," Artagán said, though he lowered his bow, his gaze trained on Aidryn. "You owe me this, at least."

"There is something I need from him first," Aila answered, black hair ruffling in the breeze. "Back away while I perform the rite. Then, you may do what you want with him."

The archer's glare darkened—an expression that made Aidryn's stomach churn. "Then let's get on with it."

Aidryn took a step back, and Aila's attention snapped back to him. She lifted a hand, curved her fingers into a claw, then twisted her wrist. Aidryn's feet swept out from under him, and he landed hard on his back. His head hit a large root, and for a moment, he saw stars. The heady scent of moist earth filled his nostrils, and he nearly gagged at the intensity of it.

What would Aila do to Lira if she were still here? Aidryn was profoundly grateful she wasn't.

Aila moved to his side, crouching next to him. The sun was suddenly too bright, the colors too vivid as he dragged himself onto his hands and knees.

"Now, my child," she murmured, catching his chin in her grip, "when you were a boy, you agreed to give up your power to save Caitir's life."

"Yes, and you deceived me," Aidryn managed to say through the pounding pain in his head. He jerked away from her touch and rocked back onto his knees. "She was never ill."

"You agreed to give up your power," Aila repeated, "but you lied."

Caitir joined her then, looking down on Aidryn. For a moment, he thought he spotted a flash of conflict in her expression, but it vanished as quickly as it had appeared.

"You promised me that power," Caitir said, "but you kept some for yourself. Didn't you care? I could have died."

"You can't die from having too little magic," Aidryn answered, "but you *could* die from too much. Don't you know that's what killed Eremon?"

Caitir's lips parted in surprise, and Aila's attention snapped to her golden-haired daughter. Aidryn took the opportunity to stand, managing to back away several steps before Artagán aimed the arrow at him again.

"You're lying," his sister said, though her voice wavered.

Aidryn raised his hands, palms outward. "If you hadn't gotten yourselves barred from the festival the night before, you would have seen it yourself."

Caitir turned to her mother. "You said Lira was responsible for Eremon's death," she said accusingly.

"So you would believe your lying brother over me?" Aila said. "Remember who gave you everything, Caitir—certainly not *him*."

The girl's expression hardened as Gerallt joined them, hand on the pommel of his sword. "Are you going to get the key, or do you plan to waste the day bickering?"

Realization swept over Aidryn. Of course they would try to use him—his magic as Clan Tarlach's Key Keeper—to gain access to some otherwise impenetrable place. Aside from the clan's inborn metalworking magic, Aidryn had been born with an extra measure as its anointed. And he'd managed to keep that fact hidden from his family for most of his life.

"What makes you think I'll give you anything?" Aidryn asked, leveling with Gerallt's angry stare.

"If you do not cooperate willingly," Aila said, black lighting crackling between her fingertips, "then we will take what we need by force."

Behind Aidryn, the lush mountain forest gave way to moss-covered cliffs that tumbled and rolled into Acton's Cove far below. His heart pounded as he surveyed the four people who surrounded him—all equipped with corrupt, dark magic. Getting past them was his only hope of escape, and he wasn't keen on being shot with that arrow of Artagán's.

Still, Lira was alive and safe—and truly, Aidryn had nothing left to lose. He weighed his options, his breathing suddenly ragged, and knew what he had to do.

Fear clawed at Aidryn, but he made his decision, then met Aila's dark stare. "Then I dare you to try."

CHAPTER 2

SILIRA MÓR

Eastern Rodhlan
7 Days Later

A rough wind from the eastern seashore tore across the sandy plain, whipping dust into the air and scattering it across Silira Mór's skin before she could cover her face. She held her breath and squeezed her eyes shut until the wind died down, blinking furiously to clear the grains from her eyes. Her skin was coated with a layer of sand and grime from days traveling on foot, her dark curls a tangled mess.

The sandy grasslands near Rodhlan's coast were unforgiving as the cool spring days yielded to dry summer heat. Though Lira walked for miles, her body grew increasingly restless, her pent-up magic begging for release. Her fingers tingled, as though pricked by thousands of tiny pins. As the days wore on, the sensation became ever-present—as insistent for relief as her power.

A week had passed since Lira abandoned her grandmother, Skelly, in the meadowlands. Guilt gnawed at her for leaving the elderly woman alone and vulnerable, but Nevala and Mytr, her friends from Va'hesk—the remnant of Clan Tarlach—had managed to get word that Skelly was safe with Lord Irem Énna on the western coast.

Skelly had been desperately ill with an overflow of magic when she'd given so much of it to Lira. Now, Lira was Rodhlan's Witness Tree—the living vessel of history for her people. And this mass of power, which should have been gifted to Clan Mór's people generations ago, was a force whose demands multiplied in intensity and ferocity from one day to the next. She desperately needed to disperse it, but with Aila, Gerallt, and Caitir now leading Clan Mór toward certain disaster, there was no one Lira could trust with the power.

After her grandmother's haphazard gifting, and knowing she was weakened, Lira used a *turas* traveling spell to escape Rodhlan Ridge, the sprawling mountain range to the south. But the *turas* had somehow wounded her magic, and she'd spent two weeks at Va'hesk recovering before setting out in search of Aidryn.

If only she had fled Iathium with him the first time he asked.

Come with me—let me protect you. Please.

Lira gasped softly at the memory of Aidryn's touch—the way he'd cradled her face in his hands as he begged her to leave everything behind. But then, he'd been the one to give everything up by trading his freedom for hers. He'd allowed himself to be captured on the Ridge so Lira could escape, and she had mourned every moment since.

She shook her head and began to move again. If she continued becoming distracted enough to stop in her tracks like this, she would never make any progress toward the mountains.

"Should've never sent Tudur back to Va'hesk," she sighed. The borrowed pony might have been good for something, had he not been enchanted to take her directly to Clan Beran's fortress. That was the last place she needed to go.

If she'd thought to ask Aidryn's magic for a way to direct the pony herself, Lira would not have spent the past week on foot. But the Binding spell that tied her to him was so new, she had not considered all the ways it could be used.

Before they'd parted ways, Skelly described the Binding as the outdated marriage rituals the clans still performed. Lira once thought Bindings were only symbolic, and certainly not magical. But everything she'd believed before had been turned on its head, so why not this, too?

Lira's ears perked at the sound of horses' hooves in the distance. Sentries were known to patrol the wilderness from time to time, but she hadn't happened upon anyone yet.

Quickly, she skimmed the area around her, then sank into the high grasses, pulling the hood of her rough-woven gown over her head. There had been no one nearby, though the wind continued to carry the sound in her direction. That meant there was time to hide herself well.

She pressed her fingers into the dry, sandy ground and whispered for willows and brush to spring up around her. The feeling of magic rushing from her hands into the earth was nothing short of bliss. Lira sighed and lay on her side, reveling in the feeling of the earth against her cheek, and closed her eyes. The tingling in her fingers had ceased, and she relaxed into the sudden absence of discomfort.

It wasn't clear how much time had passed when she was awakened by the sound of those distant horses approaching her willow grove. She pulled her hood completely over her face and hid her hands beneath the rough brown fabric, praying it would camouflage her, and listened. By the clink and scrape of metal on metal, the riders were certainly sentries.

"D'you remember that grove of trees being here last week?" one of them asked, his voice tinny inside his helmet. Lira held her breath and lay perfectly still.

"I don't know," the other answered, halting her horse. "Didn't that girl from the archive have some sort of tree magic?"

"*Witness Tree*, Gara, not tree magic," the first replied,

bringing his horse alongside Gara. "It's something to do with Clan Mór, anyway. This is Tarlach territory."

Lira held her breath, sure they would dismount and come to investigate. She wouldn't be able to escape if they found her.

"Well, I don't know what any of it means," Gara said, swearing. "Nobody told me I was signing up to deal with some sort of wild magic—I thought it was a myth!"

"So did everyone else." The other sentry's horse stomped nervously, and he clicked his tongue at it. "Come on, let's go."

Lira remained where she was, tense and silent, until they were far out of earshot. When she was satisfied they'd gone, she began to gather her meager belongings: her satchel, which contained scrolls of Clan Tarlach's folklore for Aidryn, as well as a few stale pieces of bread she'd managed to save.

Her stomach growled, so she opened her bag and broke off a piece of bread, chewing it slowly to soften it. Waving her fingers over the grass, she conjured a bush laden with ripe blueberries and picked a handful, savoring them in the late-morning warmth. The plant wouldn't survive for long on this terrain, but at least she could feed herself as she traveled.

Suddenly, the tingling sensation returned to her hands, then rushed up her arms and into her chest and shoulders. As the feeling reached her throat, she began to panic—but then, her eyesight failed and a witnessing took hold.

"If something happens to me, see to it that the key is sealed inside my vault." Rí Corlan extends a hand to his son, Eremon—a boy of about twelve. He gives an ornate, golden key to Eremon, and the boy cradles it gingerly.

Eremon looks up at Corlan then, his angular, gray eyes wide, silken black hair sliding across his forehead. "Nothing is going to happen, Father," he said, his fingers tightening around the key.

"Still, we must think ahead." Corlan rests a warm hand on Eremon's shoulder. "Iuchair unlocks a power no human should ever access. Keep it safe, and above all, keep it out of your mother's hands. When I am gone, it goes with me."

The boy nods once, searching his father's face before he asks, "Why should no one access the power?"

Corlan inclines his head slightly, a shadow crossing his expression. "That knowledge dies with me."

Lira lost herself to the same memory, which played out in her mind over and over.

It was midday before the witnessing finally released her. She blinked rapidly as her eyes adjusted to the sunlight again, willing her vision back into focus. Sweat beaded on her forehead and ran into her eyes, stinging where the rough sand had ground into them earlier.

Eremon. The young ruler had been responsible for the Binding spell that connected Lira to Aidryn now. But it was Eremon who'd captured her heart first. Lira had allowed herself to dream of ruling at his side, working with him to bring the true histories back to Rodhlan. To help him give magic back to the people.

Her eyelids drifted shut again. *Even in death, you demand my attention,* she thought wearily.

Eremon's own dark magic had killed him—along with a mix of power his forefathers had stolen from the clans over many generations. After his death, Lira was stripped of her Defender of Histories title—the archival post in the city she'd worked so hard to achieve. Now, there was no way she could do anything of significance to help the city she loved so much.

Suddenly, she was keenly aware of the ring she still wore. In Eremon's mind, his ring made Lira heir to the throne. But there was no way Iathium's council or its citizens would honor that whim. She was better off fading into Rodhlan's wilderness and vanishing for good. And she would do that, once she rescued Aidryn.

With a pang, she thought of the ring's other purposes: protective magic, for one. It was said to shield its wearer from the dangerous dark power that had killed Eremon—the same magic his mother, Raní Macha, wielded. But Eremon had also managed to thread the Binding spell through the ring.

It was a strange sort of contingency plan, for Eremon to marry Lira off to her dearest friend. Apparently, Eremon had created the spell to respond to mutual love in the event of his death, which was all the more puzzling. Lira and Aidryn had been friends since childhood, but she struggled to grasp how and when they could have possibly fallen in love.

Still, her magic found its power in truth. Even if she couldn't understand it, she felt the truth of the Binding down to her very bones.

DAYS PASSED, one blurring into another.

Memories and dreams mingled and haunted her sleeping and her waking; what little rest she did get was fitful. Whenever she dozed, she saw Aidryn's face, twisted with grief and pain—and her abdomen clenched excruciatingly until she could rouse herself enough to stop the images from coming.

The visions didn't manifest through her memory magic as a witnessing might. Instead, she feared the Binding spell might be giving her glimpses of Aidryn's suffering in the moment. Most of the time, she avoided sleep until she was too exhausted to fight it.

I'm coming for you, Aidryn. I promise.

During the day, fragmented visions of the past began to cloud her sight, forcing her to stop wherever she was until they passed. Most of the memories she witnessed were fleeting, but one of them visited her over and over.

Each time Lira witnessed Eremon's memory, she keenly felt his disappointment. And each time she lay eyes on him through the witnessing, she relived the brutal death he'd suffered at the hands of his own power.

Lira ran her fingers over Eremon's ring. They'd loved one

another once, but it already felt as though a lifetime had passed.

As Lira traveled, it wasn't long before she found herself locked in an increasingly exhausted haze, unable to progress more than a few miles at a time. On the fourth day, she started planting trees as soon as her fingers began to tingle. Then she'd curl up beneath them, pull up her hood, and try to blend in with the dry terrain as she gritted her teeth through each vision.

Sometimes, she could interpret fragments of the memories. But the histories she'd spent her life learning bore little resemblance to the events she witnessed. Just like at Va'hesk, she could not follow a full memory from start to finish. She saw the continent's histories in short bursts that left nothing resolved— and reconciled with nothing she'd known before.

Then, alongside her power, her own memories began to fracture. At first, she noticed herself struggling to recall the names of important places. Then, people. Their faces flashed before her, but she could not recall their names, nor exactly what they meant to her.

There had been a married couple back at the tent village who helped her. They'd given her a pony, which she had sent away. Now, she wished she had not.

There had been a gray-eyed young man with raven hair and a kind voice, whose face made her stomach twist with grief.

There had been a dear friend who sacrificed himself for her freedom, whose touch she craved and whose presence she desperately missed.

Sometimes, she wished she had someone who could answer her questions. Someone who could help her piece together these broken memories.

She thought she'd had someone like that, once. But she could not recall his name, any more than she could remember her own.

ANOTHER WEEK PASSED. Lira's sight faded almost completely, replaced by a nearly endless cacophony of unfamiliar voices and sounds. During her few remaining lucid moments, she sat beneath her trees, staring out across the vast continent.

One warm afternoon, she rested in the soft meadow grass, her visions gone for the moment. When her palms met the ground, a grove of willows burst up around her, shading her from the scorching sun. The grass was tall, cool, and lush, and she lay down in it, looking up at the clouds that drifted lazily across the sky.

From somewhere in the memories that flooded her sleeping and her waking, she heard a lilting song. It was a song that had come to her more than once during these long weeks. And though she didn't recognize the language—though she hadn't lifted her voice in song since she was a small child—she lay beneath the clouds and began to sing.

> 'Tis setting sun, and light of day
> Gives way to all things dusk and dim.
> The sentries 'round us draw their blades,
> And fight we now for life and limb.
>
> But you, my friend, meet fatal blade
> And drift off to some distant shore.
> And if I could, I would yet trade
> My freedom for a moment more.
>
> To feel the wind blow through your mane
> And watch the sunset as we go.
> To fly breakneck across the plain
> Abandon thoughts of war and woe.

I care not, tho' the foe may win.
My sorrow rises like the tide.
I only wish for you, my friend,
To take me out on one last ride.

Tho' sword may clash with axe and shield
And armies raise their battle cry,
Still I would race across the field
To guide you home, where love abides.

Her own voice felt foreign to her as she formed the notes and syllables—softly at first, then more confidently as she grew comfortable. Lying on her back, watching the wind ripple through the willows' leaves, she sang the song to herself over and over. It was as soothing as a lullaby, as sweet as the wildflowers that grew abundantly across the rolling meadowlands.

An hour passed, or maybe two; yet, Lira never tired of the song. And somehow, singing it kept her tethered to the day and the land that spread out before her. So she continued, afraid to be silent—terrified of the nightmares that would overtake her once again. Gradually, her voice grew weak, wavering more each time she began to sing, until it became a whisper.

Tears began to spill from the corners of her eyes, rolling down the sides of her face once she realized that her voice wouldn't hold any longer. The dread that had been gnawing at her insides roared to life, and she nearly gave in to it...

Until a massive shadow blocked out the sun overhead and something soft, velvety, and warm came to rest on her forehead.

CHAPTER 3
LIRA

Lira held her breath and lay perfectly still as a great beast stood over her and nuzzled her face. Blinking tears away, she placed her hands on the soft muzzle and met the kind eyes of a large gray stallion with a white mane. It huffed, stomping impatiently above her.

And then, everything came surging back. The broken visions that filled her mind suddenly dissipated, and Lira gasped, taking in the stallion's familiar face. This wasn't just any horse—it was Fannin. *Aidryn's* horse. And the song she'd been singing was a ballad of Clan Tarlach. She remembered transcribing the words herself not long ago, though she wasn't sure where she'd gotten the melody.

Her heart swelled with affection as Fannin gently nipped her fingertips.

"I thought I'd never see you again," Lira rasped, looking up at the stallion from where she rested.

Fannin nosed her palm once, then dipped his head, nudging her side as if to say, *Get up.*

Lira pushed herself to sitting, then got shakily to her feet.

She had not been lucid enough to realize how weak she'd become, despite being able to feed herself during her travels.

Draping her arms around Fannin's neck, she rested her head on his coarse mane. They'd lost him in the mountains weeks ago when Lira, Skelly, and Aidryn tried to escape. The saddle and bridle he'd worn on their journey into the mountains were long gone. His matted coat smelled of mud and mildew, as though he'd been on his own for weeks, just like she had.

He'd clearly escaped from the paddock at Rodhlan Ridge, where they'd kept him when they sought asylum. But it wasn't like Fannin to leave Aidryn's side. Even if the horse and his master were separated, surely Fannin would have felt Aidryn's presence and remained near him.

Still, it wasn't outside the realm of possibility for Fannin to look for his master. After all, he was descended from a line of magical horses brought from Iteloria—the continent across the sea—centuries ago. Famed for their intelligence and magical speed, Clan Tarlach tamed Itelorian stallions, bred them with the wild horses that roamed Rodhlan's meadowlands in times past, and named them the Seanlaoch.

Aidryn had kept two of those stallions at his family's home in Iathium—Fannin and Edan. Lira had caught glimpses of Edan from time to time, but Aidryn favored Fannin. It was the horse he'd called to help Lira escape the city after Eremon's death... and the other disasters that had followed.

Insistently, Fannin nudged her, then nipped at the leather pouch that hung at her side. Inside the pouch, she carried a handful of trinkets and small heirlooms Skelly had given her as a child.

It was a wonder she'd managed to keep up with anything she had been carrying at all.

"I don't have any treats, boy," she said, stroking Fannin's forelock.

The horse nipped the pouch, then gave it a hard tug.

Suddenly, the bag took on a weight that Lira hadn't noticed before.

"All right." Lira patted the bag, then opened it and reached inside.

Her eyes widened; the pouch was filled with keys.

"By Nami," she whispered, withdrawing her hand and opening the bag's mouth wider. "What's this?"

She closed her fingers over a handful of keys, taking them from the pouch and examining them in her palm. Then, she looked into the bag again, flabbergasted. There were keys of all shapes and sizes; silver, iron, bronze, and gold. Some were gilded; others, plain. A few of the keys were uncut, as if their bearer had been saving them for... she wasn't sure what.

Fannin studied Lira's every move closely, as if waiting for her to understand.

As long as you stay alive, he lives, Skelly had said. *And perhaps, in the meantime, you can learn to harbor his magic for him.*

Her heart began to race as she dropped the keys back into her pouch and pulled the drawstring tight. The magical connection between Lira and Aidryn was said to allow each to harbor—even wield—the other's power. Even if she hadn't believed in the Binding before, there was no other explanation for why his magic had suddenly transferred to her.

She had not reached for his Key Keeper power—had not realized she was calling Fannin. Yet, it seemed to have come to her unbidden, as though sentient. As though it had been seeking *her*.

Lira shook off the thought. Perhaps the song had summoned Aidryn's power. She had seen Aidryn call Fannin, and even the kelpies in the Moravon River, through song. It made sense that singing the ballad could have both called Fannin to her, and somehow summoned Aidryn's power at the same time.

But her heart sank as she realized she'd never seen him use

music to command locks and keys. That power had always manifested as a tendril or burst of crimson magic.

Had Aidryn's suffering taken a dire turn?

"Eremon's ring is supposed to *protect* him," she said quietly, more to herself than to Fannin. "Skelly said so. That's—that's what she said."

Nervously, she twined her fingers through Fannin's mane. Dread gnawed at her, and she didn't want to think about how much time she'd wasted in the stupor her overflow of magic had created. She had Skelly to thank for that.

Her fingers shook with anger as she summoned her magic then, fashioning a bridle of tightly braided vines. She hadn't had much practice using her magic outside of instinct, so her handiwork was clumsy. It took four attempts before she finally created a bridle she could use.

As she worked, she considered her next moves. Aidryn was still in the mountain valley, she assumed. If her uncle Gerallt was holding him there, could she command trees to swallow the keep?

No, she thought with a shake of her head. She didn't want to endanger Aidryn further. It was possible Lira could sneak into the valley, get near the keep, and *turas* in. Surely, if she wasn't traveling far, the spell could succeed.

At this point, it was her best option.

Lira slipped the bridle of vines onto Fannin, patting his withers as she prepared to mount him. But a thought tugged at her: Could she use her magic to witness the recent past—recent enough to see what had happened to Aidryn?

Sinking to the ground, Lira sat on her knees and closed her eyes. She couldn't stop the swell of fear that washed over her. After she'd finally regained some grasp on reality, she was afraid to tap into her magic. But if it could help Aidryn, it was a risk she was willing to take.

She closed her eyes and let the power of the Witness Tree rise.

"Show me Aidryn Tarlach's most recent memory," she whispered.

The now-familiar tingling sensation began in her fingers, rushed up her arms, and devoured her sight.

Aidryn is chained in a familiar tower room in Gerallt's keep—the same room where the master held Skelly for two years. His body aches from days—weeks?—of living on the filthy stone floor, sleeping in the moldy straw that covers it.

The shackles around his wrists and ankles are charged with dark magic. Every time he attempts to tap into his power, the restraints burn into his skin, sending a jolt of scorching darkness through his body.

He has long since stopped struggling.

Aila stands over him again, black power crackling in her palms, charging the room's atmosphere once more. He's intimately familiar with the feeling of that power now, and his terror mounts as she releases a bolt of black lightning.

The magic enters his chest with a crack, as though splitting Aidryn's sternum in two. He cries out as the bolt probes and burns beneath his skin, seeking that final remnant of his power.

He has managed to keep it from Aila this long. Surely, he can manage it once more. Gritting his teeth, he fights against her magic, but he quickly loses control, his body convulsing violently as Aila sends another surge into him.

"Give it to me, and this can end." Her voice is almost soothing in contrast to the terrible, scorching magic.

Aidryn's body feels as though it's on fire, burning from the inside out. Blisters erupt inside his mouth and throat, the taste of blood thick on his tongue. He chokes on it, barely managing to roll onto his side to spit a mouthful onto the stones as Aila releases the surge.

Aidryn remains on his side, panting, for a long moment before Aila blasts him with another wave of dark magic. Through the searing pain, he can feel the power's desperation. It carries the rising panic of an entity that seeks, but cannot find. He cries out before he can stop himself, enraged at Aila, and at himself, for coming undone so easily.

Still, he has managed to hold onto the magic she desires so badly. But he won't be able to for much longer.

Artagán shoulders into the chamber then, bow and arrows slung over his shoulder. He jerks his chin at Aila, who releases her magic to acknowledge him. She is panting now, beads of sweat rolling down the sides of her face.

"What is it?" she asks, breathless.

"The master requires you," Artagán says. "Says Caitir is being uncooperative."

"As is her way," Aila answers with a scowl. She glances at Aidryn, who is back on his side, his knees curled to his chest. "See what you can do with him. He is exhausting me."

"With pleasure," the archer says, leering down at Aidryn.

Suddenly, Lira lost her grip on the memory. It dissipated like mist, leaving her trembling. She pressed her palm against her forehead, cursing her broken power. Now, there was a tremor in her right hand—an inexplicable new symptom amongst a host of others.

Her power was still too new, and she was too inexperienced in exploring memories to follow them through to any conclusion. It didn't help that she also had the magical wound to contend with. But it was clear that Aidryn was in grave danger. If this was part of his last memory, it was anyone's guess what Artagán might be doing to him while she prodded at her magic like an amateur.

"Fannin," she said, her voice strangely thick in her own ears, "let's go to Rodhlan Ridge."

In answer, the horse knelt. Lira shimmied onto his back, clamping her legs around him and taking the reins. She steered him southward, but he tossed his head uncertainly, stomping his hooves. Rather than moving forward, he backed up a step.

Lira pressed her heels lightly into his sides to make him

move, recalling a casual command she'd heard Aidryn give the kelpie they'd ridden downriver weeks ago.

"*Ano je*," she murmured, patting the stallion.

Without warning, Fannin reared, turned, and bolted full-speed in the other direction—not toward Rodhlan Ridge, but instead in the direction of Iathium.

CHAPTER 4
AIDRYN

Rodhlan Ridge

Aidryn lay curled on his side on the tower's stone floor in Gerallt Mór's keep, the metallic tang of blood still filling his mouth. The chamber door clicked shut as Aila left him alone with Artagán. The archer paced before him, as though stalking wounded prey.

Aidryn rolled onto his back and exhaled slowly, hoping to avoid the stabbing pain between his ribs. No such luck. The excruciating pain had begun after Aila's first torture session, and hadn't eased up in days. It didn't help that she'd let Gerallt pummel his ribs over and over, kicking Aidryn as hard as he could until the master was left winded and exhausted.

"I don't think you'll find me a sporting hunt," Aidryn groaned.

"It's no fun to shoot a wounded cur," Artagán answered, propping his bow by the chamber door. "There's no glory in it."

Aidryn inhaled as carefully as he could, stopping and starting until he'd drawn a full breath. "Then why are you here?"

Lira's cousin crouched before Aidryn, propping an elbow on his knee. His long, auburn hair fell over one shoulder, contrasting with the green jerkin he wore to hide himself among the trees. "Why are *you* still here? You're the Key Keeper. You could have unlocked your chains and left on the first night."

Aidryn swallowed, then grimaced, blood and saliva burning his raw throat. "Because the longer I keep Aila occupied here, the more time Lira and Skelly have to find safety."

The archer tilted his head, swearing softly. "You're the only one of us who's not a monster, aren't you? And I hated you the moment you set foot here."

Any other time, Aidryn might have been prepared with a quip akin to, *I told you so.* His eyelids felt sluggish as he closed them for a moment, then opened them again, blinking away the blur that followed. "Because I goaded you," he answered weakly.

"You did," Artagán agreed. He lowered himself to the floor, sitting cross-legged at Aidryn's side. "You're going to die," he said matter-of-factly, though not unkindly.

Aidryn wondered at the change in the archer's demeanor. He'd noticed a gradual shift since that day in the clearing, but was feeling rather disoriented by this exchange.

"I wish I could," Aidryn admitted, his voice gravelly and low. He'd certainly felt close to death more than once these past weeks.

"Lira can't protect you with the ring here," Artagán said. "And I don't want them to have that key."

"What do you know about it?" Aidryn asked. Aila had mentioned a key more than once, but had never said what it was for.

The archer shrugged. "There's some sort of power in Iathium—they think they can get to it if they have this ancient key. *Iuchair*, they keep calling it. It has something to do with the crypt under the city.

"You know the mistress—more magic. Always, more magic. And your sister, with all her talk of goddesses and divinity. She thinks she can just *make* herself into a goddess?"

Artagán scoffed, propping his chin on a fist before he continued. "I almost feel sorry for that one—what they're doing to her. If she weren't so—"

"What are they doing to her?" Aidryn asked quietly. He hadn't allowed his mind to wander too far into the implications of the marriage arrangement with Gerallt, but something about Artagán's tone made bile rise in his throat.

The archer's eyes shuttered, and he looked at the floor. "I don't think you want to know. There's nothing you can do about it, anyway."

Aidryn squeezed his eyes shut. For years, he had tried to protect Caitir from Aila's machinations. Eventually, though, he'd had to let go. There was nothing about Caitir's situation that he could control, and he'd had to choose where he could be of the most help.

"I have a sister, too," Artagán continued. "Watching what Papa is doing to yours..." He shook his head. "I'm leaving tonight, to look for Ellwyn. I can't keep this up."

Aidryn finally looked at the archer again, tearing his gaze from the ceiling. "I wish you could get Caitir out."

Artagán bowed his head. "So do I. But I will look for Lira, if I make it off the Ridge alive."

"You'll have a lot of explaining to do," Aidryn said. He almost regretted saying it, because a sudden coughing fit seized him. It felt as though his ribs were breaking.

While he regained control of his breathing, Aidryn thought about what Artagán had just said. The crypt beneath the Dome was where all of Iathium's supreme rulers were buried. Precious few people had set foot inside it. If the history books from Iteloria were correct, the room would only open at the touch of a ruler's palm—or that of an heir. That meant that usually, the crypt only opened when it was time to bury a dead Rí or Raní.

Eremon was dead, and Lira was, for all intents and purposes, his official heir. With Lira gone, how did Aila expect to get in?

"Is it a key to the crypt?" Aidryn asked, slowly pushing himself up to sitting.

"That's just it," the archer answered. "The key is buried with Rí Corlan. It has nothing to do with opening the entrance. Aila wants it before they seal Rí Eremon inside, though. That's why she's so bent on getting it now."

Mentally, Aidryn ticked backward. "They haven't buried him yet? It's been almost two months."

Artagán shrugged. "They say he's surprisingly well preserved for having been dead so long."

Aidryn shuddered, trying to block out the memory of Eremon's violent death. "Your sister stole magic from Macha after he died. Our scouts say it took the Raní this long to recover. Even now, she's weak. Aila wants to move on the city in seven days, when they open the crypt. She thinks you can get it for them—if not here, then in the city."

Aidryn swore softly. "They're really going to try it."

"They have enough allies," the archer agreed. "Papa has sentry friends who remember my uncle Arlen from his days at the armory. They hate Macha and want her gone—and they'll rally under Lira's banner."

No, Aidryn thought. He'd romanticized the idea of fighting for her once, before this had all become so real. But Lira didn't want the throne. She didn't want bloodshed in her name, and neither did Aidryn.

When it came to protecting Rodhlan, they would both be on the battlefield in moments. But a quest to rule was lost before it began. And perhaps that was why Eremon had given Lira the ring, beyond his desire to marry her.

With the ring in Lira's hands, there was no bloodline heir to the throne. The magical authority once secretly enjoyed by the ruling line had ended with Eremon, at least for now.

Perhaps Eremon wasn't as naive as Aidryn had once thought.

Aidryn felt for the remaining tendril of his power. It was weak and failing, just like him.

"I can't keep holding Aila off," he said, his heart sinking at the truth of the words. "She'll break me soon. I can feel it."

"Whatever that key is for, it doesn't sound good," Artagán said, his voice laced with alarm. "Tell me what to do—I'll find a way to get you out of here."

Shaking his head, Aidryn answered, "I'll just slow you down."

Artagán didn't miss a beat when Aidryn's gaze flicked to the bow he'd propped by the door.

Aidryn jerked his chin toward it meaningfully. "Make it quick," he said, his heart beginning to race.

Slowly, the archer rose and headed for the door, picking up his bow. "Are you sure?" Artagán asked hesitantly, as though he hadn't been itching to kill Aidryn just days ago.

"I—I think it's the only way," Aidryn answered, his words almost catching in his throat. "Whatever Aila wants in that crypt, we have to keep her from getting it."

"What about Lira?" Artagán pressed. "What happened in the clearing..."

Aidryn shook his head sadly. "Just tell her I love her, when you see her again. That's all I ask."

"Aye," the archer whispered. "I will."

Over these past weeks, Aidryn had let go of the idea that he might reunite with Lira one day. His purpose had been to delay Aila for as long as he could. But now, the greatest danger was allowing his stepmother to harness his magic to carry out her scheme in Iathium—whatever that might be.

When he thought about it, what had his life ever been but an inevitable sacrifice? He'd been foolish to dream it could be otherwise.

He noticed Artagán's fingers trembling as he withdrew an arrow, then nocked it on the bowstring. Aidryn took a shallow breath, willing himself not to despair. These past few weeks had been torturous; finally, it would all be over.

"Use one with a poisoned tip," he said softly, sitting up on his knees to expose more of his torso. "Make sure it gets the job done."

Artagán nodded once, double checking the arrow he'd selected. Then, he stepped into the center of the chamber, across from Aidryn, and raised his bow.

"Go quietly in peace," the archer said, his voice breaking as he pulled the bowstring taut.

Artagán released the arrow with a soft huff, and the world around Aidryn slowed. He thought only of Lira—of her dark eyes and the scent of wild roses and morning dew on her hair. Of the way she'd leaned into him, pressing her back into his chest for warmth as they rode Fannin across the meadowlands. Of the way her skin felt when he touched her face. As the memories etched themselves into his mind, he felt terribly hollow and utterly alone.

When the arrow pierced Aidryn's stomach, the inoxia spread quickly, burning much like Aila's magic. He collapsed, the toxin taking hold in seconds, paralyzing him. As he waited for death, he felt his magic *flee*—as though the poison was chasing it from his body. Everything around him went suddenly dark, and all he could hear was the archer's ragged breathing from across the chamber.

Long, silent minutes passed, and he could still feel himself lying on the stone floor of the tower room. He couldn't open his eyes—it was as if they were sealed shut. The void his power left behind was like nothing he'd ever felt, aching and scrabbling for the lost magic that had been there moments before.

Strange, the sensation of death. Aidryn couldn't feel himself breathing, but he was somehow still sentient, locked inside a body that no longer responded to his thoughts or commands. He thought he heard the archer leave the chamber, the door shutting with a soft click, but he could not call for help.

CHAPTER 5

LIRA

Meadowlands

It was a wonder Lira managed to stay astride Fannin as he galloped across the meadowlands at full magical speed. More than once, she thought she might fly from his bare back. His mane whipped her face and tears streamed from her eyes until she managed to dip her head, shielding them from the driving wind.

When she'd gained control over her racing thoughts, she visualized vines encircling the stallion, intertwining to form a sort of harness to help her stay on his back. She succeeded in creating a crude, twisting tangle of them, which wound her legs to his sides. It eased the cramping in her back and thighs and allowed her to think, if only a little, given her precarious hold on the horse.

Fannin's hooves pounded the earth, kicking up a thick cloud of dust as they moved. At this pace, it would be mere hours before they reached the city.

"Fannin!" she cried, tugging the bridle in an attempt to steer him toward the mountains again. "Don't!"

The stallion drove harder toward the city.

"Not there!" Lira shouted. "Go back!"

Fannin jolted hard and charged to the right, nearly losing his footing as he changed course and instead headed toward Clan Beran's territory. Panic began to overtake Lira; the horse was clearly determined *not* to return to the mountains.

"Fannin!" she screamed. "Stop!"

The horse seemed to pick up speed instead. Lira finally gave up calling to him. She tried to tune in to each breath he took, each powerful stride, as they rode through the afternoon and into the night.

Despite the long, punishing ride, Lira was grateful to be lucid. As they passed through land she'd traversed these past weeks, she recognized little groves of trees she'd left behind. A trail, perhaps; she thought fleetingly that she may as well have left signposts leading straight to her. She hadn't been able to think clearly enough to do anything besides feed herself and tend to necessities. And she was surprised she'd thought to use her now-filthy gown as camouflage.

Lira thought about her rash desire to go back to Rodhlan Ridge, to the territory and the people Aila had claimed. Every time she thought of the memory she'd witnessed, she panicked; but she would never be able to get Aidryn out on her own. She was more likely to get them both killed than to save him, and Skelly had told her she should stay alive.

If staying alive meant he would survive a little while longer, then that's what she should do.

What she needed was help. Once Fannin stopped to rest, she would regroup and decide what to do next.

Dawn broke before the horse finally slowed, shifting from the charging gallop into a rolling trot. He was only just getting winded; Lira patted his neck gently, running her fingers through the wind-whipped mane. Her back and legs cramped as she pushed herself up to sitting.

They were less than a mile from Beran's Gorge, a day's journey from Fortress Halgeir. It was the last place she wanted to go—next to returning to Iathium, of course. Her mother, Iva, was married to Clan Beran's imposing overlord, Artur. In theory, Lira should want to ask for their help, but she knew Artur's aversion to outside alliances well enough to guess she might not be welcome.

She still resented Iva for marrying Artur, leaving Lira and her brother, Talfryn, motherless in Iathium. But Lira had been determined to remain in the city. And she supposed Artur did not *have* to pay her late father's debts…

It was possible she had been wrong about Artur before. She had been wrong about so many other things.

Perhaps she should consider completing the journey to Halgeir, after all. She was already so close. It might be a risk worth taking, if it meant getting help for Aidryn.

If she listened closely, she could hear the river shallows lapping its pebbled shore. The mouth of the gorge—the outlet from the river into the meadowlands—was far from where Fannin now walked. But the ledges that overlooked the vast canyon below could still be traversed.

The crag-rams that roamed the gorge were the only beasts sure-footed enough to scale the steep rock walls—but it was unlikely to encounter a tame one running free. She would have to travel on foot, then find passage downriver. It wasn't unusual to see dinghies and rowboats making the trip up and down the Moravon. Perhaps a fisherman could take her as far as the fortress in the morning.

When they reached the gorge, Lira called Fannin to a halt. He slowed gradually, and she breathed in the scent of the river, her gaze darting around them. They hadn't encountered anyone during their journey. Travelers were not usually so scarce in the meadowlands—especially this close to Clan Beran's territory. Fortress Halgeir loomed in the distance, miles upriver. Lira could hear the distant roar of the waterfall outside Iathium's walls—the one she and Aidryn had ridden down astride a kelpie during their escape from the city.

With a sinking feeling, Lira realized she wouldn't be able to take Fannin down to the fortress with her. She gave his neck a scratch. "I don't suppose I can ride you down. Perhaps I can call our kelpie friend."

Slowly, she worked her way free of her vines and slid from Fannin's back. Her legs were unsteady beneath her, and she gripped him for support, resting her cheek on his velvety withers.

"What do you think I should say to Mam and Artur when I arrive?" She frowned. "If I arrive."

Fannin snorted.

"Probably as effective as anything else," she muttered, patting his neck.

She came around to face him and stroked his muzzle. "What did you get me into, old boy? You Tarlach horses."

Fannin nuzzled her cheek, and tears pricked her eyes. She fought them back, speaking softly to the stallion. "There are grazing pastures to the east of the fortress, that way," she said, pointing.

The horse followed her gaze. "There are cattle and horses out there, but no entrance to the Fortress. You can go make friends with the ponies while you wait for me."

The stallion nosed her palm, nipping at it gingerly. A smile spread across her face.

"Carrots," she whispered. "Of course."

Dropping to one knee, Lira pressed her fingertips into the soil. She felt the satisfying sensation of magic leaving her body as she willed several long, fat carrots to grow beneath the soil. Then, she pulled them up, one by one, and presented the largest to Fannin with a smirk.

"Let's see if Aidryn can find you a better carrot than that," she whispered, her voice breaking.

The ache of his absence slammed into her full force. She'd shed so many tears these past few months that now, it seemed like a waste of energy. The more time she spent falling apart, the longer it would take to bring him back.

Lira gave Fannin one last pat, then used a seed to grow a large willow tree where they stood. She lay the carrots at the tree's base; the stallion eyed her curiously.

"If Aidryn calls you, go to him," she whispered, backing away a step. "Bring him back if you can."

Fannin took one tentative step forward, then another, and another. He closed the gap between them, draping his head over her shoulder and pulling her close. She wrapped her arms around his neck; he sighed, his hulking form practically melting against her.

"I won't forget your song; I promise," she whispered, squeezing her eyes shut as she pressed a kiss to his mane. "I'll call you again, my friend."

For a long moment, all she heard around them was Fannin's soft breathing and the breeze rustling the leaves. Then, the wind seemed to still. Fannin tensed, holding his breath. The world around them grew deathly quiet as a hulking shadow loomed over them.

Lira trembled as she, too, tried not to breathe. Whatever had joined them beneath the willow was at least as large as Fannin, and *warm*. She could feel its hot breath puffing on the back of her neck. A low growl emitted from the creature, but Lira froze, determined not to move. Her hair stood on end.

The beast sauntered up to her, nosing at her back. She bit down on her lips, a little cry of fear escaping before she could stop it.

Something inside Fannin snapped. He bolted, throwing Lira off balance as he fled. She fell hard onto her back. The impact knocked the breath from her, and she rolled to her side, groaning as she turned her head to look up at the beast that towered above: a massive, brown bear.

CHAPTER 6
LIRA

Beran's Gorge

Lira couldn't scream; she'd barely drawn a full breath since she landed. Instead, she lay still. But it was too late; she and the bear had already locked eyes. Its dark brown fur was flecked with gold, and it might have been beautiful, had it not been so terrifying.

The bear huffed and rose onto its hind legs, towering over her. Lira began to scramble backward, choking and whimpering.

It only took the bear one long stride to catch up to her, close enough that she could feel its breath on her legs. She cried out, kicking the beast as hard as she could in an attempt to deter it.

Instead, the bear stomped its gigantic front paw down hard on her leg and pinned her to the ground. Its claws sank into her thigh, and her scream was drowned out by the bear's booming roar—a sound that reverberated into her bones and was at once as guttural as it was shrill

The monster loomed over her; she was sure it would tear out her throat any moment. She braced herself, praying her death would be quick. But before the bear could make its next move, a deep male voice barked, "Yrsa!"

To Lira's relief, the bear stood down immediately, moving away from her in deference to the tall, muscular man who had burst from beneath the willow's branches. He was nearly as big as the bear, with long, thick, blond braids that tumbled over his back and shoulders, and he carried what appeared to be a heavy rucksack. Lira recognized the ceremonial beads he'd woven into each braid, the runes tattooed on his forearms, the leather bands he wore around his wrists.

"Beran," she said, trying to rise. The edges of the world went white as he made his way toward her, lowering his pack to the ground and kneeling at her side.

"Be still," he said gruffly, tearing off a strip of his tunic to tie around her leg. "You will bleed out."

Lira pressed a hand to the wound; when she withdrew it, it was indeed covered in hot, sticky blood. "No..." she gasped, shaking her head. "No, no, no, I—Aidryn—he—"

"Hush." The Beran man wrapped the cloth tightly around her leg, tugging on the ends before he yanked a knot right next to the wound.

Lira hissed; the man ignored her, instead rummaging in the rucksack. He produced a leather flask and more cloths; he opened the container, held it above her wound, tipped it, then waited. A moment later, thick, golden honey began to flow slowly out of the flask. The man directed the honey into the gash; it burned as it made contact with the broken skin, and Lira's eyes filled with tears.

"It stings," she whispered.

He nodded. "Yes. It will clean the wound; help it heal."

Using the cloths, he bandaged her leg snugly, binding the honey into the wound. The bandage felt like it might cut off the circulation in her entire leg, but Lira was too stunned and nauseated to react. Instead, she lay back as he worked, her mouth and throat suddenly parched as she stared at the sky overhead. She licked her lips and swallowed before whispering, "Am I going to die?"

He snorted. "Not now."

"But later?"

"Do not be stupid. What I mean is—how do you say it?" He busied himself with checking her wrap again. "Two minutes more with Yrsa..." He gestured vaguely with one large hand.

"Two more minutes with the bear. Or two more minutes without a tourniquet..." Lira ventured.

The man gave her a curt nod. It was curious, she thought, that Athi didn't seem to be his first—or only—language. She had always noticed than Clan Beran's people spoke with a thick, guttural accent, but had assumed that their self-isolation had caused them to retain the ancient cadence. In her few short visits to the fortress, she had never heard her mother or stepfather—or anyone else—utter a word in Brylla.

"I see," she breathed.

He jerked his chin toward the bear. "Yrsa is the least of your worries. Others hunt you—human beasts."

Lira's stomach clenched. "Yes. Though... I haven't encountered anyone besides you in days."

"But you left a trail," he said. He slapped the large leather satchel he'd been carrying; he was hauling at least sixty honey-filled flasks in it, perhaps more. "I harvest honey out here in the spring and summer. Yrsa thought she must search every new tree for a hive."

Heat crept up Lira's neck and spread into her cheeks and ears. "The trees were shelter and—" She clamped her mouth shut; she'd already said too much.

"Don't worry; I already know your secrets," he said matter-of-factly.

The first thought that came to her mind was the Binding—it was, quite possibly, the only secret she guarded, if it was still a secret at all. Her heart began to pound. "Such as...?"

"You harbor too much power for one person to handle," he

said, reaching out to prod her shoulder. "Planting the trees is like medicine for you—expending the power."

"Yes—more like a release of pressure," she said. "Otherwise, I... I shouldn't talk about this. I don't know you."

"But I know *you*," he said, leaning forward conspiratorially. "And you know my father."

Lira's eyes narrowed; now, she was truly curious, though also mildly irritated that he was making her ask. "Who is your father? And who are you?"

"I am Thorne Beran, son of Ljós."

"Eremon's healer?" she cried, grasping the soft fabric of his tunic. "Your father is alive?"

Thorne nodded. "He returned to Fortress Halgeir two days ago—brought word that you were missing somewhere in the wilderness. Sentry patrols are searching for you. I'm glad I found you first."

"I owe my life to Ljós," she said. "And now, I suppose I owe it to you as well."

"You owe me nothing," he said, scooping her up with ease. "But it seems that it takes half of Rodhlan to keep you alive. The other half—they want your head."

"Did you really have to remind me?" she whispered, curling in on herself. She wanted to bury her face in the crook of this stranger's arm and never emerge—a realization that was as disturbing as it was appealing. She was so very *tired*.

Thorne heaved a sigh. "I am not strong with speaking Athi. It is no help that I say whatever is between my ears."

"You mean you're painfully honest."

He chuckled. "Brutal with the honesty, so I am told."

Lira refrained from saying that Clan Beran wasn't exactly known for its tact.

"When did Clan Beran begin speaking in Brylla again?" she asked instead.

"When did we not?" Thorne smirked, waving his hand vaguely in Iathium's direction. "No one in Beran followed that law. I learned Brylla as a child. But we do not speak it in front of outsiders."

Lira felt taken aback at his admission. She wasn't sure why she was still surprised at each new revelation. Rather than being a great seat of knowledge, Iathium had instead insulated her from truth—the very opposite of what she'd always striven to uphold. Still, she couldn't help wishing she could skip the shock of each new truth and just simply... know everything as it truly was.

Thorne clicked his tongue, and Yrsa ambled over to him. Lira drew her feet up, shrinking away from the bear as she neared.

"What are you doing?"she gasped.

"I will not carry you to Halgeir," he said, scratching behind Yrsa's ear, "but Yrsa will."

"No, she will not."

He waved her off. "You are safe; she obeys me."

The bear met Lira's eyes as if to confirm Thorne's words. Lira searched Yrsa's expression, expecting to find some sign of the vicious creature that had sunken its claws into her moments ago. Now, all she could see was a subdued gentleness, and for a moment, she felt remorseful for kicking the beast.

Reluctantly, Lira nodded her assent, and Thorne lowered her to Yrsa's back. The bear was soft and warm, and she sighed at the welcome comfort.

Thorne hefted the large satchel over his shoulder and began to walk. Yrsa padded along behind him.

"You should not have been traveling alone, Silira," he scolded. "Someone should have been with you."

"I was trying to get back to the ridge," she said, "to save my —my friend. He was captured. My uncle is holding him there. I think they're torturing him."

"Gerallt Mór?"

Hearing her uncle's name felt like being bludgeoned. "Yes."

"He and his women are going on procession soon. They are building an army to overthrow Macha."

"Do you think they might leave my friend in the mountains when they do?" she asked, hope swelling in her. "Could he be saved once they've gone?"

As the words left Lira's lips, she felt ashamed. Perhaps she should care more about Iathium's fate, but for the moment, Aidryn was infinitely more important to her. She'd dedicated her life to that city, and it had spat her out without a second thought.

"You must not go near the ridge," Thorne said sharply. "It reeks of dark magic. No one knows what has truly happened there. But now is not the time to find out."

He was silent for a moment before he added, "I'm sorry about your friend."

"His name is Aidryn Tarlach," she said quietly, draping herself over Yrsa's back. Her leg throbbed in protest.

"Then I will listen for his name," Thorne promised.

They moved toward the mouth of Beran's Gorge, the Moravon roaring below. Gradually, Lira allowed herself to relax into the bear's thick fur. Yrsa's gentle swaying made her drowsy, and she fell asleep before she could ask any of the questions that swirled in her mind.

CHAPTER 7

LIRA

Beran's Gorge

Thorne shook Lira's shoulder to wake her when they reached the bottom of the gorge. She sat up on Yrsa's back, her leg throbbing in protest. Night had fallen and the world around them was silent, save for the water's gentle lapping against the smooth stones.

The river flowed clear and quiet here, branching out into the streams that ran through the meadowlands and to the south, into Acton's Cove. Thorne bent to fill the flask Lira had been traveling with, took a swig, then offered it to her.

"We will take my boat into Halgeir," he said, nodding to a small dinghy he'd tethered on a tree that jutted out of the canyon wall. "Keep your leg dry."

He extended his arms, and Lira allowed him to lift her from the bear's back.

"What about Yrsa?"

Thorne grinned. "She likes to swim. And she can fish along the way."

He waded into the river, Lira in tow. When they reached the

dinghy, he carefully set her down in the bottom, lowered his pack in after her, then climbed in himself, taking the oars.

The only way into Fortress Halgeir was by boat; in the distant past, there were multiple points of access to their territory. But after the Felling of the Clans—after the mortal god Nami enacted so many sanctions against them—Beran had slowly reduced its interactions with the rest of Rodhlan, quietly retreating into its great stone fortress.

One by one, access points had been closed. Pathways that had once been heavily traveled disappeared as if they'd never existed. Still others were closed by violent rockslides. The gorge became unstable and unsafe to traverse. Only one entry point to Fortress Halgeir remained: an inlet cut into the massive rock wall, halfway between Iathium's towering waterfall and the gorge's outlet in the meadowlands. Reaching the inlet meant rowing upstream against the current.

For someone like Thorne—whose muscular arms rippled with effort as he rowed—getting in and out of the fortress was fairly easy. Clan Beran's people had long placed a heavy emphasis on cultivating physical strength, and it was apparent Thorne took those sentiments to heart. But for someone like Lira, who barely paid any mind to physical prowess beyond walking across town, rowing upriver would be impossible.

As old wounds were forgotten and histories were rewritten, Clan Beran had entered trade with the city like Clans Mór and Énna. Rís Corlan and Eremon seemed to have been content with the imbalance of power, offering Beran full access to Iathium while Beran grew increasingly isolated.

Beran's attitude toward Iathium had long soured Lira's impression of the clan. It was a point of contention with her mother and stepfather. Artur Beran hadn't wanted Lira and Talfryn to remain in Iathium, but when it came to their mother, he had a soft heart. If it had not been for Iva's persuasion, Lira might have been forced to grow up in Halgeir.

Perhaps it would have been better, she thought, barely

suppressing a cringe in spite of herself. *At least I wouldn't be in the center of this chaos.*

As the hours passed, the air cooled. Thick mist gathered over the water's surface. The dinghy cut through it easily, but visibility was poor. Once, Thorne stopped rowing to loosen the tourniquet that bound Lira's leg. He showed her how to tighten it again, then instructed her to loosen it from time to time to keep the blood in her leg flowing properly.

Lira began to shiver. Thorne's eyes cut to her; wordlessly, he handed her a heavy bearskin cloak from beneath his seat. She wrapped herself in the soft fur and sighed, leaning back against the bench opposite his.

Her leg throbbed under the tight tourniquet, and she was careful not to move it too much. She hoped the wound wasn't festering already. The pain came in warm, overpowering waves when she did move, even slightly.

"I am considering the best way to get you into Halgeir," Thorne said, breaking the silence. "The Arthmael has forbidden Beran from making alliances with you—or the other clans."

Lira's stomach dropped at the mention of Artur's traditional title. "But he's my stepfather."

Her argument sounded feeble. She and Artur held no affection for one another, and they'd never made that fact a secret. Why should he welcome her, especially now?

"Doesn't matter. Even mentioning your name brings trouble." He rowed in silence for a long moment before he added, "There was talk—we wondered if he would send your mother away because of you."

"What?" Lira breathed. Perhaps Artur didn't have as much affection for Iva as she'd thought.

"You know Artur. He is determined to keep Beran to itself. No outsiders—no trouble." He shot a knowing look in her direction. "But everyone knows your name, knows you belong to Iva. She has our trust, and we persuaded Artur to keep her by his side."

Lira had tried, briefly, to believe that she might have a chance at an alliance with Artur—but she'd been right when she declared there was no way he would ever ally with her. She tried to quiet her racing thoughts, and instead focus on the *diplomatic prowess* Lord Irem had allegedly praised her for.

"What would he give for valuable information about where this war is headed?" she asked carefully.

A flash of curiosity crossed Thorne's face, but he quickly masked it, heaving the oars hard before he asked, "What would you know to benefit Artur?"

"More than he does, I'm sure," Lira answered. "When was the last time he emerged from his cave?"

"You might be surprised how often he travels these days," Thorne said. He paused for a moment, pressing his lips together tightly as he propped the oars over his legs, letting the dinghy glide as the current eased. They must be near the inlet now.

"How will you convince him?" Thorne asked. Before Lira could speak, he continued. "You will not be allowed to make your case to him in private, if you get to him at all. Others will hear what you have to say."

"Get me to him first, and you're welcome to be in the room," she pressed.

Thorne set his jaw. "Tell me what is happening, and I will get you to him."

Lira narrowed her eyes at him. "Why should I trust you?" She raised a hand to silence his answer. "Don't say because Ljós is your father; that doesn't make you trustworthy. I want to know what *you* have to gain. What's in it for you, if you're the first to receive the information?"

Thorne sighed, dipping the oars back into the water, pumping them hard to drive the dinghy forward, then putting them down again. The river's lapping echoed on the canyon walls around them, and he didn't answer.

Lira slumped, running her fingers through the cloak's thick fur. She took a few steadying breaths, intent on speaking, but she was *tired*. Tired of not being able to trust anyone—tired of considering every word over and over before she spoke it. Tired of everyone she encountered having an agenda or an ulterior motive.

Finally, she said quietly, "I have spent the past few months discovering that everything I thought I knew was a lie—including most of the people in my life. If you'll forgive me, Thorne, it would be helpful to know your motives before I decide whether I will share what I've seen."

Thorne cracked a grin, then laughed at her. Bristling, Lira asked, "What's funny about that?"

"The fact that you expect me to reveal my motives just because you asked." He was still smiling broadly, despite her scowl.

She crossed her arms with a grimace. Her leg throbbed and her head ached. "So you're my enemy, then?"

"No," he said, growing suddenly serious. "But I am Artur's heir."

Lira released a surprised breath. The future overlord of Clan Beran? She drummed her fingertips on the bench where she sat. "That does complicate things," she said shakily. "You shouldn't have brought me here. You're risking—"

"I know the risk." Thorne grunted, never slowing his pace. "I also hear the rumors of war. Clan Beran has been able to keep to itself for so long *because* Rodhlan has been at peace. But if the continent is at war, war will come to Beran sooner or later. We can't afford to be weak."

Lira tilted her head, scrunching her brows. "But Clan Beran has never been weak. Besides, you're insulated from attackers—there's only one way in or out of Halgeir, and you can't get an invading army in."

His eyes slid to her. "True, but they could seal us in and starve us," he said, heaving the oars over and over.

"What do you mean, they could starve you?" Lira asked incredulously. Clan Beran had been relentlessly self-sufficient for centuries; she'd seen their fabled hanging gardens, the carefully-cultivated—though sparse—farmland that bordered the northern coast. She couldn't imagine the clan being unable to survive a siege.

"Curse my tongue," Thorne swore. He rowed angrily, clearly debating whether he should elaborate. "I spoke before I thought better of it."

"What's happened?" Lira asked, fear rising in her throat. "Why would Clan Beran be so vulnerable?"

"There has been a blight on our gardens," he answered reluctantly, "since last summer. We emptied our food stores last winter because of it. We have meat and milk from our cattle and sheep, but those will only go so far. And if Iathium were to lay siege..." He shook his head, putting every ounce of his energy into the oars. "We need allies to help us open the old entryways for more trade. We need more resources, but Artur will not ask for aid."

Lira wasn't sure what shocked her more: the fact that Artur would doom his people in the name of isolation, or the fact that Thorne had just told her so. "How did the blight begin? Did someone deliberately poison the gardens?"

"We don't know," he answered. "I shouldn't have told you so much."

They were silent for a long moment. The only sound in the gorge was the soft slap of the oars on the river as Thorne continued to row.

"What about my mother?" Lira finally asked. "What is her role in all of this?"

"In secret, she tries to make Artur hear reason. Before the clan, she must be loyal to him. He demands full dedication."

"Indeed, he does." Lira remembered a heated argument

she'd had with her stepfather when she was sixteen years old. She'd stood her ground against assimilating into his clan, and he had declared he would rather support her and Talfryn from afar than have disloyal city-dwellers under his nose at the fortress.

Water lapped at the sides of the boat as the fortress came into view. Lira gnawed at her bottom lip, wishing again that her mother had never met Artur.

She had always resented her stepfather. But it was Iva who bore the brunt of Lira's ire for giving away her identity—her family—to rule Beran beside him. Logic told her she should be grateful that Artur had let her be, paid her father's debts, and allowed her to live in the city with Talfryn. But she had never stopped wanting her mother back.

More than once, Lira opened her mouth to speak again, then indecisively shut it. The closer they drew to Halgeir, the more apprehensive she grew. She watched the large man before her heave the oars over and over. If this was to be Beran's future leader, then she would do well to forge an alliance with him.

Already, she could see that he was kinder and more empathic than Artur could ever hope to be. But because of that, she realized that she didn't want to see him stripped of his position before he got the chance to lead Clan Beran into a better future.

Lira leaned toward him. "Perhaps you should put me in irons before you take me to Artur."

CHAPTER 8

LIRA

Beran's Gorge

Thorne's rhythm faltered, and for a moment, he just let the boat glide along, the oars cutting a quiet path through the dark water.

"If you stand to rule, don't risk your position," Lira said. "I know we haven't known one another for long, but I think you would be a better—"

"Whatever you are about to say, don't." Thorne glowered at her as he rowed. "His eyes and ears are everywhere."

"Fine," Lira said, leaning on the side of the dinghy. She rested her chin on a fist and glanced sidelong at him. "So, what say you?"

"I say I am thinking," he said gruffly. "When we arrive, you will know what I've decided."

She didn't like his attempt to gain control of the situation; perhaps the trust she'd put in him had been grossly misplaced.

"I don't like that," she pressed. "How am I to trust you if you won't tell me anything?"

Thorne shrugged, holding up a hand. "I called Yrsa down when she could have eaten you. I bound your wound. You willingly got into this boat." He ticked off each point as he spoke, then leaned closer. "And now you wish to bargain with trust? You have already given me that."

"And you have given me yours. It's no use elevating yourself; we are equals who find ourselves at an impasse." She set her jaw stubbornly.

The warrior stared her down, his gaze hard. "Then how is this? I cannot promise that you have nothing to fear. But if you do as I say, perhaps you will have less."

Thorne sniffed as he rowed, but paused, his eyes narrowing as he sized Lira up once again—as though perhaps he hadn't truly seen her earlier. He pulled one of his oars into the boat and rested an elbow on his thigh, considering. Lira didn't like the way he was looking at her. It was as if he'd just solved a puzzle, and she wasn't sure she wanted to know what the answer to it was.

"You said earlier that you could smell my magic," Lira said. "Does magic really have a smell?"

"Not always." He grasped the oar again, lowering it back into the water with a knowing glance. "But there is a certain scent to a magical wound. It's hard to describe. You have so much power, but you are a mess."

Lira snorted softly, raising an eyebrow. It was true, but she didn't have to admit to it. "Are you sure you want to offend someone so *powerful*, Thorne Beran?"

The corner of his mouth pulled into a grin. "You need to work on that expression." He motioned vaguely to her face. "It's not intimidating at all."

Lira's jaw dropped.

His shoulders shook with quiet laughter before he added, "Anyway, you need someone to help you untangle the mess."

Ah! There it is. Let's see if he'll admit what he's after, now. "Who, you?"

"No," Thorne grunted matter-of-factly, heaving the oars again.

Lira had been waiting to find the thread of deceit that would lead her to his truth, assuming he was concealing it like so many others did. But his unwavering honesty made her feel off-balance. She had never known anyone who was so willing to admit they didn't know something or couldn't be of help in some way. The most well-meaning people in her life had always tried to protect her feelings by lying or omitting part of the truth.

"Are you going to tell me how your power got this way?" he asked.

"No," she echoed, looking out over the water. "I can barely make sense of it myself."

"My father can help you, if you still trust him," Thorne answered.

She kept her expression impassive, though a surge of relief tore through her. "Good."

"He's anxious to talk to you about Eremon. Says you saw everything."

Lira suddenly felt faint. "I did."

Thorne sighed softly. "I'm sorry."

The day Eremon died, Lira had called for Ljós, but he hadn't come. She hadn't spent much time questioning why. Instead of answering Thorne, she just shook her head, staring at the nearest oar as it slid through the dark water.

"Here is what I can offer," he continued. "I don't think Artur will see you himself, but I will try to persuade him. And I will do whatever I can to help you. But I would like to know more about what happened with your magic."

"You have already told me you know about my abundance of power," Lira replied carefully. "You know I also have a magical wound. Tell me, what else do you know?"

"I know you can make things grow—trees, plants, food." He nodded pointedly toward her hand. "And I've heard stories about that ring."

Lira ran her thumb over the stone. "Rumors, or truths?"

"I don't know."

"What else do you sense?" she pressed, fearful he might have already guessed she was bound to someone. She wasn't ready to talk about that with Thorne, and especially not with Artur.

"Something more," he mused, "but I don't know what to call it."

The Binding, then, she thought.

"Then call it nothing," Lira said. "It sounds like you know enough to speak on my behalf. As for the rest, I will take my time deciding how much you need to know."

Thorne nodded curtly, but didn't speak again until they reached the fortress.

Fortress Halgeir was every bit as intimidating as Lira remembered. As it came into view, she cowered down in the little boat—more and more, the closer they rowed. She hadn't planned to return to these lands any time soon. After all that had happened, she certainly didn't want to be here now.

Her leg burned and throbbed more than before, stiff from the hours in the dinghy. When they docked, she could barely stand on it.

Thorne hefted her out of the little boat and set her carefully on the rocky shore. Lira tried to walk a few steps and stretch her legs, but her vision began to go black and she swayed, the world tilting around her. He caught her before she fell, picking her back up and carrying her toward the fortress gates himself.

"I don't want anything to happen to you on my account," she said, letting her head loll against his chest. "Don't let them—"

"Quiet," he grunted. "You are too weak. Let me do the talking."

Fear took root in Lira as they neared the high stone gateway.

Its ornate carvings were ominous in the moonlight—looming sentinels whose vacant eyes seemed to follow her every movement. She remembered panic rising in her chest the first time she set foot in Halgeir—panic that bloomed anew now.

"What's going to happen?" she asked quietly.

He sighed, glancing down at her for a moment before looking ahead again. "I don't know."

"Honesty," Lira whispered. "A rare thing these days."

Thorne's grip on her was solid and unflinching—a strange comfort despite their unfamiliarity with one another. So she tried to listen to that tug in the back of her mind. The tug that told her he was a refuge in the midst of danger.

A friend.

Lira had never been quick to befriend anyone. As a child, Aidryn and Caitir had coaxed her into the friendship they'd eventually forged. She'd always been guarded with her affection. Talfryn had been the only person who had ever received it freely, without having to ask for it.

As for the others, her father was dead. Her mother chose Clan Beran. Caitir turned against Lira, and Lira against Skelly. When she'd allowed herself to truly feel for Eremon, he'd been ripped away from her. And now, Talfryn and Aidryn were gone, too.

Perhaps it was a sign of her desperation, that she would allow herself to become attached to anyone at all.

They passed under the sentinels, and the path began to curve gently uphill toward the entrance to the stone fortress. As if reading her thoughts—her doubts—Thorne began to speak in a low voice.

"I hope to take you to the healer first, but I cannot say what will happen once we are inside. The *Beravakt* will want to intervene, but they are not likely to take a wounded woman into custody."

Beravakt—the armed warriors that guarded Halgeir and the overlord.

"There are things I must say to get you inside," he said. "You will not like them. And there are things I cannot tell you before we approach Artur. I have a plan, but he will not listen if he thinks you know it."

"I don't like this," Lira said curtly.

Thorne narrowed his eyes. "Is that not what I just said?"

"You'll find that I am exactly as stubborn as the rumors suggest," she answered. "Probably now, more than ever."

"I am sure." He adjusted his hold on her. "It's time."

Lira sucked in a breath as they passed from the moonlight into pitch darkness. The cave-like entrance of Halgeir swallowed them up, the temperature plunging. She shivered, clinging tighter to Thorne as he carried her down the long, dark hallway.

The thought of the pathway closing in around them made Lira's heart race. She didn't want to panic, but a dark, heavy feeling washed over her, and suddenly, she couldn't think past the narrow walls. They felt as though they were closing in, though she could not see them.

"Almost there," Thorne said softly, as though he knew her fear. She didn't feel much calmer, but what he'd said did help ease the tension she was feeling.

It wasn't long before a shaft of light crept into the tunnel, then a little more. Finally, Thorne was emerging with her inside Halgeir's walls.

Lira remembered the wide, long courtyard that sat on the center of the spiraling stone fortress. Each time she entered there, the sheer vastness of the space overwhelmed her. Though it was night, torches illuminated the entire place in a golden glow, burning in sconces on the exterior walls every few feet.

From the outside, Halgeir looked like the result of some natural disaster—as though the earth had opened up and thrust it into existence. But on the inside, it was apparent how skillfully-crafted the place was. It was immediately obvious to

Lira that something terrible had indeed happened to the hanging gardens. They were nearly nonexistent, exposing the fortress's astounding craftsmanship all the more.

The moment Thorne set foot inside Halgeir, he was surrounded by a band of six Beravakt, all brandishing blades. They wore fitted leggings, short boots, and tunics made of leather and fur. Along their forearms they bore rune tattoos— even a few on their faces and upper arms. The men and women alike wore their long hair braided and twisted into intricate styles, some with beads and bits of bone woven throughout.

Lira tensed, but Thorne immediately began speaking quietly to the young men and women in Brylla, and they lowered their weapons almost immediately—though still wary of Lira's presence.

"Oda. Bard," Thorne said, nodding toward two of the warriors.

From within the group stepped a young, dark-skinned woman with green eyes and a pale boy—certainly no older than fifteen—with hazel eyes and a mass of auburn braids. Neither of them made eye contact with Lira, but instead deferred to Thorne.

The woman, whom Lira assumed to be Oda, looked near her age, or perhaps a little older. Her thick black hair had been gathered into long twists, which she had tied at the nape of her neck with a leather strap. Curiously, the hair that framed her face was white on one side, and those strands had been pulled into a braid and tied back with the rest.

Thorne continued speaking softly to the warriors in Brylla, to Lira's dismay. Occasionally, Oda glanced her way. Lira felt small and vulnerable next to these trained fighters, and she wished she could disappear. She let her eyes roam around the massive fortress's interior. Halgeir was the last place she'd wanted to come, yet here she was.

To their left lay the entrance to the Arthmael's Hall, the largest single space inside the fortress. It was separated from the courtyard by tall, wooden doors that boasted carved illustrations of Beran's histories and ancient fables. For Lira, the hall had served as the most intimidating room she'd ever set foot in —that was, until the events of the past spring. Now, she wasn't sure Clan Beran's imposing traditions would seem nearly as bothersome as they had in childhood.

The walls and pathways surrounding the courtyard appeared to have been carved out of a solid piece of stone, much like many of the stone stacks in the archive back home. They wound around the courtyard—and up four levels. Each exterior walkway led to a series of corridors that opened into the interior paths.

Inside the fortress's interior walls were the entrances to the clan's various homes and chambers. Halgeir's breadth was such that it could fit hundreds of living quarters for entire families, in addition to guest chambers, dining halls, and communal meeting spaces.

Thorne barked what sounded to Lira like a gruff command, abruptly breaking into her thoughts. His companions were walking toward one of the stone pathways that sloped upward and led to some of the fortress's living quarters. He followed them, adjusting his grip on Lira as they moved in the opposite direction from where her mother's chambers would be.

"What about Mam?" Lira asked, craning to look back over Thorne's shoulder.

"We tend to your leg first," he said. "Oda is opening one of the guest chambers."

"What?" Lira cried. "Why?"

"I need to speak with the overlord first," Thorne answered. "Alone."

"I should be privy to the conversation, at the very least," Lira bit out. The throbbing in her leg made it difficult to think.

"Did you forget what I told you outside?" he asked.

"No." Lira sighed. She'd just hoped, somehow, she might

see her mother tonight. Might avoid being left alone in the dark.

With a shiver, she thought of the deep darkness of those fortress chambers, windowless and carved out of solid stone. Stepping inside one without a candle was like falling into a pot of ink. Each room required a great many candles in order to achieve proper illumination—something she'd lamented on her past visits to this place. It had always been challenging to get enough candles for reading light.

It wasn't that she was unused to dark rooms—the archive and its inner chamber had been underground, after all. But they had also been generously lit with torches, wall sconces, and chandeliers full of candles. At Fortress Halgeir, inhabitants made their own candles, and there were precious few to spare besides.

Lira shuddered at the thought of spending the night in another dark, stone room—even if it was more comfortable than Iathium's dungeon. She had been imprisoned beneath the Dome briefly, after Macha accused her of killing Eremon. This was the first time she would be entering a stone room since then. Her stomach knotted at the realization.

Thorne called out to Bard and Oda in Brylla. They abruptly turned down a corridor to their right, but he continued forward.

"Where are they going?" Lira asked as they passed.

"To get supplies," he said.

She'd thought she was growing to like this man of few words, but now his short, almost-answers were irritating. But she was too tired, weak, and sore to argue or ask any more questions, so she let her head rest heavily against his chest instead.

Thorne wound them through several corridors until they came to the chamber that would be hers for the time being. When he opened the door, Oda was already inside, lighting the candles she'd placed around the room. Lira realized she'd likely brought them from her own chamber.

Straight ahead was a wide bed piled with soft animal pelts and furs. Its headboard and footboard were made from wide logs that had been smoothed to a shine. Across the room lay a bureau for storing personal items, and the doorway to a bathing chamber. The room was dim in the sparse candlelight, though not pitch-black.

Thorne lowered Lira onto the bed and stepped back to survey the room, whispering to Oda. Lira sighed in spite of herself, sinking into the dense, soft mattress. It was the first shard of comfort she'd felt since Nevala's little cot at Va'hesk, though the room itself was dark and cold.

Still, the pain in her leg raged as the rest of her body tried to relax. When she shifted to get comfortable, she could barely move it.

"Thorne?" she whimpered.

The warrior turned to her again, concern etched on face. He glanced down at her leg—seemed to note the way she was clenching her fingers around the fur she'd tried to pull over herself. His amber eyes flicked back up to meet hers.

"I'll get my father," he said, then excused himself, leaving Lira alone with Oda.

CHAPTER 9
LIRA

Fortress Halgeir

Oda moved closer to Lira, removing her sword and a large axe from the sheath she wore on her back and setting them at the foot of the bed. She carried axes and blades of all sizes strapped to her back, hips, and thighs. Her long, wide broadsword looked as though it weighed thirty pounds on its own.

"Are you in pain, Silira?" Oda asked, sitting on the mattress beside her. She was all sculpted muscle and generous curves, her dark skin flawless in the candlelight. It may have been the exhaustion and delirium of the injury, but Lira thought she looked almost luminous.

"A great deal, I'm afraid," Lira answered, gritting her teeth as she tried to shift again. "I would hate to cross Yrsa on a bad day."

"Yrsa knows better," Oda replied curtly, smoothing the fur that edged her tunic. "And you don't look like the sort of woman who threatens a bear."

"Far from it," Lira said. If she had felt better, she might have smiled. "She spooked Aidryn's—my horse."

"Who is Aidryn?"

"He…" Tears pricked Lira's eyes, and she glanced up at the ceiling for a moment, willing them away. Just as she was trying to formulate a proper reply, the chamber door opened again, and Thorne stepped back inside, his father in tow.

Oda pressed a palm to Lira's forearm, leaning close. "Tell me later," she said softly, standing and retrieving her weapons. She met Thorne and his father by the door, nodded once, and exited without another glance behind her.

Warmth flooded Lira when she looked on the healer's face again. Ljós was quite a bit shorter than his son, but they had the same kind eyes. Unlike Thorne's mass of blond hair, Ljós kept his head shaven and wore a short beard. She wouldn't have guessed Thorne belonged to Ljós if no one had told her.

"Silira," Ljós said, surveying her with a concerned expression as he stepped to her bedside.

"I'm glad you're alive," Lira said, reaching for his hand.

"Likewise." The healer clasped her fingers for a moment before opening his leather satchel. "Thorne tells me you wrestled the she-bear and survived."

Ljós took a small bone knife and cut a long slit in the fabric of Lira's filthy dress, which had stuck to the bandage Thorne had used to wrap her leg. Carefully, he loosened the ends of Thorne's bandage and began working to remove it, cutting away and discarding the fabric as he worked.

"He flatters me." Lira gasped, stiffened, and pressed her palms into the mattress, grimacing as he unwound the cloth and peeled it from the raw wound. "The bear only stood down because he told it to," she bit out.

"Yrsa is almost as headstrong as you are," Ljós said, an almost-smile playing on the corners of his mouth.

Lira pressed her lips together, groaning as Ljós finally removed the bandage and set it aside. Though the gash was deep and painful, Thorne's dressing had kept it from festering.

The healer worked in silence for a long while, applying a

salve to Lira's wound that began knitting the torn flesh as soon as it made contact. It itched and pulled as it worked its magic, repairing torn sinew and muscle from the inside out.

It did nothing, however, to soothe the ever-present pain that had settled beneath her ribs over the past few days. She'd noticed it when Aidryn's magic first came to her. And, though her mind had quieted for the moment, she was unsure when her visions would overtake her again. Her heart began to race when she thought of it, and though she tried to calm herself, she suddenly felt short of breath.

Ljós seemed to sense her churning thoughts. "Do you have anything you'd like to ask me?"

"When—" Lira's chin trembled, and she took a deep breath before she began again. "When will the pain stop?"

The healer glanced over his shoulder at his son. Lira had forgotten Thorne was still in the room. As if anticipating his father's wishes, the warrior excused himself, leaving Lira alone with Ljós.

The older man leveled with her then, his warm gaze boring into hers. "In the leg? Give it a week, perhaps. It will be tender, but you will have complete healing.

"As to the pain in your spirit..." Ljós sighed, pressing a palm to his chest. "I cannot say. The grief will pass with time. I can work on your magical wound while you are here. We have tinctures and remedies for the sadness—the racing heartbeat—and to help you sleep if you have need. But the Binding spell is another matter."

Lira cringed. "Did Eremon tell you he was creating a spell?"

"He didn't have to. He was so fearful of what was happening to him—so afraid of what might happen to you in the process. I believe he tried, in every possible way, to keep control of a situation that was out of his hands long before he was born.

"I cautioned him against manipulating magic, more than once. Better if he had left well enough alone. You would have been safer for longer, had he not tried to ensnare you."

The healer's words were soft, yet they cut into Lira. "That's exactly what Aidryn said," she whispered. She couldn't help envisioning his devastated expression when she'd refused to leave the city with him—the way he'd reached for her, touched her face.

"Aidryn was correct," Ljós answered. "As good as Eremon was, he was also too idealistic. Too young."

"He had such a pure heart." She realized this was the first time she'd ever truly reflected on him this way. "He didn't deserve to suffer. He should be alive."

"Silira," Ljós began—but paused. She stilled at his tone. It seemed cautious and heavy, as if he wasn't sure he should even *think* the words he was about to say.

"What is it?"

"You were chosen for this, for many reasons," he said softly. "Eremon could not help but be drawn to your love for Iathium. Together, you would have been the greatest rulers Rodhlan had seen since Rhona and Riku, at the city's founding."

Lira squeezed her eyes shut at that, the sheer weight of his declaration threatening to crush her as Ljós continued.

"It was never about simply obtaining your magic, but *dispersing* it," he said. "Eremon knew the power your grandmother withheld. Knew the birthright destined to be passed to you."

"Do you believe he wanted me to give my power back to Clan Mór?" she asked. "He spoke of restoring power to the clans..."

"Not only Clan Mór," Ljós answered, "but all of Rodhlan."

She looked to the healer, heart pounding. "What does that mean?"

"Not now," Ljós whispered, raising a hand to silence her. "Someone is coming."

The door to her chamber rattled, then swung open. Lira's stepfather entered the room then, flanked by a small contingent of Beravakt. Thorne brought up the rear and dismissed the warriors, who filed out, leaving Artur alone with Thorne, Lira, and Ljós.

From her vantage point on the low bed, Artur looked a thousand times larger and more imposing than the last time she'd seen him three years ago. But since then, he'd shorn his hair close to the scalp. His coarse, dark blond beard was peppered with gray, and he'd trimmed it shorter than in years past. She couldn't help noticing that his skin, usually pale from time spent in the fortress, was leathery from repeated, prolonged exposure to the sun.

"I see you finally ventured outside your beloved city's walls," he said by way of greeting, crossing his muscled arms over his chest.

"I could say the same for you, *sjeiva*," Lira answered, pushing herself up to sit. The movement made her feel dizzy, but otherwise the pain in her leg was nearly gone. She swung her legs over the edge of the bed and sat up straight, pulling one of the furs over her lap to hide her bare leg.

Ljós rose, satchel in tow, and gave Lira a little nod before letting himself out of the chamber.

"You are correct," Artur answered, inclining his head. "So, Thorne told you about our blight."

Thorne stood taller. Lira's gaze shifted between him and Artur. "Yes," she answered cautiously, "and with great reluctance."

"It is the reason I have been forced to leave the fortress more often than I'd like," her stepfather continued, beginning to pace. "I sought to bring your grandmother here to help us, but my scouts report that you took her from her territory, then abandoned her in the meadowlands."

"She is safe with Clan Énna on the western coast," Lira answered, raising her chin. "But I'm sure your scouts have learned that by now, as well."

Artur's words about Skelly didn't ring true—not after Thorne had said he was refusing to seek help.

"Indeed, they have not," Artur answered, the creases in his brow softening, "but I'll have them verify it."

"They'll find her with Lord Irem Énna and the caravan," Lira replied. "My leaving her was impulsive, but I'm afraid you don't have the entire truth as to why."

"Then tell me," Artur said. "Your mother feared the worst. It's fortunate that you both survived."

"What about Mam?" Lira asked. "When can I see her?"

"I haven't decided whether you will," Artur answered. "But you must meet my conditions regardless."

A sick sensation crept into Lira's stomach. Artur was known to be a fierce negotiator. He'd spared Lira these so-called *conditions* in the past when he'd conceded to let her stay in the city with Talfryn. But now, she was at a grim disadvantage—and he could leverage that for himself.

"What sort of conditions, *sjeiva*?" She hoped her grudging use of the title—*father* in Brylla—would soften Artur's heart, but his gaze hardened instead. Her stomach clenched.

"Endearments are no good to you here," Artur said. "You are under house arrest until I deem otherwise. You're lucky Thorne didn't have you thrown in a cell. It was the one condition I allowed *him* to negotiate for you. You have him to thank for this measure of comfort. Otherwise, I would hold you as a prisoner of war."

Lira looked to Thorne then, who leaned against the wall across from her. His gaze dropped to the floor.

"And what hoops must I jump through to lift my house arrest?" she asked Artur, turning back to him.

"To remain under house arrest and avoid the dungeon, you will use your power to heal our gardens," Artur answered.

"So I'm to be held here with no hope of release?" Lira asked, voice rising. "That's tyranny! I won't stand for it."

Artur's face grew red, and his lip curled. The near gentleness with which he'd regarded her earlier melted away to reveal the imposing man who ruled his people through ruthless fear and intimidation.

"To accuse the overlord of tyranny is treason," Thorne said quietly. "You should mind your words."

"I can't willingly give my power to this land under coercion," Lira shot back. "It doesn't work that way—it must be given freely or it will blight your land further. And I do not belong to this clan; I declare myself Witness Tree of Rodhlan. You cannot hold me!"

Emerald magic flared from her pendant at that, filling the room. Artur took a surprised step back, looking her up and down. From his vantage point on the wall, Thorne raised his brows, studying Lira curiously.

"I am not your prisoner," Lira repeated, "and I will not be held or used against my will."

"You will not leave here alive with the knowledge you possess," Artur declared, raising his voice to almost a shout. "And if you refuse to aid us, I will see both of your heads on spikes in my Hall."

He stormed out of the chamber, slamming the door behind him. Thorne looked toward the door as though he expected the overlord to burst back through at any moment, demanding that he follow. But Artur did not return.

"That was your plan?" Lira growled, rounding on Thorne. "Barter away my freedom in exchange for my magic?"

"It's better than the dungeon," he retorted, "or being beheaded, which could still happen thanks to you."

"Let me explain something to you, Thorne Beran," Lira seethed. "*Magic wrongfully taken goes to war with its host and returns to its rightful place tenfold.* It's something I learned during my studies, and it's why Rí Eremon is dead."

As the words left her mouth, they reverberated through her like the sound of shattering glass. She swallowed hard, took a deep breath, and asked, "Now, what does that mean to you?"

Thorne's expression darkened. "It means that stolen power

destroys whatever it enters, then multiplies before returning to its source."

Lira nodded. "Sooner or later—exactly. So, if I am coerced to unwillingly pour power into this land, what do you think is going to happen?"

"Why would you be unwilling to help us?" he asked incredulously. "That's your stepfather—your mother."

"What. Do you think. Will happen," she repeated.

Thorne slid down the wall and sat on the floor, considering for a moment. "It would kill what is left of the gardens."

"And?"

"And then multiply and return to you." His eyes widened then, and he rubbed a hand over his mouth. "You already carry too much magic—it would kill you."

Lira nodded. "What you don't understand is that my power was first inborn, awakened by this pendant." She touched the heavy bronze charm that hung around her neck. "Then, I received a portion of our clan's power, stolen by Eremon's forefathers. After that, Skelly forced Clan Mór's birthright onto me —not only as anointed. It was the intended magical inheritance of an entire clan."

"I didn't know," Thorne answered, squaring his jaw and looking Lira right in the eye. "For that, I'm sorry."

Lira sighed heavily. "You insisted on speaking with Artur alone, and you negotiated in ignorance. Next time, let me speak when I ask it of you."

Thorne blinked. "Next time?"

"Yes," she answered. "I want you to take me to my mother as soon as you can."

He shook his head. "I can't make that promise."

"You must," Lira insisted. "Mam has Artur's ear. Surely if she understands what's happening, she can help him see reason."

"She can't convince him to get help for his own people," he retorted. "Or did you already forget that?"

No, she hadn't forgotten—but she had no other leverage to consider. "Please, Thorne," she begged. "Even if all you can do is get me back in a room with Artur. I need time to explain everything to him so he understands.

"I will help willingly, if I am released from house arrest," she said. "Giving my magic freely *would* heal the land. Please, just try."

Thorne shook his head resignedly. "He is so afraid of exposing the clan's weakness to the outside—I doubt he will hear you. But I will try, at least." He stood, eyeing the chamber door. "I should go—it's late. You need rest."

Rage washed over Lira, but she fought it down. "When can I expect you again?" she asked.

"Tomorrow, as early as I am able," he answered. "I will speak to him and let you know what comes of it."

She dropped her eyes to the floor, offering him a resigned half-nod. "All right."

Thorne gripped the iron handle, pushed the heavy wooden door open, and stepped into the corridor outside. It sealed shut behind him without a sound, and Lira could hear a key turning in the lock. She remained on the edge of the bed, caught somewhere between raging at her stepfather and savoring the relief in her leg. The latter won out, and she slumped for a moment, thankful at least one source of pain had been relieved.

She considered Thorne, and whether or not she could truly trust him as an ally after what he'd done. On one hand, his bartering felt like a betrayal. But she also couldn't help but acknowledge the risk he'd taken in negotiating for her life at all.

As angry as she felt about what he'd done, the fact was that he'd taken many risks to save her. He'd risked his life, his father's safety, his inheritance—all to keep her alive. The matter of her imprisonment complicated things, but she would bide her time until an opportunity presented itself. It wasn't worth it to think too much about how long that might take.

For now, she was relieved to have a place to recover and to

be near her friend, the healer, again. She thought about what he'd said to her—about Eremon's vision of dispersing her power across the continent. Restoring Rodhlan's histories through memory would give truth back to the people far more quickly than teaching them through books and revised oral histories. If she could somehow pass on her own intuition for truth along with the memories, it would be harder for them to argue against change.

Still, she didn't know how this could be possible. If there were a kingdom of idealists, Eremon would have been its leader with no contest. He had been so optimistic and naïve—qualities that were both endearing and infuriating in retrospect. Qualities that had drawn her to him, that she had shared. They'd both had their ideals and their unshakeable worldviews, until everything had fallen apart.

Now, she was left scrabbling for any semblance of stability she could muster. In this moment, she knew where she was and by whom she was surrounded. But tomorrow—what then? She had no intention of staying here under Artur's thumb any longer than she had to. The horror of knowing nothing was all-consuming.

Lira's chest suddenly felt heavy and tight. The chamber around her seemed to shrink, as though its windowless walls were closing in on her. It was too quiet and too loud all at once. As the candles began to gutter, she curled onto her side on top of the furs, eyes wide against the dimming light, and tried to forget the last time she'd been imprisoned in a room of stone.

CHAPTER 10

AIDRYN

Rodhlan Ridge

Aidryn wasn't sure how long he'd been lying on the chamber floor in Gerallt Mór's keep, hovering somewhere between life and death, before the door swung open and banged against the wall. His ears rang at the sound, though he could have sworn it hadn't been that loud before. The odor of the straw he lay in burned his nostrils.

Dull pain pulsed in his belly. He still couldn't move or open his eyes as soft footsteps approached.

A voice cried out in alarm—Caitir, he realized. Aidryn noted something like real grief in her voice.

"Mother, Árchú!" she screamed, her voice painfully piercing. "It's Aidryn!" Her footsteps retreated.

Vaguely, Aidryn realized he hadn't seen his older brother since they'd arrived in the Ridge. But he was clearly here now, for he was with Caitir and Aila when they returned to Aidryn's chamber.

"No," Aila cried, moving closer to Aidryn. He sensed her kneeling by his side—felt her place her fingertips on his neck. "This is Artagán's doing. I shouldn't have let him live."

Aidryn wished they would lower their voices. There was no need to shout.

"I told you to give the archer to me and take Gerallt yourself," Caitir said. "I could've persuaded him to leave well enough alone."

"And risk the two of you running off together, like he has done now?" Aila said. "I'm not that stupid."

It was good that the archer had escaped. And it seemed Aila was still bent on keeping Caitir as isolated as possible. Without allies of her own, Caitir would be forever off-balance and reliant on Aila to survive.

"D'you want me to go after him, m'lady?" Árchú asked.

"Go," Aila answered, "and take the hounds. Make sure he doesn't leave this mountain alive."

Aidryn heard his brother leave the room, followed by Caitir's soft footsteps moving closer.

"Is he dead?" Caitir asked softly.

"No, but he should be," Aila answered, prodding the area around where the arrow had embedded itself in his stomach. The wound was strangely numb. "Inoxia usually works in seconds. We are terribly lucky in that regard."

"He can't fight you any longer," Caitir mused. "If he's still alive, take the key and let's be done with it."

"Yes," her mother agreed. "I'll perform the rite now, and we'll ride for Iathium in the morning."

"Then can we be done with this stupid charade," Caitir said.

Aila went still, her fingers resting on Aidryn's abdomen. "This is no charade," his stepmother answered, her voice deathly quiet. "This is our life now, and we are seeing it through until the end."

"But—"

"Remember what I promised you," Aila said. "If we can take it, the throne is yours. Then no one else will matter—not

Gerallt, not the armies, not Macha. No one will be able to stand against us."

Caitir was silent for a moment before she said, "All right."

Aidryn could feel Aila's palms hovering over him now as she called on her dark magic. A jagged tendril of it broke in through his arrow wound.

Where his senses had been dulled moments before, they were suddenly awakened by the raging, searing magic. This time, he couldn't fight it—couldn't cry out or grit his teeth against the pain. He was completely at the mercy of the power that wound its way through him.

Please... His thoughts shattered beneath the agonizing magic. It didn't matter that his own magic had fled from him; they did not know that, and so Aila would seek until she exhausted herself.

Help me, please!

The void inside him grew more insistent by the minute, as if scrabbling for purchase—like it yearned to latch onto any power that might fill that emptiness. Some small, hidden part of him feared that Aila's dark magic might take hold of him in the absence of his birthright. What if Aidryn woke filled with the same power that had killed Eremon—that had corrupted Caitir?

No; she and Aila were wrong. He *could* fight back, though not in a way they expected.

Aidryn dove deep within himself, mentally seeking out and sealing the raw places where that dark magic might hide and take root. Then, inexplicably, he *imagined* roots. Scores of roots, forming a tightly-woven web on his insides, sprouting vines and leaves and cool moss. A deep sense of calm flooded him as he felt Aila's power recede.

"What is this?" Aila murmured, suddenly withdrawing her power.

It's you failing to get what you desire, for once in your life. He wished he could see the look on her face.

Aila gasped. "His magic—it's gone."

"What do you mean?" Caitir asked, her voice rising in panic.

Aila placed a hand on Aidryn's chest again. "All of it—it's just *gone!* How is it possible?"

Aidryn thought perhaps he should be concerned about the sudden sense of calm that flooded him, but he found that he could feel no fear.

"Can you discern it?" Caitir said.

"Quiet; I'm trying."

For a long moment, neither woman spoke—until Aila drew a sharp breath.

"Silira's magic," Aila said, her voice cold with rage. "It's *her* power in him. She must have given him magic... of *course* she did."

"But when?" Caitir cried. "You said nothing of it before!"

She did nothing of the sort, Aidryn thought.

But then he remembered the clearing, where he and Lira had clasped hands amidst the magical storm that whirled around them. He remembered silver and green vines snaking their way around his forearms and hers, glowing with that familiar emerald power. What the archer had tried to say to him before—

Words echoed through his mind—his own words to Lira, not long ago.

The rites opened a magical bond between husband and wife that allowed their magic to flow freely, one to another.

Whatever had happened that day in the clearing had bound him to Lira. It was a magical rite. For all intents and purposes, the clans would consider her his *wife*.

He felt himself losing his grasp on the realization as his mind settled back into numbness.

"I can feel something else," Aila was saying. "I think that boy-king had something to do with this."

"Can't you just take Lira's power for yourself?" Caitir asked.

"No, I... I can't seem to touch it at all," Aila answered, her voice tremulous and weak. "It feels similar to the Binding rituals the priestesses used to perform. But I've never encountered anything like this."

"A Binding?" Caitir asked. "You mean they were married?"

"It appears so." Aila swore under her breath. "But Eremon's power is tied up in it somehow."

Caitir was silent for a moment before she asked, "Do you think Macha would know what to do?"

"Macha is our enemy," Aila snapped.

"But she wants what we want," Caitir pressed. "So we should take Aidryn to her."

When Aila didn't reply immediately, the girl barreled on.

"You could make sure word gets to wherever Lira's laying her head these days. Draw her out. She'll come for Aidryn if they're bound—I know it. And she can open the crypt. If we play our hand well, we won't need Macha except to gain entry to the Dome—and we have her power. We can use it. After that, Lira can do the work."

No... What have I done?

He had played right into their hands anyway. Now, there was no longer anything he could do to protect anyone. Curious, that it felt like a reprieve.

"It's true; she should be able to access the keys," Aila mused. "That's where his power's gone to."

"Then I say we make haste for Iathium," Caitir said. "At dawn. This clan belongs to us now, and if Gerallt wants the throne, he will do as we say. If he does not, we'll destroy them all."

CHAPTER II
LIRA

The night passed slowly, and Lira drifted in and out of dozing in her chamber. She wished she had asked Ljós for a tincture to help her rest, but Artur's interruption had driven the notion from her mind. Now, she sorely missed the relaxing teas and remedies Nevala had concocted back at Va'hesk.

Halgeir's dark interior distorted one's perception of time—of day and night. There was no sunlight in the fortress's innermost chambers, though its dwellers could walk the winding exterior paths on the outside of the structure to get their sunlight. Indoors, it was impossible to tell what time it was without being a part of the clan's daily rhythm.

Lira lay on her back, staring into the dark. In a way, being here reminded her of Iathium's dungeons—the distortion of time and place. She thought of her friends and her family—of Aidryn, Eremon, Talfryn, Irem, Ellwyn. Her mother, not far away but just out of her reach. Her father.

The thought of Da brought a cascade of memories crashing through her mind. She remembered her mother's expression the moment they learned his fate. The way Eremon had looked at her, his eyes so mournful and lonely, from across the Dome's courtyard in the wake of their fathers' deaths. That silent camaraderie they'd shared, all those years, knowing their fathers had perished together.

Just then, from somewhere in the dark, she heard a familiar voice: *They knew.*

Lira sat bolt upright, heart hammering, ears straining. It couldn't be.

"Eremon?" she whispered.

She felt the tingling in her fingertips and waited for the witnessing to come. But instead of seeing images from the past, a flood of voices filled her head. No, not voices—one voice, spoken as if a thousand, splintered and shattered but strangely unified. Eremon's voice.

They knew.

Silira, save me!

The sound of his voice—the pleading way he cried out for her—left her trembling when the witnessing released its hold on her. When he'd died in the courtyard that day, she'd tried— tried everything. But he had never once cried out her name or begged her to save him. He had known his magic was taking a catastrophic toll on him, but he'd been more concerned about making her his heir.

Had Eremon tried to call to her while his magic burned him alive? Was she hearing his final thoughts as some sort of penance for her own failure?

She'd borne the pain of Eremon's death alone in Iathium's dungeons. Alone in Rodhlan's meadowlands. And now, alone in Fortress Halgeir—with her mother so close by, sequestered in her own chambers.

Does Mam even know I'm here?

Lira lay back against the pillows, pulling the soft furs up to her chin. She guessed it was still the middle of the night, because she couldn't hear anyone coming or going in the corridors outside her chamber. So, she lay awake for a long while, trying to will herself back to sleep.

Her thoughts drifted back to her mother, and she was suddenly filled with a longing for Mam that she hadn't felt in years. She remembered Mam's embraces, too—just as comforting and warm as Da's, though Lira had distanced herself when Artur entered their life. Now, she regretted her unquestioning loyalty to the city. She regretted holding her mother at arm's length all this time.

There was so much to regret.

Anger sparked in her at the thought of Artur restricting her movements. Her mother was all she had left of her immediate family right now. There was no way of knowing when she would see Talfryn again—if he was still alive. Lira wasn't going to let the overlord continue standing between her and Mam.

I don't care what Artur says—I have to see her.

She threw the furs aside and swung her legs over the side of the bed, fumbling to light the candle that sat on the low stone table next to her. Once lit, she carried it around the room, lighting the other candles that she'd arranged around its perimeter.

Several changes of clothes had been left with her, yet she hadn't bothered to look them over. She was still dressed in her filthy traveling clothes from the night before, still caked with dirt and blood. Her leg smarted when she put her full weight on it, but when she examined the scar, it was nothing but a barely-visible—but jagged—white line.

There was a bathing chamber connected to her room; she moved toward the stone tub that sat in the center and turned a lever to fill it. Steam rose from the hot water, which slowly began to warm the room.

Fortress Halgeir had managed to engineer a few marvelous luxuries in the midst of its cultural and social isolation. Clean, heated water was one of them. Iathium's Dome was the only structure that surpassed its comforts, and it had borrowed many of its own advances from Clan Beran. If she could have combined Iathium's love for plush blankets and pillows with Clan Beran's easy, warm baths, she might never want to leave.

Various soaps and creams lined the side of the tub in crystal vials, and there were several sponges and brushes to choose from. Lira peeled off her clothes and ran a rough brush over her skin before stepping into the tub. She hissed at the heat, her skin pink and sensitive, but quickly sank into the deep bath anyway despite the water's sting. It had been too long since she'd had a proper bath like this.

At least being alone in Fortress Halgeir would be quiet. She would never be accepted among the clan, and that was for the best. It would mean recovering in solitude for a time while she worked out her next moves.

In truth, it was unsettling for no one to seek her out here. Over the years, she'd grown used to people needing her at all times—whether it was Talfryn at home, the apprentices in the archive, Irem, or Eremon. So many people had relied on her back in the city, for various reasons. It wouldn't be long before she was called on to serve Beran, unless she could convince Artur to release her and allow her to serve them freely.

One thing was certain: Lira couldn't continue existing in a state of fear. She'd been afraid and unsure of herself for so long now, she wasn't entirely sure how she would begin to break the pattern. Irem had admired her ability to be diplomatic, so she must had been a good communicator at one time. Now, she would need to call on that skill to renegotiate her freedom with Artur.

A wave of shame passed over her as she recalled her failed attempt at negotiating with Gerallt. But she tried to shake it off; besides, Gerallt's plans had already been set into motion before she arrived in the Ridge. Nothing she said or did would have changed his mind.

She wondered where Gerallt, Aila, and Caitir were now—what their next move would be. Something inside her whispered that they intended to amass more power, and perhaps move against Iathium sooner rather than later. Lira shuddered at the thought of her uncle and his two wives, and then her thoughts snagged on Caitir.

Caitir's entry into the marriage-alliance with Gerallt was so outside her character. She had always been lively and energetic. Yes, her ambition had always existed—and perhaps Lira had mistaken her competitive nature for friendly competition, similar to Aidryn's. She had never imagined Caitir would want to do real harm to anyone.

The water lapped around her in the silence, and she thought about the way Aidryn had crumpled at the full realization of what his sister had done. She missed his warmth, his familiarity, and she wished...

Lira shook off the thought as another wave of grief washed over her. The only option was to save him and keep him close. Their barely detectable connection through the Binding was the only thing that reassured Lira he was still alive.

Thinking about his fate for too long was a dangerous prospect. Panic and fear would make it difficult to focus on saving him. She tried not to think about the memory she'd witnessed the day before.

First, she had Artur to contend with. She couldn't afford to cower before the overlord. The man might be her stepfather, but Lira was now one of the most powerful magic-wielders in Rodhlan. More than that, she was a truth-bearer. Perhaps she could use her magic to persuade Artur to release her as his prisoner and ally with her instead.

She remembered Aidryn's admonition to push past her fear.

Stay on your feet, Lira, and never bow to anyone.

Lira's breath caught at the sudden memory. She squeezed her eyes shut and dunked her head under the water to wash it away.

When the bath was tepid, Lira stepped out and dried herself, squeezing excess water from her tangle of curls. Carefully, she combed through her hair, working out the snarls before scrunching a saltwater tincture through the strands. She wasted no time in donning the garb of Clan Beran, discarding her filthy gown in favor of warm leggings and a knee-length tunic-dress trimmed with fur.

She'd found a familiar pair of soft, supple leather boots that had been left in her room sometime after she arrived—boots she'd regretted leaving behind the last time she returned to Iathium. It was a welcome comfort to have something that belonged to her in this place.

Lira pulled the boots on and checked her hair in the glass. She took the time to painstakingly weave beads and fragments of bone and shell into sections of her hair as it dried, working a few strategically placed braids into her mass of curls.

There was no time to lose. She would be granted access to her mother today, and she would demand her freedom.

Her thoughts shifted immediately to *how* she was going to get through the fortress to Iva at all. There was a series of barred doors that closed off sections of the fortress, making them accessible only to those who possessed a key.

She considered ways to use her magic. Perhaps she could grow roots to break through the doors, or thick vines to crack them open. Already, she'd bent this magic to her will, using it to defend herself and her friends. Surely there was a way…

And then she remembered the *other* power she harbored.

As if summoned, Aidryn's magic surged to life within her. There was a warmth to it that her own power had never provided. His magic was a mere fraction of what he'd been born with, and she wondered for a moment what it might feel like to experience the full measure of it.

Glorious, she thought. *Glorious and wonderful and bright.*

And that was fitting for Aidryn. His presence had been a constant source of vibrance and stability in her life—something she'd realized in the weeks since she lost him. Even before then, when he'd left his post in the archive, she'd felt his absence keenly, and had mourned the unwelcome change.

She'd taken him for granted for far too long. If Lira managed to get him out alive, she'd never let a day go by without letting him know how much he meant to her.

And there it was.

She closed her eyes for a moment, her breath escaping her lips in a soft *whoosh*. The sound of his voice had made her ache for him with a longing she'd been struggling to ignore since that day in the mountains. Maybe longer than that.

Lira shuddered. This wasn't why she'd summoned Aidryn's power. Now was not the time for getting tangled in her emotions. She would sort out her feelings eventually.

Perhaps.

For now, the next step was to get to her mother.

The leather pouch she'd worn on her belt in the meadowlands sat on the floor by the bed. When she'd arrived, it had only contained her heirlooms from Skelly, but now it appeared to be full once again. She remembered how it had filled with keys the day before, and she wondered whether it was safe to hope that any of those keys might help her navigate the fortress.

Lira hefted the pouch, and sure enough, it strained with the weight of the keys within. She would have to explore her own truth power later—ask it the purpose of a magic that allowed Tarlach's anointed to hide keys in the ether and extract them on a whim. It would have seemed like a pointless power to have before she needed it.

She'd seen Aidryn fire a shot of magic at a lock before to disengage it, but she had a feeling she would fumble too much with the mechanisms. A real key would be better.

Lira dumped the pouch's contents out onto the bed and rifled through them.

"This is going to be cumbersome," she muttered to herself, looking over the different designs and makes of the keys. "How did you select just one at a time? I don't need fifty of them at once."

She strained to recall whether she'd ever seen her mother using a key on the corridor entryways here in the fortress. It wouldn't be ornate or delicate, coming from Beran. Instead, it would be practical, plain—small, perhaps, for ease of transport. Able to be used for multiple doors, because the warriors wouldn't want to sift through heavy key rings.

Finally, her eyes landed on a small iron key that met these standards. It was the size of her palm, but sturdy and plain. She set it aside, re-filled the pouch, and crept toward the door, but immediately noticed there wasn't a keyhole on the inside.

With a groan, she sat down on the ground in front of the door and placed her fingertips on it. Closing her eyes, she called on her own power. Emerald light flared around her.

"How do Clan Beran's doors open from the inside?" she asked.

She half expected not to get an answer, but a moment later, a brief vision rose to her mind.

A nameless woman is held captive in Clan Beran's fortress. She is alone, afraid—abandoned by her clan and left here as prisoner. Desperation rises as she surveys the ornately carved door before her; there is no lock to pick from the inside. Power wells within her alongside her raging terror, and she grips the door's iron handle and pulls once. Twice. On the third attempt, she stops, panting, and rests her head against it. A flash of crimson power floods her senses, and a moment later, a keyhole appears.

If only there was a key to fit it, she thinks. Again, that power flashes, and she finds one resting in her waiting palm.

The vision released Lira then, and she was relieved to find herself sitting on the floor, just where she'd begun. A sheen of sweat covered her face, and she swiped it away before standing and gripping the chamber door's iron handle herself. It took effort to seek out Aidryn's power after tapping into her own, but she found it once again and concentrated on chasing the sensation until the crimson power flared from her own hand and a keyhole appeared.

Releasing a shaky breath, she fitted the key she'd found into the hole and turned it. The mechanism within clicked to life, and an elated cry rose in her throat—one she swallowed as she pushed the chamber door open and stepped out into the dim, torchlit corridor.

Lira expected to have guards posted outside her door, but she was surprised to find the hallway empty. She hurried down the corridor, key in hand, and focused on summoning another thread of Aidryn's magic as she approached the locked door that closed off her end of the corridor.

Just as she had in her chamber, she called on the keyhole to appear, then summoned the small key back into her waiting palm. She moved through three doors similar to her own before she reached the outlet to the outside pathway.

By the time Lira reached the final door, she was beginning to feel heady with victory. It wouldn't be long before she reached the outer paths—then, she could take them all the way down to the Arthmael's Hall.

Lira grasped the handle and closed her eyes, feeling for Aidryn's magic. Once again, she fitted the key and the lock disengaged. She pushed the heavy doors open, but when she moved to step through them, she came face-to-face with a familiar pair of bright green eyes.

CHAPTER 12
LIRA

Fortress Halgeir

Talfryn froze before her, gaping in surprise. Her younger brother's hair was still tousled from sleep, and he was clad in a black tunic and leggings similar to those he'd worn beneath his armor back in Iathium.

"Lira?" he cried.

"Talfryn!"

A cry escaped her lips as she took in the sight of him, stepping forward to pull him into an embrace. But he stepped out of her reach, his expression crumpling as his gaze dropped to the ground.

She blinked in disbelief. "Tal... what..."

His face had paled. "I heard you'd been brought here, but..." He shook his head.

For a moment, she felt utterly lost at his response to seeing her. It wouldn't be surprising if he was done with her after what had happened in Iathium. But then her gaze fell to his left shoulder, and she gasped, pressing a hand to her mouth. Sometime between *Nami Mostari* and his arrival at Beran, he'd lost his left arm. It appeared to have been cut off at the shoulder.

She began to tremble. "By Nami, Talfryn," she whispered, voice wavering. "What did they do to you?"

He looked up at her mournfully then, his eyes filled with a pain she'd never seen there before. "It happened after the festival," he said quietly, "before Faolan could get to me."

Lira remembered the way General Peros had run Talfryn through with his sword, and a sick sensation overtook her. Faolan had told her Talfryn paid a price for showing loyalty to his sister. Talfryn finally closed the distance between them and pulled her into a tight hug.

"I'm sorry," Lira said, her voice muffled against his chest. "I was supposed to protect you, but I failed."

"I would do it again," he whispered, his voice surprisingly calm. "Every bit of it."

Lira shook her head. "It wasn't supposed to be this way," she whispered.

"But it is," he said, patting her back gently. "The Beran healers sealed the wound for me. I'm still a bit weak, but it's been more than two months. They're feeding me well and I'm feeling stronger. I don't want you to worry about me."

No matter what, Lira would *always* worry about her brother. But that didn't mean she had to say so.

"I'm so glad you made it out alive," she said, squeezing him around the middle. "I feared the worst."

"If it weren't for Faolan and Aeron, I wouldn't have," he replied. "It was Faolan who persuaded the Captain to spare my life. Talked him into letting them be my guards. Then, they smuggled me out."

"It seems I have a lot to thank them for," she replied.

Talfryn's expression darkened as he pulled back and said, "Whatever happened to Aidryn Tarlach? I know he was trying to help you..."

"He did help me," Lira answered, a lump forming in her throat, "but he allowed himself to be captured in the mountains. I need to get to him as quickly as possible—that's what I was trying to do when Thorne found me." She swallowed hard. "I was *trying*," she repeated feebly.

"Where is he now?" Talfryn asked. "I'll get word into the city if I can."

Lira knew he wouldn't be able to do that—not under Beran's scrutiny. Still, she appreciated the sentiment. "Gerallt had him in the valley, the last I knew. But that could be different now." Her voice broke, and she squeezed her eyes shut.

"You were in the Ridge," Talfryn ventured. "What about Skelly? Where is she?"

"Safe," Lira answered, "with Lord Irem at his family's settlement." She hoped Talfryn wouldn't pry about their rocky reunion and abrupt separation, and he did not.

"Good." Her brother looked her in the eyes. "We'll try to find a way to help Aidryn. Let's hope he can survive until then."

Lira glanced down at Eremon's ring and rubbed it with her thumb. "If Eremon's spell holds, he will."

Talfryn didn't miss the gesture. He glanced down at the ring, too, then looked at her curiously. "What do you mean by that?"

Lira looked left and right down the long corridors, then grabbed Talfryn by the sleeve and dragged him back into the shadows. "You can't repeat this, Talfryn—not to anyone," she whispered.

His eyes glimmered, a hint of levity despite the weight of their conversation. "Intrigue! I love it. What can't I repeat?"

"Well..." Lira began nervously. "Do you remember the ancient Binding rituals Skelly used to perform in the valley from time to time?"

"What, you mean like weddings?" he asked, wrinkling his nose.

She nodded and inhaled deeply, trying to control the racing of her heart. "Yes, well—Eremon did that. To me and Aidryn." She held up her ring. "He used this."

"Wait, he—what?" Talfryn grabbed her hand and scrutinized the ring. "This is Eremon's ring, isn't it? I don't—" He huffed a laugh and shook his head. "I don't understand."

"Eremon. Bound us. To one another." Lira studied Talfryn's expression carefully, attempting to gauge his response. "Me and Aidryn."

"What? You mean your intended bound the two of you into some sort of..." He shook his head again, searching for the words. "Magical arranged marriage?"

"Exactly that," Lira answered.

"But... *he* wanted to marry you—so, why?" Talfryn ran his hand through his mess of curls. "Why would he do that?"

"I'm still trying to understand it myself," she answered, "and I don't know what to do about it."

"Then do nothing," Talfryn said. "Eremon must have had his reasons. I trusted him without question—most of us did. Besides, Aidryn did always fancy you. He's a good match. I can't complain about having him for a brother."

Lira's cheeks burned. "That's not the point—the point is that the choice wasn't ours."

"It could be much worse," her brother said, ribbing her. "It could have been Lord Irem."

She made a face and shook off the notion. "No, thank you. At any rate—I hope it will all sort itself out somehow. We just have to get Aidryn out. That's all that matters right now. We can think about the rest later."

"It's not like arranged marriages are unusual," Talfryn supplied.

Lira sighed. "But I worked so hard to avoid one, and in the end, that didn't matter."

One of the most important reasons why she'd pursued a historian position in the archive was to remain self-sufficient if she wanted to. She would never have needed to marry unless it was entirely her choice. But it had never been easy to make others understand why she held such strong opinions about it.

Turning on a heel, she headed back out to the corridor outside, but Talfryn stepped in front of her to block her path.

"I thought you were under house arrest," he said. "Why are you out of your chamber?"

Lira cringed. All the talk of injuries, magic, and Aidryn had distracted him, and she'd hoped he wouldn't ask.

"I'm going to see Mam," she said, raising her chin.

Her brother's expression grew weary, and his eyes shone much older and wiser than his sixteen years now. "You are *not*. You should go back until someone sends for you."

"I will not be treated like a prisoner," she said firmly. "And I won't let Art—"

"Don't," he said, squeezing her shoulder to silence her. "Don't say it out here. You must have caught the changing of the guard. Let's get you back inside."

"No," Lira said, planting her feet stubbornly. "I refuse to be intimidated by these people. Besides, Artur needs to understand that he can't just take my magic by coercion. We'll need to reach an agreement that works for everyone."

Talfryn narrowed his eyes, scrutinizing her. She expected him to press her again about going back to her chamber, but instead he said, "You'll have to catch me up on all this magic business. I'd like to know if I will inherit any myself—that is, if Beran will still have me after I've begun wielding it."

An idea began to form in Lira's mind, but she kept it to herself and instead answered, "It's very possible. Let's talk about it this afternoon, once I've settled my case here."

"You're awfully confident about this," Talfryn said. "Speaking of which, how did you get through all the locked doors?"

"I'll explain later," Lira answered, jerking her chin in the direction of the Arthmael's Hall. "Come with me?"

Talfryn sighed. "Let's go." He led her toward the outer walkway that wound around the fortress.

When she reached his side, he smirked. "I never got a chance to tell you how incredible that was—what you did for Eremon in the courtyard, with the thorns."

Lira dipped her head, remembering the walls of thorns that had burst up from the ground, clearing a path to where Eremon lay dying. "I only wish I could have saved him."

Talfryn wrapped his arm around her shoulder and squeezed. "Anyone with eyes could see how hard you tried—how much you cared for him."

They slowed to a stop behind a pillar, hiding in the shadow of the wide stone walkway. Lira hid her face in her hands and took a shaky breath. "Talfryn, there's so much more I haven't been able to tell you," she said quietly. "One disaster after another—more missteps than I can count."

"We can't cover it all here," Talfryn answered. "If you want to put your neck on Artur's chopping block, let's get that part behind us first—then we'll talk more."

"Assuming I can speak after he's lopped my head from my shoulders?" she asked grimly.

"Just remember those vines and thorns of yours," her brother answered, "and you'll be fine."

She was surprised that a small contingent of warriors didn't appear from behind to strike them down immediately for their treasonous words. But the path remained quiet and deserted, save for the siblings. The only sounds in the corridor were their own footfalls.

As they emerged out of the shadows and onto the exterior walkway, Lira squinted against the sunlight. The late spring warmth nearly made her gasp; she had missed so much of this season. Before long, it would be summer.

They wound down three levels until they came to the base of the fortress. The entrance to the Arthmael's Hall was at the northern end of the courtyard, the land barren on the pathway to the massive oak doors. Sparse grass gave way to packed dirt as they approached the door, and four of Artur's masked warriors met them as they drew near.

Lira stopped a few feet from them, raising her chin. "I am here to see Iva Beran," she declared, planting her feet firmly as she crossed her arms. "You will let me pass."

"Return to your chamber," one of the warriors said, striking the end of his spear against the hard ground. "You have one warning."

"I will not," she answered. "Let me pass."

"Lira..." Talfryn hissed.

The warriors stood firm.

Lira felt her power gathering in her palms, and she prepared to strike them. But just then, one of the massive doors opened, and Thorne emerged stone-faced from the hall.

He paled when he saw Lira, but strode purposefully toward her without missing a beat. She scowled up at the massive young man. Talfryn stood taller, stepping to her side.

"Take me to see my mother," she demanded. "She and the overlord *will* hear my plea."

"Artur is gone." Thorne cast a sidelong glance at the warriors and jerked his chin toward the hall's entrance. "Walk with me."

"What do you mean, he's gone?" Lira asked incredulously, trotting to keep up with Thorne's long strides. "Gone where?"

"He left at dawn," Thorne answered. "I cannot tell you more until we have privacy."

Lira scoffed. "Whatever it takes. Lead the way."

Thorne's expression grew distant. He turned and strode back toward the Arthmael's Hall. "Come," he said. "She's in here."

"She'd better be," Lira snapped toward his back, trotting at his heels. "And what will my punishment be, for leaving my chamber? Certain death?"

"There will be no punishment," Thorne answered, "but if

you want allies here, you will listen to me. Just for a little while." He turned his head and met her eyes. "Please."

Lira opened her mouth to unleash on him again, but something in his voice gave her pause. He was openly pleading with her, and risking his reputation here to do so. She wanted to keep fighting him, but the subtle tug in the back of her mind hadn't led her astray yet, and it was telling her to keep trusting him.

"Just help me understand," she said. "There is so much I don't understand."

Talfryn moved closer to her, lacing their fingers together. Lira squeezed his hand, keenly aware once again of what he'd just survived. How she'd almost lost him. She bit back her emotions and looked Thorne in the face again.

The warrior's expression softened. "Then do not try yet. There is still much to learn." He turned to move again, but paused. "And be careful what you say to your mother in the presence of witnesses."

Lira's eyes narrowed. "I assume we will never be without witnesses. Why doesn't that surprise me?"

Talfryn squeezed her hand. "Wait and see. Don't assume anything."

Lira looked from her brother back to Thorne and scowled. "Why not assume the worst? Then, when something turns out well, it will be a pleasant surprise."

With that, she pushed past both men and stalked toward the towering doors that led into the hall. She thought she heard Thorne tell the warriors to stand down, but she didn't pause to give it thought. Truthfully, she'd expected him to try to stop her.

Though it had been many years since Lira had darkened this threshold, she remembered how heavy the doors were—remembered trying to push them open herself when she was an adolescent. They were ornately carved with ancient runes, depictions of Clan Beran's birth, and the construction of Fortress Halgeir. Fleetingly, she wondered if glimpsing the memories of those doors would show her the same story as their carvings did.

She wouldn't be touching the doors today, but they would certainly open for her—without Thorne's help, or anyone else's. Rather than being led in like a prisoner, Lira would make her presence known herself.

CHAPTER 13

LIRA

Fortress Halgeir

Never bow to anyone. Aidryn's words echoed through her very soul, and magic crackled between her fingertips unbidden.

When she was close enough to touch the carvings, she summoned her full measure of power, feeling it pulse into the ground beneath her feet. Roots and winding vines blasted from beneath the dirt, snaking their way toward the doors to the hall. They grew into a canopy of trees that climbed up the exterior and pushed inward, leaning in so hard their roots threatened to rip from the earth.

The canopy made its way inside the torchlit hall, growing rapidly toward a tall dais where a woman sat alone, muscular and stock straight. She wore a warrior's mask that covered her face; a mane of fur burst from its edges, and the face was carved to resemble one of the large mountain cats that roamed Rodhlan Ridge. Her attire was similar to Lira's in every other way, though she clutched a long spear.

Lira walked purposefully beneath the canopy that grew and

bloomed just above and ahead of her. Grasses and wildflowers sprouted along the path beneath her feet, and the inhabitants of the hall turned to stare as she moved toward her mother on the dais.

Just as she reached the end of the walkway, she stopped and stood tall. Protocol demanded she kneel before anyone who sat on the overlord's throne, but this time she would risk breaking it. This time, she would be treated as an equal. An authority on the situation at hand.

For a long moment, the hall was still and silent. Lira stared at her mother's mask as though she could see straight through it—as though she were looking into her mother's dark eyes. Iva remained as still as a statue.

Lira silently summoned every emotion she could grasp— grief, fear, devastation, loss. Hope. Love. Desperation. She prayed Iva would see all of that and more in her eyes.

Still, her mother remained unmoving. Lira opened her mouth to speak, but thought better of it. She had sorely tested her limits and endangered herself—not to mention Talfryn and Thorne. Perhaps her mother had changed so thoroughly that there would be no getting through to her, and Lira's boldness would hasten her own demise. Or perhaps there was another way to touch this woman's heart.

Lira closed her eyes, envisioning her childhood visits to the Ridge. She remembered the delicate white blooms that burst from the trees in the mountains every spring—her mother's favorite. Arlen had often surprised Lira and Iva with baskets full of them, and Iva would weave them crowns and necklaces and bracelets to wear.

The flowers had embodied childhood wonder for Lira. They had been everything good and pure and true and real— the only magic she'd been allowed to know in those days.

She opened her eyes and felt another rush of power careen down her arms as those same flowers began to burst from the canopy overhead, and then rain from the sky. They drifted down slowly, spinning gracefully and alighting on boots and shoulders and hair. A collective gasp overtook the massive hall.

Lira stood her ground, still watching her mother carefully. The woman had shifted ever so slightly where she sat, her grip on the spear loosening almost imperceptibly. For a moment, Lira thought she'd wasted her energy, her magic, in coming here—and then she saw Iva's shoulders hitch.

Abruptly, her mother stood and let the spear fall to the dais. The warriors posted around the hall rose and reached for their weapons, but Iva held up a hand. She slowly removed her mask, setting it on the seat she'd occupied moments before.

For the first time in years, mother and daughter locked eyes. Iva's dark brown hair—so like Lira's—fell around her face in tight curls. Most of it was pulled back into a thick braid that had been woven through with pieces of shell and bone.

Iva rushed down the steps of the dais and ran to Lira, throwing her arms around her daughter. Lira returned the embrace, and the two sank to the floor, clutching one another tightly.

"I thought I would never see you again," Iva whispered into Lira's hair, gripping her hard.

"I feared the same," Lira answered. She noted how strong Iva had become—likely a result of training with Artur's warriors, as Beran's women often did.

Though the years had changed them both, Iva's embrace was as comforting and familiar as ever. Despite her years with Beran, Lira noticed that her mother's scent was the same. Iva lovingly ran a hand over Lira's curls before her cool fingertips rested against her temple.

"Witness, Lira," her mother whispered.

Lira closed her eyes as memory after memory flooded her mind in rapid succession. It was difficult to keep up at first. Iva's memories of Lira's childhood blinked through her mind, one after the other—flashes and fragments of the life they'd known in Iathium. But the memories slowed and snagged on one particularly painful moment that Iva seemed to remember as vividly as Lira did.

Lira crosses her arms, leaning against the hearth as Iva stirs the stew that hangs over the fire. "What about Da?"

Iva's expression remains impassive. "Silira, your father would want us to be protected. Artur offers us that and more."

"But Clan Beran, Mam? Really?" Lira pushes off the hearth and stalks across the kitchen before turning to glare at her mother again. "Do you not care about the years of work I've put in to rank up in the archive? I'm a historian now, and you think you can just take that away from me?"

Iva's shoulders curl in on themselves, her features pinched now. "I'm not trying to hurt you—"

"I'm not leaving Iathium!" Lira cries. "I'm sixteen—old enough to run a household. I can earn enough to stay right here."

"Silira, if you would just consider—"

"Consider what, Mam? That you want to leave? That's not what mothers do. Mothers don't leave!"

Iva stands abruptly, angrily slamming the ladle onto the work table. "You haven't let me be your mother since Arlen died," she said, raising her voice as well. "And you've carried on his legacy, making Talfryn love the city more than his own kin—"

"Because Iathium loves us back!" Lira cries. "Our family never did."

"Those are your father's words—he poisoned you both."

"He wanted us to have a good life—"

"And I could do nothing!" Iva finally shouts, drowning out Lira's argument. "He took me from my family in the mountains and brought me here. Then, he practically sacrificed my children to the Dome. So forgive me if I want to forge my own path for once. There's no other way to protect you."

Lira took hold of Iva's memory and stopped it there,

grasping her mother's hand and gently pulling it away from her face. Her mother's grief was palpable and overwhelming.

"Mam..." Lira struggled to control her quivering voice.

Iva pulled her into another tight hug. "I'm not angry with you. I'm just glad you're here. After all this time, I feel as though I can finally protect you."

Lira returned the embrace, unsure of how to respond. She finally settled on, "We need to speak privately."

"Yes." Her mother squeezed her shoulders meaningfully. "We do."

Iva stood abruptly, offering Lira her hand. Lira took it and rose as well. Her mother gestured for her to turn to face the hall's entrance, where a large crowd had silently filtered in to watch. Thorne and Talfryn stood near the doors, tense with what Lira could only assume was dread.

Iva raised her chin. "My people," she began, her voice strong and unwavering, "we welcome a daughter. The overlord regards her as his own; so also shall you."

The declaration hit Lira hard in the gut. It was in direct opposition to the way Artur had regarded her the night before. But if the other clanspeople present—like Thorne—were aware of the contrast, they did not speak up.

A ripple of movement cascaded across the hall as the clanspeople dipped their heads to acknowledge Lira. Her heart raced and her palms grew sweaty as she took in the sheer number of people who had noticed her display of power.

"You may know Silira as the Anointed of Clan Mór: Witness Tree of Rodhlan," Iva said. "She also guards the inheritance to Iathium's throne. But first and foremost, she is my child.

"And as my child, she has agreed to help us heal the blight on our land. Her magic will give us the means to survive abundantly through any war that overtakes Rodhlan."

The people began buzzing excitedly, and Lira's eyes widened. She looked to Iva and said through tight lips, "That is what we need to speak about."

Her mother nodded curtly, then began to move. "Follow me."

Lira exchanged glances with Talfryn and Thorne as they passed. Once she and Iva had exited the hall, the two followed a few paces behind. They moved quickly down a dark pathway just to their left. It was one of Halgeir's many tunneled-out stone hallways, but it reminded her of the pitch-black dungeon paths beneath the Dome.

Lira took a deep breath and steeled herself before they entered. More than once, she found herself almost trotting to keep up with Iva's long, powerful strides. It made her painfully aware of how sedentary she'd been for so long, despite her long walks across Iathium in the old days.

As they rounded a curve in the corridor, they nearly ran headlong into Ljós. The healer nodded to Lira, then deferred to Iva, who said, "We need a place to speak."

"Of course," he said softly, steering the group toward a small chamber just off the hallway. "In here."

They crowded into the room and Ljós shut the door behind them. He raised his palms, and just as the day before, it felt as though all the sound was sucked from the room. Lira's ears popped as they adjusted to the difference in pressure. This spell the healer favored was certainly helpful for preventing eavesdroppers, but she didn't think it would ever be comfortable.

As soon as Iva was satisfied the spell had taken hold, her shoulders relaxed visibly, worry lines creasing her forehead.

"Now, Lira," her mother began—her tone so much more familiar, now that she'd escaped the scrutiny of the clan. "Tell me, what is it about your magic? I remember everything Skelly told us about how you can nurture the land. I suppose I don't understand the problem."

"The problem is that Artur declared me a prisoner, then demanded the magic," Lira said. "I don't think I can willingly honor his request as long as I'm considered a captive. The magic would be taken by coercion, not given freely."

Iva's brow knitted. The healer nodded solemnly.

"What difference does that make?" Talfryn asked.

"Stolen magic poisons its new host, then multiplies before returning to the giver," Thorne supplied. "Lira explained it to me last night."

Together, Lira, Thorne, and Ljós explained the rules of magic wrongfully taken, and what had happened to Eremon. Iva's expression grew stormy as Lira recounted the way Skelly had given her birthright, then explained her own overflow of power.

"I'm glad you're here, Ljós, because I have an idea," Lira said, looking to the amber-eyed healer. "Rather than giving my power to the land under duress, may I willingly give a portion of it to my mother and brother? As descendants of Clan Mór, it's their rightful inheritance."

Talfryn and Iva exchanged a curious glance. Iva wrapped her arm around her son and held him close.

"I think you can certainly do that," Ljós answered, "if they are willing to receive it."

"Then we could heal the land ourselves," Talfryn said, sitting up straighter.

"Yes," Lira answered with a nod. "That's what I'm thinking. That way, Artur gets what he desires, but not in a way that would harm Clan Beran."

"You will feel better, yourself, once you've given away some of your power," Ljós added. "I would recommend doing so as often as you're able."

"I would like to do that," Lira said quietly. She looked to Iva and Talfryn then, who were studying her closely. They both seemed calm and assured—not at all apprehensive of the idea she'd laid out. So she asked them, "Are you willing to accept a portion of our clan's power?"

Talfryn grinned widely. "You don't have to ask me twice."

Iva inclined her head and answered, "We would be honored."

Lira reached for her mother's hand. "Will this affect your standing with Clan Beran, Mam?"

"I'm not concerned about that," Iva answered sharply. "They know where I was born. They know who my children are. I'm no longer willing to hide the parts of myself they don't want to see."

Lira's brows rose. "Do you carry Beran's power as well? Could that interfere?"

Iva shook her head. "My husband has not granted me his magic. I'm an empty vessel, as you called it."

With a deep breath, Lira nodded. "Ljós, I have never passed power to anyone else before. Will you show me what to do?"

"Transfer of power relies mostly on your intent," the healer answered, motioning for Lira, Talfryn, and Iva to sit. She sat cross-legged on the floor, her mother and brother facing her.

Thorne remained standing against the far wall, watching them quietly. Lira wondered fleetingly whether he might be planning to tell Artur what they were doing. Let the overlord come for them; the three of them could overpower him in a moment.

"In this case, Silira," Ljós continued, "focus your intent on gifting your family their rightful portion of your clan's power. Don't try to control how much that is; you'll find that magic is surprisingly instinctive. First, take your mother's hands."

Lira and Iva reached for one another. Ljós nodded once, then continued. "Now, focus your intent. Close your eyes and allow the magic to work."

Lira allowed her eyelids to flutter closed, searching her magic for the right things to say. A moment later, the words flooded her mind. "To my mother, Iva Mór Beran, I grant a rightful portion of Clan Mór's magic. May she wield it to nurture, to protect, and to guide those whom she leads and loves."

With a little gasp and a start, Lira opened her eyes. Emerald magic flared from her pendant and filled the room.

Vines of sparkling power encircled Iva, drifting softly down onto her skin before dissipating into glittering dust that settled and soaked into her pores. Iva took a deep breath and sighed, her expression euphoric as the power took hold. Lira couldn't take her eyes off her mother; she was absolutely luminous.

Talfryn's eyes were wide. "Mam—Lira—you're both glowing!"

Lira looked down at her skin, and sure enough, it had also taken on the same glittering, emerald sheen. "So strange," she said, turning her hands over to inspect them. "Mam, how do you feel?"

"Like a missing part of myself has returned," Iva answered, eyes rimmed with tears.

Talfryn beamed. "My turn, Lira," he said excitedly. "We all know *I* could use a boost." He pointed to his left shoulder and laughed softly.

Lira smiled sadly, and Iva patted his hand. Talfryn had always been the one to lighten up the room—but to see him jesting about his injury pained her.

"I'm honored to share this power with you," Lira said, reaching for his hand.

His eyes shone in the torchlit room, and she repeated her words of intent. Magic flared once again, and when she opened her eyes, his skin shimmered with it, too.

"Is this how it feels to *use* magic?" he asked in wonder. "If so, I may never emerge from it."

Lira laughed. "It can be rather intoxicating," she answered. "The more you use your power, the stronger it grows. If you lose yourself to it, you'll be more powerful than any of us before long."

"I'm ready to heal the gardens," Talfryn declared. "What do we do?"

"It's as much about intent as the transfer," Lira answered. "I've used words to create, as well as thoughts. There don't seem to be many rigid rules so long as the intention is set. For example"—she opened her palm—"I can speak the word *leaf*..."

With a burst of magic, a long, green leaf appeared in her hand. She smiled. "But I can also think..."

Dagger.

The leaf immediately hardened into a blade. Talfryn's eyes grew wide as she handed it to him.

"Go ahead," she said.

He touched a finger to the knife's tip and flinched. "It's sharp!"

"Remind me to tell you how I made thousands of them back in the mountains," she said with a grin. Her brother's jaw dropped.

From his vantage point on the wall, Thorne chuckled, brows raised in surprise.

Ljós lay a hand on Lira's shoulder and leaned in conspiratorially. "Shall we test your power, now that you've released a bit?"

Lira nodded. Already, she felt lighter. The healer touched his fingertips to her temple.

"Witness," he said.

A gentle rush of memory overtook her then, sentient and imploring. Lira saw Clan Beran's past, as clearly as if she had stepped back in time herself.

Clanspeople tend to lush, hanging gardens that grow along the outside corridors and downstairs in a wide courtyard. Healers train people of neighboring clans in the art of medicine. The people of Beran come and go freely from their fortress—into Iathium, to and from the clan territories, into the grazing fields, onto the hunting grounds. Magic flows freely, and the people are unafraid.

The witnessing released her easily, and she blinked as the room came back into focus. There was no reeling sensation— no discomfort whatsoever. Instead, she felt calm and controlled. It wasn't at all like the chaos she'd felt these past several weeks. She felt quiet inside. Truly powerful.

This was how her magic was supposed to feel. Not violent and uncontrolled, but instead a patient guide that grasped her hand and led her into the past as a quiet observer.

"How did that feel?" Ljós asked.

Lira smiled. "Much better."

He nodded decisively, then glanced over at Iva and Talfryn. "Shall we put them to work?"

TEACHING IVA and Talfryn to wield their power was an all-day endeavor, but it resulted in fresh grass in the courtyard, with a little new garden growth on the far western side of the fortress. The trio drew a rather large crowd—something that made Lira both nervous and a bit elated.

She refrained from using her own magic and tried to focus her energy on her family. As they worked, she was able to recount everything she'd gone through since Eremon's death. When she got to the part about leaving Skelly, she braced herself for their reprimands—but surprisingly, Iva and Talfryn listened without judgment.

Lira carefully tiptoed around the story of the Binding, keenly aware of Talfryn's repeated glances in her direction. He caught her eye once when Iva's back was turned, tilting his head and raising his brows, but Lira shook her head almost imperceptibly and mouthed, "Not now."

It wasn't time to tell everything—not out here, with so many eyes and ears on them.

"Can we access Rodhlan's memories, like you do?" Talfryn asked.

"I don't think so," Lira ventured, "but I dearly wish you could. Maybe I'll figure out some way to share those, too."

As they worked, Lira couldn't help but notice the Beravakt posted nearby who changed shifts occasionally, their eyes always trained on the three of them. But none made a move to seize Lira, though they all knew she'd been declared a prisoner. She spotted the woman called Oda standing on the third level walkway, watching her closely.

"Mam," Lira said quietly, "did Artur mention where—"

"No," Iva answered abruptly. "And I know when I mustn't question him."

"Why? Does he descend into a dark mood?" Lira quipped.

Talfryn looked like he might split open with laughter, but he widened his eyes at her and shook his head instead.

Iva glanced sidelong at Lira. "He has been good to us here," she answered. "Everyone knows he has his ways. But he is a good leader and he has seen to it that I am strong and well provided for. He will do the same for you."

As his prisoner, Lira thought bitterly, but she held her tongue.

When she was satisfied Talfryn and Iva had the magic well enough in hand, she retreated to sit against a pillar on the edge of the walkway. She was lost in thought when she caught movement in her periphery, and turned to see Oda crouching beside her, spear in hand.

"How's your leg?" Oda asked, laying her spear in the grass.

"Almost as if nothing happened to it," Lira answered, pressing her palm to her thigh. "There's just a faint scar now."

"Good." The warrior nodded decisively. "I'll be back." She strode down the walkway toward the great hall, leaving the spear behind.

A few moments later, Oda returned with a cup and bowl in hand and offered them to Lira. The bowl was filled with thick porridge, the cup with strong tea. Lira stirred the porridge, which was sprinkled with dried fruit and nuts.

"Thank you," Lira said, lifting a steaming spoonful and blowing on it.

"You didn't eat anything after you arrived last night," Oda said, sitting down beside her. "So if you need more, just ask."

Lira took a bite of the rich porridge and sighed. She hadn't realized how hungry she'd been. "Thank you."

They sat together in silence for a long while, watching Talfryn and Iva wield their magic. Oda's gaze followed each flash of emerald power.

"I've never seen any magic except Clan Beran's," she mused. "We've heard stories about your magic from Iathium, but it sounded more destructive than nurturing."

"It's both," Lira answered. "It can be bent to the user's will. That's the danger in it."

"Ah," Oda answered. She propped an elbow on her knee. "What do you know about people descended from two clans? How does their magic manifest?"

"I don't know," Lira answered. "It wasn't addressed in the manuscripts I studied. But I also didn't make it through many of the books about magic before everything fell apart. I had to leave it all behind in the city."

Oda's expression fell. "Oh."

"Why?" Lira asked, eyeing her. "You must be a descendent of Beran and..."

"Clan Énna." Oda sighed. "My mother is Beran. I have a measure of her healing power, but can't seem to connect with any magic from my father's side."

"Some descendants don't inherit power," Lira said. "Or haven't yet—there's no consistency to it, the powers were stolen and suppressed for so long. But I know someone who could help you manifest it. My mentor back at the Dome was a descendant of Clan Énna."

"How would that work?" Oda asked, sitting up straighter. "I want to meet him—what's his name?"

"Lord Irem," Lira answered. "He's like a grandfather to me. I imagine he would have you write some of the clan's folklore in *Maree*."

When Oda spoke next, her lips barely moved. "I would

break you out of this fortress myself if it meant you could help me learn Énna's water magic."

"If only," Lira replied.

She liked this warrior with her bold, straightforward nature. Oda was kind, and Lira found herself hoping they might truly be friends one day.

"We love your mother here," Oda said abruptly. "We're at her service, and yours."

Then, she rose, taking her spear and walking away without another glance.

CHAPTER 14

LIRA

Fortress Halgeir
9 Days Later

Sometime deep in the night, Lira heard a knock on her chamber door. She lay awake for a moment, staring into the darkness as the light knocking continued. With a heavy sigh, she sat up, draping one of the furs around her shoulders and padding to the door.

When she opened it, Thorne stood in the corridor, a stricken expression on his face. He was still dressed in the same clothing as he'd been wearing earlier that day, when they'd shared dinner in the Arthmael's Hall with Iva and Talfryn.

"Thorne, shouldn't you be sleeping?" she whispered groggily, her eyes still bleary from sleep.

She was alert enough to half-hide behind the door. The long sleeping gowns her mother had provided were made from thin, cool fabric, the sleeves cut away at the top to expose her shoulders. She wasn't used to showing so much skin, even to sleep, but she hadn't complained. Then again, she also hadn't expected a visitor in the middle of the night.

"Yes," he said, shouldering past her to step inside her chamber. "But we must speak."

"It's not exactly proper," she ventured, glancing out into the corridor before she closed the door again. Tonight, there were no guards posted. "But you're here now, so..." She chewed on her lip as Thorne leaned against the far wall.

Lira took a seat on the bed, nestling back into the soft furs as she drew one tightly around her bare shoulders. He was completely unfazed, so she tried to stop worrying about it.

She yawned deeply. "Go ahead, I suppose."

Thorne's expression was grim. "There is something you need to know."

The deep fatigue Lira had felt only a moment before vanished, and she sat up a little straighter. "What is it, Thorne?"

A flicker of pain crossed Thorne's face. He pushed a braid behind his ear. "My scouts reported tonight. Artur went to Iathium to forge an alliance."

Lira felt herself grow cold and numb, her heart hammering and her ears ringing. "With whom?"

Thorne crossed the room to her bedside. He sat on the floor, his back against the stone bed frame. He rested his hands in his lap and stared at them. "With Macha."

"*What*?" Lira breathed. After all Iva had done to ensure their protection, Artur would willingly put his family and his clan at risk? "Was he truly that desperate?"

"There's more." Thorne closed his eyes, a muscle in his jaw tensing. "Macha was removed from power two days ago. Your uncle and his wives have taken the city, and they've captured Artur. He is being held in the northeastern tower, according to my scouts."

Lira shook her head in disbelief. *No, no, no.* "How could that be?" She couldn't imagine anyone holding Artur captive, much less unseating Macha.

"Gerallt built an army from his archers and some turncoat sentries," Thorne answered. "They did it during Eremon's burial, when Macha was off her guard. No one has seen her since."

Lira couldn't fathom why Macha had waited so long to have her son buried. She shuddered at the thought of Eremon's body lying in that tower chamber for so long.

"What about the sentries that didn't side with Gerallt?" Lira asked.

"The rest of them either fled the city or were too afraid to resist. They say Macha was injured somehow, right after Eremon died. Perhaps the usurpers knew her weakness."

Panic gripped Lira, and she struggled to make sense of what she was hearing. But she thought about that day in the tower, when Caitir had attacked Macha.

"I know what happened to her—I was there," she said. "May I share the memory with you?"

Thorne tilted his head, but nodded. "Yes," he said.

"All right." Lira rose from the bed, keeping the fur pulled around herself, and sat on the floor in front of him. "I'll need to touch your head—may I?"

"Yes," he answered, dipping so she could better reach him. She touched her fingertips to his temples and closed her eyes—and that's when the tingling in her fingers began.

Thorne opened his mouth to say something, but Lira's vision went black as a witnessing overtook them both.

"I do not serve to die."

Caitir lunges at Raní Macha, black lightning buzzing and crackling between her fingers. Macha struggles, but arches involuntarily into the girl's touch. The lightning's intensity binds the two for a moment, as if Caitir's fingertips are fused to Macha's face and back. Suddenly, the older woman's body goes limp. Caitir lets the woman fall to the floor carelessly, her limbs splayed at odd angles, her eyes open and staring vacantly at the ornate ceiling above.

For a moment, the room is silent, the other handmaidens looking on in horror. Caitir removes her veil, then turns to walk purposely toward Lira.

Lira's sight didn't return at the end of the vision, nor was she able to break her contact with Thorne. Instead, the witnessing shifted into another memory—one of Macha's.

The tower room is silent and still, save for Eremon's body lying in state and Macha's lying on the floor. Macha awakens, her eyes now an opaque white, her skin mottled with bursts of blackened veins that have risen to its once-pristine surface. Lightning bursts haphazardly from her palms as she forces herself up to sitting, and she takes in her surroundings as if she doesn't remember what has just taken place.

The vision ended in a rush, and Lira blinked rapidly, dropping her hands as her eyes adjusted once again to the candlelit chamber.

Thorne was wild-eyed and panting. "What was that?"

"One of my memories," Lira answered, "and a witnessing. I think my magic wanted me to see it. Are you all right?"

"I'll be fine," he replied shakily, though he looked like he might vomit. He dropped his head into his hands, groaning softly. "There's one more thing I haven't told you, because I fear you won't listen to me once you know."

"What?" Her heart began to pound.

"There was also a specific piece of news delivered through my scouts' channels. We believe it's a trap for you—I'm reluctant to say, but you need to know." He looked up, conflict flashing in his eyes. "Your friend Tarlach is being held in Iathium, too."

"Aidryn," she breathed. "I don't care if it's a trap—we have to get to him."

Thorne's brow furrowed, and his voice dropped so low, it was barely audible. "Who is he to you, really?" He *had* to suspect something—there was no way he didn't. Lira's stomach twisted into a nervous knot.

"He's..." she began, but she quickly shut her mouth, unsure of how to answer.

Why was she so afraid to admit the truth? Eventually, the Binding would be common knowledge. But she feared the inevitable shame that accompanied it, because everyone also knew she'd been with Eremon less than a fortnight before the Binding happened. What would they think of her?

"I know he is not just a friend, Silira," Thorne added. "I want you to feel safe enough to tell me the truth."

His amber eyes were honest, but her hesitancy to speak had nothing to do with Thorne's trustworthiness. Rather, it was saying the words aloud that threatened to break her.

Her eyes stung as she whispered, "He's my husband. We're bound."

Thorne exhaled softly, looking up at the stone ceiling. "So that's it. I sensed your Binding, but thought you'd married the Rí in secret."

"No." Lira shook her head sadly. "But Eremon did have a part in it."

She explained Eremon's spell and what little she understood about the Binding. Thorne's brows knitted in concentration, as though he was trying to envision every possible mechanism of the intricately-woven magic.

"Could the enemy use the Binding to access your power?" he asked. "Or is Aidryn just bait to lure you into Iathium?"

"I don't know," Lira admitted, "but the ring is supposed to protect me. I pray that holds true when I go to the city with you."

"I didn't say I was going to the city," Thorne said, his expression darkening.

"You didn't have to say it," she replied. "It's obvious."

He shook his head. "The cost will be too great if we're both lost. You should stay here."

"But I know the city—intimately," Lira pressed. "What paths I haven't walked myself are revealed to me through magic. And I have access within the Dome that no one else has." She held up her hand, flashing the ring once again. "This is a key. I've used it before—I can use it again. I can also access

Aidryn's power as Key Keeper. If he and Artur are in the Dome, I can get us to them."

"And if they've been moved?"

Lira chewed the inside of her lip. There were no right answers here. She could bluff all she wanted, but Thorne would see right through it. Instead, she admitted, "I don't know."

She heaved a shuddering sigh. "But I can't go on knowing Aidryn is at their mercy. They know my weaknesses, and they will do everything they can to exploit them. And it will work.

"I'll be no good to anyone until he is safe. And I know you need me—everyone needs me, in ways I don't fully understand yet. Yet I belong nowhere. I am no one's, but everyone's. The weight of it all is so heavy…"

They sat together quietly, letting the deep, dead silence of the chamber swallow them. Lira missed the merry crackle of her hearth at home. She longed to sit before a roaring fire again, sipping hot tea with Talfryn. They'd seldom shared the space during their last few years in Iathium, and Lira longed to take that time back—to undo all the days and nights she'd spent toiling in the archive, neglecting her brother and her beloved home.

But that home was gone now, and she would never get those days back.

After a long while, Thorne heaved a sigh. "We will try to get him out."

"What?" she breathed.

"I do need you to help me navigate the city." He shrugged a shoulder. "My first plan was to trade myself for Artur's freedom."

"No," Lira said sharply. "The clan needs you."

"I know. So let's go in together. The coronation is tomorrow —help me while the city is distracted. Perhaps we can get to Artur and Aidryn before anyone notices."

Lira studied Thorne's face for a moment. He was truly beautiful, a warrior worthy of Beran's throne. If he lived to rule as overlord, he would be a leader to be reckoned with.

"Just tell me when to be ready," Lira said, "and I'm at your service."

"We go at dawn," he said, rising, "through the catacombs."

The winding network of caves beneath Fortress Halgeir and the meadowlands led to the entrances of the archive and Eremon's garden, among other locations beneath Iathium. They had long gone unused but had always been heavily guarded.

"What about the sentries?" Lira asked, puzzled. Macha had always posted them at intervals both below and aboveground.

"They are friends of Talfryn," Thorne answered. "They've been helping my scouts in and out of the city."

Fleetingly, Lira wondered whether any of Aidryn's friends were among them, too. She lay down again, pulling the furs up until they almost covered her head. "I need to rest a little longer before we go," she said, her voice muffled.

"Sleep. I will wake you when it's time."

With that, he let himself out of the room.

Lira lay in the dark, her thoughts racing. She focused on her magic, searching for a memory from Aidryn that might give her a clue to what was happening. Each time she tried to grasp a recent memory, all she saw was darkness—and all she could hear were distorted voices.

The last time she'd been able to see a memory of Aidryn's, Aila was leaving him alone with Artagán. What her cousin had done next, Lira couldn't say, but she remembered Artagán's contempt for Aidryn, and she feared the answer.

CHAPTER 15

AIDRYN

Dome of Iathium

Aidryn wished the familiar smells of the Dome wouldn't assault his senses so violently.

Aila and Gerallt had bundled him into the back of some cart, and they'd bumped along for days between Rodhlan Ridge and the city. The scent of the meadowlands made him ache for the freedom he'd once enjoyed, but mostly, the smell of turned-up dirt beneath the cart's wheels made him feel nauseous. Each squeak of a rusty axle left a deep ache in his left ear.

Then, there had been the trip through Iathium's cobblestone streets. He'd first known they were approaching the city from the clank and scrape of the sentries' armor at the gate. Where there had once been the sumptuous smells of street vendors' cooking on every corner, there was now the unwelcome stench of magic.

He didn't know magic *had* a scent. But apparently, it did— and each type of magic had its own particular fragrance. With so many strands mingled together this way, it was absolutely putrid.

More than once, he'd had the unwelcome thought that perhaps he should feel hungry or thirsty. But outside of the dead weight of his limbs—had he tried moving them?—and the heightened senses of hearing and smell, he felt almost nothing at all. The few things he did sense irritated him so profoundly, he wished someone would ease those for him, too.

Sometimes, there was a dull, detached pain in his body. He thought it had something to do with his abdomen, but he hadn't asked. Could he ask? There had been no one nearby since the debacle.

At least, he thought there had been a debacle. There had been raised voices and an altercation that probably should have concerned him, but he didn't know what it was about. He wasn't sure he cared, at this point.

Once in a while, Aila or Caitir tried to wake him. But honestly, who would want to wake for such insufferable humans? Better to stay asleep—if this was sleep. Aidryn didn't know anymore.

The bed where he lay was infinitely more comfortable than the dungeon floor had been. But its sheets smelled strongly of spices and oils. Between the fragrances and his meandering thoughts, he found he wasn't getting any more rest than he had in the keep.

Occasionally, he could hear screaming. He imagined it was something like what he might do, if he could react at all to Aila's magical probing. The last time she'd tried was the day of the altercation, and she hadn't been back since.

The door to his chamber clicked open softly, and his remaining senses went on high alert. Perhaps he'd thought too soon—

But then he felt someone take his hand. It was a gentle gesture, strangely familiar. He couldn't place who it was until they spoke.

"They say you're dying." It was Caitir.

Good. It's long past due, he might have said if he could reply.

"If you have any love left for your sister, you'll help me get this power before you go." She was whispering, as though fearful someone might overhear. "I can't bear the thought of Mother and Gerallt taking it. But I would put it to good use.

"First, I would turn it on them. Perhaps it's my own doing, but you wouldn't believe what they've subjected me to."

He thought he heard her shudder as she inhaled.

"I would use it to assert my strength and secure my throne. After that, I would disperse it. There are so many who desperately want magic, and if I were the one to give it to them with no expectations, I would gain their loyalty.

"If what Mother says about this power is true, then it's pure and uncorrupted. Nothing like the adulterated dark magic. Rather than killing me, it would keep me alive—maybe forever."

Aidryn felt his sister lean closer to whisper, "And if you help me get the key, then I will give some of this power to you."

Every waking part of Aidryn went on high alert. Somewhere in the back of his mind, he was tempted by Caitir's words. How would it feel to fill that void inside of him with truly pure magic? To wake again, healthier and more powerful than before? Something about Caitir's story conjured vivid images of youth and full restoration.

Suddenly, *he* wanted that power, too—wanted it so badly, he could almost smell it.

He'd forgotten how it felt to want anything. The last thing he'd truly wanted was Lira.

But Lira, the thought of *Lira*, brought his thoughts back into sharp focus. His mind cleared, and he directed that insistent wanting back to the memory of her.

It wasn't long before Caitir's feigned patience dissipated. As his own sister filled him with that burning, seeking, adulterated power, Aidryn kept his desire trained only on the thought of Lira.

The rest of that power could stay locked away for eternity, for all he cared.

CHAPTER 16

LIRA

Fortress Halgeir

At sunrise, Thorne came to fetch Lira. She was already awake, sitting on the side of her bed, her hair braided into a thick plait down her back. It felt strange to have it pulled away from her face and neck; she had a habit of hiding behind her long curls when the notion suited her.

When she opened the door to Thorne, his hands were full. Over one arm, he'd slung a traveling cloak. In his hands, he carried two bowls of hot porridge and a large flagon of tea. Lira took the bowls from him as he stepped inside the chamber.

"We should eat now," he said, setting the flagon on the floor. He laid the cloak on the bed, followed by a leather belt and two small axes.

Lira took a spoonful of porridge and sighed contentedly. She could see that Thorne was already armed; a large axe and a sword were strapped across his back. "Whose are those?" she asked between bites, nodding toward the axes.

"They're for you," he answered. "When we return, I'll teach you how to use them properly."

"Thank you, but I'm not a fighter," she answered, "though it will be good to be armed in the city."

"If you're going to be a part of this war, you'll have to become a warrior," he said. "If not, we're better off without you."

Lira wanted to take offense to the statement, but she'd already grown accustomed to his lack of tact. "I'm sure you're right, but I don't know the first thing about combat."

"You will, though." He took a swig of tea, then offered the flagon to her. "Your mother did well enough."

"Mam is strong," Lira replied, taking a sip. The tea was strong, and so hot she scalded the tip of her tongue. "I never imagined it, honestly."

"She and Oda are already at odds over who gets to work with you in the arena," he answered, scraping his last bites of porridge from the near-empty bowl.

Lira laughed softly, setting her own bowl aside and picking up the belt. She fastened it around her waist, letting it overlap the thinner belt where her pouch hung. Then, she carefully fitted the small axes into the sheaths that hung at her right hip.

"They're both going to be very disappointed with my performance," she said absently. "I don't exercise, aside from walking."

Thorne snorted. "Come on, it's time to go," he said as he stood. "I want to know how *turas* works."

Lira's mouth went dry at that. "I... the last time I used it, the magic was broken. Your father says I *still* have a magical wound. We could end up on the other side of the continent."

"How do you expect us to get your husband into the fortress?"

"I don't know," Lira protested, cheeks burning. She sat back down on the bed shakily. "Toss him into a boat? That's what you did with me."

"Supposing we get to him *and* Artur, what then?" Thorne was stone-faced. Lira wasn't sure she'd ever seen him looking this stern. "Will I carry them both? Or will you take the smaller of the two?"

Lira looked down at her hands, tears of frustration gathering in her eyes. Thorne dropped to a knee before her, propping his arm casually on one leg. "You want to come with me, yes?"

"Yes," Lira answered softly.

"And you feel better after discharging some power." Thorne dipped his head, forcing her to meet his eyes. "Yes?"

Lira nodded. "I do."

"Then it's time to go," he said. He fished in the pouch he carried on his belt—not unlike her own—and produced a flat, sharp piece of stone. "I had one of my scouts chip this off the catacomb walls," he said, handing it to Lira. "Will it work?"

She swallowed hard, palms breaking a sudden sweat. "It should."

Thorne handed her traveling cloak to her, and she put it on, pulling the hood up over her head. With trembling fingers, she held her pendant in one hand, and the stone shard in the other.

"If this magic dumps us on the western coast, don't blame me," she said dryly. "Just remember, you insisted."

Thorne covered Lira's hands with his own, bringing the pendant and the stone shard together before she could protest. Everything went black, and for long a moment Lira waited to feel that sickening sensation of tumbling and tangling with Thorne in the void. But this *turas* was different. It felt smoother, and it was over in a blink.

When the world came back into focus, Lira and Thorne found themselves at the mouth of the catacombs, not far from Iathium's southern wall. This was a little-used entrance situated between the wall and Beran's Gorge—Lira remembered that much, though she'd never familiarized herself with these tunnels. Today, she was trusting her magic to help her navigate them.

Thorne braced a large hand against the hillside. He looked

pale, and he closed his eyes, taking deep breaths through his nose.

"The nausea gets better," Lira said softly. The warrior started, then shook his head.

"I'll be fine," he answered shakily. Then, he touched his fingertips to the insides of his wrists. Golden magic, like his father's, flared briefly, then blinked out. He sighed with relief, his features relaxing.

"I'm sorry. I think *turas* affects everyone differently," she ventured, blinking heavily against the sudden exhaustion. "It makes me feel incredibly tired when I travel long distances, like I could sleep all afternoon."

He grunted and gave her a slight nod. "Are you tired now?"

She nodded. Thorne motioned for her to hold out her hands, and he placed a small burst of magic inside her wrists like he'd done for himself. Instantly, she felt lighter and clearer-headed.

"Let's go," he said.

Lira's heartbeat sped up as they approached the mouth of the dark tunnel, but she followed Thorne in anyway. Sure enough, only a few paces inside stood two sentries dressed in full regalia. But when Thorne approached, they both lowered their spears and stepped aside, allowing him to pass without a word. As Lira approached them, they both inclined their heads to her, and it was difficult not to stop and thank them for what they were doing.

Instead, she only nodded to each, keeping one hand on the axes at her side, and followed Thorne, who hefted a lit torch from a wall sconce. For a long while, they trudged the dark stone pathway in silence.

Miles into their trek, Thorne's torch burned low, but they dared not kindle it further. Lira had never been in a place darker and more deathly silent than the dungeons at night until this. Cold terror slithered through her the deeper they descended, as though she were wading into ice water.

Lira looked to Thorne, his brows knitting as he squinted into the darkness ahead. She was glad to have a friend, but right now, she was also relieved he never had much to say. She wasn't sure she could have held a coherent conversation.

The damp, earthy scent of the underground filled her nostrils. These caverns weren't like the spacious ones directly beneath the archive or below Skelly's home in the mountains. The space was so cramped, she feared Thorne may have to put out his torch. Beran's heir hunched to keep from hitting his head on the ceiling, and she prayed the path wouldn't narrow any further. Her heart pounded and her breath came in shallow huffs, as though the air had been sucked out of this place. She couldn't seem to fill her lungs.

There was a blast of rancid, damp air, and Thorne's torch dimmed. Lira froze then, bracing against the tunnel wall. Her heart was racing out of control, and her chest tightened. One by one, her limbs grew sluggish, and she lost sensation in her fingers. The torch's crackling and her own breath roared in her ears.

This was so much worse than that dark chamber back at Halgeir.

Taking shallow breaths, she backed against the wall and slid down it, drawing her knees up to her chest. Now, her chest *hurt*. She tried to take a few long, slow breaths, but succeeded only in becoming more winded.

Thorne turned back and knelt beside her quietly, placing his warm hand on her shoulder as she struggled to calm herself. The terror of these unfamiliar tunnels—of entering Iathium again—was more overwhelming than she'd expected.

"Try to breathe," Thorne soothed. He held out the torch to her. "Hold this."

Lira looked from the dim torch to Thorne, and back again. She took it when he handed it over, staring into its glowing embers. Something about holding the torch steady, steadied *her*.

Thorne closed his eyes, taking a long breath. He rubbed his palms together and whispered something low and unintelligible—an ancient incantation of his clan, or so her power whispered. Cupping his hands, he waited. After a moment, a glowing, golden orb formed there.

Lira's magic stirred in response, and she began to regain control of her breathing. Thorne canted toward her slightly, the power he held illuminating the pathway around them more brightly than the torch. "I am not as powerful as Ljós, but he taught me." He seemed as though he were offering the magic to her. "May I?"

Even inches away from one another, Lira could feel the calming energy that emanated from the power he held. Slowly, she nodded, attempting to let her shoulders relax. He moved closer, directing the orb toward her heart. The magic all but leapt to her itself, and he pressed two fingers over her heart as it absorbed into her body. He took the torch from her and sat back on his heels, waiting patiently.

Instantly, she felt calmer. The tightness in her chest eased, and she was able to draw a full breath.

"Thank you," she said.

He nodded once, then stood, offering her a hand. "Caverns and tunnels are like dungeons."

"Yes." Her voice cracked at the memory of the dungeon below the Dome.

"This path—it feels..."

"Endless," she finished. "Like we may never see the light again. Or we could turn the wrong direction, or be lost under here..."

"I will use my power for light if the torch goes out. But you hold the memories." He began walking again, raising his torch. "Can your magic get us where we need to go?"

"I think so," she answered, trailing behind. "I have done it once before." She traced her fingertips along the wall, feeling the quiet thrumming of the stone. "Perhaps I can find a waypoint somewhere."

Closing her eyes, she called to her power: *How do we enter the Dome while bypassing the archive and the garden?*

An image sprang to her mind, and she could see their next steps clearly. There was one other way to move from here to the western towers, and they weren't far from it.

"This way," she said, and Thorne followed her for half a mile more until the path split into thirds.

Lira led him through the middle pathway, then stopped when the short corridor gave way to a yawning cavern lit all the way around with strange torches. They emitted an other-worldly glow the color of sea foam that undulated to a dark violet and back again. The cavern looked and felt distinctly like an underwater grotto—or at least, how Lira imagined one might look.

"What is this place?" Thorne asked.

"My magic didn't tell me," Lira answered. "I couldn't see it... but I was sure it had an outlet."

This cavern appeared to be the dead end of the pathway they'd been following. Lira squinted, struggling to make out the intricate etchings along the walls. The shimmering, shifting torchlight made it difficult to see exactly what she was looking at until she moved closer to the far-right wall. Etched into the smooth stone was a decorative doorway with an inscription in the center.

"Thorne," she whispered, "look at this."

The massive warrior stepped behind her, bending closer to see the inscription. "What does it say?"

Lira shook her head. "I can't read it. I think it might be written in Itelos, though I haven't seen it before."

Itelos was the language of Iteloria, the continent across the sea. It was the home of the mortal gods and the first rulers of Iathium—Eremon's ancestors.

Thorne's next words came a hush. "What is this place?"

Lira swallowed hard, her hands beginning to tremble. "I think it's the Rí's crypt." She turned to Thorne, searching his face in the strange firelight. "Could it be a trap?"

He worked his jaw, then slowly shook his head. "I don't know. What do you know about it?"

"It only opens at the handprint of a rightful Rí, Raní, or successor," Lira rattled off. Her magic confirmed the truth—and apparently, this was one of the few historical facts she'd learned in the archive that had, indeed, been fact.

"They would have used Eremon's hand to open the crypt when they brought him down—before sealing him away." She swallowed a lump in her throat at the thought of his body lying in a vault, somewhere on the other side of this wall. "That's the way of things. Which means now, I'm the only person who can rightfully open it again."

"Not his mother?"

"No," Lira answered. "He was Corlan's successor, not hers. Technically, she had no right to take the throne after Eremon died. But no one stopped her."

"If you can truly open it," Thorne mused, "Gerallt would want to lure you here. Is the crypt left open after burial rites?"

"No," Lira answered. "The rites are largely conducted in the courtyard before they bring a late Rí down here. Then they seal the crypt right away."

"But do you think they followed the same protocol yesterday?"

Lira sighed. "I couldn't say." She felt another swell of panic rising, her chest tightening, her body breaking out in a cold sweat. "It feels like I don't know anything anymore."

Thorne rested a hand on her shoulder. "Why didn't your magic show you that the crypt was in our path?"

"It showed me the cavern as though the pathway simply cut through." Her throat constricted. "But not exactly what the cavern led to. I don't know why. We should have come another way!"

"There's no other way," Thorne answered quietly. "We either push through and take the risk, or we turn back and return to Halgeir without Artur or Aidryn."

"Then please, help me bear it," she begged, covering her face with her hands. "I thought I was strong enough to do this, but I'm not. I can't stop thinking about Eremon being in there."

It didn't help that she'd continued to have that dream about him. For a moment, she wondered about the key Corlan had insisted be buried with him here. Was it something Aidryn's power could access?

Thorne draped an arm around her shoulder and pulled her to his side. With his free hand, he summoned another orb of light, which he placed delicately over her heart. As she began to feel its calming effects, she sagged against him.

He didn't release his grip on her, but instead began to speak in soothing tones. "It will never go away. In time, it will be better. For now, it might be worse for a little while."

"Yes." She nodded resignedly. "That's what I'm afraid of."

"Think on the good," he added. "Good memories heal."

Lira squeezed her eyes shut and thought about *Nami Mostari*—about the dance she'd shared with Eremon. About those long days with him in the archive, studying the secret tomes. The nea'la roses on her doorstep. The way he'd always emanated warmth and kindness.

Power surged into the ring on her finger. She opened her eyes. The stone shone brighter than before.

"Time to go in?" Thorne asked, studying the ring.

"I think so," Lira said.

She looked to the etchings on the wall again. Hesitantly, she reached out and placed her fingertips beneath the Itelos inscription. Then, she pressed her palm to the stone and the cavern wall shuddered—then vanished completely.

A rush of wind pushed them forward, and the wall reappeared behind them, sealing them inside the crypt. Before them were rows of stone vaults in a long, wide chamber illuminated with blue-gray light. Lira could make out the barely audible notes of a harp, and she looked to Thorne in alarm.

"Do you hear that?" she mouthed.

He nodded, drawing his sword. Lira followed suit, drawing her axes and falling behind Thorne. Her palms were already damp against the handles.

"Stay beside me," Thorne whispered, as though reading her thoughts. "Not in front or behind."

Lira moved into his periphery, white-knuckling the axes. They moved stealthily between the rows of tombs. There was a door on the far end of the crypt, and Lira was anxious to reach it.

She looked to Thorne and whispered, "Can't we go faster —"

But she was cut off by the whistling of arrows that began flying toward them from all sides. She clutched Thorne's arm and cerulean magic flared from her ring, shielding them both. The arrows bounced harmlessly off the magical orb and clattered to the floor.

Thorne looked from the arrows to Lira, then back again. "No," he answered dryly, "because your overlords built traps like this."

"Are there more?"

He nodded. "I'm sure."

They began moving slowly once again, keeping their eyes peeled for signs of the next trap. Lira wished then that there had been more information about this crypt in the archival records. It had always been a closely-guarded secret—perhaps because of the magic the rulers had been concealing for so long. She wanted to let her magic tell her more, but she should have done that earlier. Now, there was no time to sit and reflect.

Suddenly, a soft whisper brushed against her ear.

Touch the path and it will be made safe.

Lira froze with a gasp, her eyes growing wide. Thorne whirled to study her as she mouthed, "Eremon."

His brow knitted as he scrutinized her. "What?"

"Wait." She took a breath and knelt slowly, flexing her fingers, and pressed her palm to one of the pearlescent tiles that covered the floor of the crypt. Her power affirmed her actions, tugging ever so lightly at the back of her mind.

However impossible, Eremon was still present somehow. She had questioned her own sanity when she'd heard his voice at Halgeir. Now, he was here with her. She didn't want to think about which of these stone vaults his body rested in, and she had no intention of finding out.

Magic rushed from the ring into the floor beneath her palm, illuminating the tiles and climbing up the walls. The chamber's cool glow transformed from dull blue-gray to shimmering shades of bright cobalt.

Once it was done, Lira rose, showing Thorne her ring once again. "Protective magic. I suppose it works here, then."

"Luckily," he said, shaking his head. "We must still keep watch."

As they readied to move farther into the chamber, the eerie sound of the harp abruptly ceased. Thorne threw an arm out in front of Lira, and they remained where they were, weapons drawn.

A familiar voice rang out—one that made Lira's blood turn to ice.

"So she lives."

CHAPTER 17

LIRA

Crypt of Iathium

From behind one of the vaults, Raní Macha stepped into the pathway before them. Her appearance took Lira aback; she'd expected to see the same formidable woman who had tortured and threatened her just weeks ago. Instead, the woman before them was a shell of her former self.

Macha had arranged her silver hair in a tight bun at the base of her neck, and she was dressed in the plain, brown robes of the lowest-born servants from the Dome. The fullness had gone from her face, and she looked as though she'd aged decades since Lira had last seen her in the tower.

Lira and Thorne stood frozen as Macha weighed them.

"When we entombed my son," she began, her voice crackling, "those women locked me in here with him. Left me to die."

"Not unlike you—" Lira couldn't finish the sentence. Her throat closed over the words as she fought to keep her mind clear. She didn't want to think about that night in the tower, when she'd been locked into the chamber where Eremon's body lay in state.

"Possibly my cruelest moment," Macha answered, as

though reading Lira's thoughts. "Proudest, in some respects. Yet also, the moment I most regret."

Lira held Macha's gaze. "It seems it led to your downfall."

"Indeed." Macha's eyes moved to Thorne, and the shadow of a smile tugged at her mouth. "It appears you've moved on to Beran, then. What are you doing with the overlord's pup?"

"None of your business," Lira answered.

"Do you think I know nothing?" Macha asked slyly. "Do you think I haven't heard the overlord is captive in the Dome? I might be a prisoner myself, but I'm not without my sources."

Lira could almost feel the reeling blow that revelation had delivered to Thorne, though he'd already received the news. His expression betrayed nothing.

"What else do you know, Raní?" Lira asked.

"Haven't you heard?" she asked. "That title belongs to someone else now."

Aila and Caitir, then. And the third—

Macha was staring hungrily at Eremon's ring. A chill swept over Lira, and she shook her head vehemently. "I do not bear that title."

"Yet it was freely given, and freely received." Macha nodded toward the ring, then looked back up at Lira, eyes flashing. "What will you do with it, I wonder?"

"Nothing," Lira spat. "I never wanted it."

Macha's voice dropped—softer than Lira thought possible. "But you wanted *him*."

Against her will, Lira felt her eyes fill with tears. She tried to blink them away. "I did."

"Him, but not his power."

"Never his power," Lira answered firmly.

Suddenly, it was as though Macha's façade melted away. Her expression softened into something almost melancholy. "You loved him better than I. My eyes were fixed on his potential as a ruler and a magic-wielder. I wanted that magic for myself, but I needed to let it reach maturity. I thought I could convince him to gift a measure of it to me... and then he would have survived. But he gave you that blasted ring, and squandering its protection was his downfall."

Lira flinched. She had often wondered whether giving up the ring had led Eremon's magic to destroy him.

"I concealed what I knew from his father, but Corlan learned that our son's power was killing him. Instead of learning to distribute it, he ran to Iteloria for aid. *Your* father too, if memory serves."

"I was never told what my father was doing," Lira said, her hackles rising. "Only that he died at sea."

"Then you have much to uncover yet." Macha made a show of checking her nails, though they looked as if she'd chewed them to the quick. "Search your magic; my memory is fallible."

"Pity," Lira snapped. "I so wish to sit at your feet and hear the tale."

"I'm sure you'll find the answer on your own," Macha answered sharply. "Don't let it go to your head. Power is a funny thing; too much of it is overwhelming, as you well know, whether suppressed or misused."

Rage rose in Lira at Macha's truth, but she was tired of hearing it. She was tired of being taunted, of being belittled—and of the constant reminders of Eremon's fate. All because of her.

Lira opened her mouth to speak, but Macha cut her off. "There are two things you need to know. First, the usurpers have laid traps for both of you, and I believe you know who they're using as bait."

She bit her lips, willing Macha to hurry. Thorne looked as though he might run the woman through at any moment.

"Second..." Macha's gaze was suddenly distant. "There is the matter of my son."

"Eremon?" Lira asked, growing still. "What about him?"

Something akin to grief flashed across Macha's face for a moment, and then it was gone. "The usurpers want his power.

They contained me here in hopes that I will somehow figure out where an ancient key called Iuchair is hidden, but I know no more than they. My only hope now is for a swift death, but my magic will choose my time. It may be a hundred years from now."

"You're deluding yourself." Lira gripped her axes harder. "You'll be dead within days."

"You forget that I am a descendent of Rasu the Vile."

Lira tried not to flinch at Macha's invocation. The dead mortal god had been responsible for so much destruction so long ago. Though many of his descendants had lived longer than mere mortals, two thousand years had passed since his death. She doubted Macha could have eked out a decade more than one of her human counterparts under normal circumstances.

"Plenty of time to consider your miserable existence," Thorne said firmly. "Don't expect us to free you."

Lira nodded quietly, though a strange reluctance tugged at her.

"I am not petitioning for release." Macha raised her chin. "What good is freedom when I've been stripped of everything? I would rather rot down here than be seen on the streets like this."

Lira didn't want to pity Macha, but she did. She remembered how it felt to be stripped of everything and locked away to die. Then again, Macha found herself resigned to the same sort of fate she had thrust upon Lira.

She thought back to Macha's statement about Eremon's power. Then, the name of that key again.

"How would anyone access Eremon's magic?" Lira asked carefully. "He is dead."

"His father carried that knowledge to the grave," Macha answered, watching Lira closely, "and we are left only with desperate theories."

Lira couldn't help canting slightly toward the woman, her

body betraying her curiosity. Perhaps Macha had taken a blow to the head when she'd been shut away in here.

"If anyone can unravel my son's secret, it will be you." Macha's scrutiny weighed heavily on Lira. "It's a bitter thing that his own mother cannot. But I suppose I sealed my own fate long ago."

Lira felt her breath catch, her heart speeding the way it had in the catacombs. Thorne glanced over at her, warning flashing in his eyes.

"I'm not here for anyone's magic," Lira said, fighting to keep her voice steady. "And I truly don't know what you're talking about."

"I think you can learn." Macha tilted her head. She looked less like a woman than a hungry hawk. "The power of the Witness Tree is a truly terrible one—nearly unlimited, if one understands how to wield it. You are not merely reading history books, nor are you relegated to the role of helpless observer. You have the power of full *immersion*. The ability to look into the minds of your enemies and thwart their every movement."

Lira remained stone-faced and silent. When she didn't reply, Macha blinked slowly, then a slow smile spread across her lips. "Of course, you're too honorable to delve into it, aren't you? A pity, truly. You could have this war won before first blood."

"First blood was your son," Lira replied.

"Search your immeasurable knowledge on his behalf, then," Macha snapped. "It's what he would have wanted. Then return here once you've discovered the answer. Perhaps I can grasp some shred of peace before I die."

Lira looked to Thorne again for a moment before she took a tentative step toward Macha.

"Silira..." Thorne warned.

Lira froze but never took her eyes off Eremon's mother. "I didn't come here seeking you today. Why would I return to you?" she asked. "How could you possibly expect that of me, after everything you've done?"

"We are beneficial to one another, are we not? We are dealing a blow to the usurpers together." Macha looked to Lira again, her voice laced with sudden urgency. "Promise to return, Witness Tree, and I will tell you where the prisoners are being held."

The very real possibility of a later betrayal should have frightened Lira, but their immediate need was to get to Aidryn and Artur. She could sort out the idea of returning—or not—later. So she gave the woman a slight nod. "I will return. I promise."

Thorne tensed beside her.

"Good." Something like relief crossed Macha's features before her expression sharpened. "They're being held in the northeastern tower, on the highest level."

"How do we know you aren't lying?" Thorne demanded.

She isn't, Lira thought, feeling that tug in her mind.

"I was locked in a chamber adjoined to the overlord's before they brought me down here," Macha said. "He's the one who said you'd arrived at Beran's fortress, girl. Well—he didn't so much *say* it. His silence was answer enough. His ability to remain stoic through horrific torture is impressive; I would hate to face him in battle."

Thorne went gray, and bile rose in Lira's throat. The corner of Macha's mouth crooked up at his response before she turned her attention back to Lira.

"Artur Beran's chamber is to the right of the corridor—the second door," Macha said. "And the Tarlach boy is at the end of the hallway. As far as I know, the usurpers haven't been able to wake him for interrogation."

A wave of nausea slammed into Lira and her knees nearly gave out. "What do you mean, wake him?" she demanded, her throat tightening with fear.

"You'll have to discover that for yourself," Macha answered, shaking her head. "I cannot say."

"We've been here long enough. Head for the door, Lira," Thorne said softly, keeping his gaze trained on Macha. "I will follow at your back."

Now he held both axe and sword, blades at the ready. He towered over Macha, who was unfazed by his size—and his weapons. Lira took one last glance at the deposed Raní before she walked past, Thorne's hulking form just steps behind her. He walked back-to-back with Lira, keeping his eyes on Macha while Lira led them to the far end of the crypt, which would take them into the catacombs again, then on to the tower's base.

On that wall, there was another Itelos inscription, and another doorway etched into the wall. Lira lay her palm over it, and the stone faded to reveal the corridor beyond.

"Remember your promise, Silira Mór," Macha called just before Lira and Thorne departed the crypt. Her voice was tinged with panic. "I still have eyes and ears across the continent. If you fail to uphold your part of the bargain, I will see to it that you and your beloved clans are destroyed."

Lira didn't look back. Instead, she quickened her pace, leading Thorne into the catacombs before the doorway vanished behind them.

CHAPTER 18

LIRA

Dome

Lira and Thorne sprinted down the dark passageway and away from the crypt. As the path split into thirds, Lira kept to the center, gripping her axe handles with sweaty palms. When that path came to an abrupt end, Lira found another inscription on the wall, similar to the one she'd used to enter the crypt.

Again, she placed her hand on the stone, and again, the wall gave way for her. It opened to a spiral staircase that would lead them up to the prisoners' quarters.

They paused at the foot of the stairs. Thorne wasn't the least bit winded, but Lira was panting heavily. She could feel him scrutinizing her as she caught her breath.

"I know—" She gulped for air. "I know I need to train."

He leaned nearer, lowering his voice. "What were you thinking, promising to come back?"

Lira closed her eyes for a moment, then opened them to find that he was still studying her. "That I needed to get to Aidryn, whatever it takes."

Thorne dipped his chin in a shallow nod. "But you know it's

a trap. Not now—a trap for later, when you can no longer benefit Macha by being free."

"It might be," she admitted, "but I could feel the truth in her words. There *is* something to what she said about Eremon's power. I just don't fully grasp what it is. But I do know I don't want her or Aila getting their hands on it."

"I am sure we can find a way to avoid fulfilling that promise," Thorne answered. "Being locked inside the crypt will make it difficult for her to summon her lackeys."

"That's true," Lira hummed. She wasn't going to push the issue any further with him now. All that mattered was that they knew where to find Aidryn.

She hoped.

There was no sign of life from within the tower, and outside it was deathly silent. They wound up the tower stair until they came to a narrow window that overlooked the courtyard. Lira paused climbing long enough to peek out. Her stomach lurched when she saw the mass of subdued onlookers who filled the yard and spilled onto the city streets.

Gerallt, Aila, and Caitir occupied three thrones in the center of the platform, their backs to the tower. It was the same platform where Eremon had given his final speech to his people, not so long ago. But seeing them on the thrones wasn't what made Lira feel ill. It was what was displayed behind them.

Eighteen heads had been impaled on long spears, which were lined across the back of the stage.

"The council—"

Lira retched before she could get control of herself, but Thorne immediately grasped her wrists, turning her away from the window and pouring golden magic into her skin where he held her. The nausea abated immediately, but her eyes burned. He immediately followed with a shot of power over her heart to calm her before another wave of panic overtook her.

Thorne placed a large hand firmly on her back and steered her toward the stairs.

"Don't look out there again," he said. "We have to keep moving."

"They murdered the council," she repeated. She felt as though her body was moving independently of her mind—like she was still standing by that window, watching herself walk up the spiral staircase.

"Just a little farther," Thorne pressed. "We don't have much time."

Lira's mind raced from the thrones to the heads to the somber crowd. The people had been packed onto the grounds of the Dome with no room to spare. They had stood stone-still and painfully silent—prisoners under a reign of terror. Macha had been cruel, but Macha had also craved their love.

Fleetingly, she couldn't help wishing Macha was still on the throne.

Finally, they came to the tower's eighth—and highest—level. Thorne stopped her, holding a finger to his lips. He tightened his grip on his sword and peered into the dark corridor just off the stairwell. All was silent and pitch-black. Slowly, he began inching into the darkness, Lira two steps behind him.

She expected them to be ambushed. After all, why would Aila leave Aidryn unguarded up here during such a pivotal moment? Still, there was no sound—nothing but complete stillness in the suffocating darkness.

Almost like there was no sign of life at all.

Lira almost choked on that thought, shaking her head silently as she moved after Thorne.

I'm still alive, so he's still alive, she thought. *Please, let him be alive.*

Just as terror was about to overtake Lira, she felt a familiar sensation—as though the Binding that tied her to Aidryn had suddenly snapped to attention. As though her magic was aware that he was near.

Her heart began to pound; her palms were so sweaty, she

worried she might drop her axes. Yes, Aidryn was very much alive—and they were getting closer to him.

Rather than continuing to quietly panic behind Thorne, Lira decided to reach out with her power. There were seven chambers on each tower floor, so they couldn't be far. The lock to his room would likely be enchanted, but as long as she could still wield his power, that wouldn't matter.

Lira took a deep breath and felt for his magic. *Where is Aidryn?* she asked it.

A tendril of her power snaked from beneath the skin of her wrist and floated on ahead of them, wending its way down the corridor until it came to a chamber at the end of the hall—just as Macha had said. A thrill ran through her.

Thorne refused to let her pass, but instead followed the emerald tendril himself. But he paused before they passed the second chamber, where Artur was supposed to be. The door stood ajar, the large room empty.

"Not here?" she mouthed.

The warrior's shoulders hunched slightly, and he quietly shook his head, looking down at Lira with a mournful expression. His grief was so palpable, she could feel it herself.

"Cover me," she whispered, reaching for the door and placing her hand on it. Perhaps her magic could show her what had become of Artur.

Lira called the tendril of power back to herself and closed her eyes. A rush overtook her, and the witnessing began.

Artur is on his knees in a dungeon cell, panting. Veins of black lightning mottle his skin, and he grits his teeth against the power that rages against him. Sweat pours down his forehead. Strange, the way his chills mingle with the dark magic's scorching heat.

The surge of magic comes to an end, and he draws an anguished gasp. He braces himself on his hands and knees, trembling violently. More than physical weakness, his will appears to be waning. Suddenly, his arms and legs give way and he collapses to the floor with a groan.

"I could take your pain right now," Caitir croons as she stands over him. "It would all be over so quickly."

Her voice is deceptively soothing, her golden hair as enchanting as ever. But Artur is careful not to look into her horrifyingly icy eyes.

"Come now, mighty Bear King," she says, a dangerous edge to her voice. "You just have to give Silira to us. Then, you and your clan may enjoy our mercy."

"No," Artur bites out.

"Very well," she says softly—resignedly.

Caitir's skirts swish closer to Artur, but he does not look up. Pressure builds in the room, the crackle of static raising the hairs on his arms. He braces himself as she whispers, "We'll do it the hard way."

An agonizing surge of power hits him, and he loses consciousness.

Lira gasped as the vision released her. For a moment, she was vaguely aware that she was falling. The next, Thorne's arm was around her middle, and he was hefting her back to her feet. Warmth flared in her belly, her arms, and her legs as he went to work dousing her with healing magic. He murmured something in Brylla and the power flared brighter. Warmer.

When Lira fully returned to herself, she was trembling. Artur's pain was fresh in her mind, but before, she had felt it acutely. Whatever Thorne had done had transformed it into a memory.

"What did you see?" he asked quietly.

"They took Artur to the dungeon beneath the Dome," Lira answered. "They're torturing him for information, but he isn't talking."

"Then we will not be able to get to him," Thorne replied decisively. "The dungeon will be more heavily guarded than this place. We should get Tarlach, get out, then make a new plan."

Reluctantly, Lira nodded. "I'm sorry."

Thorne bowed his head. "So am I. But now, we must move."

They headed in the direction of the imposing cherrywood door at the end of the hallway. Lira's heart sped at the thought of being so near Aidryn—if, indeed, he was in the room. She prayed that Aila hadn't decided to move him, too.

Lira felt for his magic, then examined the door. She could feel a steady thrum of power gathering around the knob, its lock, and the mechanisms within. Whatever spell Aila had used, it extended from the foot of the door to the top, infiltrating and corrupting the very wood.

Instinctively, she knew there was no key to this door—not any longer. She would need to pick the lock using Aidryn's magic. With a deep breath, she braced herself and allowed Aidryn's birthright power to surge down her arm and into her waiting palm. Its crimson glow filled the corridor, and she directed it into the keyhole, trusting it to disengage the lock for her.

Click, click. Her satisfaction at successfully picking the lock gave way to terror as the door swung open and Lira stepped inside the chamber. The air inside was stale, the furnishings covered in a layer of dust. Heavy curtains divided the entryway from the sleeping quarters. With trembling hands, Lira pushed them aside.

When her gaze came to rest on Aidryn, she fell to her knees, biting down on her hand to contain the cry that rose in her throat.

CHAPTER 19

LIRA

Dome

Aidryn lay tucked under a crimson silk coverlet the color of Macha's favorite robes. He was frail, his skin paper-thin and pale. His hair and beard were longer and more unkempt than she'd ever seen them.

He looked like a shell of his former self.

Trembling, she pushed herself back to standing and crossed the room toward him, surveying his lifeless form. She might have thought him dead, if his chest hadn't been rising and falling with shallow breaths.

"Aidryn," she whispered, reaching for him. She pressed her palm to his cheek, which felt alarmingly cool. "Aidryn, it's me."

He didn't respond. Lira reached up to brush the stray hair off his forehead, tears blurring her vision. Thorne was gravely silent at her side. He grasped her arm, steadying her.

"Poison," he said, nodding toward Aidryn. "Pull the blanket back."

Lira reached for the coverlet with trembling fingers, gently untucking it from beneath his arms, keenly aware of every point of contact with his skin. His muscles had begun to atrophy, and he looked so much smaller than she remembered. She wished she could curl up next to him, offer him the warmth he had once given to her.

She peeled back the blanket, then the sheet. His midsection had been wrapped in a heavy bandage, and the dressing appeared to be clean. Lira looked to Thorne, alarmed.

"Injured," she said, thinking back to that day in the mountains—the archers training their arrows right at his heart. Artagán must have shot him during the part of the memory she hadn't been able to see.

"Oh no," she moaned, reaching for the bandage.

Thorne stopped her with a hand on hers. "What is it?"

"It's a poisoned arrowhead—I'm almost certain," she said, her voice rising in panic.

"Inoxia," Thorne said, tentatively placing his hand on Aidryn's stomach. He closed his eyes for a moment, then nodded. "My father can heal him, but there is not much time. He is dying."

Lira shook her head. "The ring is supposed to protect him."

The warrior pressed his lips together before replying, "I think it *has* been."

I can't panic, she thought. *Not now.*

"You can't carry him through the catacombs like this—not with this sort of wound," she said.

"It would spread the poison more," Thorne agreed.

Lira ran her fingers over her pendant. "We'll need to use *turas* again."

"Are you sure you can manage it after the witnessing?"

"I'll have to," Lira answered quietly. "We don't have another choice."

Jostling Aidryn through the tunnels wasn't an option; his injury would only get worse, and he might not survive the trauma. He'd already been moved from the mountains into the city, presumably in this state. How much more could his body take?

But then, *turas* was also a risk. It could kill him, too.

Nervously, Lira reached for one of her braids, where she had woven the ceremonial beads back in her chamber. Returning directly to her room at Halgeir seemed to be the best course of action. She took one bead out of her hair and held it in a fist.

Carefully, Thorne scooped Aidryn up off the mattress, cradling the Key Keeper in his massive arms. He was dead weight, lifeless and pale against Thorne's sun-kissed skin. Lira tried to keep her emotions in check as she grasped her pendant nervously, running her fingers along its curves and swirls.

As she moved to join Thorne, the door to the chamber banged open. Lira raised her axes as black lightning consumed the heavy curtain between the bed and the door. The curtain burned up, leaving only Caitir standing in its charred remains.

When her gaze fell on Lira, her lips parted in surprise. She was dressed in a gown of crimson and gold silk, her golden hair piled high in a mass of ringlets. Her pale eyes were rimmed with red, and they flicked to Thorne before she spoke.

"Blades, Lira?" Caitir scoffed. "Do you even know what to do with them? You look ridiculous, by the way—quite feral, honestly."

Lira pressed her lips together. Caitir spoke as though they were still friends, picking up where they'd left off months ago. But Lira could see the rage in her eyes. The eerie contrast between Caitir's casual tone and the anger in her gaze sent a chill through Lira.

"Weren't you attending a rather important event?" Lira asked, tightening her grip on the axe handles. The bead pressed into her palm. "Where is your crown, by the way?"

Caitir glanced sidelong at the floor. "It seems, in all the confusion, that only two crowns were made. One for my mother—another for that vile man she chained me to."

Lira's brows rose. "Why are you telling me this?"

"Because I want you to help me," Caitir said. "We are sisters now, are we not?"

Lira sucked in a sharp breath. Thorne watched her closely, as still as death.

How did Caitir know about the Binding?

"Oh, come now, Lira." Caitir took a step closer. "All those years you said you wanted a sister of your own, and now you have one. It's funny, though. I never realized you were so fickle. What would Eremon think if he knew?"

"I'm not talking with you about him," Lira answered shakily.

"Fine; let's change the subject, then." Caitir's gaze flicked to Thorne. "Come sniffing for your master, Beran hound?"

Thorne's expression was impassive. Caitir immediately turned her attention back to Lira, smirking. "I can secure the overlord's freedom—and yours, if you'll help me."

"No," Thorne answered in a low voice.

"I wanted to help you before, but this is the path you chose, Caitir." Lira stepped backward. Her palms were slick with sweat.

"There is a power here," Caitir said conspiratorially, "and I think you would be very interested to know more about it, Silira. It can heal corruption and grant long life. Help me obtain this power, and together, we can make things right in Iathium."

"I'm not here to pursue power," Lira replied. "I came for Aidryn; that's all."

"We can work together to heal magic for good," Caitir ventured. "Bring truth to the people."

Lira didn't miss the little pang in her chest as the words left Caitir's lips. It was clear she knew just where to strike—knew the things that mattered to Lira most.

"Work with *you* to restore truth?" Lira almost laughed.

"Silira," Thorne said softly. She thought of the bead in her hand and took another step backward, toward him.

"I've thought about ending you both," Caitir said, her gaze flicking between Lira and Aidryn. "But you're worth more to me alive for the time being."

"You're too benevolent for your own good," Lira snapped. The longer she was trapped in this room with Caitir, the more enraged she became.

Without warning, Caitir fired a blast of dark magic toward them, her black lightning surging directly for Aidryn. Lira leapt between Thorne and the crackling power as her ring released its own swell of cobalt light, encasing the three of them in a cocoon of protective power. The black lighting dissipated on contact.

Caitir locked eyes with Lira, clearly dismayed. She glanced down at her fingers, then clenched them into fists and forced an airy laugh. "When you learn the truth about that power, you're going to want it," she said, "and you'll be back. That, I can promise you."

Lira shook her head. "You can still choose the right path," she said. "You don't have to stay here. There are safe places where you can hide away until this is all over."

"Don't let them keep using you," Thorne added quietly. "You are worth so much more."

Caitir tilted her head, regarding the warrior. "I know my worth, you dog." A cruel smile played on her lips. "How do you know I am not using *them*?"

Now, Lira was close enough to Thorne that she could grasp Aidryn's hand, pressing her pendant against his skin. Thorne shifted his grasp on Aidryn to make contact with Lira's fingers. It was unnerving to feel Caitir's gaze on them from where she stood, unmoving, in the center of the chamber.

"Remember how I let you live today," Caitir said. "When I see you on the battlefield, I expect you to repay the favor."

Lira pressed the bead against her pendant, and darkness swallowed them.

CHAPTER 20
LIRA

As quickly as it began, the *turas* was over. It deposited them in Lira's chamber at Halgeir, just as she had hoped. Though this trip felt more chaotic than the last, it was still more manageable than before.

Thorne looked nauseous again, but he had managed to maintain a solid grip on Aidryn. He lay Aidryn onto Lira's bed and took a knee, breathing quietly and steadily, eyes closed. Again, he used his own power to calm himself, then to energize Lira after the *turas*.

Rescuing Aidryn had been too easy. They had been allowed to escape—had been *helped* by two of their gravest enemies. Lira wasn't fooled, though. Both Caitir and Macha had ends they wanted to achieve. And the next time she encountered either of them, Lira might be on the receiving end of their nefarious plans.

"You should have been on my first few *turas* trips," Lira said quietly, touching Thorne's shoulder. "This was nothing."

He cracked one eye open and glared at her. She smiled

wryly, then looked to Aidryn. "Will you stay with him while I get your father?"

Thorne nodded, massaging a point on his wrist. When he didn't speak again, Lira padded out of the room quietly, her own dizziness abating. She needed time to collect herself—time to register the fact that Aidryn was truly here.

When she reached the healer's chamber, she knocked on the door. Ljós opened it abruptly, sagging in relief when he saw her there. He stepped aside to let her in, then sealed their voices inside. Lira's ears popped as they adjusted.

"You survived," he said. "Where is Thorne?"

"He's in my chamber. We were able to escape with Aidryn Tarlach, but we couldn't get to the overlord. He's being held in the dungeon."

Ljós bowed his head. "I am sorry for that."

Lira sighed. "So am I."

The healer gave her a slight nod, then rose and began gathering various tinctures and salves, packing them into his satchel. While he worked, Lira said, "For months now, I've been seeing the same vision of Eremon, over and over. It's always about a key buried in his father's vault."

"Iuchair," Ljós said, grinding herbs with a mortar and pestle before mixing them into a clay-like paste. "I've run across it in my studies."

He paused his work, then led Lira to a table in the corner, which was covered by a sheet. Ljós removed the sheet to reveal a stack of tomes, many of which Lira recognized from the archive. "Aidryn helped me smuggle these out of the archive while you were in the dungeon," the healer said. "I've been reading through them myself, but many are in Itelos."

He returned to his work bench, scraping the clay paste into a ceramic jar.

Lira ran her fingers over the leather-bound cover of one of the books, then looked back up at Ljós, whispering despite his silencing spell. "Have you ever heard of a magic that can be extracted from a dead person?" she asked.

"Only in the first moments after death," Ljós answered, closing his satchel. His amber eyes—so much like Thorne's—lingered on Lira for a moment. "Why?"

"Because Macha, Aila, Caitir—they all keep talking about this power they want, but they need help getting it. Macha said outright that it's Eremon's. It doesn't make sense."

"I have a theory that I cannot prove," Ljós answered, leading the way to his chamber door. "I will need to see your memories of Eremon's death, but later. Let's go to Aidryn now."

Thorne was leaning against the wall beside the bed when Lira and Ljós returned to the chamber, looking steadier than he had before.

Ljós took a seat on the edge of the bed, scrutinizing Aidryn. He pushed away the furs that covered him and used a sharp bone shard to cut away the bandages. One look at the wound sent a wave of nausea crashing over Lira, and she swayed on her feet. The puncture itself was fairly small; it was the inoxia that had made such a deadly impact.

Sickly green tendrils spread from the wound like a corrupt tattoo. It seemed the poison had inched its way across Aidryn's abdomen before moving inward. Lira studied the markings while the healer worked quietly, passing his palms over Aidryn and murmuring to himself. He summoned a large golden orb and released it into the air over Aidryn, directing it to settle over his stomach before it absorbed into his body completely.

Despite Aidryn's pallor, the healing magic glowed from within him, illuminating his skin as if *he* were magic himself. Lira moved around the bed to sit at his side. Tentatively, she reached for his hand and grasped his fingers. She wished he would squeeze her hand, respond somehow—but that wasn't something she dared to hope for yet.

"He is on the edge of death," Ljós said quietly, opening his satchel of herbs and remedies. "The spell Eremon put on that ring is the only thing keeping him alive."

Lira fidgeted with her ring, careful not to look at the wound again. "Will he recover?"

"We will see," Ljós answered, using a small mortar and pestle to mix a pungent herbal paste. He applied the poultice to Aidryn's wound. "Some people survive inoxia, but never from a wound like this."

Her breath left her in a *whoosh* and her stomach cramped as though she'd been kicked. "How long until we know something?" she asked.

The healer grunted softly. "It may be days, weeks—if he pulls through. After that, healing will take as long as his body requires."

"Oh." Lira's gaze strayed to Aidryn's face. He had always been so full of life. Growing up, she'd envied his vigor and the raw energy he emanated. It was unnerving to see him so still, so close to death.

Lira remembered sharing Caitir's bed often in the old tower home when they were children. The girls would sleep in until the sun was high—that is, if Aidryn didn't wake them at daybreak. As a young boy, he had been an early riser, while Lira had always relished sleeping as late as she could. She could still hear him boasting loudly about everything he'd accomplished in the mornings before anyone else had deigned to rise.

Now that she thought about it, Lira realized she had never watched Aidryn sleep before. She wanted to touch his face—to curl up beside him—but she remained still, keenly aware of the healer working across from her. And of Thorne watching her closely from the other side of the room.

Ljós formed another golden orb, which hovered over Aidryn before sinking into his chest. Again, the light illuminated him from within. And again, he remained completely still.

After a long while, the healer raised his head to regard Lira, then turned to Thorne. "Take her to find food," he said, nodding toward Lira.

When Lira opened her mouth to protest, Ljós shook his head. "I need to be alone with him for a little while, Silira."

With a sigh, Lira nodded. Exhaustion weighed her down, but she stood despite it. Thorne pushed off the wall, and the two left her chamber together—but not before Lira took one more look over her shoulder at Aidryn's lifeless form.

They walked the stone corridors in silence. Lira wanted to cry—to break something, to scream—anything to release the rage that simmered within her. They'd done this to Aidryn because of her. He'd given up everything to protect her, and she had ignored his pleas until the last possible moment.

Her thoughts turned to Eremon, and a sudden surge of guilt overwhelmed her. She'd allowed herself to be drawn in, to fall in love with him. Aidryn had warned her not to get attached to Eremon, and she had ignored him. Aidryn had tried to save her, but she had refused him. Now, Aidryn was paying the price for her choices. Maybe it would have been better for everyone if she had soundly rejected Eremon and continued about her business from the beginning.

Regardless, Eremon's magic would have killed him. If Lira had never befriended him, perhaps he would have left her ignorant of her true purpose. She may have been protected from attracting attention. Perhaps she would have avoided Macha's ire, and the time she'd spent in the dungeon.

A sickly chill crawled across her skin at the thought of those dark days, and she shivered.

But Aila's agenda against Lira would have remained the same. Aidryn would have still chosen to stand between Lira and his family. He would have kept tabs on the bad actors who were involved with his stepmother, regardless of Eremon's direct involvement.

When it was time for Lira to flee Iathium—which would still have become inevitable—she would have run to the Ridge first, and then on to Beran. Aidryn would have helped her run whether she asked him to or not.

Eremon had helped Lira to harness the remnant of power she'd possessed at the time. She had been given more knowledge than she would have received otherwise.

Both men had sacrificed themselves, one way or another, to prepare her for a storm that was inevitably coming for her. Each step of her journey had been overseen until she'd escaped the Ridge. And even after she'd been separated from Aidryn, there had been help around every corner. Nevala, Mytr, Thorne, Ljós, Talfryn, her mother—even Macha, of all people —had directed her steps.

The least she could do now was to let Ljós do his healing work. Perhaps soon, she would hear Aidryn's voice again.

THORNE LEFT Lira in her mother's chambers. He was eager to separate—to bathe and rest, she assumed. They were both still filthy from their journey through the caverns. Clan Beran took great pride in cleanliness, more so than Iathium, so Lira imagined he was off to scrub himself raw.

Now, Lira was doing the same. Iva had pulled her daughter into her rooms, drawn a hot bath herself, and left Lira alone to soak while she sought out Thorne's report on Artur. She sat in the near-scalding water until her skin was pink, reflecting on everything that had happened.

It was hard to believe Aidryn was here now, under Beran's protection and once again in the same place as Lira. She wasn't sure what she would say to him if he woke—no, *when* he woke. Her eyes stung with unshed tears and she bit her lip, taking a sharp, shaky breath.

Ljós had refused to give her a timeline for Aidryn's healing, so she didn't know what to expect. She wanted all the answers, and she wanted them now.

At least he's here.

Lira had been soaking in silence for half an hour when Iva returned with a tray. It was laden with hunks of cheese, dried meat, and blueberry wine in two small ceramic cups. Iva sat on a stool beside the tub, balancing the tray on its edge.

"Eat," she urged, taking some cheese for herself.

"It's late," Lira protested, though her stomach growled so loudly she could hear it above the deep bathwater. "I'm going to sleep soon."

Iva made a face. "No, you are not. And your lying skills have not improved with age."

Lira shrugged. "Truth magic. Can't help it."

She lifted a hand out of the water, flicking the droplets from her fingers before selecting a small cut of beef. It was tender and flavorful, and she chewed it slowly.

"Don't blame yourself for what happened to Artur," Iva said. "They'll keep him alive for a time because of who he is. Perhaps we'll have another chance to save him."

"We couldn't have gone into the dungeons." Lira shook her head. "They're too heavily guarded. It was risky to go to the city in the first place."

"Yes, it was. At least the three of you came back alive."

Lira had expected a reprimand from her mother for sneaking out of Halgeir. It felt strange to be treated as an ally and an equal, rather than a child. Besides, Talfryn would likely scold her enough for the both of them.

"I hope Aidryn survives this. He was barely hanging on." Lira splashed her face with the warm water. "And I wish we could have brought *sjeiva* home for you."

A heavy silence fell over them until Iva said, "Artur keenly felt the pressure to ensure all of our wellbeing here. His decisions came from a place of desperation."

"I know." Lira had thought Artur's attempt at an alliance with Macha seemed out of character for him. After all, she'd always seen him as fiercely loyal to Clan Beran—and he was.

But Artur also took risks. He'd married a woman from outside his clan, then persuaded his people to welcome her as their own. He had seen that her children were cared for. Perhaps it was Lira who had made herself unwelcome all this time.

"It's almost impossible to navigate what's happening with any clarity," Lira said. "I'm sure he was doing the best he could."

Iva tilted her head curiously. "Why so charitable toward him now?"

"I suppose I've gained perspective on many things over the past few months," Lira answered. "And I think, in part, that I misjudged him."

She thought she caught a glint in Iva's eyes. "It's an easy thing to do."

Lira reached for another piece of cheese, though her appetite was suddenly waning. "What are you going to tell the clan about him?"

"For now, I will tell them he is traveling." Iva frowned. "Thorne's scouts are sworn to secrecy. Otherwise, news spreads slowly between Iathium and Halgeir. I think I will hold the information close until it's time to send my warriors out. They'll need something to fight for."

"It may be a while, yet," Lira said. "It appears Gerallt and Aila still need time to amass a greater army."

Iva nodded once, her gaze resting on Lira's face for a long moment before she spoke again. "Why didn't you tell me you were bound to Aidryn?"

Lira almost choked on her cheese. Her heart began to hammer. "I'll kill Thorne," she mumbled.

Iva tilted her head. "Were you not intended for the Rí?"

"Eremon did ask for my hand," Lira admitted softly, "but I was reluctant to accept."

"I see." Her mother leaned nearer, her gaze steady and intense. "How did you become his heir, if you did not agree to marry him?"

"Just before he died, he asked me to put on the ring," Lira said. "I couldn't bear to refuse him—not when he was dying right in front of me. I would have done anything to give him hope—to help him hold on a little longer."

She took a shuddering breath, biting hard on her lip and staring at the ornate carvings on the ceiling. "I knew it contained protective magic, but I didn't know I was accepting an inheritance. Eremon said I would just be the ring's custodian unless I wanted the throne."

Iva remained silent, studying Lira curiously.

"But Aidryn knew. He was there," Lira continued. "There was an incantation. He told me the words to say for the magic to take hold."

"So Iathium is truly yours," Iva mused. "Who else knows?"

"Macha and the healer," Lira answered, ticking each person's name on her fingers. "Aidryn, of course. Talfryn, Skelly, and Lord Irem, I assume. Caitir, Aila, Gerallt..."

Lira thought about how Macha had directed her to Aidryn. She told Iva how the deposed Raní had been imprisoned in the crypt, and how she had deigned to remain there. However, Lira did not reveal that Macha had asked her to return—and apparently, Thorne had not, either.

"I still don't understand where the Binding to Aidryn comes in," Iva said.

Lira sighed. "It was Eremon's doing, in part. He believed Aidryn and I would be a good match, if something were to happen to him. I don't think I'll ever forgive him for making that decision for us."

"Only the bound can make that decision," Iva answered. Her sentiment echoed something Skelly had said, but Lira was reluctant to delve too deeply into its connotations.

"Eremon enchanted my ring, and that's what created the Binding—at least, from what I've been told. It's not traditional, by any means." Lira sank deeper into the water, glancing up to decipher what her mother might be thinking.

Iva's eyes were rimmed with tears. "That is a rare magic, indeed. I have never heard of a Binding ritual that acted outside of the couple's spoken commands."

"Skelly said the spell responded to our feelings," Lira mumbled, almost unintelligibly, "for one another."

Iva raised her eyebrows. "I remember Aidryn's spirit; he was always so drawn to you," she said softly. "And you to him."

Lira dipped under the water then, hiding her swirling thoughts for a moment before resurfacing and swiping the water from her eyes.

"What a gift you've received, to have been so loved and protected."

"It's a curse," Lira said, more sharply than she intended. "Our freedom is gone. Eremon is dead. Aidryn could *still* die. War is coming. And now, I have to contend with this Binding that comes so soon after—" She faltered, a lump forming in her throat again as she pressed her hands over her face. "I can't reconcile any of this."

"What is there to reconcile? You loved Eremon, yes." Iva spoke gently, carefully. "But there is no crime in admitting that you also love Aidryn. Or would you rather waste time punishing yourself for it?"

Her mother's words were daggers, and they found their mark in Lira's heart.

"Is it not wrong of me?" she cried.

Iva shook her head slowly. "Eremon must have suspected; otherwise, he would not have created the Binding spell."

It was true. Lira had seen, in her own memories, evidence that Eremon understood the lifelong bond Aidryn and Lira had shared.

"Eremon suspected he might be dying, but he still pursued me." Lira sighed. "I don't believe he intended harm or cruelty, but that is what happened.

"I wanted *him*. Not power or attention. I fell in love with him, and he helped me dream of a world where we would work together to restore truth to Rodhlan. We could have done so much good together."

"Then you and I have something in common," Iva said, tracing her fingertips along a runic tattoo on her inner wrist. "When Artur offered me a place at his side, I knew I could provide safety for you—and a powerful alliance if the time ever came. I wish you would have come here with me back then, but I knew the risks when I accepted him."

"Even the risk that he could forge an alliance with Macha?" Lira felt sorry for asking as soon as the words left her lips. She did not, however, feel sorry that the Binding was no longer their topic of focus.

"An alliance with anyone—yes," Iva answered. "I trust Artur, and I trust Thorne. I trust my husband had good reason for going into Iathium, though I don't understand his strategy. And I trust this clan.

"Beran is ready to stand with you," Iva said. "They are sworn to it."

Lira squeezed her eyes shut. The magnitude of what Iva was telling her felt too overwhelming to comprehend. "How will we do all of this?"

"A day at a time," Iva answered. "We need Clans Tarlach and Énna in the fight. Sentries from Iathium who are loyal to Talfryn and to you. Anyone we can gather to stand against these people."

"Did you always know about Aila?" Lira asked. "About her intentions?"

"No, I did not realize what she was about," Iva answered, her shoulders curling in on themselves—a habit Lira had inherited, and an unconscious action she emulated whenever she felt deep shame. "Perhaps I should have."

Years ago, Aila had befriended Lira's mother, gaining her favor through compliments and attention. As a young mother new to Iathium, Iva had been in dire need of friends. Lira couldn't blame her mother for making friends, or for trying to help her daughter meet other girls her age.

"Don't we all believe we 'should' have done many things?" Lira forced a sad smile. "It isn't your fault, any more than it is mine."

"Something you must remember for yourself, when you dwell for too long on things out of your control."

"*Everything* is out of my control." More tears slipped down Lira's cheeks. "I couldn't save Eremon. I couldn't get Aidryn off the Ridge. I haven't even mastered my own magic. I feel like I have failed in every possible way."

"But you haven't," Iva said. "You succeeded in saving Aidryn. He has a chance at healing now. And perhaps the two of you will be granted enough peace and time to nurture your Binding before the war begins."

There it was again. Lira's cheeks were blazing, and she covered her face with her hands. "I can't think about that right now, truly."

"Eventually, you will have to," Iva said, rising, careful to turn her back to Lira as she did so. She paused before she left the bathing chamber. "You have always been so attuned to truth, Lira—from everywhere but within yourself. Don't suppress it. Let it live and breathe, and you will find your freedom there."

There was a knock on Iva's chamber door then, and she disappeared for a moment. Lira could hear her speaking with a man in low tones. A moment later, she returned.

"Ljós is here to collect you," she said. "But do think about what I told you, and don't be afraid."

CHAPTER 21

LIRA

Fortress Halgeir

Lira didn't waste any time getting out of the bath, drying herself, and dressing in the clean clothes Iva had left out for her. She worked the snarls out of her hair in the heavy silence, her thoughts straying over and over to their conversation about the Binding.

In one particular, Iva had been painfully right: Lira valued the truth, yet she hid from her own. In the past, she'd been able to hide behind her work, her position, her duty—and later, the greater purpose everyone had told her she was meant to serve.

Now, those echoes had died out. Most people didn't realize Lira was truly meant to inherit the city, and she suspected they never would. Her name would quickly be forgotten now that Iathium's throne had been stolen.

She met Ljós in the open corridor outside Iva's room. Dawn was already breaking, and they wound their way down the walkways in silence until they reached the healer's chamber again and went inside.

"How is Aidryn?" Lira asked as Ljós latched the door.

"The poisoned sleep exhausted him beyond anything we

can imagine, but I believe he has a chance," he answered, taking a seat on the floor beside a shallow pit filled with smooth, amber stones. He motioned for Lira to join him, then sealed out all sound. "I have healed him to the extent that his body will allow, and I gave him a tincture that will help him rest for a while. We will know more when he wakes."

"What does that mean—the extent that his body will allow?" Lira asked, sitting beside Ljós.

"Even magical healing takes its toll," Ljós hedged. "I will work with him every day, for as long as it takes."

"Thank you." Lira chewed her lip in dismay, suddenly wishing she could bolt out the door and back to her chamber to see him.

"There is an empty room next to mine," the healer added. "If you wish it, we can move him there—"

"No, he can stay where he is." She cringed at her own abruptness—at the desperation in her voice. "I don't want him to wake up alone."

I don't want to be alone. I don't want to be without him.

The healer nodded his understanding. "Very well. Now, to the matter of Eremon."

Lira swallowed, her throat suddenly dry. "You wanted to witness his death."

"I'm sorry to ask it of you."

She had never considered that others might call on her power to untangle the memory of tragic events. It was doubly painful that this memory was her own.

"Do you have a calming tincture for after?" she asked timidly.

Ljós nodded, his expression grim. "I'll send you back to your chamber with something to calm you, and a remedy to help you rest. You should also know that drawing on your memories in this way could make you feel unwell, particularly if you access a memory more than once. I will make you a remedy for that, as well."

She nodded and took a shaky breath. "May I ask why you weren't there, in the courtyard the night Eremon died?"

"I was in my chamber, preparing a headache remedy on his mother's orders. He was in pain every day for months before that last night." Ljós's expression was stricken. "He'd taken an extra measure of the medicine that afternoon. I couldn't keep up with the demand that day, though I wish I'd been with him in his final moments. He just wanted to live the life of a normal young man."

Lira had never paused to consider Ljós and Eremon's friendship, but she imagined they'd been close. "This will be difficult for you to see," she said.

"As it will be difficult for you to relive," he acknowledged. "I am ready when you are."

LIRA WALKED SWIFTLY down the open corridor, winding around the fortress's stone walkways until she reached the entrance to her chamber. She clutched the remedies Ljós had sent with her, desperate to calm herself after immersing both of them in the memory of Eremon's last moments. Though she hadn't grown ill, she was on the verge of full-blown panic.

She had expected Ljós to observe the memory, then immediately tell her about the theory he'd mentioned. But he'd needed to take a calming tincture too, and he'd excused himself to his bedchamber, leaving her alone by the amber stones. Finally, she'd decided not to wait for him any longer. Aidryn had been left alone for too long.

Lira reached for her door but paused, her fingertips lingering over the iron handle. Her mind strayed to the man who lay inside. If he recovered, she would find some way to repay him for everything he'd done.

Before opening the door, she dropped a dose of calming medicine under her tongue. It burned a bit, but she swallowed, feeling it soothe her frayed emotions almost immediately.

Her heart thudded as she pushed the door open and stepped into her chamber. When she laid eyes on Aidryn, it felt as though the entire world shifted, and then realigned around him.

He was still sleeping, but he looked like himself again. Whatever magic Ljós had employed to bring him this far was astounding. His skin looked healthy once more, his face fuller. Ljós had also managed to begin reversing the startling atrophy that had reduced his frame to nearly nothing.

Aidryn's tunic had been cut off to allow for the healer's work. The arrowhead had been removed, the wound was closed, and the poisoned tendrils that had extended outward from the wound had faded away to white scars.

Carefully, Lira arranged the furs over Aidryn, covering his bare chest. He was breathing easily, his body relaxed into a deep slumber, the shadow of death completely gone. She allowed her gaze to roam over his face, taking in the curve of his jawline, his dark lashes, the softness of his mouth.

Back in Iathium, at the cottage, he had begged fervently for Lira to flee with him. She'd noticed his mouth then, too. Perhaps that was the first moment she'd truly known she felt something for him, and it had frightened her. But in truth, she had loved him for longer than she could remember. Perhaps for so long, the familiar admiration had simply become a part of who she was.

How many years had she been lying to herself?

"You look better," she said softly, sitting on the mattress beside him. "Now, I need you to wake up so I have someone to goad." He didn't stir.

"I'm afraid," she admitted, her throat tightening. "My feelings are all in a tangle—so much has happened, I can hardly fathom it."

Timidly, she placed one hand on his chest. His skin was

warm. Soft. With her other hand, she brushed stray strands of dark hair off his forehead, then rested her palm against his cheek.

"I suppose we'll sort it all out a day at a time, but why don't we start with the truth."

She gazed at his face for another moment, then leaned down and softly kissed his lips.

"No more lies," she whispered.

Lira rose, circled to the other side of the bed, and crawled beneath the furs, resting her head on her pillow. Beside her, Aidryn remained in a deep slumber. As she felt herself drifting into sleep, she reached for his hand and grasped it. She thought she felt the slightest movement of his fingers, so she lay motionless, waiting for a sign from him, until sleep finally pulled her under.

AIDRYN

Fortress Halgeir

No more lies.

Aidryn's senses surged to life at the brush of Lira's mouth against his. It was the most alert he'd felt in a long while—how long had it been, exactly? He felt stiff and sore, keenly aware of each place where his body ached. And he still couldn't move, or open his eyes, or speak.

But he could feel. He'd felt that kiss, had felt her sink onto the bed beside him. If he weren't in so much pain, he might have decided it was all a dream.

He'd begun to think—to feel—again when the healer had come. And now, Lira was here, breathing steadily, grasping his hand as she slept.

Aidryn wasn't sure how much time had passed since they'd arrived, but it felt like hours. It was quiet and dark and earthy here, wherever they were. There were no pungent perfumes, nor cloying incense, to assault his senses.

Now that he was with Lira, he didn't want to sleep. In fact, he wanted to wake her—to hear her voice, to gaze at her face.

But he hadn't truly rested since the arrow, and exhaustion won out. He felt himself slip back into a dreamless slumber.

THERE WAS no way to determine what time of day or night it was when Aidryn finally opened his eyes. His first thought was of how dark this chamber was, save for the few guttering candles scattered around it. There were no windows, and the walls were made of solid stone.

Aidryn blinked the sleep from his eyes and tried to move. First, he wiggled his fingers and toes. Then, he shifted his legs and arms. Bit by bit, he let his body wake up, then painstakingly rolled onto his side to face Lira.

She was sleeping deeply, fingers curled around one of the furs. At some point, she'd let go of Aidryn's hand. He studied her soft features, her pale skin, the mass of brown curls that tumbled over her pillow. From what he could tell, she was wearing some sort of fur-trimmed tunic that looked like it came straight from Clan Beran.

Mentally, he ticked off each clue as he glanced around the chamber again. *Stone room. No windows. Furs on the bed. Beran healer, Beran clothes...*

Aidryn had never visited Fortress Halgeir before. It was a good thing Lira had allies here.

He turned his attention back to her. After all these years, she was lying next to him. And she'd kissed him. Why?

Aidryn had overheard many conversations while he was incapacitated. Few of them stood out, but one in particular...

Bits of a discussion between Aila and Caitir came flooding back, and his heart began to race.

I can feel something else. That boy-king had something to do with this.

It feels similar to the Binding rituals the priestesses used to perform.

A Binding? You mean they were married?

Suddenly, he remembered his magic departing his body, and the way Lira's had bloomed inside of him, soothing the magical wounds Aila and Caitir had inflicted. It was clear something had happened between Aidryn and Lira that day in the mountains, but he hadn't been able to sort it out.

He was equal parts elated and terrified to ask Lira more about the Binding. After all, she'd never been the type to bend to the will of others. However they had come to be bound, he was sure she would fight against it.

Except... she had kissed him. The thought sent him reeling again.

He reached for her, lightly tracing his fingers over her cheek. He'd touched her face once before, and the softness of her skin beneath his fingertips had almost broken him.

"Lira," he tried to say, but his voice was so weak, almost nothing came out. He swallowed and tried again. "Lira."

Her eyelashes fluttered, and she stirred a little. He stilled, fingertips resting on her cheek, as she opened her eyes and met his gaze.

"Hello," he said, his voice gravelly and weak.

Lira grasped his hand, eyes wide and welling with tears. "Aidryn!"

He didn't have time to say anything else before she threw her arms around him, holding him tightly as she sobbed. She pulled back enough to look at his face—*to touch his face.*

Aidryn was afraid to move.

"You're here and you're awake and—I thought you might never wake up," she cried. "You unselfish fool, you were dying, you could have *died!*"

She pounded her fist against his chest to punctuate the last word before she crumpled again, her voice rising in a broken wail that made his stomach clench. Aidryn held her against his chest, all tears and sniffles and sleep-tousled curls.

"I missed you too," he said softly, tightening his hold on her.

How was this real? Lira—the woman Aidryn had loved since childhood—was in his arms. Had slept beside him. Aidryn had long since abandoned the thought that she could ever want him, *but she had kissed him*. She had rescued him and kissed him and now...

Suddenly, the reality of what she'd risked slammed into him.

"Lira, you weren't supposed to come after me," he scolded.

She sat abruptly, breaking his grasp to press an accusing finger against his chest as he rolled onto his back. Her cheeks were splotched and wet with tears. "What else did you expect me to do? I would never abandon you."

He caught her fingers and smiled up at her. "You've made that perfectly clear."

Lira raised her chin, brushing a tear off her cheek. Aidryn didn't miss the glance she stole at their hands before she looked him in the eye again. "Good." She sniffled, then wiped her nose on her sleeve. "What else should I clarify?"

Aidryn's heart thumped erratically as he weighed what to say next. His fear told him to ask her about everything that had happened while they were separated. To show him the memories of the rescue, perhaps. Or, he could ask about all the mundanities of life with Clan Beran and just let her talk—buy himself a little time to come up with a strategy for asking about the Binding.

But his curiosity won. He *had* to know—

"Well," he answered, stroking Lira's knuckles with the pad of his thumb, "you could explain why you kissed me when you thought I was sleeping."

Her lips parted in surprise.

CHAPTER 23

LIRA

Fortress Halgeir

L ira opened her mouth to speak, but a squeak came out instead. "I—I'm sorry," she stammered, cheeks blazing. "I probably shouldn't have—"

"*No more lies*," Aidryn said, laughter dancing in his eyes. "What did *that* mean?"

She let go of his hand and covered her face, caught somewhere between overwhelming sheepishness and bursting into tears again. In truth, she had barely gathered enough composure to sit up and look at him in the first place. Her eyes were swollen, her face was mottled from tears, her hair was a tangle, and she had made a complete mess of Aidryn's bare chest, crying and sniffling all over him.

And now, he was springing *this* on her?

"Do you think you can just wake up and ask me a question like that?" Her tone was unnaturally shrill.

"Oh, how dare I," he replied. "It's a simple question, Lira. I nearly died, and you can't bring yourself to answer it?" His voice was rich with amusement.

"It's not a simple question," she said, scrunching her nose. "It's two questions."

"Both simple," Aidryn pressed, reaching for her hand again.

"Aidryn—"

"So, answer them." His knowing smirk was the last straw.

Lira pressed a palm to his chest and gave him a little shove. "You already know the answers," she cried.

Aidryn was grinning broadly now. "Yes, but I want to hear you say it." He caught her shoulder and drew her closer, laughing softly as he pushed a few stray curls aside. "Out loud. All of it."

"I kissed you because I love you!" Lira blurted. "And I'm tired of lying to myself about it. Are you satisfied?"

As soon as the admission left her lips, tears welled in her eyes again. For a panicked moment, she wondered if she'd overstepped and misinterpreted his feelings, but he was staring at her with an unguarded admiration that made her breath hitch. He cupped her face, brushing his thumb across her cheek, then pulled her to him and kissed her.

Aidryn's lips tasted of heavy sleep and traces of the healer's remedies. He seemed to realize this as quickly as Lira did, because he hesitated when she tried to deepen the kiss.

"Blast it, I probably taste disgusting—" he tried to say, but she cut him off, kissing him firmly.

"Quiet, you." She laughed. "You really don't. Just herbs."

He traced the shape of her ear and sighed, as if relieved. "Then I'll have to thank Ljós for sparing me unimaginable humiliation."

"It wouldn't matter," Lira said. "Nothing could keep me from this."

She brushed her lips against his and smiled as he gave in again, letting one of his hands roam into her curls. Her stomach fluttered, a heady rush of sensation sweeping over her as this time, Aidryn kissed her deeply.

Lira helped him roll onto his side again and lay down next

to him, taking his face in her hands and tracing his jaw. He wrapped an arm around her waist and pulled her flush against him. Warmth flooded her as they held one another, trading kisses and whispering in the candlelight.

When Aidryn's eyelids grew heavy again, Lira lay her head on his shoulder and they rested together. She dozed fitfully, waking once in a while to prove to herself that he was truly home.

Home. That's what it felt like to be with him again. And it wouldn't matter whether they were at Fortress Halgeir, in Iathium, or roaming the meadowlands. As long as she and Aidryn were together, Lira would be home.

LATE THAT AFTERNOON, Ljós returned. The creaking of the opening door roused Lira from her sleep, and she rose groggily from bed as the healer took his seat on the mattress and went to work on a still-sleeping Aidryn. He glanced curiously at Lira but said nothing as she stole away to the bathing chamber and shut herself in.

Alone and in the quiet, she braced herself against the door frame, stomach fluttering nervously as she tried to catch her breath. Every time she thought of Aidryn's touch, his kisses, she was overwhelmed by a rush that made her *weak*. She was as unnerved as she was elated.

Lira looked in the glass and wrinkled her nose. Her hair was wild from sleep; when she failed to tame it, she tied it back instead. Then, she splashed her face with cool water and cleaned her teeth.

When she emerged a few minutes later, Aidryn was sitting up in bed, sipping a mug of broth. Her heart leapt when his gaze met hers just over the rim of the mug, and he lowered it carefully, never taking his blue eyes off her.

"Where is Ljós?" Lira asked, stopping short at the foot of the bed.

"Sending for food," he answered, clutching the mug in his lap. "I asked him to bring something for you."

"Oh." She pressed her lips together, then smiled. "Thank you."

"Will you come here?" he asked, patting the empty space on the bed beside him.

Lira crossed the room and joined him, leaning down to kiss his cheek before she sat. He took another sip of his broth, but choked on it when Lira asked, "When did you realize—about the Binding?"

"The same day Aila and Caitir figured it out," he answered when he'd regained his composure. "Weeks after the fact. It was during one of their failed attempts to take my magic."

His fingertips were turning white around the mug. Her stomach flip-flopped, and heat flooded her cheeks. "So I take it Artagán shot you," she said.

Aidryn went still before answering. "I asked him to. I didn't think I'd get out of there alive, and they were just going to wear me down."

It took a moment for his words to make sense. He'd wanted to die so badly, he had asked for a mercy killing. The thought of him being in that much pain and despair made her heart ache.

"Why did he agree to that?" Lira asked. "I thought he was on Gerallt's side."

"At first, he was. But then..." Aidryn shrugged. "He couldn't stop worrying about where Ellwyn had run off to. And he saw how his father mistreated Caitir. In the end, I think he just didn't have the stomach for what Gerallt and Aila are about. He told me he was going to leave that night."

"I hope he found Ellwyn." The encounter with Caitir in that tower room still haunted Lira, and she scooted closer until she was flush against Aidryn's side. She lay her head on his shoulder. "I can't stop thinking about how frail you were. It was terrible."

He hummed. "I wouldn't know, I slept through the entire thing."

"Stop trying to be funny about it," she scolded, grinning in spite of herself.

Aidryn leaned down to press a kiss against her hair. "Thank you for protecting my magic." He sighed happily. "Please tell me you put it to good use while I was out of commission."

Lira nodded. "All over this fortress—and the Dome, as well."

He chuckled. "As you absolutely should have."

She sat up to look at him. "How much mischief have you caused with this lock-picking magic, anyway?"

"More than my share, I'm afraid." Abruptly, he raised the mug and took a swig, but a bit of broth sloshed out. A drop trickled down his chin, and he swiped it away with the back of his hand, his cheeks reddening. "But, all in all, not nearly enough. It's terribly difficult to resist using it."

Lira settled back against his side, resting her head on his shoulder again. Aidryn took another sip of broth before he said, "I don't suppose you know what happened to Fannin."

"After you were taken, I left Skelly in the meadowlands and used *turas* to go..." She shrugged. "I don't know where I meant to go. But I ended up at Va'hesk, with Clan Tarlach."

"You're joking." He tilted his face to catch her gaze. "You really made it out to the remnant?"

"I did. There was healer there—Nevala. She and her husband, Mytr, cared for me. It's difficult to explain, but between my birthright and the *turas*, it's like my magic just... shattered for a while."

"So what happened then?"

"They enchanted a pony, intending to send me here."

A little laugh rumbled in his chest. "*Intending*. You mean you did what you wanted instead?"

"You might say that." She hummed contentedly, nuzzling against him. "My magic still wasn't healed, but I thought I could get back to you. I ended up wandering near the eastern coast for weeks, like a complete fool."

"It's a wonder you didn't die out there." His voice was low. Harsh. "It *was* foolish."

"Yes, well." Lira sighed. "Somehow, in my stupor, I managed to call Fannin. He brought me as far as the gorge before I lost him again."

She told him the story of how Fannin had bolted when they encountered Yrsa—and how she'd come to know Thorne. He listened intently, finishing off his broth while she spoke.

"Fannin's a smart old boy," Aidryn said, the uncertainty in his voice palpable. "I hope he's safe."

"I'll ask the warriors to watch for him," she said. "Maybe he's not far."

Aidryn set the empty mug down and reached for Lira's hand. "I know I chided you for coming after me—and you shouldn't have—but thank you. I'd given up hope..." His words seemed to stick in his throat.

She laced their fingers together gently. "That you would be rescued?"

"Well, that, yes—but I'd long since given up on winning your heart," he admitted. "When you said no more lies... well, I've had to tell my share of them to protect you. And the worst of them all was hiding how much I love you, and how long I've felt this way."

"How long?" Lira searched his face.

He dipped his head slightly, grinning sheepishly as he answered. "Since we were children. I always admired you, but I fell in love with you when I was eleven. We got into a ridiculous fight over a doll I'd hidden from Caitir. You stomped right up to me and shouted, and I handed it over because my mind"—he laughed— "went absolutely blank."

"I remember that." Lira grinned broadly. "I thought my righteous indignation was incredibly effective."

She tried to ignore the dismayed grief that suddenly numbed her laughter. How, over all that time, had she managed to miss the signs? Lira was ashamed to admit to herself that she hadn't noted his admiration at all until many years later. And she hadn't been aware of his deeper feelings until Eremon began pursuing her.

"Lira, what's wrong?"

Aidryn let go of her hand and touched her chin, coaxing her to look up at him. She didn't realize she'd hunched slightly, her gaze drifting down to her lap.

"I was completely oblivious," she answered, looking at him again. "It's embarrassing that I never noticed how you felt."

"I didn't *want* you to know I loved you," he whispered, his gaze drifting down to her lips. "I thought in time, I would move on, but I never did. Don't shame yourself; apparently, I was very good at concealing my feelings."

"I just wish..." She sighed.

"Don't," he answered, leaning down to kiss her lips. "It doesn't matter."

Ljós entered the chamber then, carrying a bowl and mug he handed to Lira before waving her away from Aidryn's side. She moved quietly to the end of the bed, picking at her own food while Ljós worked in silence, crafting one golden orb after another.

Like the day before, he directed the magic into Aidryn's body at specific points. First, his stomach. Then, his throat. He spoke in quiet incantations, the unfamiliar Brylla words rolling off his tongue.

As the healer worked, Aidryn grew visibly drained. Although his pallor seemed to improve with each pass, his eyelids began to droop. Finally, they closed completely, and his head tipped back against the headboard.

Ljós quieted, sending one last orb toward Aidryn. This one

didn't absorb into his body right away; instead, it spread and hovered over him for a moment, then settled onto his skin, luminous. After a few moments, it was no longer visible.

"You may help him lie down, Lira," the healer said, standing and stepping aside. "Then, go and find Oda. She's expecting you in the arena."

He stooped to put his tinctures and herbs away, and Lira moved to the bedside. Gently, she touched Aidryn's shoulder. When he stirred, she helped him lower himself onto the pillows, then covered him with the furs. She turned back to Ljós, finally fully realizing what he had just said to her.

"Why the arena?" Lira asked, puzzled.

"Your bodily strength is more important than ever," Ljós answered. "It's time you valued it."

"What do you—*oh*." *The arena.* Thorne must be training the warriors. She'd known this was coming, but she wasn't ready for it today.

Ljós read her expression immediately. "You will need to be strong if you want to survive the war," he said sternly.

Lira shook her head. "Rodhlan needs its memories—my knowledge," she protested. "Shouldn't I be focused on that?"

"Your presence endangers those you love the most," the healer pressed, looking pointedly at Aidryn. "If you cannot protect yourself, you force them to keep eyes and ears on you at all times. You make them more vulnerable."

His words hit Lira hard, and she wrapped her arms around herself. She had already felt the consequences of her own weakness too keenly—yet, she was afraid she might fail at a physical test. Still, Ljós spoke true. She didn't want to put anyone at any more risk than they had to be. If she wanted to see this pattern change, it would have to begin with her.

"You're right," she admitted, shame creeping into her gut. "I suppose I'm just frightened."

"Even scholars must care for their physical form," the healer said, taking up his satchel. "What good is a trove of books when you're frail and sore? Strength benefits all things."

He stepped to the door but paused before he left. "I'll bring salts for your bath and a balm for pain—they will help as you begin your work with Oda."

Lira's thoughts drifted back to the memory she'd shared with the healer the day before.

"What about your theory?" she said. "Have you figured anything out?"

Ljós cast a sharp glance in Aidryn's direction. "Not quite. But that's a discussion for another time."

He didn't allow Lira to ask any more questions before he disappeared from the chamber.

Flustered, she cast another glance back at Aidryn. He slept peacefully; he would likely rest for some time yet. She hated the idea of training with Beran's warriors, but perhaps if her mother had survived it, she would, too.

Lira recalled Aidryn telling her the Defender role would make her feel ancient, and he had been right. Mentally, she ticked off the days and months—she would be turning twenty in a few weeks. Twenty, and she was already uncomfortably familiar with constant pains in her neck and back—and barely a shred of muscle on her small frame.

Lira shuddered. She had always been just healthy and strong *enough* to go about her business as she liked. But she wasn't strong enough for battle. She wasn't strong enough to withstand a war, and she knew it. Ljós knew it. And so did everyone else.

With a sigh, she stalked toward the door and out into the fortress. If she was going to withstand this torture, best not to put it off any longer than she already had.

When Lira arrived at the arena, Oda was waiting for her at the entryway. The warrior already had a sheen of sweat on her skin. Like Lira, Oda had also pulled her thick hair away from her face, and she seemed euphoric when she came to greet her.

"What do you know about fighting?" Oda asked, eye shining. Her gaze flicked briefly to the axes Lira wore at her side.

"Next to nothing," Lira admitted. "Just concept."

"All right—follow me," Oda said.

She took off down the wide stairs toward the circular grounds below. With a sigh of resignation, Lira followed.

CHAPTER 24

LIRA

Fortress Halgeir

The arena was a yawning, cavernous place, surrounded on all sides by rows of stone benches where onlookers gathered to watch the Beran warriors spar. Today, the seats were all but empty, and Lira was glad for it.

Clan Beran's warriors trained in shifts throughout the day, many visiting the arena more than once for various sparring and strength training exercises. Working in the arena was as natural as breathing to them. Lira felt achingly out of place among these men and women who engaged in daily combat, hefting broadswords as though they weighed nothing.

By contrast, Iathium did not prize physical strength so much as hard work by way of a learned trade. Exercise was best left to sentries and farmers, and was considered the equivalent of manual labor.

"I thought of training you to be Thorne's shield-bearer," Oda said over her shoulder as they picked their way down the stairs. "But his shield weighs as much as a small mule. So I thought that Talfryn's might be better."

"Talfryn's?" Lira asked in alarm.

"Yes," Oda answered. "How else do you think he'll be able to fight? He can wield that sword well enough, but he needs protection on his left side. You're perfect for that."

Lira froze, skimming the arena floor until her gaze fell on Talfryn. He was fully engaged in swordplay with Bard. She almost called out to him, but then she squinted, taking a closer look at her younger brother. He was *grinning*, and with each clash of his sword against Bard's, his smile grew broader.

"See there?" Oda asked. "He can hold his own. It's you we're worried about."

Lira gulped. "*I'm* worried about me," she admitted.

"You should be." The warrior gave her a little nod. "Now get down there."

They entered the training floor, and Lira was overwhelmed immediately by the noise and clash of activity all around. Oda seemed to sense this, and she steered Lira across the floor, between pairs of fighters and toward the far end of the arena, where an array of weapons and weights had been laid out.

"This is our area," Oda said. "Every day at dawn, you'll meet me right here."

Lira gawked. "Dawn?"

"Yes, dawn. Then again at midday. You have a lot to learn. And don't worry about the pain—that's where our healing powers come in."

Lira relaxed a little. "I hadn't thought of that." It was less crowded here, and she blew out a nervous breath. "Where do we start?"

Oda spent the next two hours teaching Lira a set of basic strengthening exercises and fighting stances. She seemed most concerned with helping Lira build her balance and her ability to stay on her feet during combat. They started slowly, but Lira was a good student—however reluctant. By the time they were done, she was panting and exhausted, yet somehow exhilarated.

Together, she and Oda went to the great hall for their meal.

They took mugs of water and bowls of steaming meat out into the courtyard, which was now thick with the lush grasses Talfryn and Iva had enchanted there. The gardens grew abundantly again, vines and vegetation climbing up the columns and railings of the fortress's interior walkways. It was more beautiful than Lira had ever seen it, and she was grateful her clan's magic was a part of that transformation.

The Beran clanspeople had grown used to seeing Lira around the fortress now, and they no longer watched her with suspicion. They spoke freely in Brylla—something they had not been allowed to do in past years with outsiders among them. Though Lira still had little interaction with most of the people of the clan, their apprehension seemed to have calmed to a quiet rapport. Perhaps eventually, she would feel more comfortable around them as well.

Lira lowered herself slowly to the ground, hissing at the pain in her thighs. Her legs trembled as she sat. Oda joined her, setting her mug and bowl aside and placing both hands on Lira's knees. Her magic flared to life, immediately soothing some of the pain.

"Thank you." Lira sighed, taking a drink.

"While you are learning, I'll heal you just enough to make the pain bearable," Oda said, popping a bit of meat into her mouth. "But you need to be able to work through it and overcome it. Training is predictable, but a battlefield is not. If you come to rely on full healing after every training, you won't be able to withstand the pain of battle."

"I appreciate a little soothing," Lira said. "Otherwise, it's going to be difficult to continue."

"You get used to it. In time, you'll even welcome it. The pain is a sign that we're honoring ourselves and those we love."

"Honoring ourselves through pain?" Lira scrunched her brows and took a bite.

"Honoring ourselves through challenge and perseverance,"

Oda said. "It's not the same thing as self-destructive pain. It's strengthening pain—necessary pain."

They finished their meal in silence. Lira's thoughts turned to Caitir, and how she had seemingly dedicated herself to suffering for the sake of amassing power. No matter how strong she believed herself to be, that strength would always be built on the basis of self-destruction. In the end, Caitir was attempting to build a legacy on a fragile foundation.

Thorne padded across the grass from the great hall and sat cross-legged beside them, interrupting Lira's thoughts. "I spoke with Tarlach this afternoon," he said. "I like him."

Lira smiled. "Good." She took a sip of water. "He's much improved."

"Yes," Thorne replied. "He asked my father about a separate chamber. I think he fears crowding you out."

His words bludgeoned Lira. "He isn't crowding me out," she mumbled, her cheeks growing hot.

Why would Aidryn want to be alone, after the way he'd kissed her? After admitting he loved her?

Oda perked up, looking between Thorne and Lira. "Who is Tarlach? I didn't see anyone come in during my patrol, and the Beravakt didn't report him."

"Aidryn Tarlach," Lira answered absently. "We brought him in through *turas*—you wouldn't have seen him."

"*Turas*?" Oda's eyes widened. "That's a rare power—I want to know all about it. But tell me more about this Aidryn." She tilted her head curiously. "Why do you want to keep him in your chamber?"

Lira opened her mouth to answer, but Thorne grinned and blurted, "Because he's her husband."

Oda's jaw dropped, and she let out a little squeal. "*What*?"

Lira crossed her arms and scowled at him, but he just laughed softly and replied, "You were just going to dance around it. Oda hates dancing." His amber eyes sparkled with amusement.

"I hate dancing, and small talk, and avoiding important conversations," she said with a shrug. "Just say what you need to. Now, with that out of the way: why didn't you tell me you were married?"

"It's a very strange situation," Lira answered, shifting uncomfortably.

"All right—hold onto that for a moment," Oda said, rising. "I'm getting us more to eat. Then you can tell me everything."

She grabbed their mugs and bowls and headed back toward the great hall. A moment later, she looked back over her shoulder and shouted, "He's daft if he wants his own chamber!"

Lira smiled nervously, and Thorne chuckled. "I think he wants to stay with you," he said quietly, nudging Lira's shoulder. "But you'll have to sort that out with him."

LIRA'S LEGS still shook slightly as she walked down the corridor toward her chamber. The nearer she got, the more nervous she became about Thorne's comment.

To her relief, Aidryn was still sleeping when she arrived. His back was turned to the door, so she padded through the room and into the bathing chamber as quietly as possible. Ljós had left her with a little jar of herbal balm and some healing salts, so she prepared a hot bath.

She piled her curls into a messy bun atop her head and sank into the tub to soak her sore muscles. Afterward, she massaged the balm into her thighs and upper arms, praying the concoction would help her find stamina the next day.

This life was so different from her existence in Iathium. At best, she'd taken baths once a week in the city. When she wanted a full bath, the process of filling and heating the tub was tedious and exhausting. She'd had a small washbasin in her chamber back at the cottage, and she had cleansed herself daily. But soaking like this whenever she liked was something she only got to do when she was at Fortress Halgeir, and for the first time, she dreaded the thought of giving it up when it was time to move on.

Lira looked to the basket that held her clothing, but her dirty tunics and leggings had been taken, presumably for laundering. There were only two sleeping gowns in the basket. Her cheeks heated, and she took a shaky breath as she lifted one of them—light lavender, like the wildflowers that grew in the rolling hills of Skelly's valley—and slipped it over her head. Like the other gowns, it exposed her bare shoulders.

Lira had never felt so unsettled by a sleeping gown before. And this was Aidryn—he'd seen her in nightgowns more times than she could count, when they were younger. But she'd always had some sort of robe or dressing gown to cover herself. And they weren't married back then, either.

She took a shaky breath.

Perhaps he does need his own chamber.

As she moved to open the door, Lira caught her reflection in the looking glass on the wall. Lavender did suit her. It wasn't a prominent part of her wardrobe back in the city, but perhaps now it should be. She liked the way it looked against her dark brown curls and pale skin.

Slowly, she undid the cord she'd used to tie her hair up and let her curls tumble down her back. It had been so long since she had bothered to look in a mirror for more than a glimpse. Now, she leaned nearer in the candlelight, scrutinizing every feature: wide, brown eyes; pink, full lips; small, round nose with a scattering of light freckles across its bridge. She'd never thought of herself as beautiful before, but perhaps her reflection wasn't so bad.

"Lira?" Aidryn called from the other room.

A little gasp escaped her, and she squeezed her eyes shut for a moment, taking a deep breath before she pushed the door open and peeked around at him.

Aidryn had managed to pile up every pillow on the bed and

now sat propped against them, holding a small, leather-bound book. His lips stretched into a warm smile when he saw her.

"Hello," he said softly.

Lira tightened her grip on the door, still hiding her body behind it. "Hello. What are you reading?"

"One of the books Ljós managed to get his hands on after everything in Iathium went sideways."

"Oh." She didn't move.

"I feel better," he ventured.

Lira nodded, trying to smile. "Good. I—I'm glad."

Aidryn's nose crinkled, mischief glinting in his eyes. "Why are you hiding behind the door?"

"It's my gown," Lira answered. "It's a bit immodest—I don't have a tunic or a dressing gown, just this."

He raised his brows. "Oh?"

"I mean..." Her face blazed. "It isn't immodest by *Beran's* standards, just..."

Aidryn grinned. "You mean it shows your forearms or some nonsense. Come out—I'll cover my eyes or give you one of these ridiculous furs, whatever you want."

"All right," she said, stepping out from behind the door. "It's just the shoulders. I—I don't know why I'm so worried about it."

Lira walked across the room toward Aidryn, who remained silent. Her legs were still stiff. She tried to bite back a grin when she noticed his cheeks turning bright red. The blush crept up to his ears as his eyes roamed from the hem of her skirt up to her face. He scooted over, making extra space for her.

Lira scowled at him. "You said you would cover your eyes."

"*Or* give you a fur," he said, resting the book in his lap. "You're moving like you were thrown from a horse."

"Careful, or I'll throw *you*," she muttered, glaring at him. She sat beside him, leaning against a pillow and pulling one of the furs up to her chin.

"It won't be long before I'm in the arena, too." Aidryn kept his gaze trained on the book. "Ljós is giving me a week."

Lira paused. "That doesn't seem like nearly enough time."

"I don't know." He shrugged. "He's good."

"Yes."

An uncomfortable silence descended on them. Lira looked over at him, trying to catch his gaze. "Thorne said you asked about a chamber of your own," she said quietly.

"I did," Aidryn answered slowly, finally looking her in the eye again, "only because I wasn't sure if I would need one."

"Well, you don't *need* your own chamber," she said, "unless that's what you want."

He inched nearer, scrutinizing her. "You're saying you want to share a room. With me."

"Yes, Aidryn," she answered, holding his gaze. "I don't want you to go."

"You know the implications," he said, a warning tone in his voice.

"I do." Lira rested a hand on Aidryn's chest. "Half of Clan Beran knows about the Binding already. It's partly why Thorne agreed to help get you back."

He set the book aside and opened his arms to her. She threw her legs over his lap and shimmied closer, letting the fur fall away from her shoulders.

"That Thorne is an intimidating fellow," Aidryn said softly, the corner of his mouth turning up. "I wouldn't want to cross him."

"You're lucky he likes you." Lira brushed the tip of her nose against Aidryn's.

He cupped her face, drawing her in for a kiss. "So if we're embracing this Binding... does that mean I can call you my wife?"

"Well, it *is* a marriage." She touched his beard lightly and smiled. "An arranged one, apparently."

"When I realized *that* part, I thought you would run screaming—as far away from me as you could get." Aidryn traced his fingers over her bare shoulder, leaving gooseflesh in the wake of his touch. Her cheeks warmed. "What do you know about this Binding? How did it happen?"

Dread gnawed at Lira—she did *not* want to talk about Eremon, but there was no way to avoid it completely. "All I know is Eremon was behind it. Some sort of spell he cast on the ring responded to our feelings for one another."

"Oh." A shadow crossed Aidryn's expression. "So he knew the entire time..."

"Yes," Lira admitted. "He knew my feelings for you better than I did myself. Which brings up other questions I'd rather not think about."

"Then don't." He took her hand and brought it to his lips. "I dreaded talking to you about the Binding. Actually, I thought I might just... never bring it up at all. But then you kissed me, so I didn't have to agonize over what to do."

"It's a complex situation." She fiddled with the collar of his tunic, letting her fingers linger on the bit of skin that peeked between the laces. "We could spend time deconstructing all the finer points of the Binding, but I think what matters is that we chose one another."

Aidryn licked his lips. "Well," he began, his gaze straying to her mouth again, "is this the first time we've agreed on something without debating it first?"

"Mm," Lira hummed, "I'm not sure. I'll have to consult the histories."

"Fair enough." He dipped his head and kissed her again.

"It feels strange to call you my *husband*," Lira giggled against his mouth. "It seems like a lifetime ago that I was trying to outpace you in the archive."

He rested his forehead against hers and laughed softly. "Never stop trying to outpace me, Lira. And I don't care what you call me, as long as you stay right here."

CHAPTER 25

LIRA

Fortress Halgeir

L ira was stiff and sore when she woke the next morning, the previous day's exercise with Oda having settled into her muscles. Aidryn was still in a deep sleep, one arm slung across her where she lay. Like the previous night, fatigue had dragged him down, and he'd nodded off mid-sentence.

She couldn't imagine him being well enough to walk the corridors, much less train, within seven days. He had exhausted himself just kissing her.

Her cheeks heated and her stomach fluttered, a grin spreading across her lips. Rolling over to face him, she lay there and simply watched him sleep. She had always secretly admired his slightly softened features, his full lips, the way his hair fell into his eyes. But until now, she had never allowed herself to enjoy him without reservation.

Reaching for him, she brushed his hair off his forehead. He stirred a little but didn't wake.

The still-new sensation of touching him gave way to a tingling in her fingertips. She lay back on the pillow and relaxed, allowing the witnessing to wash over her consciousness.

Arlen Mór grips the railing of Iathium's fastest ship, squinting against the salt spray as ferocious waves crash against its sides. Lira stares at him in wonder; her only memories of him have grown painfully distant, yet here he is before her, vibrant and alive.

His auburn hair is tousled by the ocean wind, brown eyes glassy and bright. Iteloria looms ahead, a jagged string of islands jutting up between the cold, mountainous main continent and the open sea.

A tall, black-haired man joins him at the railing—Eremon's father, Rí Corlan. Lira has never seen him clad in anything but court regalia. He is wearing a chain mail shirt, a simple gray tunic, black pants, and rugged work boots. His hair is bound in a low bun at the base of his neck, and one of her father's swords is strapped at his side.

"Where do we disembark?" he asks. His voice is deeper than Eremon's, though it has the same softness.

"We dock on the eastern isle," Arlen says, pointing toward their destination. "Then trek west toward the settlement."

Tears well in Lira's eyes at the sound of her father's voice.

"I wish—" Corlan's fingers tighten around the wood, his knuckles going white. "I wish they were here with us. I can't help but worry that we've taken a grievous risk in coming here without them."

"You well know what might happen to your boy if he set foot here." Arlen levels a knowing gaze at Corlan. "And to you, for that matter."

Corlan's hands tighten on the railing. "It's a risk I must take. I'm glad he is safe in Iathium for now, as Silira is safe in the archive."

"She has no inkling of what's happening." Arlen sighs for a moment, his shoulders sagging. "I fear I did my job too well."

"We have done what was required of us," Corlan answers firmly. "We work from our understanding in the moment, and nothing more."

"I'm sorry about Eremon," Arlen says softly. "It's hard enough knowing the weight of responsibility Lira will carry as Witness Tree. I can't imagine what you must be going through."

Corlan sets his jaw, but his voice breaks when he says, "All I can do is look for answers here. There is no one in Rodhlan who can help him."

"Who else knows his fate?" Arlen asks.

"His mother suspects," Corlan answers grimly. "She may well learn for herself while we're away."

"A calculated risk."

"A terrifying one." Corlan's expression is mournful now. "I did everything I could to keep magic suppressed—to save him. To save us all. Now it's out of my hands, and we must begin to make things right, even in the midst of the coming chaos."

"Who says there must be chaos?" Arlen furrows his brow.

"It is the way of things," Corlan answers. "When the natural order has been interfered with for so long, the world cannot right itself quietly."

Lira's sight returned. Aidryn remained silent at her side, his back turned to her now. It had been so long since she'd been close to Da—and it had never occurred to her that she might be able to learn the truth about what had become of him.

Reaching for her magic, Lira shut her eyes again and followed a thread of power back to the ship. She found it again, this time docked at what she guessed was Iteloria's port city.

Arlen steps off the dock at Najyn, pulling his heavy coat tighter around his shoulders. The temperature has plunged in the short hours since they cleared the barrier islands and docked the ship. Ice sparkles on the walkway before him, and snowflakes drift lazily through the air.

"Mind your step," he calls over his shoulder. "The ground is frozen."

Four sentries accompany Corlan down the gangplank, surrounding him once they exit the narrow dock.

Lira pulled herself out of the memory for a moment. She'd leapt forward by hours, but she needed to go farther. More than once, she had been admonished to search her power for memories. Perhaps she had more control over her magic than she gave herself credit for.

"Show me what happened to Corlan and Da," she mouthed silently, setting her intention for the witnessing.

Magic swept over her again.

Corlan stands before the circle of crystalline willows, Arlen one step behind him, a hand resting on the pommel of his sword. A Tai'Ceru chieftain waits, his flowing white hair and pale blue eyes standing in stark contrast to his dark skin. He wears white leather breeches, but no tunic. White markings are tattooed beneath his eyes and around his wrists. There is a young king beside him—La'hiran—wearing a circlet of white gold and a richly woven tunic of orange velvet and silver cord.

The chieftain speaks to Corlan in Itelos, and La'hiran translates.

"If what you have confessed is true," La'hiran says, "then Eremon is the first in nearly two thousand years."

"I am aware." Corlan raises his chin defiantly.

"And rather than bring him to us as an infant, you deigned to conceal him."

"Surely you understand why." Corlan's voice wavers. "He is my child."

"Yet you would risk your continent and ours by seating him on your throne." La'hiran does not try to conceal the rage in his voice.

"Eremon is no threat, to you or anyone else." Corlan's voice is calm and assured. "He has a kind heart and a level head; he is no warmonger."

The king shakes his head. "Only because he does not yet know what he is. Once he learns the power he possesses, he will be lost to it."

Corlan levels a hard stare at La'hiran. "I know my son, and I know he will not be devoured."

"Then let us negotiate," the king says, taking a step forward and extending his hand, "for there must be a way to reach commonality."

The chieftain is glaring at Corlan. Arlen tightens his hold on the sword. Palpable tension sucks the air from the clearing as Corlan takes a breath and moves toward the king.

The moment the Rí steps into the circle of willows, his body seizes. He crashes to his knees, crying out in pain as the trees around them begin to glow, casting a spectrum of colors across the men in the clearing. Shimmering, bouncing arcs of light illuminate his skin before a violent surge of black lightning bursts from his palms and into the ground.

Veins of the black power etch outward, burning their way up the willows' trunks and illuminating the crystals that hang from each limb. Corlan cries out again, pale and trembling, still planted on his hands and knees.

Sword drawn, Arlen closes the distance between himself and Corlan.

"Forgive me, my friend," he cries, raising his blade.

Before La'hiran and the chieftain can get to him, he has run Corlan through in one swift strike.

"No!"

The king and the chieftain rush Arlen, drawing their own blades. Arlen takes them on, fighting with the skill and agility of a young sentry. Still, the chieftain's warriors are positioned around the willow grove, and one flings a throwing knife at Arlen, striking him on the back of his neck—right above the collar of his chainmail shirt.

Arlen collapses as the chieftain reaches him. The dark-skinned man catches him as he goes down, barking an order to one of his warriors—a young girl who steps timidly into the grove, her gaze flicking between the dead Rí and Arlen. Her silver hair is braided into a coil around her head, and her eyes are the color of sea foam.

The chieftain fingers Arlen's chainmail and murmurs something to the girl, who places a hand on Arlen's forehead. Her eyes glow emerald as she uses her power to take. Arlen cries out in pain, but she holds firm until her magic has done its work. Then, she reaches for the chieftain, touching his temple, the same glow emanating from her eyes once again.

Arlen is lying on his back now, the blade in his neck removed, color draining from his face.

"N—negotiate," he is saying. "For the tomes."

La'hiran looks down at him and solemnly shakes his head. "It's true that your histories have been thoroughly erased, or your Rí would have known to remain outside the grove. Still, Iteloria required a sacrifice for his grievous sin. For now, the land is satisfied."

"Leave the child," Arlen rasps. "Leave Rodhlan be."

"The boy's magic will claim him in due course," the king says. "Your continent does not concern us. Let it be what it will."

The chieftain turns from the young girl and says something softly. La'hiran's eyebrows rise and he looks to Arlen again. "So Rodhlan has one too. The Armorer's mother; curious, indeed."

He raises a curved dagger, and Arlen has no time to speak before the king brings it down on him.

Lira emerged quietly from the witnessing, her body trembling. When she opened her eyes, Aidryn was lying on his side, watching her intently. She felt rattled as she turned to face him, her eyes stinging with tears.

"What did you see?" he asked softly, reaching for her hand.

"I saw my father die," she answered shakily. Her right hand still tingled, the magic's sensation lingering longer than she was accustomed to. "And Corlan."

Her mind raced as she recounted the dream. Of all the possible scenarios, Lira would never have suspected her father of mercy-killing the last Rí. She tucked away most of the details involving Eremon; this love she'd found with Aidryn was so new, so tenuous, she didn't want anything to interfere with it.

Eremon is the first in nearly two thousand years.

She shook the thought off, allowing Aidryn to gather her into his arms while the vision's lingering emotion slowly faded.

Lira had almost drifted back to sleep again when someone banged loudly on the chamber door. She awoke again with a start, sitting up abruptly and crawling off the bed. Her legs were shaky and sore as she crossed the room, cracking the door open.

Oda stood outside, arms crossed, her feet planted in a wide stance. She looked as though she were trying to maintain some semblance of sternness, but one look at Lira had her cracking a wide grin. Suddenly, Lira was keenly aware of her sleeping gown, her tousled hair, and Aidryn lying in the bed behind her.

"I was going to reprimand you for being late, but it's clear you forgot," Oda said, unable to suppress the giddy ring in her voice. She took in Lira's lavender gown and smiled wider. "You look *good*."

"I'm in an incredible amount of pain," Lira replied wryly. "Even with your magic and the healer's concoctions, I can hardly walk."

Oda craned past Lira, peeking inside the candlelit chamber. "Is he asleep in there, or can I meet him?" She grinned slyly and waggled her eyebrows. "Is he decent?"

"*Of course* he's decent," Lira said, trying not to smile. "He's still recover—"

"Lira?" Aidryn called from where he lay, his voice thick with sleep. "Who is it?"

"It's Oda. She wants to ogle you."

"She's right, I do," Oda declared, and Lira finally grinned, too.

"Fine, but there's not much to see," Aidryn replied. From behind her, she could hear him shuffling the furs and pillows to sit against the headboard again.

Lira stepped aside for Oda to enter, then turned toward Aidryn again. He'd hastily tied his hair back and had pulled the furs up.

"So you're the husband," Oda said, striding straight to his bedside and sticking out her hand. Aidryn took it with a wide smile.

"So you're the Oda," he replied, squeezing her hand.

"I'm the Oda." She plopped onto the edge of the bed beside

him as though they'd known one another for a decade. Leaning in slightly, she added, "Listen, sir—Lira has a rigid training schedule to uphold. If you plan on distracting her at dawn, you'd best recover quickly so I can punish you both in the arena."

Aidryn snorted. "If the healer has his way about it, I'll be right in the thick of it soon. We'll see how that goes."

"You will," Lira said, leaning down to kiss his forehead. "I'm counting on it."

"While I'm here, I want to show you something," Oda said. "Talfryn needs a shield he can bear himself, and I have a few ideas."

"Talfryn's here?" Aidryn asked as Oda pulled a piece of folded parchment out of her pocket and handed it to him. He opened it to reveal several sketches. Lira squinted at them in the candlelight.

"A shield he can wear?" she asked. If Oda's idea was workable, it would mean Talfryn could fight independently, without needing another person to carry his shield for him.

Aidryn looked up at Lira in alarm. "Why would he need to wear a shield?" he asked softly, his voice heavy with the realization.

"Peros took his arm, back in Iathium," Lira answered, a lump forming in her throat. "There hasn't been time to catch you up on everything."

Aidryn pressed a hand to his mouth, studying the sketches more closely. When he remained silent, Oda said, "I was hoping we might utilize your metalworking magic to fit him properly."

"I have a little experience with metalworking—mainly with fitting shoes for my horses," he answered absently. "But let me think on this. Perhaps I can practice when I recover." Aidryn folded the paper again and held it up. "Can I keep this?"

"Please," Oda said with a smile.

He stuck it inside his book and closed it slowly, sighing

heavily and shaking his head. "How has he borne it?" he asked Lira, his gaze mournful.

"He arrived here before she did," Oda answered gently. "At first, he didn't bear it well at all. He's so young. But once we got him healed and into the arena, he transformed. He has a good humor about him; he didn't want the injury to destroy his spirit. And it hasn't."

"I always thought his disposition was better than my own," Lira added. "He knows how to find the light in everything. I wish I could, as well."

"He perked up when you gave him some magic to work with," Oda said.

They spent the next hour neglecting their training, filling Aidryn in on the finer points of the past few weeks. Lira told him of her stay in Va'hesk, and hearing about his namesake clan seemed to perk him up. But he was still weary, so Lira tucked him back into bed before she dressed for training and slipped out with Oda.

She was disconcerted as they headed down the walkway together, still preoccupied with what she'd seen in the witnessing.

"I need to speak with Ljós before we train," she said quietly.

Oda's attention snapped to Lira. "What for?"

"I can't say just yet," Lira hedged. "I just need to talk to him."

The warrior raised her eyebrows. "Now?"

"Give me half an hour," Lira said, stomach fluttering.

Oda paused, resting a hand on Lira's arm. "Lira, what's the matter? Is it something I can help with?"

"I don't know." Lira's gaze dropped to the ground. "But it's deeply troubling. I wouldn't know where to begin, were I to say it aloud."

"Then start with someone you trust," Oda admonished, jerking her chin back in the direction of Lira's chamber. "Surely you can talk to Aidryn."

Lira sighed. "It's not that easy."

Her friend gazed at her for a long moment, then set out walking again. "Then let's get you to the healer first. Perhaps he can help ease your mind."

Something deep within Lira told her that, whatever was about to unfold, peace of mind would not be part of the equation.

CHAPTER 26

LIRA

Fortress Halgeir

Lira was winded by the time she reached the healer's chamber and banged on the door. Ljós pulled it open swiftly, expression stricken, but he relaxed when he saw Lira standing there.

"You are supposed to be in the arena," he said, stepping aside to let her in.

"Yes, but I need to speak with you now." Lira wrung her hands, pacing nervously back and forth past the pit of amber stones. They were glowing with the healer's golden power, illuminating the room more effectively than the candles he normally used.

Ljós poured Lira a mug of tea and handed it over, halting her with a hand on her shoulder. "Slow down. Take a drink. Then we'll speak."

Lira sipped her tea, steadying herself. "I asked my power for a witnessing. It showed me how Corlan and my father died." She sat beside the pit. "But there's something more."

The healer nodded as he joined her. "I thought there might be. Do you need my help deciphering it?"

"Yes, and I have an inkling it might somehow fit with your theory." She took another sip. "I was hoping you might share that with me."

Ljós's expression was near unreadable. "It might." He reached for a small amber stone near the pit—one the size of a pebble—and handed it to Lira. "I want you to practice something while you're here. Try projecting your power into the pebble, and it should send your memories to the stones, just there." He motioned to the pit.

"And do what with them?"

"You'll see." The healer cast his silencing spell over the room. "This is a spell I was crafting with Eremon before he died. If it works as planned, it will aid us in teaching the true histories."

Lira called on her magic, directing it into the small pebble. Down in the pit, the amber stones shone with traces of emerald and gold magic. A shaft of pure power burst up from the pit, flooding the chamber with light.

"Now, ask your magic for the memory you witnessed." Ljós placed his hands on his knees and waited.

With a deep breath, Lira whispered the same request to her power, more specific this time: *Show me what happened to Corlan and Da in the grove of crystal willows.*

Rather than losing her sight, Lira was able to watch the stones as her hands began to tingle. Then, in the shaft of power, figures began to form. There was Da and Corlan, La'hiran and the Tai'Ceru chieftain in the willow grove. She and Ljós watched in silence as the memory unfolded before them—as Corlan hit his knees and his magic was siphoned from his body.

Lira squeezed her eyes shut when Arlen drew his sword, but she could still hear the sickening squelch, the thud of Corlan's body. And she couldn't stop tears from rolling down her cheeks as, once again, her father died before her.

When the memory flickered out, she set the pebble down

and swiped at her face. Ljós had gone pale. His chin trembled as he whispered, "I thought so."

Lira turned to the healer and scooted closer to him. "Thought what? Ljós, you've kept me in the dark—I need to know what you've figured out."

The healer's expression was grave when he met Lira's gaze. "I hesitate to answer because in this case, truth will be more painful to bear than uncertainty. And not only for you—this truth will test you and those you love in ways you haven't yet begun to imagine."

Her stomach twisted. "I need to know, Ljós, *please.*" But the moment the words left her, she regretted saying them. Still, the more she recoiled, the harder her magic tugged at her, pulling her toward the truth. "What did the king mean when he said Eremon was the first in nearly two thousand years?" she heard herself say.

"Eremon was born a mortal god," the healer said quietly.

Lira's eyes widened, and she vaguely felt herself shaking her head. Eremon was the one who taught her about mortal gods, but he'd been one himself all along?

"No one ever told him, did they." The remark came out as more of a statement than a question. Just as she had been kept in the dark about her magic, Eremon had been lied to about his own.

"No one." The healer stood and moved slowly toward his tinctures, returning after a moment to where Lira still sat in stunned silence. He offered her a little vial, and she accepted it.

"What a terrible fate, to have never known his true potential," she said quietly, before knocking back the tincture in one gulp. It warmed her insides, soothing her as she listened to her power. Rather than affirming the truth Ljós had spoken, her magic tugged at the back of her mind. *There's more.*

Then what is it? she asked her power. Somewhere deep within her came a great shudder, and her magic pulled her back into Nevala and Mytr's tent at Va'hesk—back to something

Mytr had said that Lira barely recalled, and hadn't once questioned: *What do you think happens to a mortal goddess when she dies?*

Lira gasped, snatching the amber stone off the floor, attempting to tap into her power again. But this time, no magic burst from the stones. She squeezed her eyes shut, probing with her power. *What am I supposed to be looking for?*

Nothing. Lira opened her eyes again and sighed, frustrated. "What happens when I can't find one of Rodhlan's memories? Can I search a person's?"

"I don't think it would be wise." Ljós watched her carefully. "If a memory comes to you of its own accord, that's one matter. It's another thing entirely for you to sift through a person's memories without their consent."

"If I ask my magic, and my magic consents...?" She remembered asking her power for Aidryn's last memory, and her request had been granted.

"Then it may be allowed."

She closed her eyes again and asked her power: *If there is a memory that will lead me to Iuchair, show it to me freely.*

The stones surged to life again as a witnessing poured from them.

Rí Ulan, son of Nami and third supreme ruler of Iathium, stands in his father's crypt, clutching Iuchair. He climbs atop Nami's vault, where a keyhole opens up, spilling cobalt magic into the room around him.

"As Riku fell, so falls Nami the Furious," he says, plunging the key into the hole and turning it decisively to the left. Immediately, the magic dissipates.

His father was responsible for suppressing magic in Rodhlan for one hundred years. And perhaps the magic of the clans shouldn't flow freely. Ulan could level with that sentiment. What he doesn't understand is his late father's thirst for unlimited power. After all, Nami had taken on the magic of three mortal gods when they'd perished— his mother, Rhona; his father, Riku; and his uncle, Rasu the Vile.

Then, he'd spent his life making sure the clans couldn't freely access their own power, taking it for himself instead.

Ulan has seen far too much destruction for the love of unlimited power. While he is almost as strong as a mortal god, he is not quite strong enough. And perhaps that's for the best. Sealing away his father's power seems the best first step toward bringing some semblance of balance to Rodhlan.

Tears trace down Ulan's cheeks, but his expression is determined, his angular black eyes fixed on the vault before him. He slips the key inside the front pocket of his robe with trembling fingers and kneels unsteadily, bowing his head.

"Never again will limitless power threaten Rodhlan. I swear on my own death, there will be no more mortal gods."

The witnessing winked out, but Lira poured more magic into the stone. Her right hand began to shake, but she tightened her grip on it. "Show me Ulan's first memory of Iuchair," she said aloud. Another memory played across the shimmering power, older than the first.

Ulan stands on one side of the table in his audience chamber, leveling a hard stare at Iteloria's king—a man of middle age, much older and more refined than Ulan is himself. The table's wood creaks slightly beneath Ulan's weight, and he lets up a little, never breaking eye contact with the king.

"You're proposing we seal away our mortal gods' magic, and you'll sign the treaty," he says. "Why? When has Rodhlan ever posed a threat to you?"

The king inclines his head. "You are well aware that your father was a descendant of Iteloria—of two mortal gods. Now, his descendants will sit on your throne until your dynasty ends. Do you think we wish to make our lands vulnerable to the unchecked magic you now wield?"

"I have no interest in Iteloria," Ulan says decisively. "I have my city and the four clans to attend to. Suppressing magic is my highest concern."

The king raises his eyebrows. "Then if you wish to keep it contained, you will do as I ask. If your clans were to learn that mortal gods could be resurrected, the magnitude of that truth would upend your rule. Any control you believe you possess will be nothing more than a vapor."

Terror floods Ulan as he considers the king's truth. His grandparents would not have wanted to see their clans' powers stolen and suppressed. They would have been livid at the absolute power Nami seized upon their deaths. And they would urge Ulan not to sign this treaty today, but instead to give the clans their rightful power once again.

But they are not here to protect him, so he must make his best choice in this moment.

"And if they never know?" His voice comes out softer than he means for it to.

"Then the dead gods and goddesses remain so, and exist in spirit only. Their magic will be bound to their tombs in your crypt." The king slides an ornate golden key across the table toward Ulan. "They will not cease to exist, but will be prevented from returning to the mortal world forever."

"How does it work?"

"Set your intention, then turn the key," the king says.

Reluctantly, Ulan picks up the quill, signs the treaty, and takes the key.

The witnessing flickered out. Suddenly, a wave of nausea slammed into Lira, and she retched. The healer moved swiftly to her side and grasped her left wrist, applying a bit of golden magic to the inside, where she'd seen Thorne do it before. Immediately, her stomach settled. But then, Ljós grasped her other hand, which was now trembling more violently.

"Has this happened before?" he asked softly, studying the movement for a moment before he doused her hand in healing magic, and it stilled.

"Once," she said, trying to squash the memory of her sudden illness. "Right after a witnessing. I thought it was because I had so much magic at the time."

"I think it's an effect, then," Ljós mused. "Try to avoid delving into others' personal memories. If Rodhlan doesn't give them to you as significant to our past or future, do not take them for yourself. Yours is a power that could be horribly misused in the wrong hands." The tremor returned to her hand, and again, he bathed it in magic. "In fact, before the clans' powers were suppressed, the Witness Tree was considered the most fearsome of the anointed ones."

Lira gave him a shallow nod, recalling Macha's words in the crypt: *You have the power of full immersion. The ability to look into the minds of your enemies and thwart their every movement.*

"No wonder there's a target on my back." She tried to laugh, but couldn't manage to force a smile.

"As frightening as your power is, there is one greater." The healer rocked back on his heels. "And we must decide what to do about it."

"Eremon's power," she breathed. "What is there to do, but lock it away?" She noticed Ljós watching her carefully, so she dug deeper. "If Iuchair locks the power of the mortal gods, I imagine it can also unlock it. Locking the power meant separating it from the dead gods' spirits. But unlocking it..."

Her stomach lurched, and she thought she might be ill again as the realization settled over her. "Eremon can be resurrected, can't he?" The truth tore through her like a seaside gale.

"I believe he can, yes," Ljós replied slowly. "The question is, should he be?"

"Of course not," Lira answered abruptly, though emerald magic burst across her vision in protest. She blinked it away furiously, which also succeeded in containing the tears that suddenly pricked her eyes. "What good is there in bringing back a dead man?"

"I think the question has more to do with the extent of his power than anything," the healer said.

Lira's magic tugged at her mind in agreement. "Is this why Aila wants Iuchair? Is she trying to resurrect him?"

"Doubtful. Most likely, she thinks she can take his power during the locking process. I wouldn't know how to begin guessing at the mechanism."

"If he's resurrected, would that prevent them from taking his power?"

"I believe it would," Ljós answered slowly, "though my greatest concern would be whether he would still be *Eremon*. With unlimited magic, he could become a greater threat than a help to us. His power is infinite, Silira. He would rise an immortal."

Lira swayed, and the entire chamber seemed to tilt. The thought of seeing Eremon in the flesh again—of him being anyone other than the kind young man she'd known—made her skin crawl. How was it possible?

"There've been no mortal gods here for—for centuries," she stammered. "I doubt most people believe they existed. So how..." Suddenly her head ached. "What am I supposed to do with this information?"

"I don't know."

Lira sighed, exasperated. "That doesn't help, Ljós! You led me to this revelation, yet you have no advice on what to do?"

"I can't help believing he could take back his throne—defeat the usurpers. Perhaps restore peace to Rodhlan."

She pressed her fingertips between her eyes. "The people will never believe it."

"They will if he rises as the Eremon they knew. The problem is in the unknown. Many clanspeople would oppose bringing back such a dangerous power."

"Why? Don't they want peace?"

"Beran and Énna have always been wary of concentrating extra power in one individual. They would likely make up your greatest opposition. Your clan will be difficult, as so many of them followed Gerallt to conquer Iathium.

"There was always a sharp divide between the four clans. Your clan and Aidryn's always had the most powerful anointed ones. Beran's anointed might have an extra measure of physical strength, but not always more magic. And Clan Énna has held its anointed power close over the centuries. I have never seen it demonstrated."

"Who is Énna's anointed now?"

"They have not revealed their chosen one in many generations," the healer answered.

Lira turned the amber stone over and over in her hand, running her thumb along its smooth surface. "Is bringing Eremon back worth the risk of losing allies?"

"Let your magic discern that, if it will. The first thing I want you to do is tell Aidryn about what we've learned."

Lira recoiled. This wasn't a conversation she was ready to have—with Aidryn or anyone else. "I need time to think," she said.

The idea of bringing Eremon back made her feel dizzy. Besides, the risks of doing so seemed equal to the potential rewards. As long as the key was sealed away, Aila couldn't reach him. And as long as Lira and Aidryn stayed far away from the crypt, there was no way to unlock the vault.

Lira thought about Macha and the promise she'd made to return to the crypt, and squeezed her eyes shut. She didn't want to feel compassion for Macha, but for a moment, it pierced through her like a shot of visceral pain.

"There's something else to consider in all this." The healer leaned nearer, ever so slightly. "We can't assume that the only access to Eremon's tomb lies here in Rodhlan. It's likely that Iteloria holds another key like Iuchair, or that their magic-wielders have other methods of accessing and sealing the gods' power. Without a ruler to seal away Eremon's power, Iteloria may decide Rodhlan has breached its treaty. If King La'hiran were to strike, this would be the time."

Lira's mouth went dry, a chill skittering across her skin. "So we may have far greater worries than usurpers in the city." It wouldn't matter whether *Aila* was denied access. Iteloria may be coming.

Ljós inclined his head. "That's what I fear."

Terror seeped into the pit of Lira's stomach as she stood, suddenly unsteady. "I need a little time to think this through," she repeated.

"Naturally," Ljós agreed. "It is shocking news, indeed."

Her stomach twisted harder as she moved toward the chamber door, then paused. "When you work with Aidryn today, please don't say anything about this. I need to decide how I should approach him."

"Aidryn is a reasonable man. Given the entire truth, he would understand why Eremon's return might be the most beneficial option."

"But the Binding," Lira said softly. "What would it do to us?"

"The two of you need all the time you can muster to steel yourselves together." Ljós's eyes darkened, and he sighed. "But I do not recommend delaying the truth for long."

Oda was standing in the corridor, arms crossed, when Lira emerged on shaky legs. She looked as though she was ready to snap about the long wait, but her shoulders sagged when they locked gazes. Concern washed over her expression. "Lira, what is it?"

"Let's get to the arena." Lira strode purposefully down the corridor.

Oda trotted to keep up. "Whoa, wait a minute—"

"You need to distract me," Lira said over her shoulder, her chin beginning to tremble. "I can't think about it, I can't talk about it—"

"Running from something will get you hurt," Oda said, resting a hand on Lira's shoulder. She squeezed, but Lira shrugged her off. "You need someone to—"

"I can't think about it," Lira repeated, hot tears gathering in her eyes. She wasn't sure she could hold herself together for long enough to keep the truth to herself.

Oda trotted to keep up. "So you're going to power through our routine and talk to Aidryn, then?"

"No, I—I don't know," Lira stammered. "I don't think I can."

"How much does it affect Aidryn?"

"It will affect him profoundly," Lira said, fighting to keep herself from crying. "I need time, Oda. Eventually, I'll be able to talk about it."

They walked together in a tense silence for a few moments longer before Oda grabbed Lira's hand again, tugging her to a stop. "Lira, are you with child?" she blurted, green eyes shining.

"What?" Lira burst out laughing in spite of herself, her cheeks suddenly burning. She wiped away the tears that had begun to trickle from the corners of her eyes and sniffled. "Whenever could that have happened?"

Oda grinned sheepishly, biting her lip. "I mean... you're married. You're sharing a room. And you ran off to the healer without telling me why. You came out distraught. And you said you didn't want to talk to Aidryn about it, so... I reasoned it out."

As embarrassing as Oda's assumption was, it was a relief to set thoughts of Eremon aside.

"By *Nami*, Oda." Lira sighed. "No, I am not having a baby. There's absolutely no way I could be. I'm not going to detail all the reasons *why* that's not possible—but I'll trust you to believe me."

The warrior pressed a hand to her middle and exhaled heavily, apparently relieved by Lira's answer. "Good, because you can't train if you're carrying a child. You also can't travel or fight—you'd have to stay here at the Fortress. And, forgive me for saying so, but this would be a terrible time to bring a child into the world."

"Yes," Lira agreed, her thoughts straying to Aidryn. She hadn't had time to think about what it might be like for them to have children together—or whether she wanted children, for that matter. Did Aidryn want children? How many, and how soon? Suddenly, she felt lightheaded.

"Our female healers make a tincture for the women who aren't ready for children," Oda ventured as they began walking again. "I can get you a vial if you want, but you'll have to take it at the same time every day."

"I probably should," Lira said slowly, "though I don't know when I'll truly need it."

"Lira." Oda stopped her again, clapped both hands onto her shoulders, and looked her dead in the eyes. "If you haven't *consummated* things already—"

"Stop it, I *hate* that word!" Lira cried, laughing with embarrassment.

Oda laughed, too. "Well, anyhow, I don't think it's going to be much longer."

"That's none of your business, Oda!" Lira covered her face with both hands. "It was a wholly unconventional marriage to begin with. You can't expect it to follow the usual *timeline*."

"You didn't *have* to tell any of us you two were married, but you did. And that's the natural conclusion, so don't blame me."

Oda linked arms with Lira and pulled her in the direction of the arena, chattering away. She seemed to have forgotten her earlier questions, and Lira was grateful for the distraction. For the rest of the morning, she threw herself into her training and tried her best not to think of Eremon, Ljós, or the truth they'd uncovered.

CHAPTER 27

LIRA

Fortress Halgeir
3 Days Later

Lira spent the next few days ruminating on what she'd learned from Ljós and her magic. She took every possible moment alone to explore her power, gleaning bits and pieces of information about Ulan, Iuchair, and Eremon.

At first, she didn't understand why the Itelorian king would have given up the key if it contained the power to access the gods' magic. She had come to believe he'd taken a calculated risk because he understood how deeply Ulan desired to bury the power and erase the histories. That king had bartered on the assumption that there would be no more gods. And apparently, so had Ulan.

That was why so many of Rodhlan's magical texts had survived Iteloria—had been stored there. They were reference material for the Itelorian king if another god were to be born.

As Lira dug deeper into her magic, she discovered that there had been factions of magic-wielders over the centuries who had attempted to raise themselves to the power of the ancient mortal gods. None had succeeded. And what surprised her most was that neither Macha or Corlan had held these ambitions when Eremon was conceived. The exact mixture and depth of his power were formed completely by chance.

Her memories kept snagging on one detail—a memory she'd witnessed months ago, when she was still in Iathium. She'd seen Corlan lying in a coffin with a glass lid, holding Iuchair. More than once, she'd wondered how they managed to get the key past Macha. One day after training, she paused in the corridor shadows and whispered, "Show me Eremon on the day of Corlan's burial."

Her magic swept her into one of Eremon's memories before she could stop it.

The boy-king and a contingent of sentries march along the underground corridor toward the crypt. Ahead of Eremon, six sentries shoulder Corlan's glass coffin. He lay in state in the Dome's throne room for more days than Eremon can remember. He is exhausted from standing vigil, and ready to fall into bed as soon as they are finished here.

Eremon has never been to the crypt before. The cold, damp underground air makes him shiver. When they reach the corridor's dead end, the sentries step aside and he approaches the wall, where an Itelos inscription appears.

He freezes when he reaches that wall. His mother told him to recite an incantation in order to open the wall, but he can't remember what it is now. With a deep, shuddering breath, he squeezes his eyes shut and wracks his memory. It can't be that difficult to recall.

She isn't allowed down here—his mother. Only the heir of the last Rí may enter with his guard. On any other occasion, Eremon would be pleased to be shed of Raní Macha, but it is embarrassing to forget something so important at a time like this. She would have helped him.

One of the sentries—an older man called Beolf—steps forward. "If I may, my Rí," he says tentatively, "I was here with Rí Corlan when his father was entombed. Simply place your hand on the wall below the letters."

"But Mother told me what I should say, and now I've forgotten it," Eremon replies, looking up at Beolf. He prays the sentry can't see the panic in his eyes.

"There is no saying," Beolf says. "You are the rightful heir. The imprint of your hand will do."

Eremon lets out a breath, closes his eyes, and places his palm upon the wall. Suddenly, the wall vanishes completely, revealing the yawning crypt beyond. It's lit in a strange sort of gray-green hue and filled with rows of stone vaults. One stands empty on the far left wall, its lid set aside and ready for Corlan's coffin.

As Eremon drops his hand, he feels something heavy on his finger. Carefully, he traces it with a thumb—a ring that he was not wearing a moment before. If his guess is right, it's his father's ring. The mark of a true heir.

Eremon lets the long sleeve of his robe conceal the ring as he leads the way, his trembling chin held high, toward the open vault. The sentries march in formation behind him. When they arrive at the vault, Eremon stands aside to oversee the sentries placing his father inside.

The young Rí's mind races. How did his father expect him to get Iuchair into the coffin with him? Eremon breaks out in a cold sweat, sensing the weight of the great key in his pocket.

How did the ring come to him at the entrance? It simply appeared. The boy sways on his feet and squeezes his eyes shut, wishing against all sense that the key might simply appear in his father's hands.

And when he opens his eyes, he catches a glimpse of its golden glint as the sentries lower Corlan's coffin into its vault. He presses a hand to his pocket where the key was a moment ago, and finds that it's gone.

Pain pierced Lira's temples as she pulled herself from the memory. The intensity of Eremon's grief was too much to bear, and she was grateful she'd had enough control to end the witnessing. She suspected Macha had punished the boy for disobeying her wishes. Most likely, she had ordered a servant to be whipped in Eremon's stead, as she'd been known to do before he had come of age.

Lira's thought strayed back to Iuchair's vanishing act. How had Corlan accomplished it posthumously?

"Perhaps it was rigged in advance," Lira muttered to herself, crossing her arms and leaning against the corridor wall. Her hand was trembling again, but barely. She pressed it against her side, willing it to stop. "Always a trick with these rulers."

"Who are you talking to?"

A startled shout caught in Lira's throat as Aidryn stepped into the shadowy walkway with her, leaning heavily on a cane. He was clad in fitted brown trousers and a tunic the color of the sky, with a leather belt slung 'round his waist. His dark hair was gathered in a loose bun at the nape of his neck, his short beard neatly trimmed.

Her heart leapt at the sight of him—for more than one reason. She hoped he hadn't heard exactly what she was saying. "Myself," she stammered, reaching for his hand.

"As you do." Aidryn slid a palm up Lira's arm and onto her shoulder as he bent to kiss her. She warmed at his touch.

"It's good to see you walking about," she said, wrapping her arms around him. Over the past two days, Aidryn had begun walking again—first around their chamber, then venturing into the corridor just outside the door. To her knowledge, this was the farthest he'd wandered yet.

"It feels good." He sighed, pulling back to regard her. "Who's pulling tricks?"

So he *had* heard. Now, her heart was pounding. "I'm working through some memories," she hedged, "trying to decipher something Macha said to me in the crypt."

The moment the words left her lips, she wished she could take them back. In the days since they'd retrieved Aidryn, she'd withheld the story about her encounter with Macha—especially since learning the truth about Eremon.

Aidryn's lips parted, and his brows knitted in confusion. "The crypt?"

Suddenly, Lira's mouth and throat were achingly dry. "When Thorne and I came for you, we had to pass through the Rí's crypt. Macha was being held prisoner there."

Now, his eyes were wild. "*What?*"

"Aidryn," she said, fighting to keep her voice steady, "*so* much happened, and you're still recovering. I didn't think it wise to drop everything onto your head at once."

He exhaled sharply, giving her an equally piercing look before he softened. "I suppose I can't argue with your reasoning. I did keep quite a bit of important information from you."

"For quite a long time," Lira reminded him. She was relieved when, instead of pressing her harder, he kissed her hair instead.

"How did you get past Macha alive?" he asked. "Is *she* still alive?"

"She is," Lira answered, looping an arm through his and leading him out into the sunlight. Aidryn tipped his chin back and closed his eyes, breathing deeply as Lira continued. "She told us where to find you, then let us seal her back inside. Said she'd rather die down there than have people see her deposed."

He raised his eyebrows and braced his hands on the railing that overlooked the now-lush courtyard. "Then she was absolutely pulling tricks. But it was quite a gamble on her part. She'll starve to death before anything comes of her scheme." With a soft snort, he added, "As always, we must both be a means to an end."

"An astute observation—apparently, we're worth more to everyone alive," Lira teased, nudging him.

"What did she want?"

"Revenge on the *usurpers*," Lira said ominously. She watched him closely, carefully sidestepping the bargain she'd made with Macha, or the topic of the dead Rí. "There's more, of course. Caitir let us go, too."

"I remember that part." He sighed. "I heard it."

"What else did you hear when you were asleep?" Lira asked.

"Everything's so fragmented." Aidryn shifted uncomfortably. "It might be easier for me to give you my memories. Then, we can try to sort things out together."

"Are you healed enough to use magic?"

He smiled ruefully. "I don't know. Every time I try to summon my power, I *ache*. The torture exacerbated the old magical injury."

Lira frowned up at him. "Well, what did the healer say?"

Aidryn shrugged. "Haven't asked. Honestly, I don't think I want to know the answer."

She shook her head. "We know your power still works, because I've used it. So I'm sure there's a way to heal you."

"I'm on my way to see Ljós now," Aidryn said, adjusting his cane. "Do you want to come along—hold me accountable for asking the right questions?"

Lira giggled, hoping he couldn't detect her nervousness. "I would, but I'm on my way to take a salt bath. Oda slaughtered me in the arena." She stood on tiptoe to kiss his cheek. "I trust you to get some answers."

She hoped the healer wouldn't mention anything to Aidryn about Eremon—but it seemed less likely if Lira avoided the encounter altogether.

CHAPTER 28

AIDRYN

Fortress Halgeir

Aidryn emerged from the healer's chamber feeling better than he had since before he'd been captured. It had taken Ljós less than an hour to restore enough strength to Aidryn's gait that he no longer needed the cane. Still, he held onto it in case he grew weak or winded while they continued to work on his healing.

He had finally worked up the nerve to ask Ljós about his magical wound, and the older man's answer had been surprising in its simplicity.

"A Binding between two clans can heal magical wounds."

"It's that easy?" Aidryn had asked, laughing in spite of himself.

"All I know is theory, so don't assume it will be easy." Ljós had busied himself with a mortar and pestle, mixing a tincture to help Aidryn rest. "Some people believe that the clans' powers were meant to be merged, rather than kept separate. Evidence of past healings plays into that belief.

"Both of you have suffered with unique injuries I have not

been able to heal. I don't think there would be any harm in attempting it."

Aidryn thought again about how Lira's magic had soothed him from the inside out when he'd been captive. He'd leaned against the work table. "How do we try it?"

"Like any other magic, try setting your intention for healing." Ljós had handed the bottle of medicine to Aidryn. "Be open to feeling whole. One of the most important keys to recovery from any ailment is believing you can be healed in the first place."

Aidryn pondered his friend's words as he strode through a sunny patch on the walkway. He paused for a moment, soaking in the sunlight, before heading toward his chamber again. Lira would be waiting for him. A rush of excitement washed over him at the thought. Cautiously, he picked up his pace bit by bit until he was moving at a pleasingly steady clip.

Eagerly, he gripped the handle and pushed the door open, only to hear Lira call from inside, "Wait, I'm not decent!"

"Oh, come on, Lira." He laughed, stepping inside anyway. "I've seen your *ankles*—"

He stopped short at the sight of her and dropped his cane, his jaw falling open in surprise. Lira was standing in the middle of the chamber, and she was not the *least* bit decent. In fact, she wasn't dressed at all. She shrieked, ripping one of the furs off the bed and covering herself with it.

"Did you not hear me?" she shouted.

Aidryn's cheeks blazed. He knew he should react, should turn around, should do *something*, but he found himself unable to function at all beyond the strangled noise he managed to make at the back of his throat. After a moment, he backed toward the door and leaned against it, letting it click shut behind him, and pressed a palm to his face.

"I, um—" he tried to stammer.

Lira stomped angrily toward him, wrapped in the fur now.

Her cheeks were as red as Aidryn imagined his own to be. "Couldn't you have waited another *fifteen bloody seconds*?"

She looked so tiny standing before him, yet so adorably enraged. Inexplicably, Aidryn began to laugh. He didn't want to invite her wrath, but he couldn't stop himself. While Lira stood there scowling, he dissolved into a fit of uncontrollable laughter.

"What's funny about it?" she demanded. "Do I look that ridiculous?"

"No, it's—" He wiped the tears that had pooled in his eyes and tried to catch his breath. "It's the fact that you're so beautiful shouting at me, wrapped in that stupid fur." He doubled over again, laughing so hard his stomach ached. "Something is *profoundly* wrong with me."

"No..." Lira said quietly, finally noting the cane lying on the floor. "Something is *right*. You're walking without it—how are you feeling?"

"Oh, now you're concerned," he teased, crossing his arms. "If you must know, the healer took great care of me today. I have to say, I'm glad you didn't accompany me after all." Laughter burst from him again before he could contain it. "I might not have experienced this fantastically embarrassing moment—Lira, I'm so sorry."

She smirked, taking a step closer to him. "You are *not*."

He reached for her, brushing his fingertips over her cheek. "No, I'm not," he said softly. "You are truly beautiful, even when you're ready to twist my ears clean off my head."

"That's a fair assessment," she replied, leaning into his touch. "The twisting of ears, I mean."

"I *am* your husband," Aidryn said, trailing his fingers down the side of her neck. Lira's eyelids drifted shut, and she tilted her head to the side slightly as he took a step closer. He bent forward—heard her breath hitch as he pressed his lips to her throat. "I suppose it's not a crime for me to see my wife undressed," he whispered, moving lower to kiss her bare shoulder.

Lira shivered against him and made a little noise that sounded suspiciously like a whimper. "Yes, well." She backed away with a teasing grin, pulling the fur tighter. "The next time you see me naked, it will be entirely on my terms."

She strode off toward the bathing chamber, snatching a bundle of clothing from the bureau as Aidryn caught her full meaning. "What—wait, next time?"

Lira stuck her head back out and made a face. "Are you daft? It's like you said—we *are* married." She shut and locked the door, but a moment later Aidryn heard her call, "Maybe something *is* profoundly wrong with you."

He smiled at the laugher in her voice, then tried to pull himself back together while he waited for her to emerge again. When she did return half an hour later, Aidryn was lounging atop the furs, eyes closed. He listened to her soft footsteps as she padded across the room toward him and sat on the edge of the bed at his side.

"Aidryn," Lira whispered, nudging him. "Are you sleeping?"

He cracked an eye open and grinned up at her. She was wearing another of those Beran tunics, and her still-damp hair was slung over one shoulder. "How could I possibly fall asleep at a time like this?"

She blushed. "I'm sorry I shouted at you. You caught me by surprise."

Aidryn sat up, crossing his legs. Lira scooted farther up onto the mattress, mirroring him. "I didn't mean to embarrass you," he said, reaching for her hands. Her touch was light as she traced his palms with her fingertips.

"I was so excited about not needing the cane—and I learned something from Ljós that sounds promising. And then I burst in here like a complete idiot..." He shrugged, letting his mouth tug into a grin. "All in all, I'd say it has been a *very* good day for me."

Lira swatted his arm, but laughter danced in her gaze. "What did you learn from Ljós?" She leaned forward eagerly.

Aidryn explained the theory behind using the Binding to heal their magical wounds. Lira closed her eyes for a moment. He could feel her searching her own power for truth.

After a long moment, Lira cracked an eye open. "I've found something. Do you want to see?" she asked.

"Yes."

Lira pressed her fingers to his temple and shared the brief flashes of memory she'd dredged up. Indeed, bound couples had healed one another before. Each scene was similar: the couple, sitting face to face, with magic flaring brightly between them.

When Lira released the memory, Aidryn said, "So there's no incantation or ritual?"

She shook her head. "Not that I've seen."

"It backs up the healer's story," he ventured. "Ljós seemed to think the healing is based on intent."

Lira laced their fingers together and squeezed lightly. "Then I intend for my magic to heal your wound."

"And mine, yours," Aidryn answered, feeling silly as he made up his own words for the spell. "Through our Binding, let us both be healed."

Lira's eyes glowed emerald. Her magic surged across the Binding and into Aidryn, awakening his own power before it swept back to Lira.

The first sensation Aidryn felt as his magic stirred was searing pain. He was still raw on the inside from weeks of torture. So he called on Lira's cool, soothing power to calm him. Their magic mingled together and danced across the Binding spell.

He gasped, tightening his grip on Lira's fingers as the rush of power overtook him. Tendrils of emerald and crimson magic surrounded them both, intermingling with one another as they snaked their way around their torsos, through their hair, and around their arms and legs.

Every painful place within him was sealed, and for the first time since he was a child, he felt completely whole. The yawning void that had become his constant companion finally closed. Serenity flooded him, and he relaxed.

They allowed the magic to do its work as long as it willed—until the tendrils of power faded and sank into their skin. When it was over, Aidryn was panting softly. His eyelids fluttered open and he found Lira quietly studying him. Aidryn met her gaze, and she didn't shy away.

"Well?" She took a breath, eyes shining. "Do you think it worked?"

Aidryn smiled. "I can't remember the last time I felt this complete," he said, pressing a hand to his middle. "Maybe when I was a boy. How do you feel?"

Lira was radiant as she returned his smile. "Wonderful," she said breathlessly.

She shifted to her knees and crawled toward him. Lira brushed her nose against his, then kissed him, trailing her fingers along the back of his neck. The world slowed as Aidryn reached for her, his hand sliding from her waist to the soft curve of her hip.

"About those terms you mentioned," he whispered.

She laughed softly. "What about them?"

Aidryn was about to make a joke about starting negotiations when there was a loud knock at the door. Lira startled, then abruptly swung her legs over the side of the bed and rushed to answer it. He followed at her heels to find Oda standing in the corridor, expression stricken.

"Oda, what's wrong?" Lira asked, her voice tinged with panic.

"We have news of Artur," the warrior said solemnly. "Follow me."

LIRA

Fortress Halgeir

There was a sparse crowd in Ljós's chamber when Lira, Aidryn, and Oda arrived. The group had assembled around the pit of amber stones in the center of the room. Iva, Thorne, and Talfryn sat together by the pit, holding mugs of hot stew and talking quietly. A handful of other Beravakt were present, whom Lira recognized from the arena—most likely Thorne's scouts. Oda peeled off to join them.

Talfryn leapt up at the sight of Aidryn, rushing him from across the room. Warmth bloomed in Lira's belly and tears pricked her eyes as Aidryn opened his arms to her brother, and the young men embraced. They spoke in hushed tones for a long while, and Lira stepped aside to join her mother, whose eyes were also rimmed with tears.

Iva rose to grasp Lira's hands, and she realized her mother was trembling. "What's happened?" Lira whispered, her throat clenching in fear. She felt Ljós's silencing spell take hold of the room, and her ears popped.

"Thorne's scouts received word that Artur has been executed," Iva answered softly.

Lira suddenly felt nauseous, her heart pounding, but a tug at her magic gave her pause. "Do they have evidence?" Her voice rose slightly, betraying the panic roiling in her belly. "Who told them?"

Thorne stepped forward, resting a hand on Iva's shoulder. "They only heard rumors, but the talk was widespread. We have no witnesses to confirm it."

"Well, you have me," Lira said. "We'll look into my power—see what we can find."

She tried to ignore the nervous trembling in her legs as she moved closer to the stone pit and picked up the small amber pebble Ljós had given her to project her power. The healer seemed to understand exactly what she was doing, for he strode to the edge of the pit, too, and sent an orb of his power into it, illuminating the stones. Chatter in the room quieted as everyone turned their attention to Lira.

Ljós deferred to her. "Silira, please address the room. Explain what we are about to attempt."

She nodded slightly, taking a shaky breath. "Ljós and I have developed a method for projecting memories. We're going to attempt to determine what has happened to Artur, and whether the rumors of his death are true. If they are not, perhaps we can also look into the motivation behind the rumors."

Aidryn moved to her side, resting a hand on the small of her back. They sat together beside the stones, and Lira clenched the pebble, taking a deep breath.

"Please speak the questions you are asking your magic, Lira," the healer said softly. "It will help everyone in the room understand what you are seeking."

Lira nodded, then let her eyes drift closed. "Show me, Rodhlan: what has happened to Artur Beran?"

She hoped invoking the continent would keep her from accidentally delving into the man's mind. The amber stones burst to life with bright, raging magic, and an image appeared in the light that shone above the pit.

Artur Beran sits against the stone wall in the dungeon of Iathium. He is ill, his body aching and undulating between chills and cold sweats. There is a basin of dirty water and an untouched bowl of gruel beside him. Besides the occasional sentry patrolling these corridors, the cell is silent. His skin is mottled with black veins from persistent torture.

The memory winked out, and Iva shuddered. "So they were rumors meant to draw us into the city."

Lira's magic tugged in agreement. "It appears so," she answered. "I'm going to ask my magic another question." She took a deep breath. "Show me, Rodhlan: did Gerallt falsely report Artur Beran's execution?"

Her power answered with a decisive *no*. "Then what is the enemy planning?" Lira's fingers tingled around the pebble, and another image appeared in the light.

Caitir and Aila face off in the Dome's throne room. The high noon sun casts an array of colors on them as it filters through the stained glass oculus. Aila's hands are clenched, her expression enraged as veins of black lightning crackle around her fists. She wears a gown of sleek ebony that pools around her feet, as though she's being swallowed by an abyss.

"You were the only person who could have possibly seen Silira in Aidryn's chamber," Aila shouts. "And you let them escape. Stupid girl!"

"Your accusations are beyond the pale, and I will not stand for it," Caitir rages. "Why would I let them go when that power was nearly in our grasp? You failed to post guards outside Aidryn's chamber during the coronation—that's your fault."

"I enchanted the door! There was no need for a sentry." Aila raises her chin. "It should have remained sealed. There is only one person who can unravel that spell, and he was completely incapacitated."

"Yes. He was. But Silira came," Caitir says, eyeing her mother's face carefully. "And they are bound. Don't you remember?"

Aila's eyes widen in surprise, and the hint of a grin tugs at Caitir's mouth. The girl smooths the bodice of her pearlescent gown languidly. "Do you honestly believe I would have allowed Lira to slip through my fingers, knowing she could access the power in the crypt?"

Her mother's glare suddenly shutters, and her countenance softens. "No, my dear. I do not."

Caitir takes a step closer to her mother, lowering her voice slightly. "So we must draw her back into the city. She came once already to save someone she loves. And we are still holding another who is dear to her."

Aila's face hardens again. "She cares nothing for Beran."

"Do you really believe that?" Caitir studies the intricate stitching on one of her gown sleeves. "He is sheltering her. We have surmised that much."

"And he will continue to do so," Aila answers. "They are likely holding her prisoner."

"There is more than one way to get to her," Caitir says. "That clan is bloodthirsty. Suppose we draw their warriors into the city instead, set an ambush. We are playing a very long game, Mother, and we are patient. Weakening their clan could give us an opportunity to get to her. Besides, she can't stay there forever. She'll pretend she doesn't want your throne until she gathers enough allies, and then she will come for it. One way or another, we must harness the power of the gods. It is the only way to break her."

Aila scrutinizes her daughter for a moment, then slowly nods. "Then we shall make sure Clan Beran gets word their overlord has been executed. They are a ruthless rabble. If they believe he is dead, they will come to avenge him."

"Why only make them believe it?" Caitir says. "Why not have the deed done?"

"Because if Artur believes his best warriors are coming for him, we might have use for him yet. He protects his clan. When we show *him we have captured his most prized fighters, he will break. We will trade them to him in exchange for Silira, and we will have the magic we desire."*

When the memory faded from the stones, the tremor had returned to Lira's right hand. Aidryn reached out to grasp it gently. "What's this?" he whispered, his eyes full of alarm.

The healer was at their side in an instant, pouring magic into her hand as she quietly answered, "It's happening when I go into a person's memories. If I ask Rodhlan for a memory, it doesn't happen."

When the trembling ceased, Aidryn laced her fingers together and brought her knuckles to his lips. "Then you must be more careful."

Warmth filled her at his touch. Suddenly, Lira was aware of the silence in the room—of everyone's attention on her and Aidryn. She looked to Thorne. His expression was stony, his massive fists clenched.

"We will have to leave Artur where he is for now," he said grimly, glancing at Iva. "I'm sorry."

Iva's eyes filled with fresh tears again, but she did not allow them to fall. "He won't survive much longer this way. He is ill."

"I know," Thorne said softly. "But I learned strategy from him. We can't afford to lose any warriors to the city. If he were here today, he would say ignore the rumors. Draw Gerallt's army out of Iathium. Don't walk into a trap knowing it has been set for you."

"Then I defer to your training, Thorne." Iva said.

He inclined his head solemnly. "And I defer to your leadership. I want you to continue leading the clan in the overlord's stead. I ask that you keep me in charge of the warriors."

"Thorne, you need not ask." But Iva straightened her shoulders and nodded anyway. She and Thorne clasped hands. "Of course, you have my blessing."

Lira wanted to embrace her mother. She looked from Iva to Thorne, who gave Lira a tight smile and stepped toward her.

"Silira, we will protect you," he said. "I give my word, *sjeinga*: you will never be traded to Iathium, for any price." *Sister*.

Warmth enveloped Lira at the sentiment. "Thank you, *sjeovi*." *Brother*.

Iva turned to Lira. "Witness Tree," she said softly, "your magic is magnificent."

Her cheeks heated. "Thank you, Mam."

Iva gave her a small smile, then raised her hands to the room. "There are some things to put in order before we leave here tonight. First, Thorne and I will be calling the clan to announce Artur's imprisonment. We will dispel any rumors and call the warriors to prepare for a coming battle. If we are to draw out the usurpers, we will need to gather allies. For now, our people will be put on alert, and we will double our training efforts."

She turned to Lira. "What do you know of this magic they want?"

"Not as much as I'd like just yet," Lira answered, trying to hold her voice steady. Her palms were clammy with sweat. It was true; she did *not* know as much as she wanted to. "I've been searching Rodhlan's memories for answers. I know they believe they can access the magic of the dead mortal gods. There is a key called Iuchair, which they believe unlocks this power."

Aidryn turned to stare at Lira and worked his jaw as though he wanted to ask a thousand questions. But he closed his mouth when Oda spoke instead.

"Who are these mortal gods?" she asked, crossing her arms.

"That is a story for another time," Ljós answered. "For now, let us focus on today's most pressing matters."

Oda inclined her head and turned her attention to Lira, as if she wanted to ask, *Why haven't you told me any of this?*

"Aidryn," Iva said, "when you were held prisoner, did you glean any information about this power?"

He appeared startled as he looked from Lira to her mother. "I did. It wasn't much, and I was hardly in a position to decipher all of it. But I gathered that they wanted a key to obtain power, and they needed my magic to get it.

"They believe it will grant them immortality—or unnaturally long life, at the very least. If it truly comes from the mortal gods, I wouldn't be surprised." He shrugged. "I imagine that's why they want Lira. She can access my magic through the Binding, and I hers. If they can't go through me to get the key, then they'll try to use her."

Lira perked up at Aidryn's description of the magic. She wondered why he hadn't mentioned it to her, either, but it was unlikely he was concealing important details; after all, he had only gleaned fragments. A guilty pang twisted her stomach, but she pushed aside thoughts of Eremon. There would be another opportunity to expand the story later.

"Yet Caitir made no attempt to take Lira when we encountered her at the Dome," Thorne said. "She let us go."

"The memory we just witnessed indicates Caitir has deeper motives." Iva looked pointedly at Lira. "Would you agree?"

"Yes," Lira answered. "I agree. She was beside herself because Aila and Gerallt were crowned, but she was not. They lured her into that marriage with the promise of a crown. My magic affirms she is planning to take control of the throne, one way or another."

Aidryn nodded. "Most likely, she plans to play the victim, access that magic, then overthrow her mother and husband."

"That explains why Macha struck that bargain with Lira when we passed through the crypt," Thorne said. "She wants the same power."

"Lira, you did *what*?" Aidryn's eyes were wild with alarm now. "What did you promise her?"

She inhaled sharply, keenly aware of everyone's eyes on them. "I promised to return with information about the magic in exchange for your location," she answered, her voice wavering. "Aila and Caitir put her there to access it, but she knew little about it—just that it exists. And apparently, it sounded attractive enough that she wanted to try getting it for herself."

"I *told* you," he said, his voice pleading, "you shouldn't have come for me. What kind of danger did you invite by bargaining with that woman?"

Lira scoffed. "None. She's a prisoner down there, Aidryn. No one can get to her, and she can't get out. She was locked inside the crypt during Eremon's interment, and I'm the only person who can open it again. I don't *have* to go back."

"You absolutely don't, and you won't," he said firmly. "Like Thorne said, we're going to protect you. Macha can live out her sentence among the corpses. It's what she deserves."

There was a dangerous edge to Aidryn's voice that she'd never heard before. Lira reached for him, resting a hand on his arm. "Aidryn, I'm safe. We made it back alive. But in that moment, I would have done *anything* to get to you."

His expression was almost mournful as he touched her cheek. "I know, but I wish you hadn't endangered yourself on my account. I don't know if I can ever forgive myself for it."

"There's nothing to forgive," she whispered.

Iva moved toward the chamber door then, looking to Bard, who sat across the room between Talfryn and Oda. "Bard, blow the battle horn. It's time to call the clan."

Bard gave her a little bow and left the room. Talfryn, Oda, and the remaining Beravakt followed behind him. Oda stole a last glance at Lira before she left the chamber. Lira wanted to go after her—to explain everything—but there were still details she wasn't ready to reveal. Truths that must be guarded until they could no longer be held close.

Iva turned to Lira. "Lira, Ljós—it seems there is still much to unravel, so I trust you to see it through. Aidryn, you have yet to enter the arena, so your job will be to begin strengthening yourself for battle. Thorne will work with you."

Aidryn nodded deferentially. Lira's mother looked to the door as though she might leave, but doubled back and crossed the room toward him. He rose to meet her and she reached for his hands, leaning in to kiss his cheek.

"It's good to see you again," Iva said with a soft smile. "I'm honored to have you as a son."

Aidryn returned her smile, warmth radiating from him. "I have loved Lira for so long." Lira stood and stepped toward them, and Aidryn reached for her, grasping her hand. He pulled her in, and the three embraced. "I promise I will protect her until my last breath."

Iva kissed Lira's forehead, then Aidryn's. She grasped one of Aidryn's hands, then one of Lira's, and brought them together before letting go. "We are living an uncertainty none of us have experienced in our lifetimes. War is coming, and we don't know what new dangers tomorrow will bring."

Lira looked to Aidryn, who met her eyes and raised her fingers to his lips. There was a heat in his gaze that nearly brought her to her knees. She released a shaky breath, her stomach fluttering.

Iva took a step back, smiling sadly at them. "Don't waste a moment of the precious time you have together." With that, she strode from the room and didn't look back.

"Let's go?" Aidryn asked softly.

Lira nodded, feeling suddenly weak. She allowed him to lead her from the chamber. On the way to the door, she caught the healer's steady gaze. Ljós's expression contained questions she wasn't ready to answer, for him or anyone else. So she turned her attention back to her husband, letting her thoughts about the mortal gods' magic scatter.

Aidryn pulled her into the dark corridor and pressed her against the wall, kissing her with an intensity that made her forget where they were. Lira traced her fingers along his jawline and into his hair, returning his kisses with equal fervor. He braced his hands on her hips and trailed his lips down her neck. She shivered, heart pounding as she tipped her head back to give him better access. He returned to nip at her bottom lip before deepening the kiss again.

Lira gasped lightly, grasping his face. One of her hands wandered to the laces at the collar of his tunic, and she worked her fingertips beneath them to touch his warm skin. She had always thought of herself as an independent soul who didn't require romantic love to have the life she wanted. But the need Aidryn had awakened in her was so overwhelming, it was almost painful.

"Aidryn," she breathed, pressing her palm to his chest. She could feel his heartbeat hammering beneath.

He rested his forehead against hers, cupping her cheek. Then, he traced his fingers down her throat, over her collarbone, and finally over her heart, where he paused. "Please, Lira..." he whispered, leaning in to press his lips against her jaw, then to her mouth again.

Suddenly, she was keenly aware of his body pressed flush against hers—of every place where his hands had been, and exactly where he was touching her now. "Not in the corridor," she laughed quietly.

Her cheeks felt warm, her lips swollen from their fevered kisses. Reaching for her hair, she unwound a bead from one of her braids. Aidryn kissed her again as she pressed the bead to her pendant, and the *turas* spell swept them back to their chamber.

They landed on their feet, just inside the door. Lira fired a little shot of Aidryn's magic at it to engage the hidden lock before returning to his arms. The room was almost uncomfortably dim, the candles burning dangerously low in their stands.

Aidryn laughed, his voice rough with desire. "Why is that the most attractive thing you've ever done?"

She grinned mischievously, but before she could reply, he was kissing her again. Her breath caught as his hands roamed, his mouth never leaving hers as they moved toward the bed.

Lira had spent every day since Aidryn returned denying

herself this—in part, to give him time to heal. If she was being honest with herself, she'd also feared the raw vulnerability that would come with making love to him. But with war on the horizon, her fear suddenly seemed insignificant.

As evening wore into night, Lira allowed each kiss, each new sensation to chase away the thoughts of war and power and mortal gods. And when the rolling boom of Clan Beran's war horn tore through the fortress, they ignored its call. For tonight, everything else could wait.

CHAPTER 30

LIRA

Fortress Halgeir
2 Weeks Later

For a fortnight, there was no word from Iathium—no news of Artur, nor of Gerallt and the army he was building. Once the people of Clan Beran were allowed to process the news of their overlord's capture, they threw themselves into training. Although the warriors worked the longest and hardest, it wasn't unusual for entire families to cycle through the arena for training throughout the day, children included.

Lira and Aidryn spent the bulk of their days building their strength and honing their magic in the arena. Otherwise, they stole away to their chamber at every opportunity. Lira felt as though she could drown in her own happiness, and in the pleasure she and Aidryn shared. When she was younger, she had tried to envision what it might feel like to love someone this deeply—but her imagination, she'd quickly realized, had fallen profoundly short of reality. What she felt for Aidryn surpassed any semblance of affection she'd ever held for anyone or anything.

It hadn't been difficult for them to make a habit of arriving late to dawn training sessions. This morning, they'd lingered in bed longer than usual, reluctant to give up the cocoon of warmth they'd created. Aidryn braced himself over her, studying her unabashedly as she trailed her fingertips along his back.

"We're late again," she said, grinning up at him.

He smiled lazily. "And?"

"Oda's going to throttle me. I promised her I'd run drills with some of the magic-wielders."

Lira had spent long periods of time searching Rodhlan's memories for magical battle tactics. She'd found many examples of how the clans had used magic on the battlefield in the past. Using the memory-projection trick she and Ljós had devised with his amber stones, she had been able to teach the fighters—both from Clan Beran and the refugee camp—how to apply their magic for offensive and defensive battle.

Aidryn chuckled and kissed her nose. "Well, I think I'm safe from Thorne. He just pretends he has no idea what goes on in here."

Lira snorted. "I wish Oda would pretend. One day, she's going to waggle her eyebrows right off her face."

They rose and dressed, then stepped out into the cool morning air. The sun was already blazing, its bright rays spilling onto the stone walkway as they strolled toward the arena.

"I never asked you," Aidryn said, reaching for her hand. He was wearing a sleeveless leather tunic like Thorne's, a broadsword sheathed at his hip. "You remember that council, where we spoke of the mortal gods' power. Why didn't you mention it before?"

Lira faltered, but managed to keep pace with him. She'd been content to let thoughts of Eremon and the magic slip into the back of her mind over the past few weeks. "Got distracted," she hedged, grinning at him. He returned her smile. "You were recovering, for one thing. And with Aila and Caitir and Macha, it's always about more power, more magic. Always more."

"You're not wrong," he replied.

"At the council, you implied that you knew about the magic they wanted, too," Lira said, nudging him. "Why didn't *you* bring it up?"

"Partly because I only heard fragments of conversations." He paused to tuck a curl behind her ear. "But also because when Caitir described the magic to me, I realized I *wanted* it—desperately. And I thought, if a power is that alluring, it should probably stay locked away, right where it is.

"No human should ever wield magic that potent. And if they can't access Iuchair through you or me, there's little chance they'll ever get their hands on it. The farther we stay from Iathium, the better."

Lira tried to ignore the pang in her chest. "I suppose the fact that it's sourced from mortal gods is why it's so powerful."

"Tell me more," Aidryn said, kissing her knuckles. "How did you figure that part out?"

"Ljós and I pieced it together." She took a shaky breath. "I was able to access some memories from Ulan's reign. It seems that Iuchair was part of a treaty he signed with Iteloria. The Itelorians were rather invested in suppressing our magic, and they knew the mortal gods' power could be accessed after death somehow.

"The key can be used to lock the power away, or to awaken it once again. Some people believe the gods can be resurrected for a time. But from what I saw in my vision, Ulan locked away Nami's magic. Nami had power of his own, but he'd also taken Rasu, Riku, and Rhona's power when *they* died. I think Iuchair separates the magic from their spirit when the locking spell is applied. The magic is sealed away permanently, from what I understand."

"So who locked Ulan's magic away when *he* died?" Aidryn

asked with a cheeky grin. "Did he think about that before he did it to his father?"

"No one, probably," Lira said. "Besides, I think he was just a powerful mortal. He wanted to end the line of gods with Nami."

"And did he succeed?"

She swallowed hard. "Apparently not, or we wouldn't have all these self-proclaimed rulers clamoring for this magic."

Suddenly, Aidryn stopped in his tracks and rounded on her. "What does your magic feel like when it's discerning truth?"

Lira felt the blood drain from her face. *This is it—he knows, he knows.* "Like a subtle tug at the back of my mind. It feels like intuitive affirmation, I think. And when something is not true, it gives me a little nudge in the other direction."

"Oh," Aidryn said, smiling. "I felt that tug when you were describing all this. It's the first time I've noticed it."

She resisted letting a relieved breath whoosh out of her. "It's exhilarating, isn't it?"

"Quite." He leaned down, brushing a light kiss against her mouth.

As he withdrew, Lira grabbed the front of his tunic and pulled him back to her, kissing him deeply. With a low groan, Aidryn snaked his hands around to the small of her back and pressed her body to his. She let the sensation chase away her nagging guilt for staying silent about Eremon.

We've faced so much for so long... I just want to enjoy this while I can.

Besides, she wanted to speak to Ljós again before giving Aidryn the rest of the details. She'd been avoiding the healer since the last war council.

"Do we really have to go to the arena?" Aidryn murmured against her mouth.

"Not *really*," she said with a smile, "but we probably should."

He cupped her cheek, brushing his thumb over her bottom

lip before kissing her again. "Don't give me options or I'll haul you right back to bed."

Lira's cheeks heated. "We'd likely be interrupted by a certain warrior kicking down the door." She laughed softly. "Let's go."

They set out walking once again, the sunlight warming their skin. Lira, too, had taken to wearing training tunics similar to Oda and the other warriors. It had taken time to get used to exposing her arms, but she found it was much easier to move her body and practice with her axes without sleeves getting in the way.

"Have you figured out whose magic they want?" Aidryn asked. "Who the other mortal gods are?"

Again, Lira's insides lurched. She wondered if she should just tell him outright, but her fear of his reaction outweighed the urge to come clean. Eremon had been a sore spot between them in his first life. Bringing him back would be painful for all three of them.

It felt irrational to run from the truth like this, but the past few weeks had been the happiest of her life. If she could delay putting Eremon in the center of their conversations for a little while longer, she would.

"It's hard to say," she finally answered, "but Ljós and I have been trying to glean answers about that, too. It's funny; I don't always think to explore the histories for all the answers."

It was all true; it *was* hard to say. And Lira did often forget to sift through the memories at her disposal—a fact she was ashamed to admit. Aidryn seemed satisfied with her answer, and he didn't ask any more questions before they reached the arena.

Oda met them at the door, throwing a mock kick at Aidryn's shins. He jumped backward with a grin, and she advanced on him, cuffing his shoulder. "I was just about to come after you two," she said, looking to Lira with raised eyebrows.

"See what I told you, Aidryn?" Lira laughed.

He cracked a crooked grin. "Right, as usual."

"I'd say I hope you got plenty of rest, but we all know that didn't happen." Oda winked at Lira.

Lira groaned, but Aidryn threw his head back and laughed. They trekked down the stairs together, laughing and chatting. On the way down, Oda glanced back over her shoulder. "Some of your friends from Iathium arrived at dawn. Thorne's already down there breaking them."

"Who?" Aidryn craned his neck to see.

Lira followed his gaze down to where Thorne was training. On the arena floor, Faolan Énna's expression was stoic and determined as he blocked and parried Thorne's broadsword with a blade of his own. Next to them, a sweat-slick, grinning Aeron—Faolan's cousin—was fighting with Talfryn.

Aeron had shucked his tunic off at some point and was fighting shirtless. From Lira's vantage point, she could see three long scars that marred his chest—markings he must be proud of, she thought. She trained her focus elsewhere; not even the men from Beran ran around bare-chested like that.

Faolan and Aeron had helped Aidryn and Lira escape Iathium in the spring, before they'd run to the mountains in search of Skelly. The young sentries had later helped Talfryn flee the city, too, making sure he reached Fortress Halgeir safely after his injury.

"Énna!" Aidryn shouted, rushing down the rest of the stairs toward Thorne's group.

Faolan swore loudly, dodging Thorne's oncoming blade. "What are you trying to do, Tarlach, get me killed?"

"That's the idea," Aidryn said as Thorne called a halt to the drill.

Faolan rushed Aidryn and the two embraced. He clapped Aidryn's back before abruptly extracting himself from his friend's grip. "All right, that's enough," he snapped gruffly, his gaze immediately shifting to Lira.

"It's good to see you, Faolan," she said with a smile.

"I'm surprised you made it this far alive, little bookworm," Faolan said dryly. His black curls were slick with sweat, his tan cheeks pink with exertion.

"Sometimes I am, too," Lira answered truthfully.

Faolan reached for her then, tugging her into his arms while Aidryn and Aeron spoke quietly. "I'm glad you did," he said curtly, though there was a tenderness in his voice she hadn't expected to hear.

He lay a hand on her shoulder and gave her a nod before stepping back again. His hair was longer than the last time she'd seen him, and he pushed away the stray curls that stuck to his forehead.

Aeron took his cousin's place, pulling Lira into a hug as well. He was uncomfortably sweaty, and she stiffened against his embrace. "Hello, Aeron," she squeaked.

"Nami's bones, Aeron, put on a tunic next time," Aidryn swore. "I didn't let you near me, and you think you can put your stink all over Lira like that?"

"Sorry," Aeron said, stepping back abruptly. "I didn't think —I'm just so glad to see you both."

"Don't apologize." Lira laughed, though she was grateful he'd let her go. "Where did you get the battle scars?"

Mischief glinted in Aeron's eyes. "If I said battle, would you believe me?"

Lira wrinkled her nose. "Not for a minute."

"If you must know, it was a dog," Faolan said.

Aidryn grinned, glancing between the two sentries, then finally at Lira. "But he likes it when ladies notice, so good job." He picked Aeron's wrinkled tunic up off the ground and chucked it at his friend's face. "Put it back on. You got your attention."

Aeron winked at Lira and tugged the tunic over his head. When he'd straightened it, he leaned toward Lira conspiratorially and asked, "What's this I hear about a Binding?" His hazel eyes glinted, sweat beading down from his hairline. "I want to know everything that's happened."

"Sounds like Aidryn's been filling you in," she said, her cheeks heating. Aidryn offered her a warm smile.

Faolan stilled, looking between Lira and Aidryn. "You two?" he asked incredulously.

Lira was puzzled by the shadow that crossed Aidryn's expression before he nodded. Faolan sighed. "Well, that's going to complicate things."

"Why would it?" Aidryn asked. He seemed suddenly uneasy, and he rubbed the back of his neck.

"It won't," Aeron said under his breath, glaring pointedly at Faolan. "Come on; let's see what Tarlach has in him after training with this Beran fellow."

Aidryn unsheathed his sword as the young men strode off to join Thorne and Talfryn again. Lira suddenly felt ill as she watched them cross the arena.

"What was that about?" Oda muttered.

"I don't know," Lira said. "Faolan's an odd one. Maybe it's just his way."

The warrior hummed. "I don't know," she echoed. "Come on—we're running drills with axes this afternoon."

Lira gripped the axes on her belt instinctively. She'd grown used to training with them now, though she was still working to refine her aim. The axes worked for hand-to-hand combat, but they were also designed for throwing.

Warriors on the front line in battle could throw their axes at the ground, toward the feet of the enemy. The axe blades were carefully weighted, so that when they hit the ground, they bounced upward, beneath the enemy's shields. At the very least, they could damage the shields in the process. More than once, Lira had searched her memories to see what it looked like to use them in combat.

Oda had lined several dummies up against the far wall and mounted shields to them. She picked up a pair of axes, twirling them between her fingers. "All right, Lira," she said. "Let's have another go today."

But Lira's attention had wandered. She watched Aidryn, who appeared to be engaged in a spirited conversation with the Énna boys as they sparred, two-on-one. Their strange exchange from before nagged at her, and she chewed her lip nervously.

"Lira." Oda stepped into her line of sight. "I'm sure it's nothing. Let's get to work now—throwing a few axes should take your mind off your worries for a little while."

She met the warrior's gaze and nodded numbly, but her magic was setting off warning bells no training session could erase.

LIRA

Fortress Halgeir

That evening, the war council convened in the healer's chamber. Lira was careful to avoid being pushed into conversation with Ljós for fear of someone overhearing. Instead, she found a seat next to her mother and Oda. Aidryn had disappeared with the sentries after training, but Thorne had assured her they would be back for the council.

Her nervousness had only increased over the course of the day. Faolan's cryptic remark still rattled around in her mind: *Well, that's going to complicate things.* What had he meant?

"I met your friends from the city today," Iva said when Lira sat. Oda brought her a mug of tea, lowering herself onto the floor beside them.

"Oh?" Lira said, taking a sip. Ljós's tincture had taken the edge off her anxiety, but she still felt uneasy.

"They've brought a large group of former sentries with them," her mother continued. "Nearly six hundred people, all told."

"What?" Lira sputtered. "Surely not six hundred *sentries.*"

"Most of them are clanspeople or city-dwellers who can't be bothered with your uncle's nonsense," Oda said. "No offense."

"It is what it is. Where are they all staying?" Lira asked.

"Some of the warriors are erecting a war camp in the eastern pastureland," Iva answered. "A few of the Beravakt are clearing out the old tunnel your stepfather filled in forty years ago. That way, the soldiers will have easier access in and out of the fortress."

The tunnel served as a path from inside Halgeir to the pastures. It would prevent Beran's people from being forced to use the river inlet for all their transportation, and would greatly ease the trouble it took to get fresh meat and other supplies inside.

"Lira," Thorne barked. She looked up, startled, to see him standing over her. "Walk with me."

Did Thorne know what was going on with Aidryn? Was he going to tell her? Suddenly, Lira felt faint, but she got up and followed him into Ljós's adjoining chamber, where he shut the door behind them.

"What's wrong?" Lira asked. Her voice was unnaturally high-pitched, and she fought to steady herself.

"You've been withholding important information," he said accusingly.

And there it was. She couldn't help shrinking beneath Thorne's glare—though he seemed more disappointed than angry. Her heart sank; she had never wanted to upset him this way. Beneath the realization that her friend was disappointed, a deep fear of Aidryn's reaction surged, swallowing her thoughts and making it difficult to breathe. His reaction to her lies would surely be much worse.

When she finally opened her mouth to answer, Thorne cut her off. "Don't dance around it, Silira. I already know. But I want you to confirm it."

"Ljós told you about Eremon." She could barely get the words out.

"Yes," he answered sternly. "He gave you time to do it yourself, but it looks like even your husband doesn't know. You left us all in the dark."

"Why does it matter who the power belongs to? The important thing is that Aidryn and I stay away from the crypt. As long as they can't use our power to obtain the key, there's nothing they can do about the gods' magic."

"Until they ally with Iteloria in a bid to get the other key," Thorne answered. "That girl is cunning and smart. You know that if she can't get Iuchair from you, she'll find another way to the magic. And if she is going to overthrow Aila and Gerallt, she will need allies. Who else will side with her?"

Panic clawed at Lira. Thorne was right. Iteloria would be lured into Rodhlan with the promise of sealing away Eremon's power. But Caitir and the others—unless she did, indeed, overthrow them—would devise a way to get that second key. Suddenly, she felt daft for waiting to share that bit of information.

"I'm sorry," Lira said, her heart beating erratically. It was hard to draw a good breath. "I'm sorry. I didn't think it through."

Thorne's expression softened, and he fashioned an orb of that healing magic to calm her. "Quiet now, *sjeinga*. Time has not run out. But you have to tell Tarlach before this goes any farther. I'm giving you until tomorrow to do it. If you don't, I will tell him myself at afternoon drills."

Lira exhaled shakily and nodded. "Understood."

"For what it's worth, I think he will understand why you did not tell him," Thorne said. "In time."

She squeezed her eyes shut and nodded. Thorne's blunt truth wasn't helping her remain calm. Lira wondered how she would manage eating stew during council, the way the group had begun to do. Right now, she felt sick to her stomach.

Suddenly, she remembered Aidryn's puzzling exchange with the sentries again. "When Aidryn was with Faolan and

Aeron, did you happen to hear what they were discussing? There was something odd about it..."

The warrior shrugged. "All I know is that Tarlach was asking about his horse. They said they hadn't seen him."

"Oh." News like that *would* be incredibly upsetting to Aidryn. But it still didn't explain why their Binding would complicate things.

Thorne rested a hand on Lira's shoulder and steered her toward the door that opened into the main room. "You are courageous," he said quietly. "If you can face down both Macha and Caitir in the same day, then you're strong enough to do this."

With that, he crossed back into the chamber where the war council was gathered. Lira took a deep breath to steady herself, then followed him out.

Aidryn and the sentries had come while she was speaking with Thorne. From across the room, Aidryn caught her gaze, and something about his expression set her heart pounding again. But this time, it wasn't desire or admiration—it was suspicion. His gaze flicked to Thorne, then back to her before he took a seat between Faolan and Aeron, near the exit into the corridor.

Trembling, Lira went back to her own seat with Iva and Oda. Her friend frowned when Lira settled back in.

"The tension is thick," Oda said. "You're going to have to tell me what's going on."

"I can't yet," Lira answered. "But soon."

She drew her knees up to her chest and wrapped her arms around them. Oda looked as though she wanted to speak again, but instead, she turned away from Lira as Iva called the council into session.

Lira struggled to pay attention to what her mother was saying, stealing glances in Aidryn's direction from time to time. His expression was entirely unreadable, though she caught

Aeron's eye once or twice. The first time, he gave her a tight-lipped smile. He did not acknowledge her again.

"We've received word that Gerallt Mór plans to march on Clan Énna's caravan in the west, to absorb them into his army," Iva was saying. "The scouts report that Lira's grandmother and Lord Irem Énna are of interest to Gerallt. They are being guarded, but Clan Énna's fighters are too few to withstand an entire army."

Lira sat up straighter as Iva continued. "Our scouts believe it could be weeks or months before they march, so we must be ready to go at a moment's notice."

Though they'd originally discussed marching toward Iathium to draw Gerallt's army out, Thorne, Iva, and the other warriors had eventually decided against it. The best option, they'd concluded, was to wait until they gleaned more information.

"Our hope is to meet them in the meadowlands, heading them off somewhere between the city gates and the coast." Iva continued. "At best, we surround them by the ocean and force their surrender. At worst, we drive them back into the city. We expect to march out in four weeks' time."

Faolan spoke up, earning a hard glare from Thorne. "Any less than six weeks is alarmist," he said.

"Wait until you're spoken to," Thorne reprimanded, but Iva raised a hand.

"Let him speak," she said, keeping her gaze trained on Faolan.

The sentry inclined his head. "Gerallt's people are disorganized and sloppy. They've handed out portions of that dark magic to the archers they brought from Clan Mór, and the sentries who joined them. It's complete chaos in the city right now. They'll have to gain control of their power, not to mention their people, before they can execute an organized march anywhere."

"Tell us what you know about their numbers," Iva pressed.

"All told, Gerallt has an army of thirteen, fourteen hundred, including archers," Aeron cut in. "More than a thousand fled. The rest scattered—many of them are either hiding out in the city, or they've run to the clan territories. We've recruited as many as we can along the way."

"Some are moving across the continent in small groups," Faolan added. "And we heard a large number of them boarded a ship for Iteloria, though no one can confirm it."

"How many are camped outside the fortress?" Thorne asked.

"Five hundred eighty-three," Aeron answered.

"We have seven hundred warriors to lend ourselves," Iva said. "If it's possible to recruit more from the clans and sway those who fled to Iteloria, we could quickly outnumber Gerallt."

"Clan Énna's settlement is small," Aeron said, "but if we can recruit from there, we stand a chance of adding at least another hundred."

"Lira, you've been to Va'hesk in the east," Iva said. "How large do you estimate their settlement to be?"

"It's hard to say," Lira answered, "but perhaps three, four hundred tents were erected there. Larger than Énna, but smaller than Mór."

"What news of Clan Mór?" Aidryn asked.

"Most of the men and fighters went with Gerallt," Faolan answered. "They left a score of women, children, and elders behind in the mountains."

Iva swayed where she sat, and Lira felt the same. Though they farmed crops, Clan Mór depended on its men to hunt, fish, and gather throughout the year.

"Talfryn," Iva said, "I want you to ride for Rodhlan Ridge in no less than three days. Take two of my men with you and plant more gardens there, the way you did for us. I'll send a group of warriors behind you to establish extra protection for the settlement."

"Yes, Mam," he answered softly. Lira's heart suddenly ached for her brother. Being sent into the mountains meant Talfryn would be kept far from the battlefield—safe. She'd seen him fight well in the arena and hold his own. Being relegated to magical gardening wouldn't please him in the least. Still, his safety was one less thing for Lira to fret over.

Clan Mór was likely to be insulated from army invasion for a while yet. Accessing the mountain valley was quite a feat in itself. Gerallt would be more likely to target the Énna caravan and Va'hesk before trying to take a large army back into the Ridge.

"I'll go to Va'hesk," Aidryn said. "We're going to need their riders and any of the Itelorian stallions they possess."

Lira felt like she'd had her legs swept out from under her. She opened her mouth to protest, but Iva beat her to it.

"Not yet," Iva said kindly, but firmly. Aidryn's countenance fell. "I've sent two summons to their assembly, but have not received a reply. Wait until we hear something first. It's possible they could come to us."

He nodded, but didn't say anything more. And when Lira tried to catch his eye, he did not glance in her direction.

WHEN THE COUNCIL meeting was over, Lira slipped back into the adjoining room where Thorne had scolded her. She'd kept to the back wall of the main chamber, in hopes that she wouldn't have to pass Aidryn and the sentries on the way out. Her heart was pounding too erratically, her thoughts too scrambled to face them right now.

With trembling fingers, she unwound a bead from her hair and readied to *turas* back into her chamber. But Aidryn burst through the door angrily and stalked toward her before she could render the spell.

"You've gotten better at lying," he said. "When did *that* happen?"

Lira shrank away from him as he reached for her. "I haven't lied—" she said before he grasped her hands and pressed the bead to the pendant himself.

Turas deposited them in their chamber, where he locked them in. "No, you haven't lied outright, but you have omitted plenty. Your magic told me something was wrong this morning, but I didn't want to believe it. So I left the arena with the sentries, then came here alone to search the histories myself."

Lira was taken aback. "You used my magic?" She couldn't help feeling like he'd invaded her privacy.

"I *tried*," he said, raking a hand through his hair. "Turns out I need lessons. But something's wrong here, and I want to know what it is, Silira. I can't help protect you if you're leaving out bits of truth."

"I didn't tell you because you're going to be angry—I know it," Lira said. "And now you're angry that I withheld it, so it doesn't matter. I should have just told you—but I couldn't make myself. We finally had peace and rest and *happiness*, and now..." Her chin began to tremble. "Now I've ruined everything."

"You *can* tell me, Lira," Aidryn said softly, his expression pleading. He cupped her elbow gently and trailed his fingertips up her arm before resting a hand on her shoulder. "Please tell me. I promise, even if I'm angry, I will never reject you. I love you. Just—let me help."

"Why do you want to leave for Va'hesk?" she asked abruptly. "Is it because of me?"

His brow knitted, and he shook his head. "No, I—that was for another reason entirely. It has little to do with you."

"Then what is it?"

Aidryn looked stricken. "Let's sort one thing out at a time."

Lira bristled at his dodging. "So you can press me, but I can't ask questions? What are *you* hiding?"

"I'm not—" He pressed his lips together for a moment, then started again. "I promise I'll explain. But you go first."

Lira studied him warily. This wasn't the first time Aidryn had withheld something from her. He'd guarded quite a lot of information over the years. Perhaps since he'd held back before, he might understand why she had—especially now that he was clearly doing it again. So she swallowed her questions and nodded her assent.

Aidryn moved to the bed and sat down, inviting Lira to join him. She sat across from him, limbs trembling, and took a deep breath.

"You know as well as anyone that some details need to be withheld for a time, having done so yourself," Lira said shakily. "I trust you'll understand why I waited to tell you this."

He reached for her hand. "I'll try. I promise."

Tears gathered in Lira's eyes and her throat tightened as she answered, "The mortal god is Eremon."

CHAPTER 32
AIDRYN

Aidryn swore softly, running a hand over his beard. No wonder she'd been keeping this a secret.

Eremon, a mortal god.

The realization clanged through his mind, a chaotic racket that drowned out Lira's next words. He squeezed his eyes shut, opened them again, and refocused on Lira.

"I'm sorry, what?" he asked numbly.

"I said their original plan was to use you to get Iuchair from the crypt," Lira said. "It didn't work. And I was surprised Macha didn't know much about any of it. They locked her in with Eremon anyway, thinking she could figure out how to reach him."

Aidryn still felt numb, as though his mind was suddenly detached from his body. "I'll guarantee she knows more than she let on, or she wouldn't have made that bargain with you."

Lira laughed nervously. "No, she likely would not have."

He was almost relieved until Lira's truth magic pushed him harder. *Ask more questions*, it said, and his heart sank. "There's more, though, isn't there?"

Aidryn tried to remain calm, observing Lira's expression as it transformed into full-blown panic.

"Yes," she said, her voice breaking with emotion. "Think back to what Caitir told you. About this particular magic."

It's pure and uncorrupted. Nothing like the adulterated dark magic. Rather than killing me, it would keep me alive—maybe forever.

Aidryn remembered the way he'd felt when his sister described the power, too—as though just a measure of it could heal him in moments, if he could only take a little bit.

"She believes it could make her immortal," he said softly, brushing his thumb over Lira's knuckles.

"Now dig deeper," she urged.

Despite his attempt to stay level-headed, Aidryn was growing agitated again. "Stop avoiding it, Lira—just say it. *Please.*"

A tear slipped down her cheek. "Iuchair's use is at least threefold, based on intent," she said. "It can seal away magic and prevent it from joining with another host. Under the right circumstances, I believe a person with ill intent could take the magic themselves, though I don't understand the mechanism."

She took a deep, shaky breath before adding, "It can also resurrect a mortal god as an immortal in the flesh."

Truth surged through Aidryn. He dropped Lira's hand abruptly, as though her touch was suddenly scalding, and stood, pacing like a caged animal. How had he not figured this out already? All the signs were there. With a jolt, he remembered something he'd heard Caitir say to Lira: *When you learn the truth about that power, you're going to want it, and you'll be back.*

Lira was still sitting on the bed, staring at him, wide-eyed. She wasn't trying to hide her fear.

"Nami's rotting bones." Aidryn thought he might vomit. "You want to bring him back."

She closed her eyes with a shuddering sigh.

Aidryn's mind was reeling. "In what reality is it natural or advisable to bring a person back from the dead?"

He felt equal parts relief and horror. As much as he'd resented Eremon, it had been terrible to watch him die. Perhaps the kindest thing would be to give him another chance at life. But the thought of reuniting Eremon and Lira so soon made Aidryn feel as though he were tumbling headlong into Beran's Gorge.

Lira shifted uncomfortably. "There's something I want you to consider."

"Enlighten me—it's not as though I've had weeks to think this through, like you have," he snapped.

Lira recoiled as though she'd been struck, and he immediately felt a pang of guilt. But he shook it off, remembering the look on Thorne's face when he'd emerged from that chamber with Lira an hour ago.

"We might need Eremon's help to win the war against Gerallt," she finally answered.

"That's possible," Aidryn agreed. "But I still don't know that we should tamper with death."

"But what about Iteloria?"

"What *about* Iteloria?" Aidryn's heart was racing—arguing with Lira was the last thing he wanted to do.

"Eremon's existence violated a peace treaty Ulan made with Iteloria in the third age," Lira replied thickly. She wrapped her arms around her middle and dropped her head. "According to the treaty, Corlan should have taken Eremon to Iteloria as an infant, but he did not."

"To Iteloria?" Cold dread seeped into the pit of Aidryn's stomach; he wasn't sure he wanted to know the answer. "For what reason?"

"I suspect they would have put Eremon to death—taken his magic."

Aidryn's stomach clenched. "They would kill an infant for its magic?"

Lira nodded. "Somehow, King La'hiran knew Eremon's magic would kill him. So he sat back and let it happen." She chewed her bottom lip. "There's another key like Iuchair in Iteloria. I think La'hiran will eventually try to come for Eremon's power. And Iteloria is stronger than us—they'd have the upper hand in a war."

He leaned forward and rested his chin in his hand. "If we lock the power away first, we're in compliance with the treaty, right?"

She released a shaky breath. "I want to think so, but I saw something in a witnessing that made me think otherwise."

It seemed as though it took great effort for Lira to speak now. Though Aidryn didn't want to listen, he couldn't help but be drawn in by the rasp in her voice and her beautiful, mournful expression. He wanted to move closer to her—to kiss away this nightmare—but he restrained himself.

"Do you remember when I witnessed my father and Corlan dying?" she asked. Aidryn nodded as Lira continued. "They'd figured out what Eremon was, and they knew he was dying. That's why they went after the books."

She explained how the Itelorian king had stood down, anticipating Eremon's death. But Aidryn's attention snagged on something she'd said about a crystalline willow grove. He remembered seeing it in one of her visions, long ago.

"What did you say happened to Corlan's magic?" he said.

"I think the land took it," Lira said. "Or the willows. I'm not certain. But the moment he stepped into the grove, it's like all his power was siphoned out of him."

Another realization washed over Aidryn. If he'd just thought more deeply about it, he could have figured more out on his own. "I read something about this in the books the healer brought from the archive. But I was so focused on learning about Rodhlan's power, the information didn't really stick."

"What was it?"

He stared up at the ceiling. "It's not much—old legends, sparse records. But they suggest that Iteloria—the land—somehow replenishes itself with magic."

Lira murmured something unintelligible.

"Could you repeat that?" he asked.

She started. "Yes," she said. "It's something La'hiran said to my father before he was killed: that Iteloria required a sacrifice for Corlan's sin. The sin of concealing Eremon, I think. But he also said, 'For now, the land is satisfied.'"

"For now," Aidryn echoed. A theory was forming in his mind—and he didn't like it a bit. "That magic can't just dissolve into the ether when the power is locked away. Something has to happen to it; it has to *go* somewhere."

"Well, it probably goes back to their land, doesn't it?" she replied.

Again, her magic hummed to him in affirmation. A sudden weight settled on his chest. "If his magic became some sort of pure power after he died, that's not something we need to give away. It should benefit Rodhlan, one way or another, if it's to be accessed."

"So that leaves us two options: bring Eremon back soon, or wait to see if Iteloria makes contact," Lira said. "If we wait, we'll need spies to report on the ambassadors' dealings."

"If we wait," Aidryn said slowly, leaning against the far wall, "then we risk Iteloria coming to lock away the magic themselves. If a weakened Iathium isn't enough to attract their interest, Eremon absolutely will be."

A look of horror crossed her face then, as though she'd realized the same truth as Aidryn, in the same moment. "They'll come for us no matter what we do, then. And when they come, we're going to need all the help we can get."

Aidryn sagged wearily. "Then we don't have two options, Lira. We only have one."

He stared at Lira—who remained where she was, unmoving—for a long moment. *We finally had peace and rest and happiness,* she'd said. Yes, they'd had *everything* for a wisp of a moment. And now he faced losing it all to the same man who had taken Lira before.

Suddenly, the staggering unfairness of it all gripped him—took the breath from his lungs. Lira's expression crumpled, but Aidryn turned on his heel and stalked from the room. He slammed the door behind him before his sympathy could get the better of him.

Aidryn moved swiftly in the direction of the training arena. He needed to break something—someone—*now*. His body trembled, his breathing ragged as he moved. Though he was accustomed to living with a low-lying, ever-present anger that simmered constantly below the surface, he was rarely livid.

For three years, he had quietly raged at Eremon because he knew the Rí would take Lira for himself, no matter how Aidryn felt about it. That was the way the world worked. Kindness and loyalty never compared to power and money. Especially not to a crown—and certainly not to an immortal.

Two years before Eremon began pursuing Lira, he had known Aidryn was in love with her—and he hadn't cared. Instead, Eremon had backed Aidryn into a corner, coercing him into agreeing that he would not pursue Lira as long as he was still Lord Irem's heir. For two long years, Aidryn had done his best to forget he wanted her, but every effort to do so had failed miserably. And he had stood by and watched as Eremon romanced Lira, then irrevocably upended her life.

Instead of moving on and forging a life of his own, Aidryn had remained close to Lira, learning to better hide his feelings for her in the process. He'd despaired over a future he had never truly believed to be possible. Now that Lira was finally his, Eremon was going to shatter it all again.

And it wasn't only the inevitability of Eremon's return that stoked Aidryn's terror. It was the fact that Iteloria would undoubtedly be a factor in the greater war. Their involvement was something Aidryn had never considered, and Rodhlan was no match. Even if they had an immortal on their side, would it be enough to withstand La'hiran's legions?

Aidryn found himself in the arena a few moments later, unsure as to how, exactly, he'd gotten there. His walk across the fortress was a blur. There weren't many warriors training; most would be at their evening meal now. But Thorne was on the floor, and Aidryn made a beeline for him, drawing his sword.

Thorne seemed to sense his approach long before Aidryn reached him, for he turned, drew his own blade, and waited. "This is your fourth visit to the arena today, Tarlach," he said, his voice booming across the training floor. "You should rest."

"Damn all of it," Aidryn growled, advancing on Thorne and raising his blade.

Thorne met his strike with ease, moving back smoothly as Aidryn drove forward. His lungs were already burning, his arms and back screaming from the effort of hefting the broadsword. He was better, but not yet healed. Still, Aidryn pushed himself harder, sparring with Thorne until his side cramped and his tunic was drenched with sweat.

He was near collapse when Thorne disarmed him. The broadsword clattered to the ground, and Thorne kicked it across the dirt floor before Aidryn could retrieve it. When Aidryn surged toward it, Thorne grabbed a fistful of his tunic and pressed the tip of his blade beneath Aidryn's chin.

"Yield," Thorne said, his voice soft and lethal, "or you're done, Tarlach. Do you have a death wish?"

Aidryn barked a laugh, his throat aching and raw. "Some days."

Thorne released him then, giving him a little shove. Aidryn stumbled backward but quickly regained his footing. He glared at the warrior, but his rage had already begun to dissipate as exhaustion set in.

"Your anger is justified," Thorne said, "but let it pass."

"She lied to me."

"You know better." Thorne stared hard at Aidryn. "She

should have told you sooner, but any fool would understand why she did not. Or have *you* never kept something from her?"

There was a knowing glint in his eye that made Aidryn's shoulders droop. "I have," he said. "More than I care to admit. Most of the time, it was to protect her."

"She believed she was protecting you." Thorne sheathed his sword and kicked Aidryn's back to him. "But I'm not your mediator. You need to work these things out together." He pressed his fingertips to one of his shoulders. "You're bleeding. Best let my father see to you."

Aidryn vaguely remembered Thorne's blade striking him during the fight, but he hadn't registered the pain. Now, it throbbed and ached. "Can you patch it up?" he asked, glancing down at the cut. He wasn't particularly in the mood to see Ljós right now.

"I can," Thorne said, striding toward the stairs, "but I'm not going to."

He took the stairs three at a time and disappeared from the arena before Aidryn could limp to the bottom step. Sparring with Throne had been a stupid idea. Aidryn would need more than a simple healing spell for the wound on his shoulder. Ljós would have to work on his entire body again, and there was no telling how far he'd set himself back in the healing process.

Until today, Aidryn had done well pacing himself. But with everything that had happened, his emotions had spiraled. It didn't help that Faolan and Aeron had shown up here at the worst possible time.

Aeron had been right. The Binding *would* complicate things, now that they were here. For in coming to Fortress Halgeir with the sentries and refugees from Iathium, they'd brought along a final secret Aidryn had yet to reveal to Lira.

As he slowly made his way toward the healer's chambers, Aidryn feared that the combined forces of his secrets, Lira's omissions, and Eremon's return would seal the fate of their Binding for the worst.

CHAPTER 33

LIRA

Fortress Halgeir

Lira wasn't sure how late it was when Aidryn crept quietly into their room and shut himself in the bathing chamber. She lay on her side in bed, facing the far wall as she listened to him draw a bath. Nestling deep beneath the furs, she pulled them up over her shoulder, until they almost covered her face entirely.

She'd spent the afternoon lying here in silence, going over and over each detail of their confrontation. Aidryn had responded how she expected him to—worse, really, And he wondered why she wasn't an open book in this particular situation.

All this time, she'd been expecting to make the case that bringing Eremon back was the right choice. But in the end, she hadn't had to. They'd come to that conclusion on their own. Whether Iteloria came to avenge the broken treaty or to punish Rodhlan for raising Eremon, they would eventually come.

When the bathing chamber door clicked softly open again, Lira shut her eyes tightly. She wondered if Aidryn would leave again, but instead she felt his weight sink into the mattress beside her. Lira kept her breathing shallow and pretended to sleep.

"The sleeping act would have been convincing, if you hadn't covered your head with a fur as soon as I opened the door," Aidryn murmured from behind her.

"Oh," she said softly. Frustratingly, her body began to tremble, and she hugged her arms tightly around herself. The heaviness in her chest was overwhelming. It might have been a relief to cry, but she found that she couldn't.

"Lira..." he whispered. "May I touch you?"

She peeked over her shoulder at him. "Please."

Aidryn curled against her and wrapped his arm around her body, pulling her close. Lira let out a shaky sigh and relaxed into him, letting his warmth envelop her. They laced their fingers together and lay quietly for a long time before either of them spoke again.

"I'm sorry I didn't tell you sooner," she said.

He kissed her hair. "I know why you didn't."

Lira rolled over to face him, trailing her fingertips over his back. "We shouldn't keep secrets from one another. I don't want this to happen again."

His expression was pained as he kissed her forehead. "Neither do I. But I know what it's like to hold something close for fear of hurting the person you love. And in this case, it was a rather upsetting revelation."

"Aidryn," she said, touching his face and guiding him to look at her. "You know I love you. I chose you, and I will continue to choose you—even if Eremon returns. You are my husband, and you're the man I love. We can't let fear of the past spoil what we have right now."

He squeezed his eyes shut and let out a shaky breath before dipping to kiss her. For the rest of the night, they remained there, holding one another in the dark, quiet chamber. Lira desperately wanted to believe that they could go on as they had before, but something between them had broken, and she wasn't sure how to repair it.

"Lira!" Talfryn bounded across the courtyard toward where Lira and Oda were eating their afternoon meal the next day. "Bard's found Fannin."

"What?" Lira squealed, jumping up to greet her brother. "Where is he?"

"Out in the east pasture," he said, the color high in his cheeks. "Where's Aidryn?"

"I'm not sure." Oda turned to scrutinize her, but she ignored the warrior. "Probably in the arena with Faolan."

"I'll go get him," Talfryn said. He took off toward the corridor.

"What's going on between you and Aidryn?" Oda asked when Talfryn was out of earshot.

Lira sighed. "It's complicated."

"All right," Oda said, standing. She offered a hand to Lira and pulled her up, then set out walking toward the tunnel that led to the pasture. "You can explain the complications on the way to visit the horse. I know you want to see him."

Lira released a shaky breath, but took Oda's hand. As they traveled down the long pathway—which had been generously illuminated with torches, to Lira's relief—she explained the mortal gods' magic and the predicament with Iteloria. Oda listened quietly, never responding with judgment or contempt. In fact, she seemed to understand why Lira had kept the details about Eremon a secret for so long, and empathized with her.

"Most people would have made the choice you did," Oda was saying as they emerged into the sunlit pathway. Lush, rolling pasture land surrounded them on all sides, fenced in on either side of the dirt road where they walked. In the distance,

Lira could see the tents the warriors had erected for the refugees. "I would have."

"The last thing I wanted was to hurt Aidryn," Lira said softly. "But I did anyway."

Oda rested a reassuring hand on her back. "He'll be fine once he realizes you aren't going anywhere."

Lira paused on the road, skimming the fence line for signs of Fannin. She let out a squeal when she spotted the stallion several yards from where they stood. There was a dark-haired girl standing by the fence, hand outstretched, smiling as the horse nipped her open palm.

"There he is," she said.

She went to trot in Fannin's direction when she heard Aidryn shout, "Lira, wait!"

When she turned toward his voice, Aidryn was trotting toward her, looking panicked. "It's all right, Aidryn, they found him! He looks good from here."

She caught his hands, but he was staring past her, shaking his head wordlessly. "Is something wrong with him?" Lira asked, turning toward the horse again.

But Aidryn grasped her elbow and steered her away, back toward the fortress. Oda scrunched her nose, looking befuddled, before she wandered to the fence line and clicked her tongue. A brown mare approached, and Oda stroked the horse's nose, looking back at Lira and Aidryn worriedly.

"Lira, I need a word," Aidryn said, rubbing the back of his neck nervously. "It wasn't supposed to happen like this."

"What wasn't?" she asked, puzzled. "Are you not happy to have him back?"

"Yes, it's—it's not Fannin I'm worried about." He stole another glance in the horse's direction as Faolan and Aeron emerged from the tunnel.

Aeron stopped short when he saw Lira, clapping an arm out to halt Faolan, too. Faolan took another few steps in Aidryn's direction, but Aeron grabbed him and dragged him back into the tunnel.

"Those two," Lira said. Aidryn's expression was stricken as he watched the sentries retreat. "What's going on with them? You've all been acting strange since they arrived. I thought it was all about you-know-who…"

"No." Aidryn sighed. "I was angry about that, but this is a separate matter." He closed his eyes and sighed heavily. "It's the reason I panicked and asked to leave for Va'hesk."

"Why?" Lira studied his face. "I don't understand. Why would you want to leave?"

Why would you want to leave me?

"Aidryn Tarlach!" an unfamiliar voice called.

Footsteps approached from behind, and they turned to see the black-haired girl standing before them. She was smaller than Lira, with skin the color of sand and small iron earrings dangling from her lobes. Her face was upturned toward Aidryn, and she wore a pained smile.

For a moment, Lira struggled to remember where she'd seen the girl before. But she'd come to visit Aidryn in the archive once, a few years ago. She had asked about a ballad Lira was transcribing, and had brought a set of new horseshoes for Fannin.

Fannin.

This girl knew Aidryn's horse. She knew *Aidryn*. And, from the way she was looking up at him, she knew him well. Lira's knees suddenly grew weak as she tried to piece the answers together.

"Hello, Fiadh." Aidryn took a step closer to Lira and cupped her elbow.

"Fiadh Énna," Lira heard herself say. "I remember you."

"I'm surprised," Fiadh answered lightly, taking in Lira's outfit from her boots to her hair. "I almost didn't recognize you outside the archive."

"Fortress Halgeir isn't a place you expect to cross paths with old acquaintances," Lira said, eyeing Aidryn. He winced and looped an arm around her waist. She stiffened in his grasp, but did not pull away.

"Hardly." Fiadh glanced down at Aidryn's hand on Lira's waist, then back up at his face. "Well. Looks like you finally caught her attention."

Aidryn went completely still for a moment before he answered, "I did."

Fiadh crossed her arms, tapping the toe of her boot on the packed dirt road. "I'm glad for you, truly. It's what you always wanted." She kicked a pebble into the grass.

"What brings you here?" Lira asked. Aidryn squeezed her waist and gave her a subtle nudge, as though he wished to leave.

"Helping at the smithy. I'm here with my brother and cousin." She jerked her chin toward the tunnel entrance, where they'd been standing a moment before. "You know Faolan and Aeron."

"Yes, they saved me back in Iathium." Lira scrunched her nose. "I didn't know Faolan had a sister."

"Twins," Aidryn said warily, keeping his eyes trained on the girl. "Fiadh used to make horseshoes for Fannin."

"I remember," Lira said softly, recalling the way Fiadh had gone out of her way to see him in the archive. At the time, Fiadh's interest in Aidryn had been obvious—and Lira had encouraged him. Her cheeks warmed as she recalled the exchange.

"*She likes you,*" Lira had said. "*What are you going to do about it?*"

Aidryn had seemed uncomfortable with the suggestion. "*I don't have time to think about all that.*"

"*Excuses. You must have someone else in mind.*"

"*I do,*" he had answered, "*but I find her quite out of reach at present.*"

"Then maybe you should consider someone who is right in front of you, showing her interest."

Fiadh nodded—one too many times—and tucked a strand of hair behind her ear. "In truth, Aidryn, I came here looking for you. I was worried after everything that happened, then I heard you'd been captured. It's good to see you're well."

"I am," he said softly. He pulled Lira closer and kissed her hair. "Fiadh, Lira and I are married."

Fiadh inhaled sharply and pressed her lips together, looking to the sky, the dirt, the pasture—anywhere but back at him. Her chin trembled slightly as she rested a hand on the nearest fencepost. "Well, that's unexpected."

"I thought Faolan would have told you," he said weakly.

"Faolan doesn't tell me anything—just as you never did." Fiadh's voice quivered. She looked to Lira then, tears gathering in her eyes. "I suppose Aidryn never told you we had an understanding, more than two years ago."

Lira tensed, pulling out of Aidryn's grasp and turning to face him fully. "No, he did not."

"Ah," Fiadh breathed. "Then I suppose I'm not the only person he kept secrets from."

Lira's magic tugged in affirmation, and her heart sank. She took another few steps away from Aidryn and rested her hands on her hips, studying him closely. "I suppose not."

Aidryn's his eyes grew wide, his expression stricken. "Lira, we did *not* have an understanding."

"I knew that's what you would say." Fiadh hugged herself tightly. A bitter little laugh escaped her lips. "I'm sorry I thought I could hold you to it. But you're like those horses of yours—*no one* can hold you for long before you're fighting against the tether."

Suddenly, Lira felt hot. Her stomach churned and her palms grew clammy. "Forgive me, Fiadh. I—I didn't realize."

Fiadh closed her eyes and scoffed, her chin trembling. "It's just as well. I was never his first choice, and I've learned to accept that. I just didn't think he was the disloyal sort." She opened her eyes to look at Lira, but her chin trembled violently. Turning on her heel, she walked briskly toward the camp, swiping at her eyes.

Lira crossed her arms, glaring at the ground. "So that's what you've been hiding."

He stepped nearer. "Lira…"

She couldn't look at him. Instead, she stared after Fiadh, her curls blowing wild around her face in the summer wind. "Is it true, Aidryn? Were you to be married?"

"No," he answered pleadingly. "Though I suppose I led her on."

"You *suppose.*"

"I did—lead her on." He heaved a sigh. "I believed I could never be with you, so I allowed her to pursue me anyway. But my heart was never free, and I'm deeply sorry for it."

His truth resonated with her magic, but it didn't soothe the ache that had lodged itself deep within her chest.

"That wasn't fair to her," Lira said, her anger rising. "It wasn't right."

Aidryn's voice was almost inaudible when he said, "I know."

"And it wasn't right for you to keep her presence a secret. You *knew* she was here. Have you been coming out to see her? Is that why you've been disappearing?"

"No, I would never!" he exclaimed. "Lira, what have I ever done to make you question my loyalty?"

"You've lied to me before—many times. I understand lying about your family and the histories to protect me, but this?"

"Lira, I—"

"It was humiliating, running into her like that. I was completely unprepared—the *least* you could have done was give me a fair warning."

"I'm sorry." Aidryn looked like he couldn't decide whether to plead with Lira or stare at the dirt. He reached for her, but Lira dodged him and took off toward the tunnel. "Lira, wait—"

She picked up her pace and ignored Aidryn's calls, almost trotting now. Just as she approached the tunnel's opening, Faolan and Aeron stepped out of the shadows. They had, apparently, been watching the entire debacle unfold.

"That could have gone better," Faolan quipped.

Lira whirled on Aidryn, stalking back toward him. He nearly collided with her, and scrambled backward a step. "Do you think I'm an absolute dolt? How long did you think you could skulk around, pretending she wasn't here?"

Aidryn looked at the ground. "Maybe a little longer than this?"

"Wrong answer, Tarlach," Aeron said.

"You made me look *stupid*." Lira jabbed her finger at his chest. "If I'd known the two of you had a history—"

"History." Aeron chuckled. "Probably the only history you've ever wished to forget."

Lira turned on Aeron then, glaring at him. "We could do without your commentary. You helped him hide this." She shoved past him and moved toward the tunnel, but doubled back and added, "And you are *not* funny."

"Lira," Aidryn called.

"*Don't* follow me!" she shouted over her shoulder before plunging into the shadows again.

Tears stung her eyes as she broke into a steady clip. It wasn't long before someone caught up with her. As footsteps approached, she slowed, whirling. "I told you not to follow me—"

But instead of Aidryn standing there in the tunnel, it was Faolan.

"No, you told *Aidryn* not to follow you," he said, crossing his arms and moving to her side. "I'm free to do as I please."

"Well, you can do it alone," she snapped, trying to lose him.

But Faolan reached for her, his touch surprisingly gentle. "Lira, stop."

She stilled, turning to face him. His black eyes glinted like flint in the torchlight. The last time they'd been in a dark corridor together, he'd been escorting her from a dungeon cell beneath the Dome—before she'd known he was secretly helping Aidryn. He had been rude and abrupt with her, though he'd shown some semblance of relief that she had survived. Now, he felt more like her peer than her captor.

Lira shut her eyes and took a breath. "Fine."

"I don't do this often, so consider yourself lucky."

"Don't do what?" she snapped. "Have a civil conversation without hurling debilitating insults?"

He raised an eyebrow. "I can be pleasant company." She was surprised to hear a hint of amusement in his voice.

"The most accommodating and gracious," Lira added dryly. "Whatever happened to sibling loyalty?"

"I'm stingy with my loyalty. Being related isn't part of the criteria." Faolan smiled ruefully.

"Oh."

"I told Fiadh to leave well enough alone years ago." He kicked a pebble down the pathway. "Aidryn was always stuck on you—nothing about that ever changed. He wouldn't have looked at Fiadh twice if he hadn't made that deal with Eremon."

Lira turned to Faolan in surprise. "What deal?"

He leaned toward her conspiratorially. "Eremon made Aidryn swear not to pursue you for two years. He had to stand down until you were anointed Defender of Histories in his place."

She remembered the sudden change in Aidryn back in the spring, after she was made Defender—the way he'd shown up at her cottage and begged her to run away with him. How he'd suddenly cared who she gave her heart to. After years of holding back, pretending not to feel anything but friendship for her, he'd finally felt free to love her.

Faolan's words rang true.

"No wonder," she said. Aidryn must have felt so hopeless, to have been outmaneuvered by the supreme ruler. Suddenly, she felt a rush of anger toward Eremon.

Faolan seemed to understand what she was thinking. "What sane person would try to compete with the Rí? I always goaded Aidryn—told him he'd never be good enough for you. I don't think it helped when Eremon stepped in like that."

Her stomach clenched. "You told him he wasn't good enough?"

"I meant I didn't think *you* would appreciate him," Faolan said softly.

A lump formed in Lira's throat. "That's not fair—"

He crossed his arms and assumed a wide stance. "It's entirely fair. Whose love did you accept first?" Her jaw fell open, and Faolan smirked. "My point. You were always so aloof, like you had no idea how much he cared for you."

Lira frowned. "I didn't know how he felt. How could I have?"

He gave her a pinched smile and offered his arm. "You couldn't have."

She took Faolan's arm hesitantly, and he led her toward the fortress interior. Despite his attempts to be off-putting, she found that being near him felt easy and familiar, as though she'd known him her entire life.

"We used to call you The Book Wife," he ventured after a moment. "Guess it's true now."

She laughed in spite of herself. "The *what*?"

"The Book Wife." Faolan cracked a grin. "There was also Scroll Woman, Madam Tome, Mistress of the Archive, Archive Wife, Arch*wife*. That was mine." He snorted. "They were all mine."

Lira narrowed her eyes. "No." But there was a warmth blooming within her where her rage toward Aidryn had been moments before. She would have never taken Faolan for a mediator.

"The point is, you may not think Aeron is funny, but I am. I think that's all I'm trying to say."

"You were trying to convince me that Aidryn only had eyes for me, not that you were funny," Lira replied. "But it was a worthy effort."

He hummed softly. "I think he gave in to Fiadh for a little while because we all got on so well. But then, we started our work in the city with the clan descendants, and he got cold feet. Besides, we didn't want to get Fiadh involved."

"Why?"

"She can't manifest magic herself," he said. "It's a bit of a sore spot with her."

Aidryn, Faolan, and Aeron had worked together to master their own powers. Then, they'd helped to spread the clans' magic through Iathium, using fragments of the original written languages. Before Eremon's death, the three had been involved in a covert group that smuggled magic-wielders out of the city. Some of those refugees had joined them here at the Halgeir camp.

Faolan looked off down the tunnel, and Lira turned to follow his gaze. Aidryn, Aeron, and Oda were still several yards away, but were heading toward them.

"If you're still going to lose him, now's your chance," Faolan said.

She extracted herself from his grip. "How can I ever repay you," she said dryly, finally making eye contact with Aidryn. His eyes were wide as his gaze darted between Lira and Faolan. "It's fine. I'll wait here."

Faolan raised his chin, his expression hardening. "Don't expect me to come to your rescue again. That was the third go, if memory serves. More than that, and they'll think I'm soft."

Lira scoffed. "Wouldn't want to ruin your glowing reputation."

When Aidryn saw that Lira wasn't going to run again, he began to jog toward her, his expression stricken. "Lira, I'm sorry, truly," he said when he reached her. He cupped her elbows and traced his fingertips up her arms. "I can explain everything—you can look into my memories to see the truth. Whatever you wish."

"Aidryn," she said, holding up a hand to silence him, "I understand. Faolan explained. You can explain too, but later."

When they emerged from the tunnel, Faolan and Aeron peeled off toward the great hall. Oda followed, glancing worriedly at Lira before she headed into one of the corridors that branched off the courtyard. Lira reached for Aidryn's hand and pulled him toward their own corridor.

When she thought back on the two years before her magic manifested, there *had* been a subtle change in Aidryn. There had been a stretch of time when he hadn't walked home with Lira and Caitir as often. Lira had assumed he was busy training for his role as Defender, and had never questioned his absences. Further, there had been no reason to.

They didn't speak again until they arrived back at their chamber. Part of Lira wanted to shout at Aidryn more—to make him feel badly for keeping such a personal secret. But it *was* personal. It had happened before they'd chosen one another.

When they were both inside, Lira pressed her back to the door and let it click shut. She rested the back of her head against it for a moment and took a breath. Aidryn sank wearily onto the side of the bed and rested his face in his hands.

"I'm sorry," he whispered again. He didn't look up.

"There's so much you never told me," Lira said. "If I'd been paying attention, I might have noticed you were with someone."

"I wish you *had* been paying attention. I wish it had been you riding across the meadowlands with me, all those nights." Aidryn's voice was muffled. "I thought I could forget that I couldn't be with you. Instead, I ended up wishing she *was* you. It wasn't fair to either of us then, and it's not fair to you now."

"It also wasn't fair that Eremon forced you into that agreement."

Lira was surprised at the anger she heard in her own voice. Aidryn must have noticed it too, because his head snapped up. He met her gaze with uncertainty. "Faolan told you."

"Why didn't *you*?"

He shrugged halfheartedly. "Because it didn't matter."

"Why not?"

Aidryn looked at Lira as though she'd sprouted an extra nose. "Who was I to compete with Eremon?"

"My dearest friend," she answered, her voice rising. "My Aidryn."

"Your Aidr—" He cut himself off, laughed lightly, and shook his head. "There's no shame in having loved him, Lira. But you must understand why I was resigned to never having you. Eremon is the reason we're together now. Who's to say he won't come back and break the Binding just because he can?"

"I won't let that happen," Lira said.

Aidryn rose then, crossing the room to meet her by the door. "We may have no choice in the matter, just as we had no choice in the spell taking hold in the first place. *That's* the kind of power he will wield, Lira."

She stepped to the side to cover the door's handle, though he made no move to leave. "Don't go," she whispered.

"I wasn't going to." He leaned one shoulder against the wall and gazed down at her, cerulean eyes stormy. "I wanted to be nearer to you."

She closed her eyes and sighed, a weight lifting from her chest at the words. The previous day's distance had worn her thin, and Lira didn't want to spend another day hurting and isolated. They didn't have the luxury of time to hold grudges against one another. So when Lira felt the urge to step closer to Aidryn, she didn't resist it. She closed the distance between them, pulled him against her, and rose on her toes to kiss him.

He immediately broke away, searching her face. "You aren't angry?"

"Of course I'm angry," she said, kissing him again. "If you keep asking stupid questions, I'll be absolutely livid."

"Then why—"

He shut his mouth when she grasped his belt. "Because I don't want to think about it," she answered, working the buckle loose. Then, she tilted her head up to meet his eyes. "I just want you—right now."

"Are you sure?" he asked, though he didn't stop her from freeing him of the belt and scrabbling at the hem of his tunic. Together, they worked it over his head. Questions were still swimming in his eyes when he emerged from the fabric, and he opened his mouth to speak again.

"Quiet." She tossed the tunic onto the floor and pressed a palm to his heart. "Just—make me forget, *please.*"

Aidryn obliged her. For a little while, she allowed him to chase her thoughts away. But the problem with being a vessel of memory was that she could never truly forget anything. And despite her efforts to erase what had happened the past two days, Lira was afraid she might never be able to let it all go.

CHAPTER 34
LIRA

Fortress Halgeir
7 Weeks Later

Lira raised her sword and grinned as Oda advanced on her, bringing her blade down from overhead. The heavy *clang* of metal on metal reverberated into Lira's teeth as she blocked the warrior's strike. She stepped to the side, pushing her blade down the length of Oda's as she forced her opponent's sword downward.

"Good." Oda adjusted her grip on the broadsword. "Again."

They repeated the drill. This time, though, Oda broke the pattern they'd been following, disarming Lira and letting her own blade clatter to the ground. She drove her shoulder into Lira's, planting her right foot firmly behind Lira's as she followed through.

Lira's feet flew out from under her, but she broke her fall the way Oda had taught her, careful to keep her head from hitting the ground. The next moment, the two were grappling on the arena floor. More than once, Oda pinned Lira down, but each time, Lira extracted herself from the hold.

She thought that once she'd escaped a handful of times, they might stop to rest. But Oda didn't let up.

"Simply getting me to let go of you isn't your goal," Oda said after one such escape. "It's useful, but look how quickly I can entrap you again, because you aren't getting far enough away." To demonstrate, Oda shifted position and ensnared Lira again, straddling her stomach and pressing her weight down.

Lira struggled against the warrior, panting as she slyly planted her feet in position. "You want me to put more distance between us?" she asked.

The Brylla words still felt foreign in her mouth, despite the fact that she'd been speaking it for weeks now. Ljós had insisted on gifting the language to everyone on the war council to prevent sensitive information from spreading to eavesdroppers from the camp. Lira enjoyed practicing it during training.

Oda nodded. "Yes, enough that I can't reach out and grab you straightaway."

"You mean like this?" Lira let go of Oda's tunic and pressed her fingers into the arena's dirt floor, willing vines to burst from beneath the ground and wind around the warrior's ankles. Oda's eyes went wide as she registered what was happening.

Lira thrust her hips up and to the side to throw Oda off her. The vines did the rest of the work, dragging Oda halfway across the arena floor before receding again at Lira's command. Oda shouted the entire way, jumping to her feet the moment she was free and sprinting toward Lira, half-wild with delight. She retrieved one of Lira's small axes from the ground—discarded after target practice—and threw it at Lira.

Time seemed to slow as the weapon sailed end over end toward her. Lira swiftly conjured a shield of hardened leaves and raised it to protect her head. The axe bounced harmlessly to the floor.

Oda whooped and broke into a fit of triumphant laughter, resting her hands atop her head while she caught her breath. "Lira, that was *wild*."

From across the arena, Lira caught a glimpse of Aidryn. He had stopped what he was doing and was ogling her, slack-jawed, while Faolan pretended to impale him from behind with a long spear.

Her cheeks heated. "Children, the lot of you," she muttered to herself, though she couldn't help but enjoy the reactions she drew from him.

Oda stood, brushing herself off. "Best yet," she said, striding toward Lira. "You're so much stronger than you were, and your magic—amazing." She motioned vaguely toward the ground, where Lira's weapons had landed haphazardly. "Axes now."

She retrieved her axes and followed Oda toward the dummies on the far wall. Oda had replaced the shields a week ago, and already, they were splintered and split from the warriors' practice.

Lira set her stance and threw one axe, then the other. One lodged itself in the center of the shield. The other missed its mark and glanced off the dummy's arm. She groaned, watching the other warriors around her for a moment. When the others finished their throwing rounds, she could make a break for it and retrieve her blades. Until then...

She turned her palm upward and summoned long, narrow leaves into her hand, which she then fashioned into a small, sharp axe. Tendrils of magic shaped the leaves, twisting and curling them into the shape of a handle and a blade. When Lira was satisfied, she used her power to harden the weapon and weighed it in her hand before throwing it toward the dummy, too. Like the other axe, it bounced off the shield with no damage.

A flash of black caught Lira's eye, and she glanced to her left, where Fiadh was delivering sharpened swords to a group of sentries working with Bard. She usually spent most of her time in the camp outside the fortress. Fiadh was cordial enough when they came face-to-face, but her mood seemed to darken from one week to the next. Lira made it a point to avoid her as often as possible.

She'd learned that, before Fiadh, Aidryn had attempted to court several other young women who were part of Faolan and Aeron's social circle back in Iathium. None of them had held his interest for long, though, except for Fiadh. And perhaps that was what troubled Lira so deeply.

Even though they'd discussed the past at length, it hurt to know that he'd kept so many parts of his life from her, carefully compartmentalizing them and protecting them from bleeding into one another. He'd had his life in the archive, his life at home, his life with his friends, and his romantic life... and they had all been separate lives unto themselves until everything fell apart.

When Lira thought for too long about it, she couldn't help but understand why Fiadh had accused him of keeping secrets. That statement had haunted Lira relentlessly, even after she and Aidryn had gotten everything out in the open.

Fiadh approached them, and Lira tensed. She tapped her foot impatiently, looking from side to side for an opening. Looking anywhere but directly at Fiadh.

"Making the rounds?" Oda asked, though the warrior kept her eyes trained on Lira.

"The usual." Fiadh answered. "Working with Clan Beran's broadswords is a far cry from the sentries' blades in Iathium."

"You should come train." Oda glanced from side to side, noting at the same time as Lira that there was an opportunity to grab the axes. "I'll be back." She trotted off and left Lira standing there with Fiadh.

Lira had to bite back an indignant yelp. Oda was usually the buffer between Lira and Fiadh—the excuse Lira had to turn her attention elsewhere, to let someone else lead the conversation.

"She didn't let me finish." Fiadh rested her hands on her hips. "These heavy broadswords are no match for Iathium's.

They're powerful, yes. But the sentries' swords are light. Sharp. Perfectly balanced." She turned her attention to where Aidryn, Faolan, and Aeron were sparring. "It has been ages since I watched those three at swordplay."

"You should see them with Thorne. Three on one." Lira glanced around to see where Oda had disappeared to. Apparently, she'd retrieved the axes, but was now on the other side of the arena, showing the axe of leaves Lira had made to Aidryn, Faolan, and Aeron. Lira bounced anxiously on the balls of her feet.

"I admit, I was surprised to see you down here training." Fiadh made a show of unwrapping the last sword she held and polishing a smudge in the curve of its fuller. She ran her fingers over the pommel before wrapping it again and glanced up at Lira, a glint in her eye. "Until I saw you demonstrate your throwing, I was going to offer to sharpen your blades. Perhaps I should dull them for you instead."

Lira froze, unsure of how to respond. She wondered if Fiadh had inherited that same penchant for scathing humor as Faolan's, but something about the way she'd said it gave Lira pause. If it had come from Faolan, Lira would have snapped back with a sarcastic response—which would have earned a proud smirk from her friend. But coming from Fiadh, the dig hadn't sounded like a joke at all.

She finally settled on, "It's just practice. How's your throw?"

"I don't throw," Fiadh answered curtly, "but I can fashion a weapon that finds its mark every time—in the right hands, of course. My strength isn't in striking the target, but in giving someone more skilled than I the right tools to do so themselves."

Lira breathed in the now-familiar scent of stirring dust. She'd grown to enjoy the heavy clang of sword on sword, which had once made her flinch. Her gaze strayed across the arena to where Aidryn was driving Faolan toward the far wall. Their blades slid one over the other with a loud screech as Faolan managed to fend Aidryn off.

"If you were going to pair me with the perfect weapon, what would it be?" Lira asked absently.

Fiadh threw her dark braid over her shoulder and fiddled with one of her earrings. "A dagger, I think. Perfect for close combat, like an axe—but with the capacity for far more damage."

Lira held her hand out and summoned more of her emerald magic. Fiadh stared, wide-eyed, as Lira crafted a dagger of leaves, then hardened it before handing it over. The young woman weighed it in her hand, brushed a fingertip along the blade, then looked at Lira in surprise. "It's near perfect."

"I might not be much of a thrower, but I can craft a dagger well enough." Lira fought back a smirk.

Fiadh raised her chin and handed the dagger back. "A useful skill—well done." She hefted the sword she'd been carrying. "It's too bad you won't be on the battlefield to use it."

With that, she turned and walked briskly away. Before Lira could call her down, Oda returned to her side, handing over the axes. "What was that about?"

"I don't know."

Fiadh didn't look back as she reached the top of the steps. She paused to speak to Thorne before exiting the arena.

"She said I won't be on the battlefield, like she's an authority on the matter." Lira flipped an axe in her hand, catching it easily by the handle.

Oda shrugged. "We need as many people in battle as we can get. I can't understand Thorne passing up perfectly good fighters."

The noise in the arena abruptly died down, and everyone's attention turned toward Thorne as he made his way to the training floor. Several members of the war council gravitated toward him, and he spoke to them in hushed tones. His expression was grim.

Lira exchanged a glance with Aidryn as all of them made their way toward the warrior.

"It's time," he said when they reached him.

Lira's breath whooshed from her as though she'd been struck. "What?" She rested a hand over her heart and looked to Aidryn, who moved to her side immediately and wrapped an arm around her.

"Gerallt marches to the coast next week," Thorne said. "We're leaving in the morning and we'll face him before he gets to the Énna settlement. Council is meeting in my father's chamber tonight."

A hush fell over the arena as word began to spread. Faolan and Aeron exchanged a tense glance, and Aidryn tightened his grip on her.

"Tarlach," Thorne said, jerking his chin in the direction of the stairs, "a word with you and Silira."

Now, it was their turn to exchange a glance. Aidryn took her hand. They followed Thorne up and out of the arena, then through the fortress to the healer's chambers.

When they arrived, the chambers were empty. Thorne cast his father's silencing spell before he spoke.

"We've had word from Talfryn," Thorne said, motioning for them to sit at the table on the far end of the room.

Talfryn had been in Clan Mór's mountain settlement for nearly two months now, overseeing the care of the women, children, and elders Gerallt had left behind.

"Clan Énna has left its caravan and taken the forest route into the mountains on foot. They are planning to make camp in the valley until they can come back for their wagons." He picked up a mug and took a sip. "Some of my men are camping out in the settlement with Énna's fighters to keep the place stirring."

"That's good news," Lira said.

"We're spread thin already," he said curtly, setting the mug back down. "And I don't want to ask this of you because we need all the help we can get."

Aidryn tensed beside Lira. "What would you have us do?" he said.

"We need to move both of you as far from the fighting as possible." Thorne almost looked remorseful as he added, "And away from one another."

"What?" Lira cried.

"No." Aidryn grasped her hand. "I can't protect her if we're separated."

"Because of who you are—and because of the Binding— you both make us more vulnerable," Thorne said.

"No—Thorne, we make you stronger," Lira protested. "We're both anointed. Having our magic on the battlefield could mean the difference between victory and defeat."

Thorne raised a hand. "I know the ring protects both of you, even from a distance. But you each have the power to access that key, and our enemies know it.

"Gerallt is bringing his wives to the battle, and they've made it no secret that they are hunting powerful magic-wielders. They're using Artur as bait. Given what you figured out about Eremon and his power, neither of you should be in the heart of the battle."

"Then don't put us in the heart of the battle. Let us bring up the rear, protect the warriors from behind." Panic clawed its way into Lira's throat. "Thorne—"

"We need a chance to get to Artur, and we can't risk either of you getting captured or bartered in exchange for his release. We must remove everyone the enemy has taken a special interest in so we can focus on retrieving Artur, rather than using our energy to guard you."

"But—"

"You're both targets, Silira, and that's the end of it!" Thorne growled. "This isn't up for debate."

Aidryn's grip on Lira's hand tightened. "Well, where do you propose we go?" she cried, raising her voice. "Halgeir is the most fortified location in Rodhlan. Can't we stay here together?"

The warrior clenched a fist, the muscles in his forearm tensing. "No. The moment we march, the fortress becomes more vulnerable than ever. I can't trust that there aren't spies among the refugees. Any of them could betray you."

She looked to Aidryn. The terror in his eyes took her back to the courtyard in the spring—to the way he'd looked at her after Eremon died.

"Where will you send us?" he finally asked. He sounded resigned. Lira recoiled at the sound before she could stop herself, and he closed his eyes mournfully.

"Talfryn arrives tonight," Thorne answered. "Lira, you'll *turas* back to the mountain settlement with him in the morning."

"No," Lira said through clenched teeth.

How had she not seen this coming? She'd been relieved when she learned Talfryn would be kept safe, but hadn't anticipated that Thorne, Iva, or anyone else would use her brother's presence in the mountains as an excuse to send Lira there with him.

Thorne ignored her. "Aidryn, it's time for you to ride for Va'hesk. The Tarlach Assembly has twice denied us aid. I believe you can convince them if you go in person. With Gerallt's attention on the western coast, you're more likely to survive the journey. I'll prepare a traveling company for you."

Aidryn nodded once, but remained silent. Lira wracked her thoughts for something—anything. And then an idea began to form.

"You would prepare me for war, only to discard me in the mountains," Lira said. "There is an alternative, *sjeovi*. Hear me out."

"I will listen, but I'm certain this is the right course," Thorne answered.

"Send us into Iathium together," she blurted. "Into the crypt, while Gerallt and his wives are on the battlefield. It's the perfect time to awaken Eremon. We can do it quickly and return to the coast before the fighting begins. There's no way Gerallt can defeat the clans if we have an immortal on our side."

Thorne shut his eyes and shook his head. Her heart sank.

"Lira, there are too many unknown variables." Aidryn sighed, letting go of her hand to rub his eyes wearily. "Besides, there may be a reason we got word that all three will be at the battle. It could be a ploy to lure us into the crypt while we think they're all occupied."

"Don't forget, Macha is also lying in wait like an asp," Thorne said. "We don't truly know what she knows. If we're lucky, she's dead by now. But I doubt we're that lucky."

Their words resounded with Lira's power, but this time, Lira did not care about the truth. She ignored Thorne's words completely. "Aidryn, you *know* it's a good idea. Why are you siding with him?"

"I didn't say it was a bad idea," he said, "but I trust Thorne and I believe he has our best interests in mind."

"I trust Thorne too," Lira said softly, looking to her friend as she said so. "But I don't have to agree with him."

"You may not agree," Thorne said, "but I'm your commander."

"And who's commanding *you*?" she pressed. "Just now, in the arena, the girl from the smithy said I won't be on the battlefield. How did she know before I did?"

"It was a good guess," Thorne said.

"Fiadh's not on the war council, Lira," Aidryn said quietly. "She wouldn't know."

"She was awfully confident," Lira pushed back.

"Enough!" Thorne's voice boomed through the small chamber, and he raised a fist as though to hit the table—before he thought better of it and carefully lowered his hand. "I'm the authority here, Silira—no one else. If you want this clan's protection, you'll do as I say."

Lira's face grew hot, and she clenched her fists. "There it is. Just when I thought the next overlord would be a better ruler than Artur, you embody him to the letter."

"Lira," Aidryn said sharply.

Thorne stood abruptly and stalked to the door, throwing it open. "Get out."

Lira pushed to her feet, ignoring Aidryn's bewildered expression. Thorne's face was stormy, and Lira did her best not to shrink from him as she passed. It was, perhaps, the first time she had ever felt a trace of fear toward him.

Aidryn took Lira's arm and steered her down the corridor. "Do you have to attack everyone who tries to protect you?"

"He's trying to separate us. And it's obvious he's not the only one who wants us apart."

"What's that supposed to mean?"

"Fiadh!" Lira pressed her fingers to her brow. "She tells me I won't be on the battlefield, then half an hour later Thorne is saying the same thing? It's obvious she wants us apart. She spends so much time ogling you, it isn't funny."

"Sounds like she was goading you, Lira," Aidryn said, a current of thinly-tethered frustration rising with every word. "She's a lot like her brother—you just have to know how to take her personality. And if you're letting her get to you, then she's winning."

"You had to be there to hear what she said—how she said it." Lira tried to tether the growing fear that was gnawing at her. "You know what it's like to spend your days with people who wear different faces depending on who is watching."

Aidryn flinched almost imperceptibly. "You're right. I do. And two months ago, I understood why she might still be bitter. But she should be used to the truth by now."

"Well, she's not. She's going to love watching Thorne order us to opposite sides of the continent."

"She's not on the war council, so she won't know our every move," he said. "Besides, I think Thorne is onto something with this idea. We didn't think about the Binding making us vulnerable."

"Aidryn, you know we're better together—stronger, too. If he separates us, we can't protect each other. How many times have we both nearly died?"

He squeezed his eyes shut for a moment. "I know."

"There's something else Thorne didn't consider. We are one another's weakness. Our enemies can exploit that."

"You're right," Aidryn said. "And Thorne's right."

"Thorne is not right. He is so *afraid* of Eremon." Lira clenched her fists, her body beginning to tremble. "He's making all his decisions based on his fear of someone accessing that magic."

"It's not an unfounded concern."

Lira sighed heavily and shook her head. "You should be defending me, Aidryn, not sitting by while he orders us around."

"By advocating for your protection, I *am* defending you." He seemed to realize how loudly he was speaking, and abruptly began to whisper. "We *are* a liability. If one of us is captured on that battlefield or in the crypt, they're that much closer to obtaining the magic."

"So you're afraid of Eremon's power, too," she said accusingly.

He held a finger to his lips. "Of course I am, and you should be, too," he hissed.

"Having him on our side could help us win. If everyone fears him, will we ever be able to bring him back?"

Aidryn pressed his lips together and sighed. "I don't know. But I say we do as Thorne says for now, then regroup and figure out when to go to Eremon. Maybe wait for evidence Iteloria is on the move."

"We decided waiting wasn't an option."

"Well, perhaps it is."

Lira bristled. "We *have* waited—two months! How do we know La'hiran hasn't already sent spies into the city with Iteloria's key?"

"We don't," Aidryn answered, "but it's not likely. I still think Thorne is right: you go into the mountains, let me go to Va'hesk, and let's get on the other side of this battle before we go to the crypt."

"So you're content to leave the warriors vulnerable when they could have help?" Lira cried. "All because you're afraid of Eremon. I thought this was about the greater good."

He rounded on her and grasped her by the shoulders. "Lira, stop!" She froze, wide-eyed at his enraged desperation. "This isn't like you, and it's not going to work on me. If you're afraid, just say so. I'm afraid, too. But you will *not* manipulate me."

"Aidryn, I'm afraid." Her lip trembled and he pulled her into his arms, cradling her head as she cried against his chest. "I don't want you to go. I wanted us to do this together—all of it —the battle, Eremon, Va'hesk. I thought we could stay together for everything."

"So did I," Aidryn whispered, rubbing a soothing hand over her back. "But I wasn't thinking strategically. I was thinking with my heart. And sometimes you need a friend like Thorne who can use his tactical mind to make hard decisions."

"I still hate it," Lira said, her voice muffled against his chest. "I felt so helpless when I was alone and couldn't get to you. I never want to feel that way again."

"Then we'll make a plan," he said softly. "I'll go to Clan Tarlach—try to convince them to join us. Then I'll ride straight for the Ridge—straight to you. No battles in between; I swear."

There was no way he could guarantee that, but knowing he

meant to skip the battle was comforting. She tilted her head to look up at him. "At Fannin's full speed?"

"Faster."

She pressed her face against his chest again and hugged him close, breathing in his scent. "I'll hold you to it."

"Please do." He reached for her hand and laced his fingers with hers, breaking her grip to tug her along. "Come with me."

Lira sniffled. "But—"

He glanced over his shoulder, blue eyes glinting. "I have something for you."

When they arrived at their chamber door, he paused for a moment, closing his eyes and pressing his fingertips to the carved wood. Lira felt a rush of magic and gasped as it flowed through the Binding and flared from Aidryn's hand. When he opened his eyes, he leaned down to kiss her, then pushed the door ajar.

"Oh..." Lira sucked in a breath when she saw what was inside.

The chamber looked like a flower garden, adorned with climbing ivy and flowers of all hues. Vines wound their way up the bed's headboard, little white blooms bursting from them. Lira's magic pulsed and glowed from each leaf, each bloom, bathing the room in a soft, emerald shimmer.

"This is lovely." Lira looked up at him to find him smiling down at her warmly, despite the way she'd spoken to him in the corridor. She took a step forward, pressing her palm to his chest. "Aidryn... I'm sorry. I—"

"I know." He dipped his head to kiss her lightly, then pulled her down to sit beside him on the bed. Opening the pouch he wore on his belt, he reached inside and withdrew his closed fist.

Aidryn opened his hand to reveal a pair of silver rings. The larger band was solid and smooth. Lira gasped at the detail in the smaller ring—it looked like it had been woven from delicate vines, with tiny, intricate leaves gilded into the design.

He searched her face as she gasped softly, brushing her fingertips over the rings. "These are beautiful."

Aidryn rested his forehead against hers. "I've been trying to perfect them for weeks. Metalworking isn't my strongest suit."

"I'd say you underestimate yourself," she breathed.

"I wanted to work on them a little longer, but there's no more time." He kissed her brow. "I want you to have yours now. And I want you to remember, always, how much I cherish you."

Lira reached for his ring, but hesitated, her fingers hovering over it. "May I?"

"Yes," he whispered.

Lira slipped the band onto Aidryn's finger, then offered her hand to him. When he slipped her ring on, she didn't give him time to speak. Instead, she pushed him onto his back and kissed him fiercely. He pulled her down to him, and they lost themselves for a long while.

Already, Lira was mourning this—the tenderness in his voice, his touch, all the quiet time they'd enjoyed alone. Halgeir had cocooned them from real life, but in a matter of hours, reality was going to shatter it all.

CHAPTER 35
LIRA

Lira grasped Aidryn's hand tightly as they passed through the tunnel and out into the open air of Clan Beran's pasture. Dew still sparkled on the soft grass, the early morning sun blazing over the eastern horizon. In the distance, Lira could see a group of warriors and sentries saddling their horses near the camp tents—Aidryn's traveling companions, she assumed.

"I hate this," Lira said quietly, tightening her grip on Aidryn. "We could *turas* out right now—you and I. Just... find somewhere to lie low until this is all over."

Aidryn paused along the dirt road, pulling Lira to him and smoothing loose curls away from her face. "I want to. I wish we could." He leaned down to kiss her, and she wrapped her arms around his neck, standing on tiptoe to return his kisses. "I wish we didn't matter to this cause."

"I know." She took a step back from him and dug in her satchel, which she'd slung over her shoulder. "I have something for you, too."

From the bag, she withdrew a tight roll of scrolls. "This is folklore from Clan Tarlach," she said, handing the scrolls to him. "I transcribed it from stories Mytr and Nevala told me while I was there. I've been waiting for the right time to give them to you—something to read on your journey."

"Lira..." He looked as though he couldn't decide where to look—at the scrolls, or at her. Finally, he moved back in and embraced her fiercely. "This is perfect. Thank you."

She held onto him, breathing in his familiar scent, and pressed a kiss to the side of his neck. "I'll miss you," she said softly, resting her head on his shoulder.

"And I, you," Aidryn whispered against her hair.

"It's going to be hard to distract myself until I see you again." She looked up at him pleadingly. "I hate not knowing how long it will be."

"A fortnight, at least." His gaze was tender. "That is, if the assembly agrees to help us. It may take longer than that to get their cavalry ready. Or they might turn us away, and I'll see you again in a few days."

Aidryn held his hand out, and Lira took it again. They made their way toward the camp, where Thorne and Talfryn were waiting for them. Yrsa stood at Thorne's side, turning her attention to Lira and Aidryn's approach. The dawn light played across the flecks of gold in the great bear's brown coat.

"Who's traveling with you?" Lira asked, squinting against the sunrise.

"There was talk of Bard and Aeron coming along last night," he said, "but other than them, I'm not sure."

Thorne strode down the road and away from the tents to meet them as they approached, Yrsa ambling along beside him. He barely glanced at Lira before nodding to Aidryn, though the bear nuzzled her side gently. She ran her fingers through Yrsa's soft, thick fur, whispering to the gentle beast.

"Oh," Aidryn breathed, slowly stepping closer to Yrsa. "You're a beautiful girl, aren't you," he murmured in Brylla.

The bear turned her attention from Lira to Aidryn, looking

him right in the face and growling softly. Though Lira tensed, Aidryn remained calm. Yrsa blinked at him slowly and tilted her head, as if she understood every word. Then, she bent to nuzzle her forehead against his chest. Aidryn's lips turned up in a blissful smile, and he looked to Lira in wonder.

"Lira, just look at her!" he crooned softly. "Nami's bones!"

Slowly and easily, he raised his hands to rest them behind her ears, allowing her to nudge at him as he continued speaking to her. Aside from his horses and the kelpies, Lira had never seen Aidryn interact with other animals. She and Thorne watched him in silence until he muttered *big lout* loudly enough for them to hear. Thorne frowned as Lira suppressed a giggle. Aidryn grinned and waggled his eyebrows at her.

"Your people are waiting, Tarlach," Thorne said with an exasperated sigh. "I've given each of them a task to help you. Bard will see that they stick to their duties, and nothing beyond. Aeron will work negotiations with you."

"I understand," Aidryn said.

"You each have provisions for the journey," Thorne said. "Fiadh packed all of your saddlebags with meat and bread."

Lira scratched behind Yrsa's ear. The bear leaned into her touch. "Sounds like you're making her useful."

"I am," Thorne said, looking pointedly at Aidryn. "She's going with you, to help with the horses. Says she can make and fit shoes—and handle the Itelorian stallions. If Clan Tarlach agrees to send their horses, you're going to need as much help as you can get."

Lira blinked, then stepped into Thorne's line of sight. "You're not serious."

"I am." Thorne tried to sidestep her and double back to the tents, but she followed at his heels. Yrsa hung back beside Aidryn, who stood hesitating on the road.

"Absolutely not," Lira cried. She thought she heard Aidryn calling from behind her, but she stalked after the warrior anyway. "Why would you send her across the continent with Aidryn?"

Thorne whirled on her and grasped her by the arm, steering her away from the camp and out to the fence line. "There are six people going with him. *Six*. Her cousin is one of them—he can keep an eye on her. They have a job to do, under my orders. And Tarlach is a grown man—he can handle himself."

"Something's not right about her," Lira protested. "I've felt unsettled since the moment we met."

"I understand why," Thorne said, "but you're also a grown woman, and this is war."

"Do you care nothing about my feelings on the matter?"

"This isn't about you, *sjeinga*. It's about how we can help your husband gather his clan. We need them."

"I can't believe you let her talk you into this." Lira sighed, glancing tersely at Aidryn as he joined them, Yrsa following behind.

"Silira." Thorne's tone was sharp, and Lira couldn't help shrinking back. "You can't undermine me at every turn. I am commander, but many of the refugees look to you as a symbol of the cause. They know you're Iathium's rightful heir. If they see you openly defy every decision I make, they will not trust me."

"If I can't trust you to protect my interests, maybe they can't, either," Lira snapped.

Thorne stepped closer and glared hard at her. "*Your* interests? If it weren't for me, Tarlach wouldn't be here—and neither would you." She'd imagined an enraged Thorne would tower over her, red-faced, growling like some feral beast with muscles bulging and weapons drawn. But *this* enraged Thorne was deathly calm, his voice barely audible, his expression stricken. "And if it weren't for you, I'd have damned well left him in Iathium to rot. It's a good thing you convinced me. He, at least, lives by the loyalty and honor he claims to value. If I were you, I'd start looking past my own nose before I opened my mouth."

The warrior turned on a heel and left Lira standing by the fence, tears in her eyes. Thorne barked for Yrsa to follow, and she reluctantly left Aidryn's side.

Aidryn placed a hand on Lira's back as they departed. "You have to stop pushing him, Lira."

Lira whirled on Aidryn. "Did you hear what he *said*?"

"I did."

"Why didn't you protest Fiadh going along?" Her voice was unnervingly high, and she fought to breathe deeply—to calm herself.

"Because I'm trying to follow orders," Aidryn answered, rubbing the back of his neck.

"*Just following orders*. I can't believe you. It shouldn't be hard to change *one* person in your traveling party."

"But he's right! She *can* shoe horses, and we're going to need help filing hooves and shoeing the clan's herd if they agree to help us. We'll need as many people who can help as possible."

Lira nodded slowly. "And she can handle your stallions."

"Yes..."

"Because she used to go riding with you. On *your horse*." It stung to say the words aloud, even though she'd known for a little while. She'd also learned that Fiadh stole Edan, the other Itelorian stallion Aidryn's family owned, and rode him out of the city when Gerallt took over. "And now, she's taking your horse on a journey with you to *your clan*."

"It's not about you and me," Aidryn said, stepping closer and stroking her shoulders gently. Lira closed her eyes, resigned to his touch. She didn't have the heart to pull away— not when they were about to be separated. He cupped her cheeks and kissed her. "It's going to be fine."

"Something's not right about her," Lira pressed. "It might be my own feelings getting in the way—I don't know. Just be careful. I don't trust her."

"You know me—I can count the number of people I trust on one hand. I'll keep my eyes open."

Aidryn looped an arm around her waist, and the two of them trekked back over to the tents, where the horses were waiting. Talfryn was engaged in deep conversation with Aeron when they arrived, but he broke away to greet Lira, all pink cheeks and tousled curls.

"Is it time?" he asked, eyeing her pendant. "I've never been on *turas* before."

"Soon," Lira said, watching closely as Fiadh approached.

"We should go," Talfryn said warily, "right about now." Aeron must have filled him in.

Fiadh had a small smile on her face as she halted beside her cousin and looked to Aidryn. "Are you ready?" she asked, not bothering to look at Lira.

"As ready as I can be, given the circumstances," Aidryn answered, reaching for Lira's hand. "It's going to be a hard journey. I hope you're prepared."

"I don't think Fiadh knows a thing about sleeping outdoors," Aeron scoffed.

"You'd be surprised," Fiadh said. "It's quite nice, lying under the stars in the meadowlands. Wouldn't you say so, Aidryn?" Her gaze flicked to Lira, then back to him. "It'll be just like old times."

Aidryn's ears turned pink, and color rose in his cheeks. "Fiadh, that was wholly inappropriate."

There was an edge to his voice that made Lira pause to study him. Seeing Aidryn angry and embarrassed by a woman he'd once romanced was as dismaying as it was intriguing. Aeron and Talfryn backed away, clearly uncomfortable with the sudden tension.

"I'm sorry—I wasn't trying to offend you," Fiadh answered, shrinking. "I was only stating fact. We went stargazing before; don't pretend you can't remember." She laughed nervously.

"I do remember, but the way you phrased it sounded like..."

"*Not* stargazing," Lira finished for him.

Aidryn shot her a sharp look, then shook his head. "I'm going to saddle Fannin. Best get your horses ready too, Fiadh. Aeron." He strode off toward the pasture without looking back.

Lira was torn between following him and whirling on Fiadh. She settled on the latter. "That *was* inappropriate. You owe me an apology, as well."

"I owe you nothing," Fiadh said softly, stepping closer to Lira. "You heard Thorne. Aidryn is a grown man. I'll make sure he does what he likes while we're away." Her voice dropped to a low whisper. "And it's a good thing I know what he likes."

Lira slapped her across the cheek with a loud *crack*, so hard her hand stung when it was over. Fiadh's head snapped to the side and she stepped back, stunned, raising her fingers to the now-tender skin. She hurled some obscenity at Lira, tears in her eyes—but her ears were ringing with rage, and she didn't register what it was. For a moment, Lira thought she caught sight of a strange, faint scar on the side of Fiadh's neck, but when she turned her head, it disappeared beneath her collar again.

"That's enough," Aidryn barked, stepping between Lira and Fiadh. He pushed Lira behind him gently. "What did you say to her?"

"Nothing," Fiadh protested. Tears welled in her eyes. "She just lunged at me!"

"Aidryn..." Lira warned.

"I *saw* what happened, Fiadh," he said. "You're disgraceful." His shoulders tensed, fists clenched at his sides.

Suddenly, Fiadh's tears were gone, replaced with overblown indignation. "You're not going to say anything to your wife about attacking me?"

Aidryn paused, then turned toward Lira. "You're a grown woman, Lira; you know when someone needs a good slap."

Lira bit back a grin. Fiadh opened her mouth to reply, but

Aidryn leered down at her angrily. "Lira warned me about you, but I didn't listen. I'm rectifying that problem right now.

"You have a job to do on this mission, but that's where our interaction ends. As the only woman in the traveling party, you'll sleep in the center of the camp with protection on all sides. You will not keep night watch, and you will stick to your duties and nothing more."

Fiadh raised an eyebrow, though her lips formed a thin line. "I wonder if you'll order me around like a dog when your little *scholar* isn't standing here for the spectacle."

"Let me make myself clear," Aidryn growled. "Thorne may have approved the traveling party, but this is *my* mission, and I'll lead as I see fit. You follow my orders, or I'll leave you in the wilderness to rot."

Fiadh didn't reply, but whirled and stalked back toward the camp. When Aidryn turned back to Lira, he looked weary. "Lira, I..."

"Aidryn, she's *horrible*. How are you going to tolerate her?" Lira tilted her head, trying to picture Aidryn and Fiadh together in the past, but shook off the thought. "How did you tolerate her *before*?"

"I don't know. She's come a bit undone since then." Aidryn looked distressed before he added, "She'll be wishing she were back here after the first night. I'm sure I'll have a whole load of miserable stories to tell you when I return."

Lira couldn't help but laugh lightly as Talfryn stepped to her side. "Thank you for stepping in like that," she said. "I'm glad you saw it happen."

"I'm sorry I didn't understand before," Aidryn said, stepping nearer. He'd trimmed his beard shorter, and he was wearing the sky-blue tunic again—the one that made his eyes almost glow like magic. "I'll keep a close eye on her. You need not worry."

"I trust *you*," Lira replied, pressing her fingertips to his chest, just beneath the laces on his collar. "It's her I'm worried about."

"I understand why."

"Let's not talk about her any more. Just... be careful out there." She tilted her face up to regard him.

Aidryn pulled her to him, his familiar scent enveloping her. Lira melted into his arms. "Silira." His voice rumbled against her ear. "What are we calling you these days? Silira Tarlach has a nice ring to it."

"Mmm." She pulled him closer. "Silira Mór for official business. Lira Tarlach otherwise."

"I like that." Aidryn smiled warmly and cradled the back of her head, guiding her into a soft kiss. A surge of desperation tore through Lira, and she deepened the kiss, pouring every bit of her love and desire and frustration into him. She stood on tiptoe and wrapped her arms around his neck as they shared one kiss, then another, and another.

"Aidryn!" Aeron called from the camp. "It's time!"

Aidryn's lips lingered over hers, pressing soft, yearning kisses against her mouth. Lira gasped softly as his other hand slid to the small of her back to draw her in, and she was suddenly weak with the sensation of it all. She clung to him as though he might disappear.

"Aidryn, I love you," she said, her voice breaking. "*Please*, come back safely."

"I promise," he whispered, tears glistening in his eyes. "Wait for me at Rodhlan Ridge. I'll come for you there."

Reluctantly, they released one another. Lira stepped away from him and grasped Talfryn's hand. From the pouch at her hip, she withdrew a small gilded leaf—one of the heirlooms Skelly had given her in childhood that would now *turas* them out to Clan Mór's mountains. With a final look at Aidryn—who was now staring helplessly—she pressed the leaf to her pendant. She never broke eye contact with her husband until the spell swallowed them up.

CHAPTER 36
AIDRYN

Meadowlands
5 Days Later

Aidryn bundled into his bedroll to fend off the autumn chill. The nights were beginning to grow cool, and he couldn't help but regret the timing of this trip for many reasons. He'd thought traveling to Va'hesk would help him feel purposeful—powerful, even—but instead, he felt as though he floundered through each decision and every move along the way.

Along with Aeron, Fiadh, and Bard, Thorne had sent three other warriors: Gidri, Mjit, and Rynd. He couldn't keep the three young men's faces and names straight, to his endless humiliation. So he tried his best to avoid addressing any of them by name, instead doling out general instructions when circumstances called for it.

He'd expected his first time riding across the meadowlands since Lira saved him to be an equally freeing experience. Instead, Thorne's orders had chained him to Fiadh and the old memories he'd tried to escape. Aidryn had managed to keep interactions with her to a minimum, but his mood grew darker by the day.

Lira was right; he shouldn't have gone along with Thorne. But after she'd openly challenged the warrior—more than once—Aidryn had wanted to make peace with him. Now, he deeply regretted agreeing to this arrangement, but there was nothing he could do about it.

The group's progress had been slower than Aidryn expected. He and Fiadh had the only Seanlaoch in the party, so it was no surprise they needed to keep pace with the slower horses. But Fiadh was more poorly equipped for travel than she'd let on, and had not proven herself the least bit useful beyond the promise of horseshoes.

Bard had taken over cooking in the evenings after Fiadh's first few disastrous attempts.

"It's a good thing you know what you're doing, Bard," Aeron had said around a mouthful of hot porridge on the third evening. "We'd starve otherwise."

Fiadh had pulled her knees up to her chest and sulked before she left the fireside to visit Edan.

More than once, Aidryn thought to say something to her about taking the black stallion for herself. But he bit his tongue each time and forced himself not to. She'd bonded with Edan, and had known she could get out of Iathium faster with him. Still, it gnawed at Aidryn that she'd felt comfortable enough to take ownership like that. He was caught between gratitude that someone was caring for Edan, and resentment that it was Fiadh.

On the fifth evening—another two days' ride from Va'hesk—Aidryn sat by the fire, sipping water after a hot meal. It was dusk and almost time to snuff the fire when Fiadh took a seat next to him, resting her hands on her knees. Aidryn spared her a glance out of the corner of his eye, but kept his face turned toward the fire.

"I suppose you hate me now," she said softly, poking at the guttering campfire with a stick.

"No," he ventured, taking a drink. "I've never hated you."

"Then why do you refuse to look at me?" She scoffed softly. "You never made me feel inferior before you had *her*, but now..."

"You know I don't think you inferior." He pressed his lips together before replying. "I know what it's like to feel that way—like you'll never compare to someone. I've come to believe that feeling goes away when you've found the right person."

"Does it go away when the person you love has no choice in your arranged marriage?" She leaned forward, trying to catch his eye. "Or just when the first suitor is dead?"

Aidryn finally turned his head to look at her, and her eyes were bright with a sharp glee that made him recoil. Lira was right—there was absolutely something unsettling about Fiadh. He stood abruptly, walking toward Fannin to stash his cup and retrieve his bedroll from the saddlebag.

Draping his arms over Fannin's back, he hung his head and tried to gather his thoughts. But he heard her footsteps halt a few feet away from him, and he whirled on her.

"Before we were together, you *knew* I was in love with Lira," he blurted. "I never hid that from you. I was honest when I said I wasn't ready to ask for your hand. But you weren't honest about who you really are. I've never seen this side of you, and it's disturbing."

"And what side is that?"

"Spiteful, calculating, manipulative."

"Oh, Aidryn, I've always been strategic." She crossed her arms and shrugged. "I wouldn't call that manipulative."

"Then we have wildly different definitions of the word *strategy*." He tugged at one of the buckles that held his bedroll on Fannin's saddle, thinking back to their days in Iathium. Fiadh had once asked him what he looked for in a woman, and he'd answered honestly—and listed Lira's attributes. That was before he and Fiadh became... whatever they had been. They'd blurred the line between friends and lovers, never quite landing firmly on either side.

The more he'd begun paying attention to Fiadh back then, the more she seemed to embody so many of the traits he admired in Lira. Perhaps that's what had made him pause and pay closer attention. He'd thought he could find a similar sort of woman to move on with. But as he considered Fiadh's admission to being strategic, as she put it, he wondered whether she had simply mirrored Lira to ensnare him.

"We also have wildly different definitions of the word *honor*," Fiadh said softly.

"*Stop* accusing me of dishonor and disloyalty." Aidryn was on the verge of shouting now. "Unfairness, yes. I'll give you that. I wasn't fair to you, or to myself. For that, I'm sorry."

"Sorry's not enough. I *loved* you. I still love you. I thought I would be your wife. I came to the fortress hoping to win your affection again, and then I found you with her—*married* to her—and I can't..." She squeezed her eyes shut and a tear rolled down her cheek. "Do you know how humiliating that was?"

"You're not the only one who was humiliated." He loosened the second strap and removed the bedroll, tucking it under his arm. "You deliberately tried to turn Lira and me against one another. She did nothing wrong; you should have let her be."

She sighed. "No, she really didn't. I can't blame her for giving in to you." Fiadh opened her eyes again, and her gaze was as hard as granite. "She had no better option."

"You know *nothing* about what happened between us," Aidryn said, though her words tore at his insides. Lira's magic was silent, but that didn't stop his mind from racing—from questioning. "And I don't owe you an explanation for it. I broke from you last summer, so stop deluding yourself. You will *never* change my mind."

"You don't mean that," she said, moving closer. "I think you still feel something for me."

Her proximity was overwhelming, and he suddenly felt overheated. It was unnerving to feel his body betray his heart and mind this way. *This* was why he'd distanced himself; she stirred unwanted feelings and memories he'd made a concerted effort to forget. He took a step back, but she closed the space between them again.

"Do you think it's convenient for me to be here, making a fool of myself?" she asked. "I love you because I am incapable of anything else. My heart is like glass; it's unchanging. You can break it, over and over. It may tear me apart inside, but it will still be yours—every shard."

It suddenly grew darker, as though the sun had abruptly dipped below the horizon. Aidryn glanced back toward the camp, where Aeron was busy putting out the fire. Bard and the other warriors were nowhere to be found; they must have been scouting the perimeter.

His momentary lapse of attention had given Fiadh the chance to move in on him again. When he turned back to her, she grasped his hand and set it on her waist, raising her own hand to trace his cheek. He shivered at the contact.

"Stop pretending you don't miss this," she whispered. "I'll give you everything, with no expectations. Just... *please...*"

"No," Aidryn said sharply, stepping away to break her hold on him. "Lira was right. You have no business being here. The only reason I agreed to this was to stay on good terms with Thorne. It had nothing to do with wanting *you.*"

"Aidryn..."

"No!" he repeated. "Your only value here is horseshoes. You're dead weight otherwise. From now on, keep your distance and don't say another word to me."

The words were cruel—cutting—and Aidryn knew it. He normally kept his temper on a tight leash, but he'd had years of practice both dealing out and absorbing sharp, heartless words. Suddenly he realized, horrified, that hurling them at Fiadh made him feel better. In some sickening way, cruelty briefly reconciled some of the pain that twisted his insides.

It hurt that he'd wounded Fiadh, and that she had never recovered.

It's her fault she wouldn't accept the truth when I gave it to her.

It hurt that she'd deliberately used their past to wound Lira —and that by trying to erase the past, Aidryn had hurt Lira, too.

I should have told Lira everything years ago.

It hurt that Eremon had made Aidryn feel so defeated that he couldn't imagine Lira ever loving him.

I should've never been with Fiadh at all.

Most of all, it hurt that Aidryn could be so easily betrayed into feeling desire for Fiadh again, however fleeting and unwanted.

I wish I'd never agreed to this.

"Horseshoes," Fiadh said, taking a shaky breath. "That's all I ever really meant to you, isn't it? I thought we had something more than Fannin's stupid shoes."

"There *is* nothing more," he said. "We were finished long ago."

She nodded and laughed bitterly, stepping near enough to shove him. "You used me as a distraction and discarded me the moment something better came along. Maybe you were finished with me, but I never stopped loving you. I think that's my lot, though—I've never been anything of significance to anyone. But you'll see—I'll make something of myself yet, and you'll wish you'd never crossed me."

Aeron stepped between them, grabbing hold of his cousin's shoulders. "Fiadh, what are you doing?"

She jerked away from him, still glaring at Aidryn. "You think I don't know Silira wants to resurrect her dead lover? What are you going to do when he returns, more powerful than you could ever be?"

As her words hit their mark, Aidryn thought he might collapse. "How do you know about that?"

And then he looked to Aeron, whose expression had shifted from frustration to horror. "I'm sorry, Aidryn. I—"

"That information was never supposed to leave the war council," Aidryn shouted, advancing on Aeron. He drew his sword, and Aeron responded in kind. Their blades clashed hard, and Aidryn drove his friend into the center of the camp.

"I didn't mean to repeat it," Aeron said, scraping his blade down Aidryn's before blocking his next strike.

"How could you?" Aidryn pushed harder. "What were you thinking?"

"I don't—" Aeron sidestepped Aidryn— "know!"

Aidryn rushed him again, this time placing a foot behind Aeron's and knocking him to the ground, disarming him. He held the tip of his blade to Aeron's throat, panting hard. But he softened at the terror in his friend's eyes.

"Stop!" Fiadh cried. She had mounted Edan, and the stallion stamped nervously into the middle of camp, trampling the campfire embers.

Bard and the other warriors approached then, weapons drawn. "What's going on?" Bard demanded.

Aidryn held his blade steady, though his rage was abating. "Trouble from these two. It won't be repeating itself. Fiadh, dismount. I'll deal with you in the morning."

"You won't be *dealing* with me like some unruly house pet," she said. "I'm finished here."

"I said dismount!" Aidryn shouted, stepping away from Aeron and sheathing his sword. "You will *not* leave here on my horse." He gripped the reins for emphasis.

Fiadh blinked slowly, then leered down at him. "I hope Silira causes you *every* ounce of the pain you've inflicted on me, because you will *never* compare to Eremon." Then, she leaned down and patted Edan's neck, letting her gaze slide to Aidryn as she whispered, "*Ano je.*"

The horse bolted, ripping the reins from Aidryn's grip, and he watched in disbelief as she steered Edan toward Iathium at his full, *magical* speed. He could barely think as he crossed the camp to where Aeron was pushing himself to his feet. Aidryn grabbed a fistful of Aeron's tunic and yanked him close.

"Did you give her the incantation for the horse, too?" he seethed. His hand burned from the reins.

"No!" Aeron cried. "You spent enough time with her out here—she might've picked that up for herself."

Aidryn swore, shoving Aeron away from him. "I should never have trusted you and Faolan on the war council. I gave Thorne my *word* he could trust you."

Aeron flinched, his gaze dropping to the ground. "Leave Faolan out of this, it's my doing."

"You've made a fool out of me." Aidryn untethered Fannin, hastily stuffing his bedroll back into the saddlebag. "And now you've endangered everyone."

"How?" he asked. "What difference does it make if my cousin knows what Lira wants to do?"

"Because your cousin could take that information anywhere! Fiadh knows all our movements, all our locations. If she wants to take us down, she has everything she needs to do it."

"She wouldn't do something like that," Aeron said, though his voice broke as he said it. "She's likely running back to Faolan."

"Why, so he can comfort her?" Aidryn snapped.

Aeron took a step back, hanging his head. "I'll go after her."

"You damn well better—but good luck catching up." Aidryn mounted Fannin easily, settling into the saddle.

"Tarlach," Bard called. "We need to make camp here. It's too dark to keep going."

"Not for me," Aidryn said. "I'm riding ahead to Va'hesk. You lot can catch up at your own pace."

"Thorne said—"

"I'm done with being delayed." Fannin shifted, as though he knew Aidryn was finally about to unleash the stallion's full measure of magic after so many months of separation. "Who knows what she's after. But we can't waste any more time."

Before Bard could protest, Aidryn nudged Fannin into a gallop, then spoke his clan's incantation. He was enraged at himself for failing to stand up to Thorne. Aidryn had wanted to keep the peace—had gone along with the warrior's plan to send Fiadh with his traveling party. But Thorne had known better. There was no way he hadn't.

Aidryn hadn't spoken up because he'd doubted Lira's instincts about Fiadh. With a sinking feeling, he realized his fear of bringing Eremon back had tainted his trust in Lira's warnings. He'd convinced himself that he could play by Thorne's rules without disastrous consequences. Instead, he should have snuck out of the fortress with Lira—gone with her to the crypt like she'd asked. Now that Fiadh knew about Eremon, it felt as though their time to wait had run out.

Fannin picked up speed, and they rode through the night with terrifying fury. Aidryn was dismayed that this ride held no joy, but instead a deep, driving fear that their plans were about to go terribly wrong.

CHAPTER 37

LIRA

Rodhlan Ridge

L ira's screams tore through Skelly's little cottage in the dead of night, so loudly she woke herself. She sat bolt upright, panting, her heart hammering as Talfryn skidded to the door and peeked into the bedchamber.

"What's wrong?" he asked frantically, crawling onto the bed beside her.

"Something's happening," she gasped, her fingers tingling. She remembered flashes of a nightmare—swords clashing, bonds breaking. The tingling sensation rushed up her arms, and she fell back against the pillows as a witnessing overtook her.

She saw Aidryn. Fiadh. Aeron. Fannin galloping across the meadowlands in one direction, Edan in the other. One after another, memories slammed into her, and her head *ached*. It was as though the witnessing was being forced into her mind.

Somewhere on the edges of the vision, she could feel Aidryn's presence. The essence of his magic shimmered against the memories, and suddenly, she knew what was happening: Aidryn was sending his memories to her through the Binding.

As she emerged from the witnessing and her sight cleared, she looked to Talfryn in alarm.

"Aidryn's broken from Thorne's traveling company," she said, rising and throwing a dressing gown around her shoulders. "Because of Fiadh—she knows about Eremon."

"What?" Talfryn demanded. "What's he trying to do?"

"He's..." Lira was trembling too hard, her hands shaking as she tried to start a pot of tea over Skelly's hearth. "He's—I think —I—" A sob broke from her, and she almost dropped the pot.

Talfryn placed his hand on her shoulder. "Lira. Stop for a moment." He tugged his sister to him and embraced her. She was shuddering, fear tearing through her as the memories fully registered. Once she got control of her breathing, she told Talfryn what she'd seen.

His expression darkened. "Can your magic tell you how long it's been?"

"Tonight, I think—maybe a few hours ago."

"We need to know where Fiadh's going," Talfryn said. "And Aeron. If Aeron thinks he can come back to Thorne's army after this, he's sorely mistaken. Thorne will have him executed."

"Then he won't be back," Lira answered softly, "and neither will Fiadh."

Lira sat heavily on the work table bench while Talfryn finished the tea and poured each of them a cup. His hand was steady, his demeanor alarmingly tranquil.

"How are you so calm?" she asked.

"This was part of our sentry training," Talfryn said. "Expect deserters. Don't let your judgment be clouded by your emotions when someone defects—especially if it's a friend. I just..." He stared into the fire, cracks finally appearing in his composure. "I didn't expect it to be Aeron."

"Who did you suspect might run?" Lira asked.

"I don't know, but not him. Fiadh? Absolutely."

Abruptly, Lira rose, setting her mug on the table. "I'm going to have to do it; there's no avoiding it," she muttered to herself, heading back into Skelly's room. Talfryn followed.

Her brother leaned against the door facing. "Do what?"

She swallowed hard, heart pounding. "First, I need you to swear you won't talk me out of it."

"Why? What are you doing?"

Lira arranged the pillows and sat on the bed. "I can search Fiadh's recent memories, but there's a cost."

"What cost?" Talfryn took a step closer. "I don't like the sound of that."

"A tremor," she answered, holding up her right hand. "Sometimes, I feel ill. I just need you to be ready to help me if it gets worse."

"Worse like how? Like the way you get tired when you *turas* cross-continent?"

"I don't know. I worry that using the magic this way too often, or for too long, could have a much greater cost than nausea or a twitch. Like it could consume me from the inside if I'm not careful."

Talfryn paled. "But—"

"Doing this will give us the answers we need." She took a shaky breath. "I can't think too much about it, or I might not have the courage. Just—be here, all right?"

Her brother's eyes were wide as he nodded. "All right." He sat down beside her and held her hand. "What if you do lose yourself to your magic again? How do I help you if that happens?"

"Then get me back to the healers at Halgeir, whatever it takes," she answered. She'd felt her own overabundance of power and knew the rush of wielding it all too well. Something within her insisted that she could easily be consumed—*too* easily. The instinct set her on edge.

Talfryn must have sensed the same. His expression held a hint of awe—and fear, perhaps. "You could be a real terror. You know that, right?"

"I will be no such thing." She lay back on the pillows, gripping her pendant, and let her eyelids flutter closed. "Rhona, forgive me. Give me the strength to emerge from this."

Feeling for her magic, Lira asked, *What are Fiadh Énna's intentions?* Then, the power swept her under.

Pain jolts Fiadh's knees as they hit the marble tile of one of the Dome's many audience chambers. Her head throbs from the blow she took from a sentry's gauntlet on her way into the paddocks at the Tarlach estate. She isn't sure whether she was carried or slung over a horse's back as an afterthought, but her entire body aches.

Panting, she braces herself on her hands and knees, dropping her head before the golden beauty who stands before her.

"What have we here?" Caitir crouches before Fiadh, coaxing her to make eye contact. The new Rí's second wife has pale blue eyes, nearly devoid of color, that are both terrifying and unusual, and Fiadh finds it difficult to hold her gaze. She has seen Aidryn's sister from a distance before, but doesn't recall noting those eyes.

"Fiadh Énna," she says, her voice barely above a whisper. "I'm at your service."

It turns Fiadh's stomach to be here, pathetically begging another Tarlach for something. The thought is surprising as it rattles through her mind, and she tries not to focus on Aidryn's many rejections.

No, no, no. Always with Aidryn, it was no. Just when Fiadh had thought he was truly hers, he'd turned her away.

"I know who you are." Caitir's voice is cold, refined by nearly two decades of grooming for a place of royalty. "Twin to the traitor Faolan."

"Yes." Fiadh's own voice sounds foreign to her ears.

"Did my men catch you at espionage, or are you a simple horse thief? You tried to leave the city on one of my brother's prized stallions."

"I bonded with Edan, my lady," Fiadh answers. "The horse trusts me."

"How did you manage that?" Caitir raises her eyebrows. "Aidryn lets no one near those beasts unless they've earned his utmost regard."

Fiadh swallows hard, her mouth suddenly dry. What is she thinking, betraying Aidryn this way? Putting Faolan and Aeron in danger? But the boys have made their own beds. They've all followed Silira into a rebellion. So perhaps it's really Silira she is betraying.

She will do anything to destroy Silira.

"Because I was Aidryn's lover," Fiadh says, the lie flowing easily from her mouth. *It's only a hair's breadth from the truth.*

Caitir straightens, her gaze hardening. "He always was secretive," she muses, "but I can't see that. He would've died a monk before he took a lover who wasn't Silira."

"Then perhaps he was ashamed of me." Her words emerge in a garbled, quivering mess. "I'm the daughter of a blacksmith, you see. I forged shoes for your family's horses. He kept me a secret from Silira, just as he kept me from you and the rest of your family."

She doesn't have to fake the pain that shatters her inside as she says it aloud. And now Caitir is listening, fully intent on Fiadh's every word.

"I took Edan because I wanted to look for Aidryn," she lies. "I heard he was being held prisoner here, and I thought I could save him."

"Aidryn is alive and well," Caitir replies, her gaze sharp on Fiadh's face. "He is being held at Clan Beran's fortress, and I hear talk of a refugee camp going up in their eastern pasture. Your brother is among the traitors escorting clanspeople to the camp. Why don't you join him? Find out what you can about my brother and Lira—what the army is doing. Then report back here."

Fiadh might vomit. As much as she hates Silira, it wasn't her intention to be made a spy. She'd wanted a horse to get out of Iathium—that was all. But perhaps she can convince Aidryn to run with her, and this can all be reconciled.

She swallows hard against the bile creeping up her throat. "I..."

"If you want to live, I suggest you take my offer," Caitir whispers. "I seldom release thieves, to the dungeon or anywhere else."

"I'll take your offer, on one condition," Fiadh says, leveling with Caitir.

"You're bold, but I'm curious. What is it you want, besides my brother's attention? Which you'll never get, I assure you."

"I want magic." Fiadh raises her chin confidently. "And I want a place of significance at your side if I'm going to spy for you."

Dark magic crackles around Caitir's fingers. "I should kill you right here."

Fear surges through Fiadh, but she forces herself to remain still. "Perhaps. But we have something unfortunate in common, Caitir." She pauses a beat before adding, "Aidryn chose Silira over us both."

Lira released the memory, panting hard as she opened her eyes. Talfryn was nearly hovering over her, looking deeply troubled. The tremor had begun, and her hand shook violently.

"What did you see?" he asked anxiously.

"Fiadh is allied with Caitir," she said, grasping her right hand to steady it. "Since before Halgeir. She was there to gather information."

"By Nami..." he swore.

Lira clutched the pendant and dove back into her magic, seeking more.

Fiadh screams as Caitir withdraws the dark magic again, pain searing her insides. Her skin is mottled with black veins that fade to jagged, white scars as the magic leaves her. They've tried all manner of spells and incantations, but the power will not hold. Each time they attempt to give Fiadh magic, her body soundly rejects it.

"I'm sorry," Caitir pants, sweat beading on her brow. "This has never happened. You're an anomaly, and we have no healer, no elder who can guide us. If we keep trying, I'll end up killing you."

"Once more," Fiadh rasps, the taste of fresh blood on her tongue. "Just... once more."

Caitir sits down in a chair beside her chamber bed, where Fiadh is lying. "And I thought I was ambitious."

Fiadh looks up at the gilded ceiling then, contemplating. She's come too far to walk away with no power. "Bring a prisoner from my clan. Let's meld your power with my birthright."

Caitir calls for a sentry, and a few minutes later, he escorts the prisoner into the chamber, whom he claims to be a descendant of Clan Énna. It's a young girl with matted blonde hair and a blank expression. Caitir and Fiadh meet them at the chamber door.

The sentry commands the prisoner to her knees, stepping back to latch the door. Caitir steps forward then, seeming to glide as she closes the distance between herself and the girl, who shudders with terror. She places a hand on the girl's forehead, and she begins to sob.

"Quiet—you'll be fine," Caitir murmurs, turning her head to glance back at Fiadh. "Fiadh, you must open your intention to receive the inheritance you are due. I will assist with power of my own, but the end result is really up to you."

"Please…" the girl begs, attempting to pull back from Caitir's touch.

Caitir bares her teeth, and her dark magic ignites.

Static fills the room, raising the hair on the back of Fiadh's neck. She shuts off the thoughts that roil in her mind and forces herself to watch as a distant observer. The smell of burning flesh sears her nostrils as Caitir sends her black lightning into the girl, who begins to convulse. Caitir never breaks contact with the prisoner's skin as the girl slumps to the ground, her vacant eyes wide open.

Fiadh sucks in a breath. "Is she—"

"No. Magic can be taken without killing the vessel."

Caitir whispers something in a language Fiadh has never heard: "Sva'ceros." A moment later, the dark magic splits a wide fissure in the girl's chest. Suddenly, she is awake and fully aware again, and a tattered, gurgling scream rips from her throat.

Fiadh closes her heart to the sound. Caitir's eyes widen.

A column of violet power bursts from the girl's chest, and it flows toward Fiadh like a raging current, little black sparks licking at the pure magic of Clan Énna. For a moment, she realizes perhaps she should be afraid of accepting dark magic. But it is too late now.

Fiadh opens her palms to receive the power, but it slams into her chest, knocking her backward. She cracks the back of her head on the wall before slumping to the ground.

The magic burns as it pours into her, and she screams. It scalds her insides, as though her blood has ignited into an inferno of that horrible popping, sparking black power. And then that power suddenly fuses itself with her clan's magic.

She can almost feel the two strands of power hardening within her, adhering to her organs and veins, as hot as the heated blades she hammered for her father, for so many years. Hot and smooth like the blown glass she fired and shaped to perfection, over and over and over.

This magic is shaping her. Refining her. Honing her into something far beyond what she's ever been before. Hardening her heart to chase away her doubts, her fears, and the remaining scraps of pity she held for her friends in the clan army.

Let them face her now.

Let them be afraid.

As the power dissipates, the euphoria suddenly vanishes. The child from her clan is dead. Caitir kneels beside her, looking stricken.

"Rasu's bloody corpse," she mutters, checking for a pulse with trembling hands. "This has never happened before."

Fiadh looks down at the girl's body, and the horror she was expecting to feel does not come. In fact, she feels nothing at all.

There is a heaviness inside her chest that wasn't there before. For a moment, she wonders at it—wonders whether taking a life, taking magic, puts such a weight on the taker. She grows lightheaded and sways on her feet before collapsing. And in the final moments before she closes her eyes, she realizes her heart is no longer beating.

Again, Lira emerged from the power, her body humming with it. But something about the magic felt decidedly wrong. Both of her hands had gone numb, and the room felt as though it was spinning. She heaved herself over the side of the bed and vomited.

"What's happening?" Talfryn cried, his voice laced with panic as he rubbed her back. "Lira?"

She lay still, attempting to steady her ragged breathing. Her eyes stung with tears, her mouth and nose burning. With a moan, she spat out the taste of vomit and dragged a sleeve across her mouth. Then, she pushed herself up shakily and lay back again, holding the pendant.

"Lira, stop this," Talfryn said, lunging for her hand. "Please, tell me what you've learned so far. You could—"

"Once more," she said, panting. "Just once more."

And she immersed herself before her brother could beg her to stop again.

Fiadh has learned to marvel at the depth and breadth of her anger. Each time she attempts to call on the power Caitir stole for her, she can feel the dark magic stirring. But it never emerges. Instead, it's trapped inside her veins, her heart.

Those few blissful, emotionless moments she felt after she received her power are gone, replaced by this simmering rage. Rage that she lost Aidryn. Rage that she can't wield magic. Rage that she's enslaved to Caitir, bound to spy on her own family in exchange for a magic she can't use. The only hope she has left is to make herself into someone to be feared. And Caitir is still the only person who can give her that.

It took weeks to get used to the heart that had replaced her human one. When her power devoured her, she perceived it as blown glass, and still thinks of it as such. It's fitting for a blacksmith's daughter.

She dons the new black tunic and leggings Caitir gifted to her, belts a sword at her side, and strides to the audience chamber to meet Caitir. Her face is uncharacteristically gray, and it takes a moment before she acknowledges Fiadh.

"Gerallt has decided to conquer a Clan Énna settlement on the western coast," Caitir says. "My mother wants access to Lira's grandmother, who is staying near there. If you help me, we can overthrow Gerallt and Aila together and spare your people."

"You don't want to conquer the clan yourself?" Fiadh fights to keep her expression impassive.

"Conquering by force only inspires more rebellion," Caitir answers curtly. "I would rather earn their loyalty and have them come to me to serve." She fills a glass with water from a crystal

decanter, then offers it to Fiadh before pouring one for herself. "These outlying clan settlements are small, Fiadh. Left to their own devices, they will not rise against Iathium. It's the army of clans that concerns me. But perhaps we can use them to our advantage."

"How?"

"If they see infighting amongst our leadership, they will strike at the top but spare my men. Use logic: Gerallt's army has no loyalty. His archers and fighters followed him from Clan Mór in Silira's name, not his. But where is their figurehead now? Nowhere to be found. And I can assure you she will not be allowed on that battlefield, though Gerallt and Aila fully expect her to be.

"The sentries only care about preserving our way of life in Iathium—they fear prolonged chaos, or worse yet, permanent change. And Clan Beran just want their overlord back, so they can crawl off to their hole in the mountain and beat each other with tree limbs, or whatever they do at Halgeir. If we play our hand well, we can have everyone back in their own territories within a week."

Fiadh shakes her head, incredulous. "I don't understand. I thought this war was about bringing the clans to heel."

"I don't have the respect or the leverage to do that properly—but what you fail to understand is that Gerallt doesn't, either. He has the resources to slaughter the clans in battle, if he can keep his men in line. But what then? How long will he really be able to hold the throne?"

Caitir sits on a plush chair, settling back thoughtfully. "No, Fiadh, this war isn't truly about the clans at all. It's about securing a rightful inheritance to the throne. It's about magic beyond your wildest comprehension. And Lira has the key to all of it. How do you think we draw Lira in? Not through slaughter, but through careful strategy. In the meantime, it's up to me to inspire loyalty from Iathium. If they love me, they will not care that I did not descend from Nami's bloodline. And the clans have never changed. They wish to be left to their own devices, so I will give them that."

Logically, Caitir's words make sense. But the rage roiling inside of Fiadh demands something more. Begging endlessly for love is not a strategy, but rather, a weakness. But perhaps patience is in order. Perhaps a solution will come in time.

"What can I do to help you see this through?" Fiadh swirls the water in her glass slowly, rhythmically—water she should be able to command.

"Reunite with your brother, and get yourself into the war camp at Halgeir. Make sure Clan Beran knows exactly where our army is marching, so we can draw them there. We'll catch Gerallt by surprise and give back their overlord."

"What else, my lady?" Fiadh asks softly. Before, her heart might have been pounding, but right now she's reveling in its silence.

"Learn Fortress Halgeir. Glean every detail you can about where Thorne Beran is stationing his warriors. Every piece of information you can gather about their plans and their movements, do so and bring it back to me."

"Yes, my lady. How long do we have?"

"Two months, at least. It's going to take Gerallt time to recruit more sentries, so many left before." She looks to Fiadh, pain flickering across her features. "I hate him, you know."

Fiadh takes a small step back, regarding Caitir. "I do know."

Black lighting crackles around Caitir's clenched fists. "Before this is over, I will make them suffer. Gerallt, my mother, and anyone who opposes me. I am no conqueror, but I will be a force to be reckoned with."

Fiadh bows, grateful her heart can no longer wage war against her desires. "Then I will help you, my lady. Whatever it takes."

When Lira released the third witnessing and opened her eyes, she couldn't feel her own body. Everything felt disjointed, as though she were floating in the center of Skelly's room. But she could see Talfryn's face—only just. And his mouth was moving.

The world rattled as though it were coming apart entirely. Vaguely, she felt a tug on the chain around her neck. She caught a glimpse of the bronze pendant as it thumped against her brother's chest, and thought perhaps it suited him better than it did her.

"Lira," he was saying. His hand moved toward her face, but she could not feel it.

What she did feel was a tug on her waist. As she came to herself, her vision began to clear little by little, and she could make out Talfryn dumping the pouch of Skelly's heirlooms onto the mattress beside her. He was holding the items in front of her face, one at a time.

"Clan Énna?" Talfryn asked, grasping one of the smooth stones. She managed to shake her head weakly. He repeated the action until finally, he came to the gray pearl. "This one? Clan Énna?"

"Yes," she rasped, the feeling of pins and needles creeping into her toes.

Talfryn lay flush against her, grasping the pearl and the pendant in his hand. "Hold onto my back," he ordered, "and don't let go."

Lira did her best to put her arms around her brother, her fingers pricking with pain as they made contact with him. Talfryn touched the pearl to the pendant, and *turas* swallowed them.

CHAPTER 38

LIRA

Western Seashore

By the time the *turas* dropped Lira and Talfryn, she could feel her limbs again. They tumbled, one over the other, into a thickly wooded area not far from the western seashore. She could smell the salt in the air and hear the waves crashing in the distance.

Talfryn sat up, groaning as he put his head between his knees. Lira rolled heavily onto her side, trembling. The moonlight glinted off her bronze pendant, which still hung around Talfryn's neck.

"Tal?" she asked weakly. "Where are we?" Her hand still shook, but the nausea was beginning to abate.

"Near the war camp, I hope," he said.

"Why?"

"I'm taking you to Thorne." He finally looked up at her. "I thought you were going to die back there."

"I told you to take me back to Halgeir," she protested, though she didn't have the energy to be angry with him.

"We need a healer to see you here—now." Talfryn swayed slightly as he pushed himself to crouching and moved to her side. "Énna was a shorter trip. Besides, Thorne needs to know what's happening, and we know we can trust him."

He helped Lira sit up, then removed the tree pendant and looped the chain around her neck once more. Once he'd pushed himself to his feet, he offered her his hand. "Come on. Let's get you to the camp."

SUNRISE WAS PEEKING over the horizon by the time they reached the war camp. Talfryn had spent the past few hours hauling Lira through the woods in the relative direction of the seaside camp Thorne and his army had set up. She was so weak, they were forced to stop and rest every half hour. But each time she felt sleep trying to claim her, she demanded that Talfryn take her farther. And so her brother supported her weight and patiently helped her walk, one step at a time, through the woods until they finally caught sight of the tents.

Lira breathed in the scent of the morning meal cooking over a campfire, and her stomach gnawed. At best, the army had only been here for a day or two. It would have taken at least four days' time to travel here from Beran, and that was only if the army traveled at top speed with no delays.

As they approached the edge of camp, a familiar figure rounded the corner between two tents, then froze. Artagán Mór's mouth dropped open, and his hood fell back as he rushed toward them.

"You're supposed to be in the valley!" he cried, not bothering to greet them properly before he clapped a hand to Talfryn's shoulder. His gaze flicked down briefly as he noted Talfryn's missing arm for the first time. "What are you doing here?"

"I could ask you the same," Talfryn answered, his expression guarded as he studied their cousin. "We need to see Thorne."

Lira swayed on her feet, willing herself to remain steady just a moment longer.

"I'll take you to him," Artagán said. "I've been staying here with Skelly. We heard the overlord needed as many fighters as he could get, so here we are."

Just then, Artagán's twin, Ellwyn, emerged from one of the tents, red hair bright in the morning sun. She cried out when she spotted Lira and ran to meet her. When she reached Lira and Talfryn, she threw her arms around them, and the three embraced.

"Ellwyn..." Lira whispered hoarsely.

"You're alive," Ellwyn cried. "I feared the worst."

Lira lost her balance then, falling into her cousin, who caught her with a grunt. Talfryn steadied his grip on her and together, the two of them helped her into Ellwyn's tent. Ellwyn lowered Lira onto a bedroll as Artagán and Talfryn took off to find Thorne.

"What's happened to you?" Ellwyn asked as Lira allowed herself to relax beneath the warm blanket.

"I used my magic to gather reconnaissance, of a sort. I had to"—she yawned deeply—"pay a heavy price for it."

"You poor thing," her cousin whispered, smoothing Lira's hair away from her forehead. "And poor Talfryn. How did he lose his arm?"

"Iathium," was all Lira could say before she drifted out of consciousness.

SHE AWOKE a little while later to the warm rush of Thorne's healing magic washing over her. But the power felt stronger than usual somehow. When she cracked her eyes open, she saw that Oda knelt beside Thorne, pouring her power into Lira, too.

"I—"

"Hush, don't talk," Oda said softly. "We're almost finished."

Lira closed her mouth and looked up at Thorne, whose expression was grim. He didn't acknowledge her, but continued crafting the golden orbs of healing power in silence. Slowly, Lira noticed that her body was beginning to feel like her own again. She still felt weak, though, and her stomach cramped from retching.

When the warriors were done, Talfryn poked his head inside the tent. "How is she?"

Oda helped Lira sit up. "Better," Lira said.

"I thought I told you to keep to the mountain valley," Thorne finally said in Brylla. "Why did you disobey my orders?"

"We didn't plan to," Talfryn answered quickly. "Lira had a mishap with her power and I didn't know what else to do. It was faster to bring her here for healing."

"A mishap with your magic. I should have known; you had that scent again." Thorne crossed his arms and glared at Lira. "Please, explain."

Lira did. She told Thorne exactly what she had seen, and why the power had weakened her. When she was done, Thorne swore.

"You were right to come to me," he said. "I'm sorry for reprimanding you, Talfryn."

Her brother nodded. Oda glanced between Lira, Thorne, and Talfryn. "We need to regroup and move everyone. I say we abandon the coast and move east, into the meadowlands. March the main army eastward, then have them double back to meet Gerallt out in the open. No ocean, no forest, no shelter. Make it harder for them to trap us or drive us into the sea."

Thorne regarded her. "And the caravan?"

"Move the caravan closer to the city. Draw Gerallt's attention there, and leave our warriors in place."

"What of the camp? They'll be able to follow our movements."

"Split it." Oda raised her chin. "Let's make it appear as

though we're breaking up our army. In so doing, we divide Gerallt's. He won't be able to resist sending sentries to each outpost, thinking he can pick off groups of warriors at each location. We'll move clusters of tents to several areas around the caravan, then move the army out without them. We don't need tents—we can take enough provisions to last us the two days it'll take for Gerallt to arrive. Then we can surround them."

Thorne rested his chin on a fist, clearly considering her words. Then, nodded toward Lira. "What about her grandmother and the old Defender? We'll leave them unguarded if we move."

With a start, Lira remembered that Irem's childhood home wasn't far from here. Her heart leapt at the thought of seeing him again. Seeing Skelly again.

Oda's green eyes glinted. "My uncle has a small ship. We can send them out on the water during the fighting, keep them out of reach."

"Yes, sail them 'round to the south," Talfryn said, motioning in the direction of Rodhlan Ridge. "That way, you get them out of sight and off land."

"Brilliant," Oda said with a grin.

"You are," Thorne said, looking pointedly at her. "The men will unseat me immediately when they find out who the real strategic mind is."

"Then don't tell anyone," she said with a quiet laugh. "I like advising you in secret."

Talfryn raised his eyebrows. Lira tilted her head curiously, trying to catch Oda's eye, but the warrior ignored her.

"So what do we do?" Talfryn asked.

Thorne sighed. "We can't send you back into the mountains now. Gerallt's people know where everyone was supposed to be."

Suddenly, Lira felt ill again. "They know where Aidryn is going because of Fiadh. We need to get to him."

"No," Oda answered gently. "He has Fannin, and no one else to slow him down. Maybe splitting Gerallt's army will keep them occupied here for now."

Lira's magic was deathly silent. "I—I don't know that that's true," she stammered.

"I know you're worried, *sjeinga*," Thorne said, "but we can't go after him. He'll go looking for you in the mountains after Va'hesk. Trust he will be there once this is finished."

The continued silence in Lira's power was unnerving. She had come to rely on it to navigate these past months—to help her feel truth. Her chest tightened, and her breath came in rapid huffs.

Oda leaned forward and grasped her hand. "Lira, let's not borrow trouble. Aidryn will be safe. We have to believe that."

"Rest for a little while, Silira," Thorne said gently. "We'll wake you when it's time to move."

He and Oda left her alone with Talfryn, who whirled to scrutinize Lira. "What else is going on?"

"I can't feel my magic." The words tumbled from Lira before she could stop them. "The discernment—it's gone."

CHAPTER 39
AIDRYN

The morning sun was high when the sprawling tent settlement of Va'hesk came into view. Aidryn had been half-asleep in Fannin's saddle until the bright white of the tents snagged his attention. He scratched behind Fannin's ear before nudging him forward. "Let's go, old boy."

Fannin picked up speed, his heavy hoof beats stirring up a thick cloud of sand. The land out here was dry and sparse, despite its proximity to the eastern seashore. Right away, he noted that the view was far less attractive than that of the central meadowlands. Of Rodhlan Ridge.

His heart clenched as he thought of Lira, back in the mountains. Everything had gone sideways so quickly, from their rapport with Thorne to Aidryn's mission. It had seemed doomed from the time it began, but as he and Fannin moved toward the tents, Aidryn thought that perhaps, now that he was here, things might take a turn for the better. After all, these were his kin. However distant they might be, surely they would listen to his case.

Four men emerged from the settlement on Aidryn's

approach. Predictably, their attention went first to Fannin before they paid Aidryn any heed.

The man nearest Fannin stepped closer, scrutinizing the stallion. He was of average height and build—gray-haired, with a short beard and a patch covering one eye. "That horse looks familiar."

"We ride often," Aidryn answered. "Or, at least—we used to. You've likely seen us out on the meadowlands."

The man crossed his arms. "Where'd you get him?"

"He was a gift from my grandfather, Pàlnos Tarlach. I've had him for a number of years."

Instead of replying to Aidryn, the man turned around to consult with the other men who had come out with him. They murmured amongst themselves for a moment, leaving Aidryn waiting awkwardly, still astride Fannin. When their leader finally turned to face him again he said, "Pàlnos. That's one of the clan deserters from a few generations back—a city-dweller. I remember his name. He had no business taking the Seanlaoch from their rightful home."

Aidryn pursed his lips, shifting in the saddle. "If you want to split hairs, their true home is Iteloria."

"And you," the man continued, glaring up at him. "You're a city-dweller, too. I can tell by the way you speak. Ever been here, even once?"

"No, I'm afraid not." Aidryn was growing more leery of this place by the moment. It was tempting to turn Fannin in the opposite direction and bolt. But he'd been tasked with a specific goal, and he was here to accomplish it for the clans. For Rodhlan. "I wish to speak to your assembly."

"Outsiders aren't granted such requests," the man said. "What's your name?"

"Aidryn Tarlach."

"Name's Terovi." The man spat on the ground before looking back up at Aidryn, squinting against the sun. "I lead the assembly."

Relief flooded Aidryn. "Excellent. I have news of—"

"I didn't say you could have an audience," Terovi interrupted, holding up his hands. "I just said I lead the assembly."

"Why wouldn't you want to know what's happening out there?" Aidryn motioned vaguely to the meadowlands behind him.

"Because none of it concerns us." Terovi jerked his chin toward the tents, indicating the other men should go back into the settlement. He turned to go, too. "Go back the way you came. Leave us be."

"No." Aidryn dismounted angrily, grasping Fannin's reins. "Do not turn your back on me. I didn't come all this way to be ignored."

One of the other men half-glanced over his shoulder. "We owe you nothing," he said dismissively.

Aidryn stayed on their heels. "We sent messengers requesting aid *twice*—"

Terovi whirled on him. "And we ignored your call. Did you think you could show up here like some city scholar and demand our compliance just because you bothered to make the journey yourself? Maybe if you'd sent your overlord, since you're so fond of Clan Beran—but you can't do that with him imprisoned, can you?"

"This isn't about clan rivalries," Aidryn protested. "You've no idea what we're up against."

"Oh, we're well aware. But my clan isn't waiting around to burn with the rest of Rodhlan."

"What are you talking about?" Aidryn skimmed the line of tents, noticing for the first time that some were being dismantled. It felt like the wind had been knocked from his lungs. "You're leaving."

"And what are we to you, besides lambs to slaughter?"

"My kin," Aidryn said. Terovi glared angrily, pale blue eyes in stark contrast to his weathered, tanned skin. "As your anointed, I'm asking you to lend your horses and fighters to the cause. Help us protect Rodhlan's clans from the tyrants in Iathium."

Terovi laughed in Aidryn's face. "This clan hasn't seen its anointed in the flesh for more than a century. Show us, then. Let us see your magic if you really are the keeper of keys. Then maybe we'll send you with an extra horse for your trouble."

The other men guffawed, and Aidryn's ears suddenly felt hot. Perhaps he'd only imagined this clan to be honorable. In truth, all they had ever been to him was a dream—some distant, idealized kinsfolk he'd fantasized about running away to as a child.

Aidryn drew a breath, the early-morning wind ruffling his hair. He reached for his magic, seeking that familiar spark he'd known his entire life. But the effort to call it forward felt more like running headlong into a stone wall than drawing on a power that had always felt real and warm and alive.

His breath caught, and he felt his eyes go wide. Quickly, he shut them and felt for that tendril of magic again. *Please!* he thought. Only once in his twenty-two years had he lost complete contact with his power—after he'd been shot with the poisoned arrow. Was this some lasting effect of that injury?

And what about the Binding? He felt for Lira's power, but found that it had vanished, too. Had something happened to her? Or was this some effect of his arrow wound that he'd had yet to experience?

She's safe in the mountains, he reassured himself. *She's safe with Talfryn.*

But his *magic*—he blinked in disbelief, staring down at his empty palm like an imbecile as the mens' laughter grew more raucous.

"I should've known," Terovi howled. His expression suddenly darkened, and he advanced on Aidryn. "Another of the city's good-for-nothing sentries. I've lost count of how many of your kind came crawling out here this spring, scrounging for information to take back to those dogs on the throne."

"I'm a historian, not a sentry," Aidryn protested. His fingers tightened on the grip of his sword.

"Even worse—you can record everything you learn here." The other men came closer, too, eyeing Aidryn with suspicion. "You draw that blade, and it's the last thing you'll ever do," Terovi warned.

"My wife—Silira," Aidryn said, holding up his hands. "She knows a couple from this settlement, Nevala and Mytr. They can tell you who I am, so you'll know I'm true to my word."

"Nevala and Mytr were cast out of the settlement this spring after harboring a fugitive—your wife, I'd wager." Terovi's eyes shone with terrible delight. "They drew far too much attention to this place."

Aidryn felt his knees begin to give way, and he turned to brace himself on Fannin's saddle. But the men moved nearer still. He kept a hand on the saddle and turned to them again. "I can see there's nothing for me here, so we'll be on our way. You may refuse to help us now, and that's at your discretion. But we won't forget it."

Terovi caught Aidryn by the tunic and drew him close. "Not so fast. Your wife is the true heir of Iathium, isn't she? Silira Mór. *Witness Tree*." His hot, stinking breath reeked like rotten meat, and Aidryn made a valiant effort not to inhale.

Aidryn broke away easily, drawing his sword and advancing on Terovi. "You'll not lay another hand on me."

Terovi chuckled, then grabbed Aidryn's blade in his bare hand. He closed his fingers over it, and the metal softened before Aidryn's eyes. The assembly's overlord twisted his fist and bent the blade handily, just as it suddenly heated and singed Aidryn's palm. Instinctively, he dropped it and it thudded to the ground.

"You'd think a true Tarlach anointed would have seen that coming," Terovi said. He looked to his men. "Take him."

CHAPTER 40

LIRA

Western Seashore

Talfryn's mouth fell open. "Your magic's gone? You're not serious."

"I am," she said softly, sitting up on the bedroll and drawing her knees up to her chest. "Probably because I took the memories."

"Can you reach any of it at all?" he whispered. "Perhaps it was just...jolted a bit. Can that happen? Can magic be set off-course like that?"

"Just—I don't know," she said sharply. "Be quiet for a moment."

Lira closed her eyes and searched for a thread of her power. *Witness Tree.* She said it to herself like an incantation. A plea. *I am a living vessel of memory. The Witness Tree of Rodhlan. Please... Rhona, please...*

Warmth emanated from her fingers and she felt her power surge to life again. She cupped her palms, allowing the emerald magic to flare in her hands, and breathed a shaky sigh of relief.

"Quick," she said, "tell me something that's not true."

"Uh..." Talfryn tore his eyes away from the magic to look at the ceiling of the tent. "Thorne sucks his thumb."

Lira giggled. "Now, something true and *significant*, Tal. Historically speaking."

He shrugged, chewing his lip. "Nami was a mortal god, but Ulan was not."

She waited for the tug at the back of her mind, and finally it responded in agreement. With a loud sigh, Lira fell back against the bedroll again. "By Riku, Rhona, and Nami! That gave me a fright."

"Lira, don't scare me like that again." Talfryn clenched his fist and set his jaw. A fire had ignited in his emerald eyes. "You can't afford to be incapacitated like that. We need your power—we need you safe. *I* need you safe. If your magic endangers you that way, it's not worth using it to take memories. Let Rodhlan gift you the visions, nothing more. We'll find a way to win this war without sacrificing you in the process."

She nodded, pressing her lips together. Ljós had warned her about delving into a person's memories. Aside from the questionable nature of taking private moments without consent, the risk of losing her magic was also a valid reason not to. "You're right. I'm sorry I frightened you."

Her brother reached forward and patted the back of her hand. "Rest now, like Thorne said. I'm going to find out what he wants us to do next."

It was late afternoon when Ellwyn knelt beside Lira and gently shook her awake.

"It's time to go," she whispered, squeezing Lira's shoulder. "The Beran commander is moving us to Lord Irem's estate."

Lira blinked groggily. "What? Why?"

Ellwyn braced a hand behind Lira's back and helped her sit up. Her red hair was strikingly bright against the dark green gown she wore, and was braided in Clan Beran's fashion. "Thorne's putting you, me, and Talfryn on the ship with Skelly and Irem."

Lira ground her teeth. "He is *not*."

"He said you'd be unhappy," Ellwyn said firmly. "Apparently, you've taken a shine to defying orders."

"Arguing against them, more like." Lira stood, her body swaying as she took a deep breath and steadied herself. "Presenting my viewpoint."

"There's talk among the warriors that you've presented those viewpoints openly and forcefully," Ellwyn said, eyeing her. "I think that's part of the reason why he wants you off land, aside from the obvious. Apparently, there are some in the ranks who would be more likely to agree with you over him because of your mother's standing with Beran."

"He takes no issue with women advising him," Lira protested.

"Yes, but have any of them defied him in front of the clan?"

"Oh."

"Anyway—the least you can do is go to the estate for appearances," Ellwyn said, the corner of her mouth twitching up. "But once Thorne is satisfied, who's to say…"

She ran her fingers over her bow absently, which lay on a woven blanket next to the bedroll. Then, she met Lira's gaze again. "Who's to say you can't join Artagán and me on a mission of our own?"

Lira recoiled. "As defectors?"

"No." Ellwyn's expression was grim. "Assassins."

WARRIORS DISMANTLED TENTS AS LIRA, Ellwyn, Talfryn, and Artagán trekked through the center of the war camp. Thorne had ordered everyone to begin moving to their new locations overnight, under cover of darkness. The group headed toward the coastline; the ship they were to board wouldn't arrive until morning.

Irem's estate was a mile up the coast from where they'd made camp. Despite the circumstances, Lira was excited to see the coast at night once again. The water glowed bright blue after dark, as though it contained magic of its own when each wave white capped.

In exchange for shelter, Thorne required Ellwyn and Artagán to swear fealty to him. He had then tasked the twins with scouting the coastline for signs of Gerallt's traveling party. As the only archers in Thorne's army, they had the advantage of fighting long-range. Their mission was to get their eyes on Gerallt, his wives, and any of the high-ranking commanders— then pick them off, one by one. Because Artagán accepted dark magic from Aila before returning to the clans, Thorne hoped he could utilize that power to their advantage.

Lira's heart thumped erratically as Irem's fortified estate came into view. It was a small stone castle located on a high, craggy peninsula that jutted off the mainland.

"You say Skelly's truly well..." she ventured while they picked their way across the beach and onto the road that led to the estate.

"Yes," Ellwyn said airily, light on her feet as she moved. "Better than I've seen her in years."

Artagán, who had mostly been silent since Lira and Talfryn arrived, adjusted the strap on his quiver. "I blamed you for what happened to her, Silira. You know that." He set his jaw and looked straight ahead.

"I do." Lira stumbled on the path, and Ellwyn grasped her arm to steady her. The seaside wind was cool and tinged with the sting of salt. "For what it's worth, I'm sorry I stayed away."

"It wasn't your fault," Ellwyn said. "You can't help what Uncle Arlen told you; you were a child. All children wish to please their parents." She glared pointedly at Artagán before adding, "It takes time to learn the truth on your own."

Artagán flinched, his gaze shifting out to sea. A muscle in his jaw ticked before he turned his head slightly toward Lira and said, "All that to say—if you hadn't come for her when you did, she would not be here now."

He stalked off ahead of the group toward the estate. "You're welcome," Lira said softly.

When they reached the house, Irem met them at the gate as though he'd been waiting all day. Lira hung back behind her brother and cousins as Irem acknowledged each of them. He was bundled in the heavy cloak he'd been wearing the last time she saw him, and he leaned heavily on his cane. When she finally approached, there were tears in his eyes.

"Lord Irem!" Lira cried, the words sticking in her throat as tears pricked her eyes, too.

A wide smile spread across his wizened face, and he opened his arms to her. Lira ran to him and embraced him more gently than she would have liked, careful not to throw him off balance.

"Silira," he said softly, patting her back.

"I've missed hearing your voice," she said, pulling away and steadying him as he braced on his cane.

"It's good to see your face again." He studied her closely, dark eyes glinting in the light from the torches mounted along the gate. "You've changed since I last saw you."

"In more ways than you know," she said, offering her arm to him.

"I hoped to see you and Aidryn here together," Irem said over the crashing waves. The water was luminous as it shattered against the rocks, scattering shimmering blue light across its surface. "I was disappointed to learn he'd been sent to Va'hesk."

"And the mission fell apart entirely," Lira said, explaining how Aidryn had ridden ahead without his traveling companions. Suddenly, it occurred to her that she hadn't seen Irem since before Eremon's death. He seemed to think of the late Rí the same moment she did, for he suddenly appeared twenty years older.

"I dearly wish Eremon were still here." He sighed. "If I had known what would happen, I would have never left you alone."

"You did what you thought was best," Lira said. "And you were able to help Skelly when she needed it."

Irem went from grieved to stern in a split second. "Speaking of Wilga, Silira—in what reality is it advisable to leave your grandmother stranded in the wilderness, with no one to look after her?"

Lira winced. "I'm ashamed of myself for that," she said quickly. "I shouldn't have done it."

"All the same," he said, "she told me not to reprimand you. But I find myself disinclined to submit. It's against my better judgment." He pressed forward, and Lira found herself trying not to smile.

When they reached the door, the others were waiting for them. Irem opened it and ushered them into the courtyard. They crossed it, entered the great hall, then made a sharp right into a candlelit chamber where Skelly was dozing over an open book. Her long, silver hair was woven into an ornate braid, and her face looked fuller than it had the last time Lira saw her.

"Wilga, your little twin has arrived," Irem announced. There was a hint of playfulness in his voice that was almost unfamiliar.

Skelly jolted awake, blinking several times before her gaze came to rest on Lira. She smiled widely, reaching for her grand-daughter as Lira crossed the room and knelt beside the chair. Lira rested her forehead on Skelly's knee.

"Forgive me," she cried. "I shouldn't have left you."

She felt her grandmother's hands rest gently on her head. "I told that old hound not to chide you."

Lira laughed, swiping at her eyes and looking up at Skelly. "Clearly, Lord Irem does what he pleases." She grasped her grandmother's hands. "I'm glad you were able to come here."

"As am I. We have much to discuss." Skelly's expression softened when she saw Talfryn hanging back by the door. "Come here, my boy."

Talfryn joined them, and the three embraced. He didn't hide his pained expression when their grandmother gently rested her hand on his left shoulder. "My warrior," she said, tears gathering in her eyes now as she gazed at his face. "How brave you are."

His expression crumpled and he collapsed against Skelly, trembling as wracking sobs overtook him. She kissed his curls, cradling his head and whispering to him. Lira sat on the floor by the chair, covered her face, and let her tears fall, too.

"All my grandchildren, together again," Skelly said after a long moment. Her voice was thick with tears. "I'm sorry we can't spend more time here. So sorry, for so many things."

"Now is not the time to drag apologies on for miles," Irem said, sitting in the chair beside Skelly's. He patted Lira's back before he settled in. "Rune Énna is bringing the ship tonight. We received word an hour ago."

Lira perked up as Talfryn sank to the floor beside her, rubbing his nose. "Oda's uncle?"

Irem nodded. "I was pleased to learn your paths had crossed. Oda's grandparents are dear friends of mine." He looked to Ellwyn. "Ellwyn, if you please, I need you and your brother to help me finish preparing for the journey. You'll find our provisions back in the great hall. If you could, please begin packing the dried meats and cheeses."

The twins shared a glance, then disappeared from the room. Irem looked to Talfryn next, lowering his voice. "Talfryn, make sure they reach the great hall, and keep them there. Make yourself useful as you see fit."

"Yes, Lord Irem," he said, pushing himself to his feet and trailing his cousins out the door. He shut it behind him.

"Now, Silira," Skelly began. "Oda tells us you have important information about Eremon. Tell us everything you know."

CHAPTER 41

LIRA

Western Seashore

"It is a grave thing indeed, to consider raising a dead mortal god to immortality," Irem said softly, a tear trickling down his cheek.

They had been in the dimly-lit parlor for several hours, hashing and re-hashing everything Lira had learned about Eremon's power and the motives of those vying for it. Lira's backside ached from sitting on the stone floor, and she shivered against the cool night air that seeped its way into the little castle.

"I imagine there is a reason for the way of things," Skelly added, looking meaningfully at Lira. "It seems someone wanted mortals to have a say in the matter."

"It's such a heavy responsibility." Lira sighed, lying down on the uneven stone and crossing her ankles. It felt surprisingly good, and the muscles in her back relaxed. She looked up at the heavy wooden beams overhead. "Who decided mortals should command the power of the gods?"

"It rather limits them, doesn't it?" Irem rubbed one of his

knees, wincing. "To have no power to overcome their own deaths."

Lira thought of Eremon, suspended somewhere between life and death, his own unimaginable power just out of his grasp. Did the nearness of his magic enrage him? Was he alone or surrounded by his forefathers? Was his spirit traversing the continents, or merely trapped within the confines of his own vault? Was there any peace to be had in death at all?

When she thought of it that way, it wasn't a great leap to imagine him returning as a vengeful, all-powerful entity. Though she always came back to the belief that Eremon would still be *Eremon*, it was easy to speculate. Easy to fear.

"I've wrestled with the question of bringing him back for months," Lira said. "I think we should. But everyone around me keeps telling me to wait. I think they're afraid—so am I. But if Iteloria gets involved in this war, we'll need to be a step ahead of them."

"Trust your instincts," Skelly said. "You're an intelligent, powerful woman—the most powerful being in Rodhlan. If you believe we need help, I think you have the authority to decide that. And as the most powerful magic-wielder, it's no small thing to willingly give up your status to another."

Suddenly, Lira had a horrifying realization. She sat back up and said, "Skelly, I'm not a mortal goddess, am I?"

Her grandmother smiled warmly and chuckled. "No. But you are the strongest of the anointed. Once you've helped Eremon return, you will need to think about how best to disperse your own magic. You and I both know mortals aren't meant to bear so much power."

Lira sighed, relieved. "Good. It was hard enough to accept that I had magic at all. I would probably make a rather angry goddess."

Irem gripped his cane, sliding his gnarled fingers over its smooth end thoughtfully. "Silira, you say that when it comes to

Eremon, everyone wants you to wait. Who is everyone—the people who know?"

"Thorne Beran, for one. He thinks I'll just get myself captured in the crypt." She looked down at her hand and twisted the silver ring Aidryn had given her. "And then there's Aidryn. He has rather hard feelings toward Eremon."

"You should have seen those two in the inner chamber together, facing off." Irem laughed richly. "They were like young bucks, butting heads over every little thing. Aidryn was usually right, but it doesn't come naturally for a ruler like Eremon to concede to anyone. I made them work together on plans for the magic and the histories because I knew Aidryn wouldn't be afraid to push back.

"The one thing I didn't anticipate was their rivalry over you. You were the one thing that put Aidryn off-balance with him."

Lira blew out a puff of air. "I know."

"I imagine that fear inspires a sort of reluctance on Aidryn's part," Irem continued. "But Skelly is right. When you're certain it's time to go to Eremon, do not hesitate."

The chamber door burst open and Talfryn rushed in, followed by Oda and Faolan. Lira stood and crossed the room toward them. "I thought you two were going with Thorne," she said.

"Change of plans." Faolan's gaze flicked to Irem and Skelly, and he nodded toward them before continuing. "Gerallt split off from his main army. He's coming here tonight with a group of archers to take the estate. Thorne's scouts spotted them about five miles up the coast."

"What?" Lira cried. "What about Artur?"

"With a different party," Oda answered.

Faolan nodded. "We think they're taking him into the heart of battle to rile up the Beran warriors."

Talfryn laughed in disbelief. "Do they have an absolute death wish?"

"Apparently," Lira said. "And Aila? Is she not coming here, as well?"

Faolan and Oda exchanged a glance. "Aila set sail for Iteloria this morning," Faolan said slowly, keeping his gaze trained on Lira.

The impact of his words slowed the world. "For Iteloria," Lira echoed, swaying. Her entire body trembled with terror.

"She must have a great deal of confidence in Gerallt and Caitir," Talfryn said.

Ellwyn and Artagán joined them, their expressions solemn.

"Why Iteloria?" Ellwyn crossed her arms and leaned against the door frame. "That makes no sense."

"No, no..." Lira shook her head. "It makes perfect sense. She's not waiting for them to come to us. She's taking control of the situation."

"She was born there," Lord Irem said. "Her late husband was the ambassador. Of course. She likely still has contacts there."

"We should have guessed she would go to La'hiran." Lira began to pace. She, Aidryn, and Thorne had all agreed Iteloria would likely come to them. Yet it had never occurred to Lira that Aila would go there *now*, just as the first battle was about to begin. "Why didn't we expect it?"

Faolan unsheathed a dagger from his belt and studied the blade. "Maybe because she was busy conquering Iathium?" He rubbed the edge of his tunic against the metal until he was satisfied with its shine, then returned it to its sheath.

"What business would Iteloria have here? Why would they come to us?" Artagán shouldered his quiver and tied his long auburn hair back with a thin strip of leather.

Lira opened her mouth to answer him, but Oda cut her off. "You're not privy to that information," she said curtly. "You were on Gerallt's side before."

"I left Gerallt *months* ago," the archer said, nostrils flaring.

"Maybe you did," Oda said, taking a step closer to him, "but you have yet to prove your loyalty to my general. Until I see it with my own eyes, you get no more information. But I can see you're smart, and you're good with a bow. Once I'm satisfied I can trust you, you'll be welcome on the war council."

"I can't imagine being welcomed by any of your people, anywhere." Artagán leered at her before he added, "I'm going to the tower to stand watch." He stormed out of the room toward the great hall.

Ellwyn looked out toward where Artagán had gone, then back to Oda. "He gave up everything to come looking for me," she said. "The least you could do is give him that."

Oda crossed her arms. "I do give him that. But we allowed someone on the council who had demonstrated trustworthy behavior without fail—until he leaked important information to a spy that compromised our entire army. So you'll forgive me if I can't find it in my heart to give your brother sensitive details about what must be done to secure this continent."

Lira couldn't help looking to Faolan. He was stone-still. The only movement she could detect was his gaze sliding slowly to the floor.

Ellwyn's eyes narrowed. "I'm taking the other tower." She whirled and followed the path Artagán had taken.

Slowly, Lira turned to Oda. "Artagán is prepared to kill his own father for the clans. You can't get much more loyal than that."

"But he hasn't yet, has he?" Oda's jab stung. She was luminous in the candlelight, her single white braid falling forward on her cheek as she leaned in. "Part of proving your worth as a warrior is the ability to accept being told no. If he can't handle my very good reason for holding information close, then he's not worthy of the council."

"Is that how you feel about me, then?" Lira asked. She had argued with Thorne more times than she could count. "That I'm unworthy?"

Oda looked shocked. "I might not always agree with your

approach, but I think you've earned the right to stand up to me or Thorne, or anyone you see fit. You're an authority in your own right."

Lira sighed heavily. "Good, because I'm about to disobey his orders again, and I'm going to need help to do it."

Faolan's head snapped up, eyes flashing. "Let's hear it."

"I'm going to the crypt in Iathium," Lira answered. "If Aila's heading for Iteloria, there's no question she'll bring their magic-wielders back with her. It's time to wake Eremon now."

Oda lay a hand on Lira's arm. "Then I'm going with you." Lira clasped her hand tightly, biting down on her lip to stop the tears that suddenly sprang to her eyes.

"As am I," Faolan said. "You'll need someone to make sure you don't die."

Lira rolled her eyes. "I appreciate your vote of confidence." She looked to her brother. "Tal, how much did *turas* take out of you? We'll need to go that way."

Talfryn shrugged. "Not much. I was a bit tired after, but it wasn't bad."

"Lira," Skelly called, "is there a reason you can't *turas* yourself?"

Lira's face grew hot. She hadn't explained her illness to her grandmother or Irem, but assumed Oda or Faolan might have. "Not normally, no. But I... discovered that certain methods of using my power have consequences."

"Oh." Skelly nodded sagely. "Taking memories from another, I assume. There are no consequences if your magic brings a memory to you. But requesting them from a specific person is dangerous."

"So I've learned." Everyone's attention was suddenly on Lira. She shifted uncomfortably.

"I suspected that's how you knew Caitir's strategy, but I did not want to accuse," Irem said softly. "It's tempting to use such a powerful ability for the greater good."

Lira closed her eyes. "I will do everything in my power to

avoid misusing the magic. But I can't promise it will never be necessary. If I hadn't drawn on Fiadh's memories, we wouldn't be here now."

Skelly rose and approached Lira, gently taking her hands. "But if you lose yourself to the magic, Rodhlan will have no more Witness Tree. You must protect yourself at all costs."

Lira squeezed her grandmother's hands. "I will protect Rodhlan, Skelly. I'll protect our people and those I love, and hope that I can survive it all. That's all I can promise you." She embraced Skelly, then turned to her brother. "You ready, Tal?"

She patted her waist, only to realize her pouch wasn't attached to her belt. She looked to Talfryn, alarmed. "Do you still have my heirloom pouch? The one with the trinkets from all the territories."

Talfryn's eyes widened, and he scrambled for his own leather pouch, digging inside. "Oh no..." he groaned. "I left them in the mountains."

"What?" Lira cried. "We need those to use *turas!*"

"I did find these in your pouch." He pulled out a small drawstring bag—the one Aidryn had left in the tower for her, back in the spring—and handed it to her. "I'm sorry I left everything else. I feel so stupid."

"Don't panic. I have all sorts of artifacts from Iathium," Irem said. "We'll find something to use."

Lira weighed the bag, relieved. "I haven't thought of these in months." Inside were a handful of seeds that glowed with Clan Mór's emerald power. Faolan had slipped them into the tower when Lira was imprisoned.

"My seeds!" Skelly exclaimed. "So Aidryn did get them to you."

"We used one to escape Iathium." She weighed the bag in her hand. "Lord Irem, can we use them to defend your home against Gerallt?"

Irem squinted at the bag, then glanced at Skelly briefly.

"Wilga and I had a contingency plan for making this place... uninhabitable for intruders. But we were reluctant to use it."

"At our age, wielding magic takes its toll quickly," Skelly said. "But with the help of the seeds, I think we can do what we have in mind."

"Faolan, how much time do we have?" Lira said.

"An hour, maybe," he said. "Whatever this plan is, we'd better get into position. Then, we get out of here before Gerallt arrives."

HALF AN HOUR LATER, Lira stood on the beach below the estate with Faolan. Oda's uncle, Rune, had anchored his ship half a mile out, and was now rowing toward the beach in a small boat. From where they stood, Lira could see a subtle hint of Clan Énna's violet magic sparkling in the water just beneath the rowboat. She guessed Rune was using his power to propel it.

"I haven't seen you wield magic since that day in the dungeon," Lira said, rubbing her arms against the cold.

"That's because there hasn't been a need to display it since then." Faolan removed his gray traveling cloak and draped it over Lira's shoulders.

She sighed, soaking in its warmth. "Thank you."

"It's not a favor. It's just practicality." He jerked his chin almost imperceptibly. "Better warm and dry on you than out in the ocean weighing me down. Besides, I'll take it back once we're finished here. You won't be thanking me then."

"Always the gentleman." Lira studied the luminous waves as they rolled in and broke gently against the shore, pulling Faolan's cloak more tightly around herself. She wished it were warm enough to swim.

"What you did... digging into Fiadh's memories. It was foolish." The wind whipped his black curls against his forehead. "You can't risk yourself like that. Tarlach would kill me."

"Oh." Lira hummed. She'd thought Faolan was angry she'd invaded his sister's privacy, but that wasn't it at all. "So protecting me isn't so much about *me*, but more about self-preservation."

"You could say so." He nudged the toe of his boot into the sand.

"I've never told you so, but you're a good friend to Aidryn," Lira said. "And to me."

"I've never thought of Tarlach as a friend," he said absently, squinting out toward Rune.

"Brother, then." Faolan had once told Lira he regarded Talfryn as a brother, too. He was selfless and loyal under his armored facade—almost painfully so.

Faolan's snapped his head around to regard Lira, narrowing his eyes before he relaxed again. "Make of it what you will." He looked back out to the horizon, rocking back and forth on his heels. "I was born with Fiadh's share of magic, I think. Mine didn't manifest until a few years ago, and like you, I wasn't aware magic was real before. At first, I didn't tell her about it. There was no sign of her having the same power. Eventually, Tarlach came to me about his own magic. I nailed him to the wall because he was acting strangely—working all the time, skipping out on me and Aeron—and he told me. It was around the time he and Fiadh..."

He shut his mouth and glanced at Lira, a pained expression crossing his face. "Anyway, you know all that. When Eremon died, that's when Fiadh found out. She came to me, demanding to know why she couldn't seem to get even a spark from a piece of verse Aeron had given her to copy. We tried more than once, but it just didn't... stick."

"She was angry, wasn't she?" Lira asked softly.

"Beyond." Faolan smoothed his fingertips over the ground to reveal the curved ridges of a small gray shell, then worked it up out of the wet sand. He took his time brushing the grains away, first from its surface, then from the underside. "It's bad enough I got my twin's share of power. If she ever found out I'm Clan Énna's anointed, she would—"

"Anointed?" Lira laughed out loud. "All four of us were in one place, and you never told anyone?"

"Thorne knows. And you. That healer figured it out when he patched me up."

She was surprised he hadn't mentioned it to Aidryn or Aeron, but she didn't pry. "You really should use your magic, Faolan. Don't let it harm you."

He arched an eyebrow at her, then handed her the shell. "What do you think I'm about to do here? Been saving it for a time like this."

Lira ran her thumb over the shell's ridges, then put it in her pouch. She glanced up toward one of the stone towers, then the next. Artagán was perched on the tower to her left, but Ellwyn was nowhere to be seen. They'd been given their instructions. For their sakes, Lira hoped they'd be able to follow them.

Just then, Oda and Talfryn came into view, leading Skelly and Irem slowly over the dunes. Faolan and Lira rushed to help. By the time they'd returned to the surf, Rune was standing in the water, holding the rowboat steady.

To Lira's shock, Oda's uncle didn't look much older than she —mid-twenties, perhaps. His brown skin was lighter than Oda's —enough that Lira could make out a spattering of dark freckles across his nose in the bright moonlight. His thick mass of tight, brown curls was tied at the nape of his neck. He looked weary as he regarded the group, dark shadows beneath his light brown eyes.

"Oda, you could've picked a better time for all this." He sighed. "It's the coolest night of the year so far."

"We're beggars, Rune," she said. "There was no other choice."

"Aye. Well, climb aboard. You, there," he said, pointing to Lira, "come hold her steady so we can get everyone inside."

Lira took his place, holding the rowboat against the gentle

waves. It was harder than it looked—particularly while several people climbed inside. Talfryn got in first, giving a hand up to Skelly and Irem while Faolan, Rune, and Oda helped from below. Oda climbed in next, then extended her hand to Lira.

Once they were all in the boat, Rune took the oars and rowed them out, using his magic to push them along. Lira looked down over the side to see that he was manipulating the surface of the water. Little ripples of violet magic pushed the boat in the opposite direction of the current, moving them swiftly toward the ship.

When they reached the ship, Rune boarded first, climbing up a rope ladder he'd hung from the port side. He threw heavy ropes down to Oda and Faolan, who went to work rigging the rowboat for hoisting. Once they were satisfied with the knots, they climbed the ladder, too, followed by Lira and Talfryn. Together, the group hoisted the boat up with Irem and Skelly inside.

Lira was exhausted by the time they got her grandmother and mentor onto the ship's deck. Rune showed them where to put their meager belongings—food and basic provisions—then they gathered at the port deck to wait for Artagán's signal.

"Do you think we planted the seeds strategically enough?" Lira asked, leaning against the railing.

Skelly pursed her lips. "Did you not notice the foundation beginning to crack?"

A thrill of excitement pulsed through Lira, followed by sorrow at what they were about to do. Irem sat alone at the starboard quarter, his back turned to his childhood home. Once events were set in motion, there wouldn't be much time to act.

The sound of an owl's hoot echoed across the water, and Lira straightened, alert. "That's him."

She squinted to make out the towers. From what she could make out, Artagán had nocked an arrow and was now taking aim. Ellwyn still wasn't standing at the top of the opposite tower.

"Gerallt breached the gate," Lira whispered. She held her breath, waiting for Artagán to loose the arrow, but he remained still.

"Where's Ellwyn?" Talfryn looked stricken. "What's happening?"

A shrill whistle sounded then—Ellwyn's signal. Apparently, she'd been crouching at the top of her tower, because she stood then, swiftly nocking an arrow and aiming down into the court-yard herself.

"Ellwyn, stop!" Artagán shouted.

But Ellwyn let the arrow fly.

"No!" Her brother turned his own arrow toward her and fired.

CHAPTER 42

LIRA

Western Seashore

Lira bit down on her hand to keep from screaming.

"She must have hit Gerallt," Talfryn murmured solemnly. Skelly joined Irem on the other side of the ship and covered her face in her hands.

Ellwyn was still standing, gripping her shoulder. The arrow had either glanced off, or she had already broken the shaft. As Artagán nocked another, she hoisted herself over the outer edge of the tower and began painstakingly scaling down the vines that had grown there after the seeds had done their damage.

"Rune, get us back over there," Oda said. "She's going to need help."

Rune hastily lowered the rowboat, and Oda climbed down to it after them. They'd planned for Rune to meet Artagán and Ellwyn on the beach. Now that Artagán was a wild card and Ellwyn was injured, she would need extra cover. Rune used his water magic to move them back toward shore—more swiftly this time, with only two people in the boat.

Artagán remained at the top of the tower for a long

moment, bracing his hands on the wall and hanging his head. He disappeared inside instead of climbing down like they'd planned. Lira's heart sank.

It wasn't long before Rune was bringing the rowboat back— and Clan Mór's archers began emerging from between the battlements on the outer wall, aiming their bows. Arrows flew toward the little boat. Ellwyn screamed, and Oda pushed her down into the floor, diving down and covering her head herself.

"Hurry, hurry, hurry, hurry," Lira chanted, eyes skimming the wall for any glimpse of Gerallt or Artagán.

An arrow sank deep into Rune's shoulder, and he gasped, letting go of the oars. One slid off the side of the boat and sank into the water. Oda dove for him, and Lira could see the warrior's healing magic flare golden for a moment before fading again. Rune sat up on his knees and plunged over the side of the boat, dipping his hands into the water to propel it more quickly. Violet magic flared beneath the rowboat, and more arrows flew.

Faolan swore, tightening his grip on the railing, before he climbed onto it and dove smoothly overboard. He hit the water with barely a splash, then emerged to cut a quiet path toward the rowboat with practiced strokes. Working his way in front of the little boat, he combined his magic with Rune's to push the vessel toward the ship. It only took a few moments for them to get out of the archers' reach, and a few moments more to scale the ladder onto the ship's deck and hoist the small boat back up.

Lira rushed to Ellwyn's side, where Oda was examining the shallow wound Artagán's arrow had made. Ellwyn was in tears, and could barely draw a breath.

"He's dead—he's dead," Ellwyn gasped. "I killed my Papa, and now Artagán's gone again. With—with the archers."

The words bludgeoned Lira, and she rushed to her cousin, pulling her into an embrace when Oda was finished. "I'm sorry," she soothed as Ellwyn sobbed against her. "I'm sorry."

"How many archers left with him?" Oda asked gently, rubbing Ellwyn's back in soothing strokes.

"Eight," Ellwyn answered thickly, her voice muffled.

"Are there still sentries and archers inside the estate?"

"Most, yes—a small—small company of them."

"And Caitir?" Lira added.

"The only women I saw were archers, and they're with Artagán."

Oda and Lira exchanged a glance. Lira led Ellwyn to where Skelly and Irem sat, and helped her find a place to rest. Skelly cocooned Ellwyn in an embrace, and the two huddled together quietly, their backs turned to the scene that was about to unfold.

When Lira returned to the port side, Faolan was leaning on the railing, catching his breath. His gaze slid to her. "So it's done?"

She nodded once. "It's done."

He sighed heavily. "Good. Now for the rest of the tyrants. But first, the spectacle."

Lira tried to smile. "I'm ready for your great demonstration."

The corner of Faolan's mouth tipped up in a grin. "With pleasure." Straightening, he schooled his face into a solemn expression and approached Irem. "Lord Irem, I'm ready. And I'm truly sorry."

Irem gave Faolan a silent nod, then turned to look back out to sea. Faolan shot Lira a pained glance before he slipped quietly over the starboard side with no fanfare.

Save for its gentle waves, the sea was silent and dark. As the minutes passed, Lira found herself holding her breath, wondering when Faolan would emerge. She and Talfryn had planted Skelly's magic seeds both within Irem's courtyard and around the perimeter of the estate. Then, they'd summoned scores of giant roots, which had shaken the earth and rattled the small castle, cracking its stone foundation and destabilizing the ancient ground beneath.

Now, Faolan was about to deal the final blow.

He emerged from beneath the surface of the water then, not far from shore. A few straggling archers still occupied the towers, but they appeared to be short on arrows, for they did not fire with abandon. Faolan used his water magic to deflect any arrows that flew toward him, wading up until the water was only knee-deep.

Summoning violet magic into his hands, Faolan let his power flare, bright and vibrant against the night sky—more beautiful than the luminous waves that crashed around him. He cupped his hands and lowered them reverently onto the water's surface. Magic burst outward from where he made contact with the sea, drawing the water toward Faolan in a great swirling pool. It rose in a wall around him, leaving his feet planted firmly on the sand as it spun, a towering whirlpool on dry land.

The sea level dropped where the ship was anchored, abruptly lowering the boat as the water rushed and roared toward where Faolan stood, enveloped in a cyclone of crashing water. Suddenly, the world around them was so loud, Lira couldn't hear his incantation—that is, if he used one at all. She strained to hear his voice amidst the chaos.

What archers remained on the castle walls gaped at the display, as mesmerized as Lira and her friends on the ship. Abruptly, Faolan released the water he had gathered, and it left him standing on wet sand as it barreled toward the estate. He directed it toward the now-unstable ground beneath the stone structure, his hands pressing against an invisible force that propelled the massive, swirling whirlpool forward.

The seawater exploded against the hillside with the force of an earthquake. Faolan didn't wait before he turned and bolted in the direction of the ship, running full speed across the now-exposed sea floor. As soon as his feet hit water again, he leapt, hurtling into deeper waves and diving beneath the surface to cut a path back to Rune's ship. Already, the initial blast of water magic was receding, pulling earth and stone with it.

Irem's castle groaned mournfully, and along with it, its sole heir.

Faolan paused half a mile out from the ship, treading water as he summoned magic into his hands again. He sent a giant wave this time. It gathered and built, towering like a castle wall in its own right as it rushed toward shore. Again, the ship dropped with the sea level. Again, the water crashed into the hillside with brutal ferocity.

The castle's towers were the first to break apart and topple down the hillside as the broken earth slid from beneath it. Faolan's wave dragged back into the sea again, and he sent another, equally forceful wave right after it. With each impact, more of the castle collapsed in on itself. Lira wished to close her ears to the screams echoing in the distance.

The castle was soon reduced to a pile of rubble and half-fallen, once-fortified walls.

Faolan was swimming back to them now, and he climbed the rope ladder up the port side, moving more slowly than before. His limbs seemed heavy as he collapsed to his hands and knees on the deck, panting. Lira rushed to his side, removing his cloak and draping it over him.

"You're going to be cold," he protested, winded.

"Doesn't matter." Lira smiled and rested a hand on his shoulder. "That was brilliant."

He laughed lightly, glancing up at her, the ghost of a smile tugging at his lips. "Couldn't have done it without you and Tal."

Oda rushed to Faolan's side and administered her healing magic. Almost immediately, his breathing slowed, and his countenance improved. He rolled over onto his back and lay flat, his arms and legs splayed on the deck, and stared up at the stars before glancing over at Lira. "Wish Tarlach could've seen that."

"He can. I can share the memory when we're together again."

"Well." He sat up again, tugging the cloak tighter. Seawater still dripped from his hair onto his nose and cheeks. "Make sure you embellish it a bit, for my sake."

Lira patted his shoulder. "I'm sure you'll do plenty of embellishing yourself without my help."

The group gathered at the starboard quarter, where Irem, Skelly, and Ellwyn still sat. Reluctant to break the silence, they let a long moment pass until Oda finally said, "I suppose the next step is *turas*, then."

A yawning, hollow feeling opened in the pit of Lira's stomach, replaced by sudden horror. She whirled toward the rubble on the hill and groaned. "We never found an artifact."

"Oh, Silira!" Skelly cried. Everyone else was deathly silent.

Without an item to get them to the city, they would have to journey on horseback—if Thorne could be persuaded to give up enough mounts to make it possible. More likely, Thorne would refuse. Most likely, they would be confined under heavy guard at the war camp to prevent them from leaving. Their only other option would be to go on foot, which would take at least five days.

Too long. We don't have the time.

Lira thought she might be ill. She rushed to the railing and braced herself on it, willing away the sudden nausea that had crept up her throat. Tuning out her friends' whispers, she looked toward the water—but then a glint of gold caught her eye.

"Eremon's ring," she exclaimed, whirling. "We can use it."

"Brilliant!" Talfryn rushed to her side. "I never would've thought of that."

"Using that ring to *turas* could be risky," Irem cautioned. "It bears a heavy magical load. Each of you must weigh the risk of using it against the reward."

"Lord Irem, do you know the risk?" Lira asked, studying the ring's cobalt stone.

"I do not," he answered. "Wilga?"

"The best objects to use are ordinary things that have not been imbued with magic." Skelly scrutinized Lira's hand from where she sat. "But you've been wearing that ring for months now, alongside my pendant. Have you suffered ill effects?"

Lira shook her head. "Not that I'm aware."

"Then there may be no reason to worry." She glanced at Irem. "Would you agree?"

"I have always been one to err on the side of caution, Wilga," Irem answered. "You, on the other hand—well, we know your tendencies."

Skelly chuckled. "Silira, you must judge what is right. Then, your friends may decide."

"My decision remains unchanged," Lira answered. She looked from Skelly to Talfryn, then Faolan, then Oda. "I'm taking the risk."

"I am, too," Faolan said.

Oda and Talfryn nodded to one another. "So are we," Oda said.

Lira removed her pendant, and Talfryn donned it reverently. The group gathered on the deck and clasped hands. Before removing the ring, Lira looked to Skelly, Irem, and Ellwyn.

"Keep yourselves alive," she said quietly. And to Rune, "Protect them."

She didn't linger over goodbyes, though she dearly wanted to. Instead, she slipped Eremon's ring off her finger, then pressed it to the pendant around Talfryn's neck.

Turas pulled them from the ship's deck as swiftly and violently as a whirlwind. Lira clung to her brother and her friends as they flew over Rodhlan. She'd never experienced this before. Always before, *turas* was like an inky shadow that swallowed her up and then spat her out at her destination. This time, the spell drew itself out, allowing her to catch fleeting glimpses of the continent below as the magic hurtled them across land and water.

The spell deposited them in the meadowlands, near the opening to the tunnel she and Thorne had used to reach the crypt on their last journey here. Lira felt lightheaded as they landed together, still gripping one another tightly. Faolan looked as though he might be sick, and Oda administered her healing power to his wrists, as Thorne had once done for himself.

An elated grin spread across Talfryn's face, his dimples deep, eyes shining. "That was incredible!"

"What, you're not tired?" Lira looked him up and down, but he shook his head.

"Not in the slightest. I feel alive," he declared, removing the pendant as Lira slipped Eremon's ring back onto her finger.

When Talfryn extended the necklace to her, she reached for it—but he suddenly went pale, grasping her hand and making a strange, strangled noise. "Was it always like this?"

"Was what like what?" She snatched her hand back and turned it over to study Eremon's ring.

Lira swayed on her feet, stunned. The ring's cobalt stone had cracked down the middle, and it glowed with only a faint whisper of the magic it had once contained.

LIRA

Meadowlands

Faolan snatched Lira's hand and pulled it almost to his nose, squinting at the ring. "That can't be good."

Oda glanced at him, annoyed. "What does it mean?"

"I... assume it means that the ring's protection may be voided," Lira answered in a small voice. "I'm not sure what else it could mean."

A heavy silence descended. The meadowlands felt wide and barren around them, and suddenly Lira felt entirely too exposed. There seemed to be much less activity in and around the city than normal—no one coming and going as they used to, and no travelers moving about between clan settlements. Even the normal sounds of nature seemed to have quieted.

From what they'd gathered over the last few months, most of Rodhlan's people were sheltering in their homes, cloistered inside city walls, or encamped with the army. There wasn't a high chance of encountering anyone out here today. But it wasn't the meadowlands Lira was worried about.

"I feel so daft," Lira said shakily. "I don't know what's going to happen once we get inside the catacombs, much less the crypt. There could be sentries posted, or all manner of traps. I don't know what will happen when I try to use this." She rubbed her thumb over the stone.

Faolan glanced at her belt and raised an eyebrow. "You're also unarmed. Oda—give her something she can use to bludgeon someone."

"You have two swords and who knows how many daggers; you give her something," Oda shot back, though she grinned and unstrapped a long-handled axe from her back. She was wearing daggers strapped to her thighs, in addition to two broadswords secured across her back.

"You're the walking arsenal," Lira said, accepting the weapon. It was heavier than her usual axes, but its weight was evenly balanced and it felt good in her hands. "But you forget, I can make my own weapons."

Oda sized Lira up, drawing one of her broadswords. "Leaf-daggers or no, I would never walk into a fight without real metal."

"Perhaps it won't come to a fight." Lira regarded each of her friends, one by one. The enormity of what they were about to attempt washed over her, and she tried to fight the weight of it as it settled on her chest. "Once we've done what we came here to do, Eremon might be wholly unrecognizable. This could be nothing more than a suicide mission for all of us, and I don't want to be the cause of—"

"Lira, we all volunteered," Talfryn cut in. "None of us would be here with you if we weren't at peace with the risks."

"We'll take each moment as it comes," Oda said gently. "Faolan, any idea who might be posted on this end of the catacombs?"

He shook his head. "Not anymore."

"Last time, the sentries were friends of Thorne." Lira glanced at the mouth of the tunnel. "I doubt that's the case this time."

Oda helped Talfryn don his shield, which he'd been wearing on his back. Aidryn had, indeed, fashioned a shield that he could wear. It curved beautifully around him like armor, covering his left side. Into its surface, Aidryn had etched leaves and vines like the ones he'd painted in the illuminated manuscripts back at the archive for so many years.

The handiwork was unmistakably Aidryn's, and warmth bloomed in Lira's heart at the sight of it. She traced her fingertips over the wedding ring he'd given her. The damage to Eremon's ring would make Aidryn more vulnerable, too.

"We have to hurry," Lira said, trying to swallow the sudden fear that engulfed her at the realization. "Faolan?"

Faolan nodded to her, and she inclined her head. He looked at each of them in turn, then said, "All right, here's how we're going to do this. I'll lead. Lira, you follow behind me. Talfryn follows Lira, and Oda covers Talfryn's back."

They each nodded in agreement. Talfryn unsheathed his sword and hefted it in his hand, a brief flash of doubt crossing his features. Lira didn't miss the subtle change in Talfryn's expression as Faolan clapped a hand to his friend's shoulder, then gripped the back of his neck.

"You were trained for this, sentry," Faolan said, fixing Talfryn with a flinty stare. "Stay with me. You'll get out of here alive." Talfryn nodded, but didn't reply as Faolan shoved off and drew both of his swords.

Lira resisted the urge to gather her brother into her arms—comfort him as she did all those years in Iathium when she had mothered him, a child herself. The young man standing before her had earned every right to be treated as a warrior. Her heart swelled with pride as she watched him brace his sword, all youthful, sinewy strength.

One by one, they filed in through the entrance Lira and Thorne had taken into the catacombs in the spring. They followed the same pathways, Lira directing their steps as the tunnels grew darker, the light from the entrance growing farther and farther away.

Lira remembered the panic that had descended on her the last time she traversed these tunnels. She felt it trying to rise up in her throat again, to stifle her movements and slow them down. But she kept breathing, kept moving. There wasn't time to consider what might happen now that the ring was damaged. There was no turning back.

Finally, they reached the open cavern at the crypt's entrance. As they made to enter it, two sentries stepped into the threshold, blocking their way. They wore full armor, visors down, and raised their swords in warning.

Faolan stopped short and threw his arms out in attempt to block the others from passing him. Oda pushed past Lira and Talfryn to stand at his side, broadsword in hand.

"If it isn't the little wolf," one of the sentries jeered, his voice muffled and metallic beneath his helmet.

"Coming to sit in your mistress's lap again?" the other crooned, shifting her weight as if readying for him to charge.

"Ah, so you confirm she's inside," Faolan said nonchalantly. "Thank you for that, Gara. As to your question, no—I was only ever beneath her shoe. Never in her lap. Though that might have been slightly more comfortable, come to think of it."

He weighed his swords in his hands, glancing between the sentries. Lira's palms were sweaty around the handle of Oda's axe. The last time she'd traversed these tunnels with weapons in hand, she'd felt clumsy and vulnerable. But after months in Clan Beran's arena, her body was strong and her mind was sharp. She took in every detail—every movement the sentries made—with a steady, trained eye.

"Who do we have here?" the male sentry asked, stepping forward. Faolan raised one sword and stepped up as well, but the sentry didn't attack. Instead, he glanced at Oda, then looked over Faolan's shoulder at Talfryn and Lira. "A dirty clanswoman, a traitor, and two deserters. Garbage, the lot of you."

Faolan rolled his shoulders. "That you under there, Stefan? Whose arse did you have to kiss for that new suit of armor?"

Stefan lurched toward Faolan, but Gara blocked her partner's way with her spear. "You'd have been better off staying where you were, Faolan," she snapped, "kissing Macha's. We'd be calling you General by now."

Lira sucked in a breath, doing her best to make as little sound as possible. That must mean General Peros had been removed from power, just like Macha. She shuddered at the memory of the horrible man.

"Dog got put down, did he?" Faolan tightened his grip on his weapons. "Good. Pups next."

Faolan lunged at Gara, his blades clashing with her spear. Stefan stepped back nervously, just as unprepared for battle as Faolan had suggested.

"Help me, Stefan!" Gara barked, pushing against Faolan's crossed blades with all her might.

The heavily armored woman might have been larger than Faolan, but he surpassed her in strength and grit. He drove hard against her, holding steady as he moved her farther into the round cavern, making a path for the others to get by. Oda pushed past him and stalked toward Stefan, raising her sword overhead. He braced himself for impact as she took the first swing, pushing him farther back against the cavern's far wall.

Lira and Talfryn headed straight for the place on the wall where she'd found the markings before, keeping their backs to the wall and facing the struggle in front of them.

"Work with me—summon the roots," she said as Faolan and Oda held the sentries at bay. "Let's end this before they exhaust us."

Talfryn nodded. "Together." They sheathed their weapons reluctantly.

Lira took a deep breath and lay a palm on her brother's

shoulder. For a moment, they allowed themselves to close their eyes—to imagine scores of roots bursting from the cavern floor and winding their way across the expanse toward the sentries.

When Lira opened her eyes, roots had indeed covered the cavern floor. They gathered at its center, growing and twisting upward into a great tree whose branches and leaves burst outward. Unable to grow any taller, it grew outward, filling the room.

The tree's roots bound Stefan and Gara to the floor, first pinning their feet as they tried to move, then covering their bodies when they fell. Their weapons clattered to the ground as they shouted and struggled, desperate to escape. The roots bent and pressed their armor, leaving it weak and misshapen.

Oda joined Lira and Talfryn on the opposite side of the cavern, and Faolan made to go with them as well. But he hesitated, looking back at Stefan and Gara, who were still trapped inside the tangle of roots and warped armor. Faolan picked up their spears and turned them to saltwater with barely a thought. The weapons burst in a heavy shower, and he grinned smugly.

"I will end you, Faolan," Stefan promised, his voice a metallic rasp.

"I'd love to see you try from down there," Faolan shot back, swaggering lithely over the roots that now covered the cavern floor. He turned and stepped toward his friends.

"A pleasure," Gara said as she freed a hand from one of her gauntlets. She wrapped her fingers around one of the roots and squeezed. Clan Énna's power turned Lira's roots to saltwater, and the smell of brine filled her nose.

Faolan met the blast with waters of his own. He pushed it back with his magic, flooding the other side of the chamber until it reached the sentries' throats.

"Stay on dry ground!" he ordered, pushing harder. Sweat rolled down his brow. "Get the door open!"

"I'll cover you," Oda said, stepping between Faolan and the siblings.

Lira whirled, resting her hand below the Itelos inscription again. Eremon's ring hummed to life, its cobalt glow filling the cavern despite its damaged stone. She sighed with relief, sparing a glance back at Faolan—but dropped her hand as she took in the fight before her.

The churning water was up to Faolan's waist. When he sent a wave crashing against Gara, she went under. With a shout, Faolan forced the waters against the other side of the cavern to hold her there. Waves crashed against the far side of the room as Stefan struggled to regain his footing. Gara did not emerge.

Stefan had managed to keep his head above water, and was using the roots to keep himself from being submerged. Suddenly, Lira froze as a familiar crackle rose in the atmosphere. The hair on the back of her neck stood on end.

"Faolan..." Lira warned. "Come. The door—"

"We're almost finished here," Faolan said, shifting his swords back to both hands.

Stefan was on his knees now, salty waves battering him. He'd managed to remove his helmet, and his eyes were black with rage as he struggled against the remaining roots that bound him.

"Go ahead *Faolan*," Stefan goaded, the void in his eyes a stark contrast to his gleeful grin. "Raní Aila says death is the path to ultimate power."

Faolan's laugh rang hollow as he sent a crash of water into Stefan's face. "Then let's set you on it," he said, readying his blade as he waded deeper into the water, toward the sentry.

Lira's thoughts were driven from her mind when she saw that Stefan, too, had removed his gauntlet. Black sparks sizzled between his fingers, and his lips spread in a wicked grin.

"Faolan!" Lira screamed.

"Get out of here!" he shouted, motioning toward the crypt.

Stefan plunged his bare hand into the water, which still

lapped around Faolan's feet. The sentry uttered a guttural curse and released a surge of dark magic into the water.

Faolan whirled toward where Lira stood and tried to flee, but his eyes went wide as the current of power charged the water. His legs gave way beneath him and he hit his knees, convulsing as the power boiled the water surrounding him.

The black lighting killed Stefan instantly. He slumped against the vines that bound him, his armor sparking and popping in the electrified water.

Lira couldn't think past the horror playing out before her—past her own screams and those of Talfryn and Oda. The silent horror in Faolan's eyes as he tried and failed to crawl in her direction. The sudden, terrible memories of how Eremon had died this way, at the mercy of the nightmare power.

Lira tried to lunge for him, but Oda and Talfryn grabbed her by the arms and hauled her back against the wall.

"Let me go to him!" Lira cried, fighting against them. Oda's grip was as strong as stone.

Faolan barked out a pained, "No," as the sparks began to dissipate and he found the ability to move again. He began scooting toward them, a little at a time, until he had managed to pull himself up out of the water that remained on the cavern floor. The minute he was on dry ground, Lira broke from the others and rushed to him.

"Faolan, Faolan," she chanted, falling to her knees beside him.

He was still on all fours, his entire body trembling violently. "I—I—I'm fine," he stammered.

"Liar," she breathed, finally getting a good look at his hands. They were badly scalded and would likely blister. His palms were blackened, as though the power had burst out through them.

If his hands are this bad, I don't want to know what happened to his feet and legs. Or his insides. Her stomach lurched at the realization.

"Let's get Oda to patch you up," Lira whispered, tentatively resting a hand on Faolan's back as he continued to shudder.

"N—nothing that t—takes v—very long," he demanded, tilting his head to look at her. He blinked several times, as though trying to clear fog from his eyes.

Lira didn't have to call Oda over; she had already knelt beside Faolan, surveying his injuries. Her eyes widened as she took in what wounds she could see.

"Lira, I can't heal this on my own," she said, not bothering to hide the truth from Faolan. "You might as well understand this now: All I can do is patch you up a bit. My power's not strong enough for complete healing."

"L—leave me here, then," Faolan said, shaking his head. "I'll just s—slow you down."

His teeth clacked together, his body tensing as he continued to tremble.

"Absolutely not," Lira said, touching Oda's shoulder as she rose to join her brother. "Oda, do whatever you can. Make sure it's as unpleasant as possible so he'll remember not to make stupid suggestions."

Faolan barked out a pained laugh as Oda helped him lie down on his side. Talfryn hung back, his eyes red-rimmed and filled with tears. Wordlessly, Lira reached for her brother and he pulled her in for an embrace, holding her tightly. Lira rested her head against his chest and they stood together, shaken, for a long while as Oda spoke to Faolan in low tones and sent golden orbs of healing magic into his body.

It seemed like a lifetime passed before Oda finally stood shakily and helped Faolan to his feet. The sentry moved slowly, but he was standing—he was moving. He put on a determined grimace, allowing Oda to sheathe his swords across his back. She clapped him on the shoulder—just the sort of move he'd have expected any of his friends to make, to deflect from the state he was in.

"I told you to open the crypt, Book Wife," he said when they arrived at the wall. His voice was tired and strained. "Going to disobey *my* orders now, too?"

"What did you expect? By the way, I'll be leading now. Let Talfryn help you. Oda—cover their backs." Lira turned her back to him before he could protest, then placed her palm below the inscription. Despite its damage, the ring flared to life again, and the wall disappeared.

CHAPTER 44
LIRA

Crypt of Iathium

They stepped into the crypt, allowing themselves to be sealed inside. Lira reached down to touch one of the floor tiles and listened for the satisfying sound of the traps disarming all around them. The room's color shifted from gray to blue once again, illuminated in part by the ring's power.

"This worked last time," she whispered. "Let's hope it holds true."

Tightening her grip on the axe, Lira took the lead. Talfryn walked two steps behind her, flanked by Oda and Faolan.

Today, there was no harp playing in the crypt. The atmosphere felt heavier and more eerie than before. Briefly, Lira wondered if Macha was still alive. They made it to the far end of the crypt before they found her, huddled in a threadbare robe.

Lira sucked in a breath at the sight of the once-formidable woman. Macha was vastly thinner than before, her cheeks deep hollows against ashen skin, her body feeble.

"I was hoping you would return before my provisions failed me," Macha said, her voice weak.

"And did I?" Lira asked quietly.

"No." Macha's gaze slid to Lira, her expression contemptuous. "I subsist on nothing but my magic now—though it will sustain me a little longer, until you can bring your Key Keeper back here."

Lira squared her shoulders and raised her chin. "That wasn't part of the bargain. I won't be returning a third time."

Macha rose shakily, bracing against the wall for balance. "That boy follows you everywhere," she seethed. "Why isn't he here now?"

"That's not your concern. I swore to come back, and here I am. I want to hear what you know about this power you spoke of."

"You were meant to bring information to *me*." Macha pursed her lips and slid her gaze to Faolan. "Little Wolf. You've grown rather mangy since the last time I saw you."

"Shall I tell you what *you* look like, then, my lady?" Faolan drawled. Lira prayed Macha would miss the slight slur in his words.

"No; I quite prefer ignorance." The woman's voice was suddenly sharper, stronger. She watched Faolan with the intensity of a cat waiting to pounce on its prey. Lira thought she saw a hint of a smile tug at the corner of her mouth. "I admit, of all the sentries who served me, you're the only one whose company I have missed—traitor or not. And it seems you survived the poor excuses for guards in the catacombs."

"Indeed," he answered.

Macha shifted her focus to Lira once again, taking a step closer. Her eyes glinted. "How much do you know about my son's power?"

"I know why it's so coveted," Lira admitted, "and so powerful our neighbors across the sea made Rodhlan ignorant of it."

"My ancestors. Cunning and ruthless, they were." Macha laced her fingers together. "They were right not to underestimate this place. They knew how powerful Rodhlan's people could become, given the right tools."

"You could have helped the people," Lira said. "Instead, you were bent on controlling Eremon."

"As any good mother does when her child sits on a throne. He was not fit to rule a continent; he was too young. Too kind." She began to move, as though to circle Lira.

"You say that with contempt." Lira responded in kind, careful to keep her eyes trained on Macha, her hands braced on the axe.

"It's hard to love a child your people revere more than you." Lira thought she caught a flash of regret on Macha's face as she continued. "Yet, I'm distressed to find that I miss him."

"Perhaps you miss the opportunities he afforded you."

"As do you." Macha grew still. Her dark eyes bored into Lira. Crackling black power sparked around her fists, then winked out. "Or you would not be standing here now."

"It's true; the promise of his power is intoxicating," Lira's mind raced. *Macha must not realize Eremon can be awakened.* "To overcome the usurpers is tempting, but to unite the clans under a greater power, even more so. Iathium need not be your only stronghold in Rodhlan. Why not rule the entirety of the continent, clans included? Strip them of their autonomy, make them bow to Iathium's throne once again."

Macha's thinly-veiled rage shone on her face as dark magic wound around her fingers. "Then you should have gathered the power of all four clans here today. The Beran girl, the Énna boy. They're here, you're here. You should have brought that Tarlach boy, too, and this would be complete.

"I thought you were more intelligent than this—that you'd be able to put the pieces together yourself. You almost did, but only just! Now it's too late for me; it's too late for all of us. I will use the last gasp of my power to bring this crypt down on our heads. If I can't escape here alive, none of us will."

Macha raised her hands, as though to blast her dark power toward the ceiling, but Lira cried, "Wait!"

Her friends stood behind her, silent—waiting for her lead. The deposed Raní arched an eyebrow, glancing briefly at the weapon in Lira's hands. "What is it you want? You cannot stop what I am about to do."

"If you please, then," Lira began, heart racing, "I wish to pay my respects. I've never seen Eremon's vault; I would like to before I die. And Rí Corlan's—for my father's sake. Da's body was never returned from Iteloria, you see. We never gave him a proper burial."

Macha stood straighter. "Very well. Follow me."

She led the way down a row of vaults against the crypt's deepest interior wall. They halted before a pair of pale blue, marble vaults. Macha rested her hand heavily on one of them.

"This is my son's," she said solemnly. "I was not given the time to engrave his name upon it before I was locked in here. His father's is there." Macha nodded to her right. "Be quick about it. I am weary to my bones; I wish to be done with all of this."

"As do I," Lira whispered.

She felt a hard tug at the back of her mind as she surveyed the tomb Macha was touching. That was where Eremon rested. Her stomach clenched at the sight of it—and she felt a familiar buzz of power in Eremon's ring. She moved her hand out of Macha's sight.

Lira chanced a glance at her friends, who were watching her carefully. Faolan looked like he might collapse where he stood. She noted that Oda and Talfryn flanked him closely, ready to brace him if need be.

Please, she pleaded with them silently. *Cover my back.* Though she regretted that she'd brought them all to this precipice, Lira was comforted by their presence. She was relieved not to be alone in this tomb with Macha, who had inflicted so much suffering on them.

Lira began to kneel between the vaults, but hesitated, her outstretched hand hovering near the cool stone of Eremon's tomb. If awakening him was unsuccessful, they would all die here.

"Well?" Macha snapped. "Be done with it."

"Yes, my Raní," Lira whispered, gripping the marble and dropping to her knees before the vaults. The passage between them was narrow enough that Lira could touch both at once.

She rested her right hand on Corlan's and bowed her head, shutting her eyes against Macha and the crypt and everyone else. Once she obtained Iuchair, she would have only moments to use it, if that. She could feel the great key humming with power, *right now*, just inside Corlan's vault

Lira's palms began to sweat as she dove deep within herself, searching for a tendril of Aidryn's magic. He would understand why she'd moved ahead without him. He would *have* to.

She turned her thoughts back to Iuchair, setting her intention to receive it. The sheer power contained in the great key— this object coveted by rulers for centuries—pulsed through the marble into her bones.

Lira had Clan Mór's Anointing, and access to the anointed power of Clan Tarlach. Paired with Iuchair and the ring she wore, however damaged, this key would make her unstoppable. And what was to stop her from completing the clans' power, with descendants from Beran and Énna within her grasp? If she were to only give herself to the magic—lose herself in it—she could be more powerful than Eremon himself, or any ruler that came before him.

A yawning, bottomless well opened up inside her, and she suddenly hungered to fill it with the power of the mortal gods. Of the clans. To take and take and take, until the only thing that remained was magic, vast and unending and limitless.

Vaguely, she sensed a struggle happening nearby, but she couldn't tear herself away from the tomb. The swell of power surging through her body was intoxicating, and she gasped against it, refocusing her mind on obtaining the key. She forced a tendril of Aidryn's power through the near-impenetrable marble and felt it search—then find.

Lira felt the key dissolve into Aidryn's power. Willed it to remain hidden as she claimed it. Felt its visceral protest as she concealed it in the ether, the way Aidryn had taught her.

Finally, she tore herself away from the tomb and stood, turning to seek her friends. Talfryn and Faolan were holding Macha against the wall, their blades trained on her throat as Oda pinned her arms behind her. Macha was panting wildly as she fought the Beran warrior's iron grip.

"I see it was wise to bring companions," Lira said as she approached.

Macha laughed roughly. "Pay your respects," she spat. "I'm a fool!"

"Fool, you are," Lira answered, "and that is for you to reckon with."

"You've grown into quite the little liar," Macha said, jerking against Oda's grip. Oda applied more pressure, and the older woman groaned.

"Not lies," Lira answered, "but many closely-held truths— some kept secret from those who intend harm."

"How did you do it?" Macha demanded, her eyes roving over Lira. "Where is the key? I want to see it."

Lira did not answer, but turned back toward Eremon's tomb, approaching it slowly. It bore no carvings, no sign of ceremony or station save the rich marble it was made from.

"Hold her, Oda," Lira heard herself say as she lay a hand on the cool stone. "I don't know what's going to happen."

Macha screamed and swore, struggling against Oda's grasp. "Don't you see what she's doing?" she wailed. "She's going to take it all!"

Despite being weakened, the ring's cobalt stone raged to life, so intensely bright it illuminated the entire crypt once again. Lira drew a shaky breath, suddenly afraid to face

Eremon in his new form. Unsure of the emotions it would stir within her to see him again. But she reached for Aidryn's power once more and allowed Iuchair to appear in her hand.

The power in and around her raged so loudly, Lira could scarcely make out the renewed struggle happening nearby. She followed her instincts and let the powers guide her: the truth within her, the power of the ring, and the demands of the key, which grew louder with every passing moment. She climbed onto the marble tomb and sat on her knees, searching its smooth finish for any sign of access.

An Itelos inscription etched itself into the surface of Eremon's vault, and Lira placed her palm below it, pressing against the marble like she had pressed the wall outside. A keyhole appeared above the inscription, glowing with the same cobalt power that emanated from her ring.

Lira fitted the key into the hole and was ready to turn it when something collided into her, knocking her off the vault. She struck her head hard against Corlan's vault and saw stars as she struggled to pull herself onto her feet.

Macha was gripping the key now, but the ring's power had faded, and she seemed to be struggling with it.

"No!" Macha cried, attempting to turn it herself. The key was held fast inside the marble, and Lira thought through the pain that perhaps the stone had closed in on it.

Oda charged at Macha, but the older woman sent a shock of dark power into the warrior's stomach, knocking her to the ground. Lira heard Faolan shout Oda's name. But a moment later, Oda was on her feet again, winded but charging once more.

Suddenly, Talfryn was at Lira's side, hauling his sister off the ground. She swayed, and the room doubled as Talfryn held her up.

"Are you all right?" he asked, surveying her.

She shook her head, dazed, and Talfryn let her lean into him. Oda hauled herself onto the marble lid of Eremon's vault where Macha still knelt. The warrior wrenched Macha's hands away from the key, gritting her teeth against the black sparks that crackled and popped between them. Macha held strong against Oda, feeble though she looked.

Lira tried to move toward Eremon's vault again, but Talfryn held her back. Suddenly, Faolan leapt onto the vault from the opposite side, colliding with Macha and knocking her to the floor. Talfryn dragged a dazed Lira back to Eremon's tomb and helped her climb up.

The room spun, and Lira swayed on her hands and knees. Her head was pounding, the pain so intense she could barely think. Three keys hovered in her line of sight, the holes indeed closed around them. She wasn't sure which one to grasp.

Her brother grabbed her hand and guided her toward the key. "Show me what to do," he demanded as her fingers wrapped around it. "Where did you put your hand before?"

Three inscriptions appeared before her. Three rings flared to life. Lira tried to place her other hand down on the right one, but she couldn't manage to find where she should put it. Talfryn gently moved her hand into position, and the magic illuminated the keys once again.

Through her daze, Lira managed to set her intention: *Eremon. Come back to us, Eremon.*

Talfryn helped Lira turn the key, and the crypt went black.

CHAPTER 45
LIRA

Crypt of Iathium

For a moment, Lira wasn't sure whether she'd fainted, or the light had been completely snuffed out of the crypt. The struggle between Macha and Lira's friends ceased. Everything went deathly silent.

A low groan sounded from deep beneath the crypt, reverberating up into the marble vault. Cracks appeared in its surface, illuminated by cobalt light that burst through the fissures in dazzling shafts. Lira gasped, reaching out to lay a hand over the pulsing magic.

Talfryn looped his arm around Lira and pulled her down off the vault as the marble began to crumble in on itself. They scrambled back together, pressing themselves against Corlan's vault as the rumble of breaking stone filled the crypt.

A column of that blue power burst violently from the center of the open vault. It sparkled like stardust as it filled every space. Lira's eyelids grew heavy, her head lolling against Talfryn's shoulder as she struggled to take in what was happening. She felt nothing as she watched the magic gather in on itself in a burst of cobalt flame. And her eyesight began to fade just as the flames took the form of a man—a man who turned slowly to regard her with a curious tilt of his head.

Lira vaguely registered the feeling of her brother helping her lie back on the cool floor. Blinked hard against the darkness that threatened to pull her under. Felt the achingly familiar presence that flooded her senses as the man made of flame knelt beside her and gently cradled her head in his hands.

He whispered something Lira couldn't understand, his words scattering like thousands of voices, splintered and chaotic. She felt fingertips on her forehead. Felt magic pour into her body.

Once again, the crypt filled with that soft cobalt light. Lira gasped as the world returned and the pain abruptly left her. Her vision sharpened, and she sat up to find herself face to face with Eremon, who was on his knees before her.

Eremon rocked back on his heels, pressing a hand to his mouth as the room righted itself around Lira. He was flawless. His silken black hair fell loose over his shoulders, his angular eyes flashing silver in the glow of the crypt. He was dressed in a plain black tunic much simpler than the ceremonial robes he'd always worn before.

Lira wanted to say something to him—call out his name. Embrace him. Touch his face. Prove to herself he was real, and truly alive. But an anguished scream shattered the moment, and she turned to Talfryn in alarm.

"Macha," Lira said.

Eremon whirled, scanning the room for his mother, then offered a hand to Lira without a word. She took it reluctantly, allowing him to pull her to her feet. There was a jolt of power at the contact, and Lira let go as soon as she was steady, readying her axe. They didn't pause to regard one another again, but instead moved toward the crypt's far end, Talfryn following behind.

"Let me go to him! Let me go!" Macha was screaming as they rounded the corner to find Oda pinning her to the ground.

Oda's side was soaked with blood, her left arm covered in weeping blisters. She was holding her blade to Macha's throat. "He's my son! My son!"

"Quiet," Oda ordered, applying pressure to the blade. She jerked her chin to the right. "Get to Faolan. Now."

Talfryn bolted in the direction she'd indicated, Lira at his heels. "I'll handle her," Eremon was saying, but his words garbled in Lira's ears at the sight before them.

Faolan was lying in a pool of blood at the foot of an unmarked vault. Talfryn was already kneeling there, his hand covered in blood. He was trembling, as though he didn't quite know where he was or what he should do.

"Faolan!" Lira screamed, running full tilt toward where her friend lay.

She skidded to her knees beside Faolan and grasped his hand, searching frantically for the source of the blood. There were several deep wounds in his side, as though he'd been pierced by a blade over and over.

"Beast had a—" He gasped, turning his head toward Lira. "Had a bloody dagger on her. She was coming for you."

Sure enough, a jagged dagger lay a few feet from Faolan, covered in blood. Lira's eyes filled with hot tears as she gripped her friend's hand.

"You selfless idiot," she whispered, pushing the sweat-slick curls off his forehead. His skin was clammy and cool.

"Stop blubbering," he said. "I didn't—I didn't do it for you." He labored to take a shallow breath. "I did it for—for Tarlach. Promised him."

Talfryn let out a pained cry then—as though the reality of what was happening had just begun to sink in.

"Oda?" Lira called, panic rising in her voice. "We need you!"

Suddenly, the room filled with an otherworldly pressure. Lira's ears ached and popped. She whirled to see Eremon using a swell of that cobalt power to pin Macha to the far wall. Horror filled his mother's eyes, and Lira might have pitied her before—

might have asked Eremon to release her—but now Faolan was dying before them by her hand.

Instead of calling out, Lira watched as Eremon summoned Oda's axe into his own hand. Heard the sickening crunch of the blade as it sank into Macha's sternum. Her eyes went wide as she registered what was happening. Then, she sagged against the wall.

Oda skidded to the floor beside where Faolan lay, wincing as she held her side. Lira tightened her grip on Faolan's hand.

"Here she is now," she said softly. "Here she is. Oda's coming to help you."

"Lira," Oda protested, winded. "I—"

"She can't." Faolan gasped for air. "But don't make her feel badly for it. She's hurt, too."

"No," Lira argued, though she knew deep down that Faolan was right. He had been too badly weakened by Stefan's dark magic, and Oda hadn't been able to fully repair him then. Worse, Oda had been hit with a blast of that power herself. But Lira wasn't ready to admit defeat. "But Eremon—we have an immortal. We can save you."

Faolan tried to laugh, but just shook his head. "Let me rest now. Tell my sister..."

Tears streamed down Lira's cheeks. "Don't do this, Faolan. Hold on."

"No, listen," he whispered, squeezing her hand. "Tell Fiadh I'll haunt her—for—for what she's done."

"Stop talking," Lira pleaded. "Save your strength."

Oda's face crumpled, tears streaming down her cheeks. "I can try to ease the pain of it. I'll do whatever I can."

Scooting closer, she lay her hands on Faolan. One weak pulse of golden light passed into him, then another—enough so that he could draw a steady breath. Talfryn hung his head, his body shuddering as he wept.

"I'm sorry, Faolan," Oda cried. "I can't stop what's happening. I'm sorry."

"Don't coddle me," Faolan said weakly, relaxing beneath Oda's touch.

"Shall we insult you instead?" Lira asked, moving closer. Oda helped Lira pull Faolan's head into her lap, and she stroked his hair.

"Please." Faolan's eyelids fluttered shut.

"All right," Lira breathed. "You're a good friend."

Faolan groaned. "Stop. That's a real insult."

"I know." Lira tried to laugh, but her chin was trembling too violently, her tears coming too hot and fast. "You're loyal and brave. And even though you want everyone to think you're a terrible person, we love you all the more for it."

"Blast it," he whispered, opening his eyes a crack. "Am I so transparent?"

"Yes. To your great disappointment, I'm sure."

Faolan nodded once, slightly, and reached for Lira's other hand. Tears slid from the corners of his eyes, but he didn't bother to hide them or blink them away. Instead, he stared up at the ceiling, letting them gather in pools before they spilled over.

"I'm afraid," he whispered, his voice barely audible. "Help —help me go."

Lira crumpled then, leaning close to press her forehead against his. "I don't want to," she cried, letting her own tears fall on his face.

"Please," he whispered, rubbing his thumb across her knuckles.

With a shuddering sigh, Lira nodded and placed a kiss on his brow. She released one of his hands and pressed her fingertips to his temple.

"Faolan Énna, witness," she whispered, letting her eyelids drift shut as she called on her power.

A burst of emerald light from her pendant illuminated the room as she begged her magic for peaceful memories. For comfort. For the sound of ocean waves as they broke upon the shore.

And she poured that power into him, weeping quietly as she felt Faolan's body relax beneath her touch. Felt the tension and the fear leave him. Felt him draw one last breath, and still forever.

For a long moment, the world was a blur. Lira wasn't sure when she'd begun to wail, but suddenly, the sound of her own keening rushed into her ears as though it had been far away. She leaned into Oda and Talfryn, who had moved closer to wrap their arms around her. The three of them stayed that way a long while —perhaps too long. But they couldn't will themselves to move.

Lira didn't hear Eremon approach, but she could feel his gaze on them. On her. He made no sound as he knelt beside Faolan's body.

"He is worthy of my greatest forefathers," Eremon whispered. "I will send him to rest with them."

Lira studied Eremon, waiting for some sign that he was the danger everyone had feared. But he seemed like the Eremon she remembered—gentle, quiet, kind. She shut her eyes against the surge of relief that washed over her, the tears falling faster than before.

"You can't revive him somehow?" Oda's voice rose in desperation.

"Did I revive myself?" Eremon asked sadly, his gaze dropping to the floor.

"I'm sorry," Oda whispered, her chin trembling.

"Don't be," Eremon replied. He moved a little closer, pressing his fingertips between Faolan's eyes. Then, he murmured something in Itelos, and Faolan's body shifted to violet flame, then dissipated to stardust. The groan of stone on stone sounded from across the crypt as Eremon's vault remade itself.

Eremon gathered the sparkling magic into an orb, looking

as though he might rise. But he paused, tilting his head toward the magic. His gaze snapped to Lira. "He was an anointed?"

Lira's tears stung. "Yes. Clan Énna."

Oda gasped. "What?"

"The magic speaks to me," Eremon said. "It wants to choose another."

"Then release it," Lira answered numbly. "Let it anoint who it will."

"Very well." Eremon closed his eyes. A gentle wind rushed around him, ruffling strands of hair around his face. Then, a portion of the magic he held broke from the orb and drifted to Oda, hovering just above her heart.

She cried out softly, eyes widening. "I'm only half Énna," she protested weakly. "Why would it choose me?"

Eremon studied her closely. "Don't question it—just let it be what it is. If you don't accept the power, it will go elsewhere."

Oda hesitated, but nodded slowly. The magic sank beneath her skin, bursting into a glittering scatter of violet light. What was left of the magic in Eremon's hands remade itself into a smaller orb and he stood, guiding it toward the tomb he'd just abandoned himself. When he reached the marble vault, he directed the magic toward the few fissures that remained open on its surface. As the power sank inside, he closed the cracks, leaving the tomb as flawless as before. He lay his hand on the marble, and Faolan's name etched itself into the vault's surface.

Lira felt stunned as Eremon crossed the room to them again. She could barely pull herself up from the ground, and relied on Oda and Talfryn to help her. Her body was trembling violently, her knees weak.

She leaned on Talfryn as Oda slowly stooped to gather Faolan's bandolier, belt, and swords. Then, she headed for where Eremon stood, but stopped in her tracks with a soft, "Oh."

Across the wide chamber, Macha was alive—but barely. Oda's axe was still buried in her chest. Eremon stretched his fingers toward it and it vanished, reappearing in his hand with no trace of blood. He offered it to Oda without a word, and she passed it back to Lira, regarding Eremon curiously.

"We need to leave," Talfryn said quietly. "We've been here too long."

Lira kept her eyes on Eremon, though she hoped he wouldn't look at her yet. He seemed distracted enough by the sight of Macha. Quietly, he moved toward his mother. Oda, Talfryn, and Lira trailed behind him.

When Eremon reached Macha, he crouched before her, surveying her wound first, then her face. Her expression was one of desperation—perhaps of longing.

"My son..." she rasped. Blood trickled from the corner of her mouth. "Give me mercy."

"You've shown your hand," Eremon answered coolly, "just as you did in my first lifetime. The only mercy I can give you is a swift decay."

He stood abruptly, turning his back on her and walking toward them once again, his gaze vacant, his eyes glowing silver in the dimming crypt. Macha tried to cry out, but her voice was silenced by a surge of dark power that consumed her body in moments. There was nothing left but bones when Eremon's magic was finished with her—just as he had promised.

Eremon didn't once look back at Macha's remains, but strode purposefully toward the crypt's entrance. Lira couldn't help noticing the way his fists clenched at his sides, the tension in his shoulders. She longed to say something to him— anything—but she didn't know where to begin. A tendril of fear began to take root as she watched him go. As terrible as Macha had been, Lira had never envisioned Eremon being the one to end her.

Her mind grasped the memory of his final speech at *Nami Mostari*, before their first dance months ago. That day, she'd caught a glimpse of the deity he'd buried deep within himself.

If she had been equipped to follow the threads all the way to their conclusion, she might have figured all of this out before.

It was dizzyingly surreal to be this near to Eremon. To see him alive once again. But bringing him back had cost them Faolan's life. Even though Lira had known they could die here, it hadn't felt real until they'd lost him. Renewed grief swept through her, and she began to weep again before they reached the wall.

Talfryn wrapped his arm around her shoulders and squeezed her lightly. They stopped behind Eremon, and he raised his hand as if to touch the inscription—but then turned abruptly to look at Lira. He laced his fingers together tightly and stepped closer to her, bending to eye level. She allowed herself to meet his gaze, and to feel the surge of relief at his presence in the wake of Faolan's loss.

Eremon's silver eyes were mournful, his gaze full of longing as he whispered, "I'm so sorry, Lira. For everything."

Lira took a tentative step forward, tears tracing down her cheeks, and looked up into his eyes. There weren't adequate words to respond with, so she embraced him instead, throwing her arms around his neck and heaving a sob as he stiffened, then wrapped his arms around her, too.

"It's time," he whispered after a moment, releasing Lira and taking a step back. He grasped her hand, running his thumb gingerly over the silver ring from Aidryn. Grief etched into his expression for a moment before he closed his eyes, nodded once, and let go.

Lira sagged, and Oda grasped her hand. Eremon turned his back to them and placed his hand below the inscription on the wall. It vanished to reveal the grotto cavern. The magical waters had receded while they were inside the crypt. The dead sentries' bodies lay sprawled on the bare cavern floor, still engulfed in a mass of roots.

With a flick of his fingers, Eremon sent that same dark power to devour Gara and Stefan's bodies. Lira cringed, hiding her face. When it was over, Eremon stepped through the discarded rubble of armor and bones, gathering spears and daggers. He kept one spear for himself and extended the other to Talfryn, who sheathed his sword and took the spear from Eremon.

Wordlessly, Oda handed Faolan's swords to Eremon, then went to work tightening the straps on Talfryn's shield.

"What happened?" Eremon asked softly, looking pointedly at Talfryn's left shoulder, his expression pained.

"Peros, that's what," Talfryn answered, raising his chin. "I did it for Lira."

"She's worthy," Eremon answered quietly, stepping forward to rest his hand on Talfryn's shoulder. "Thank you."

Talfryn dipped his chin, then looked to his sister, his green eyes glassy. Lira offered him a small smile and turned to Eremon. "Let's go," she said.

They began to move down the tunnel, but Oda stumbled, then crumpled to her knees, clutching her side.

CHAPTER 46

LIRA

Catacombs

"Oda!"

Lira rushed to her friend's side. Oda managed to shift into a sitting position, propping her head against the cavern wall. She was panting rapidly, her breaths shallow, and there was a sheen of sweat on her face.

"I—I'll be all right," she said weakly. "Just need a moment." She gasped, pressing her palm to the bloodied fabric and squeezing her eyes shut.

In the chaos, they'd neglected to look at the warrior's wound. "Eremon," Lira called. "Can you help her?"

Eremon crouched beside them, placing a gentle hand on Oda's shoulder. "I can take your pain," he said softly. "I did it for Lira, back in the crypt."

Again, there was the old kindness. Lira could scarcely believe they'd succeeded—that he was here now. That he was still Eremon, an immortal god made flesh. He regarded the warrior with quiet admiration as he awaited her consent.

Oda eyed Lira suspiciously. "Apparently; that gash in her head should have knocked her out cold."

"That what?" Lira asked, instinctively raising her hand to press it to her head.

Oda reached out and caught her hand, wincing at the sudden movement. "Don't touch it! It's an open wound."

"Sit still," Eremon ordered. He pointed to Oda's side. "Lira, peel back her tunic, just there. Let's have a look."

Gingerly, Lira exposed Oda's wound. It was deep, and there was no way to determine exactly how much damage Macha's dagger had done. Oda was still losing blood rapidly, the wound refusing to clot.

Talfryn craned his neck to look toward one end of the corridor, then the other. "We need to hurry—more sentries could be here any minute."

Lira's hands began to tremble, and she felt lightheaded. "We have to stop the bleeding first," she said shakily. "It can't keep going like this."

"You need to pack the wound with something," Oda said breathlessly.

"We don't have proper dressing," Lira cried.

Eremon glanced at her and raised a cautioning hand. "Don't panic, please."

"I'm not panicking," she protested, her voice rising. "She's bleeding out!"

"You're going to frighten her," he said in a low voice, gritting his teeth.

Talfryn scooted closer to them, edging between Lira and Eremon to get a better look at Oda. "Move; let me see." He nudged Lira away and inspected Oda's wound himself, then looked to Eremon. "I need you to put your fingers into the wound—put pressure on it, all right?"

Eremon nodded silently, following Talfryn's direction. Oda winced, crying out, but Eremon held firm. Lira turned her head, suddenly nauseous.

"All right." Talfryn nudged Lira's back with his elbow. "Lira, make me some moss."

"What?" Lira asked weakly.

"*Moss*, Lira. Do it."

Lira held out her hands and conjured a mass of fresh, brilliantly green moss, then passed it to Talfryn without turning around.

"You all right, Lira?" Oda gritted out.

"If I remember correctly, that one has a weak stomach," Eremon said, his voice tinged with amusement. "I think she's trying not to vomit her guts out."

"Don't talk to me about vomit." Oda moaned. "Lira, you had better *not*. Ow—Talfryn!"

"Sorry!"

There was a bit of shuffling behind Lira as Talfryn worked on Oda's wound. Lira pressed her lips shut and breathed through her nose, trying not to think about what was happening. After a moment, Eremon scooted closer to her, wiping the blood from his hand onto his black tunic.

"She's going to be fine, I think," he said, "but we have to get her to a real healer."

"Fortress Halgeir's the closest," Lira replied, chancing a glance at him. "They've opened a new entrance 'round the eastern side. We won't have to move her upriver."

"Can't we just *turas*?" Talfryn asked from behind them.

"No," Eremon answered. "She has a magical wound from my mother's power. *Turas* could make it worse."

"Yes, it will," Lira agreed. "I've experienced it. Non-magical travel is safest."

Oda groaned again, and wave of nausea hit Lira. She sucked in a breath. "Distract me—I'm going to be sick."

"I really don't know where to start," Eremon said softly. "I have no idea what to say."

Lira tried to laugh, though the tension in her shoulders was building. "Neither do I."

Tentatively, Eremon scooted closer, sitting close enough to Lira that she could feel his warmth. "I don't think I'll ever be able to make amends for what's happened." His voice was barely audible.

Lira turned to face him. His expression was so sincere—so pained—that she almost laughed in disbelief. "You *died*, and you think you need to make amends?"

He tucked a strand of silken black hair behind his ear, then leaned on his knees. "I put a weight on you that you did not deserve to bear. And now I must live with the consequences."

"Better than being dead with the consequences," Lira said dryly.

Eremon laughed quietly, his gaze flicking down to Aidryn's ring before resting on her face again. "Well, I've already done that part." He laced his fingers together. "In all truthfulness, I don't know what was worse: dying, or waking to find that my Binding spell worked just as I intended it to."

Disbelief surged through Lira, followed by anger. "It was *your* spell, Eremon. If you didn't want it to work, you shouldn't have created it. That's yours to reckon with; I have peace."

Challenge flashed in his silver eyes. "Do you?"

"Yes," Lira said, holding his gaze. "I'm happy with Aidryn. You were right to create the spell—even though it infuriated me at first."

Eremon's brow knitted, and she thought she saw a hint of a smile cross his lips. "I know how much you like to have your decisions made for you."

His joke hit too close to home, and Lira bristled. He'd taken grievous liberties with her decisions, and with Aidryn's—and he knew it. After a moment, he added, "But the beauty is, I suppose you really made the decision yourselves. I just supplied the mechanism."

His words stung. The spell had been rigged to take hold only when Lira and Aidryn shared mutual love and acknowledged it. For Eremon to throw that in her face was as enraging as it was a relief, because that meant it was truly *him* who'd returned. Not some horrifying god-monster who would overpower the clans and conquer the whole of Rodhlan for himself, but the Eremon who would fight with them to save their land. The Eremon who had loved her—and clearly loved her, still. She sucked in a breath at the thought.

Before she could reply, Talfryn turned to them. "We're ready over here. I think Eremon needs to carry Oda—let her rest for a while."

"All right," Lira said. "We need to get her to Halgeir."

Talfryn raised his eyebrows. "How? We can't walk all that way."

"I don't know—we'll think of something," Lira said.

She and Talfryn helped to brace Oda as Eremon lifted her into his arms. Then, they made their way slowly toward the mouth of the catacombs again. No one said much as they trudged down the long, dark tunnel. When they emerged, dawn was breaking, and the soft meadow grass sparkled with dew. The air was chilly and humid.

Eremon took a deep breath when he stepped out of the tunnel, tilting his face toward the open sky. "Autumn," he sighed. "Of the same year? Or has it been longer?"

"Same year," Lira said. "You've been gone for some months."

"Months." Eremon made a noise at the back of his throat and shifted Oda in his arms. She'd dozed off against his chest halfway down the tunnel. His gaze slid down to Lira—hard and cold now. "Did you love him all along? Is that why you waited until I was dying in front of you to accept my proposal?"

"I refused because I didn't want the throne," she said. "I still don't."

"Then who is protecting my city?" He scoffed. "Not you, clearly."

"I barely survived after you died." Lira clenched her fists, her body trembling with rage. "If you'd been here to witness it yourself, you wouldn't say such stupid things."

"Then show me, Witness Tree." He glared at her angrily,

stepping closer despite the fact that he was still holding Oda. "I dare you."

"Will you two shut up?" Talfryn barked. Lira and Eremon stopped in their tracks, turning slowly to face him. His curly hair was wild, the color in his cheeks high. "You can sort out your quarrel once we've figured out what to do. Oh, and Eremon—you'll take care to hold your tongue if you can't show my sister respect."

"How dare you—"

"You're no longer the Rí," Talfryn snapped. "If anything, you should defer to *her*."

"Stop!" Lira shouted. "Just stop. I need to think."

The early morning wind ruffled her curls, now noticeably matted with sweat and dried blood. She dropped to her knees and braced her hands on the ground, hanging her head.

What should I do? I don't know what to do.

And then, Rodhlan reminded her of the spring. Of her wanderings in the meadowlands, in the days when her magic overflowed, out of control. Of a ballad she'd sung through Aidryn's magic, and the gray stallion who'd come to her rescue. In a tremulous voice, she began to sing, setting her intention on a horse that ran like the wind.

But not Fannin this time. A horse much nearer.

When the song was done, Lira stood slowly—expectantly. Eremon and Talfryn gaped.

"What was that?" Talfryn stepped nearer, as though truly seeing his sister for the first time. "When did you start singing?"

Her face heated and she crossed her arms. "Since I started using Aidryn's magic."

Eremon's jaw dropped. "You called his horses."

She inclined her head. "One of them."

He strained toward Iathium, as though listening intently. "Then why are two coming?"

"I..." Lira's heart began to pound, and she shook her head. What if Aidryn had managed to fall into enemy hands again?

How was it possible there could be two Itelorian stallions on the way?

"Speaking of Aidryn's magic," Talfryn said, fishing in the pouch on his belt, "I picked this up for you."

In his outstretched hand, he held Iuchair. Lira took it reverently, cradling it for a moment before she curled her fingers around it and allowed it to disappear into Aidryn's power. "Thank you."

Eremon looked off into the distance again. "The horses have riders." Alarmed, he looked to Talfryn. "You and Oda need to get out of sight."

Talfryn crouched, touching the ground. Immediately, trees and foliage sprang up around the mouth of the catacombs, with plenty of places for them to conceal themselves.

Oda opened her eyes and lifted her head. "I think I can walk to wherever we need to go," she said weakly.

With a nod, Eremon set her down. She swayed, her knees buckling, but he and Talfryn held her steady as they found a place to hide. By the time Eremon returned to her side, Lira could hear the pounding of the horses' hooves. She set her stance, adjusting her grip on Oda's axe.

Eremon looked to her curiously, drawing one of Faolan's swords. "When did you learn to handle a blade?"

"During the summer. Oda taught me."

He blinked several times, as though trying to reconcile the idea. Lira couldn't blame him. No one who had known her in her previous life would have anticipated this. "She seems like a remarkable person," he said.

"She is." Lira nodded. "And a good friend."

The horses came into view, galloping at top magical speed and stirring a cloud of dust in their wake. One of them was unmistakably Edan, with a wild-eyed Fiadh hanging on for dear life. The other was a smaller, chestnut horse Lira had never seen—and its rider was an equally unnerved Caitir.

"Whatever you hear," Lira said slowly, "pretend none of it

surprises you. You're in total control. Just follow my lead and I'll tell you everything when this is over."

"Diplomatic prowess," Eremon said, echoing an old sentiment of Irem's. The elderly lord had always believed Lira to be some great negotiator, but that felt laughable in retrospect. "Let's see it in action, then."

The horses halted before Lira and Eremon. Fiadh drew her sword. "What is the meaning of this?"

"Hold, Fiadh," Caitir said from her mount, motioning for the raven-haired woman to halt a few paces behind her.

Fiadh obeyed, though she looked ready to run Lira through. Her hair hung loose and wind-whipped.

"Fiadh," Lira said, raising her brows. "I was expecting the horses, but not the half-feral hounds they dragged with them."

"At least hounds know a rotting carcass when they see one," Fiadh snapped.

Caitir leered down at Lira, her golden hair bound in elaborate braids around her head—though the style had grown wild and frazzled on the ride. Her gaze darted to Eremon and she paled, eyes widening.

Eremon rested the flat of Faolan's blade on his shoulder and returned her stare wordlessly. Everything about his demeanor was perfectly steady. Calm. He didn't speak, but stared her down until she did.

"How..." Caitir blinked as though hoping to clear her vision. She laughed in disbelief. "Silira, what sort of trick is this? I've heard talk—I know you can project your power into images. You might as well give up the ruse."

"A ruse, am I?" Eremon asked, stepping nearer to the horses. He kept the blade on his shoulder, the corner of his mouth tugging up in a satisfied smirk. "Do I look like an illusion to you?"

Caitir's mare took a nervous step back as Eremon advanced on them. "Senga..." she warned quietly, keeping her eyes fixed on him.

Eremon closed the distance between them and snatched Senga's reins, holding the mount steady. He angled the tip of the sword against Caitir's cheek, and she froze, swallowing hard. "Does my blade feel like a mirage?" His voice was dangerously smooth, and so low it was nearly inaudible.

"My lady—" Fiadh began, her voice rising in alarm.

"Stop." Caitir said softly, going rigid, never taking her eyes from Eremon's face. "Don't move; don't breathe."

"That's right," Eremon crooned. "Unless you want that golden hair soaked in blood, you'll stay still and do as I say."

Caitir raised her chin defiantly. "You think you can order the wife of Rí Gerallt?"

"The wife of?" He tilted his head, applying pressure to the blade. "You mean *not* the Raní?"

"Widow, more like," Lira said, taking a step forward, "and no closer to the throne than before."

Caitir closed her eyes, taking a shallow, shaky breath. "You know *nothing*." Her expression relaxed. "I'm glad to be free of him."

Fiadh straightened in her saddle. "How did he die?"

"An arrow; dead by his daughter's hand," Lira answered.

Caitir shifted in her saddle, wincing. She smoothed her flowing, black tunic and looked down at her hands. "Good. He deserved worse."

They were all silent for a long moment. Lira's mind raced as she grasped for the next place to strike. "Was that horse part of your mother's reward for selling Rodhlan to Iteloria?"

"Senga was a *gift* from Iteloria," Caitir said slowly.

"I have a sneaking suspicion those gifts will stop, once they learn the power they sought is now unobtainable." Lira glanced at Eremon, whose expression was near unreadable. "You *do* realize his magic was never going to be yours, don't you? And you were right—I did come back for it. But I restored it to its rightful owner."

Caitir pressed her lips together, as though unsure of how to respond. *Good,* Lira thought. *Now we tighten the noose.*

"They used you, Caitir." Lira studied her former friend closely. "Over and over and over. They used you so terribly, and you don't even realize it."

Caitir looked as though she'd been struck. "You're not in my head, Silira. You don't know." Her voice was thick and hoarse, as though she was fighting back tears.

"But I could be." Lira felt a rush of power at the look of sheer horror on Caitir's face as she registered exactly what Lira was telling her. It felt heady and invigorating, almost like taking Iuchair from Corlan's vault. "My power is truth. As far as I'm concerned, your memories are fair game."

Eremon's attention snapped to her, and suddenly he was on high alert. "What in Nami's stinking tomb is *wrong* with you, Silira?"

"Sounds like someone's been tampering with her power." Caitir smirked. "Not so different, are we, Lira?"

Lira shook her head vehemently. "I'm nothing like you. I don't kill to steal magic from innocent clanspeople. I saw the Énna girl—I *know* what you did. You want people to love you, but you'll be sorely disappointed when they reject a magic-plundering murderer."

"Do you really think me some bloodthirsty killer?" Caitir looked from Lira to Eremon warily. "I would never take a life without purpose."

"Perhaps not," Lira conceded. "Maybe only when you need an ally. It's too bad your little experiment failed." She looked to Fiadh. "Still can't use any of that magic, can you? Pity. No wonder you always seemed heartless."

Fiadh nudged Edan forward a few paces, eyes wild with rage. "What is it to you? What do you want from us?"

Lira opened her mouth to retort again, but Eremon cut her off, shooting her a sharp look.

"Dismount," he said firmly. "We'll be taking the horses."

CHAPTER 47

AIDRYN

Va'hesk

Aidryn knelt in the dirt before the Assembly of Clan Tarlach, his hands bound tightly behind his back. The men and women before him spoke softly amongst themselves, occasionally glancing down at him as though he were merely in the way. An afterthought, a useless object to be discarded once they were finished with him.

His heart raced as he tried, again and again, to call the keys to him—just one. That was all he needed: one ridiculous key. Yet, he'd found himself entirely unable to access the magic at all for more than a day.

Terovi's men had overpowered and arrested Aidryn like a common thief. They took Fannin from him, setting the stallion loose with the herd of half-wild horses that roamed their territory. The overlord had kept Aidryn close, imprisoning him in his tent. Though Terovi saw to it that Aidryn was fed and allowed to take care of necessities, he didn't speak to him again until the next morning, when he'd burst into the tent and awakened Aidryn, practically dragging him out.

"Where are we going?" Aidryn had demanded.

"The assembly," Terovi had snarled. "They've asked to see you. It's not my choice, or I would let you rot."

Now, Aidryn waited for someone—anyone—in the assembly to take note of him. He felt like a complete fool, trusting in a people he had never truly known. Lira's stories about Nevala and Mytr had given him hope, but if Clan Tarlach was heartless enough to throw kind people like them to the wolves, then he wanted nothing more to do with them.

Lira. He sighed, shuddering. He wanted Lira—and to get as far away from this place as he possibly could.

"Boy—Aidryn, you say?" He snapped to attention, meeting the elderly woman's eyes. She wore teal robes, her silver hair falling in a long plait over her shoulder.

Most of the other members of the assembly were middle-aged to elderly, most were gray-haired, and all wore long robes. The fabric looked as though it had been dyed using the array of wildflowers that grew in the eastern meadowlands every spring. The robes' colors had dulled, the cloth careworn and battered by exposure to sand and wind.

"Yes." Aidryn's voice came out in a hoarse croak.

"I am Eiren," the woman said.

"That was my mother's name," Aidryn stammered.

"I knew your mother, and I remember your name," Eiren said. "When Terovi told us who you were, I could scarcely believe it."

His jaw dropped in disbelief. "Then why have I been treated as a criminal?"

"We felt it was best to prove you weren't a threat to the settlement. Yet, you have borne your treatment with great resilience, and almost no resistance." She leaned forward, her brown eyes shining with curiosity. "Why?"

"Because I have lived through worse at the hands of my stepmother and Gerallt Mór," he said, holding her steady gaze.

"I know what it's like to be tortured until you wish for death. In comparison, being tied up by your rope is merely an inconvenience until I decide how best to handle it."

"Why did you claim to be our anointed?"

"Because I am."

She blinked slowly. The corner of her mouth twitched, as though she was barely suppressing amusement. "Yet you were entirely unable to call upon your power when pressed."

"I expected Terovi to be asking all the questions," Aidryn answered. "Isn't he the overlord?"

Now, Eiren did laugh. "Is that what he told you? Terovi has always been quick to assume authority, though in this case, perhaps it was wise. I would have ordered you killed on the spot."

"Are you the overlord, then?"

"The adviser," she answered with a small smile. "Tell me, young Aidryn: what do you know of the conflict in the meadowlands?"

"The meadowlands?" he asked incredulously. "There was to be a conflict on the western coast, near Clan Énna's caravan. I came directly here from Fortress Halgeir; I did not ride out with Thorne Beran's army."

"Beran's army was split, though by what means, we cannot say. It appears to have been a strategic move." Aidryn's eyes darted from one member of the assembly to the next. Their expressions were infuriatingly well-masked as Eiren continued. "But we received word this morning that assassins from Clan Mór struck Gerallt down sometime over the past two days. There is talk that your wife was among them."

"That's not possible, she's—" But it *was* possible. He clamped his lips shut. She and Talfryn could have used *turas* to defy Thorne's orders. It wasn't outside the realm of possibility. "She shouldn't have been there."

Suddenly, he was struck with a deep, agonizing fear that

raked at his insides. He hadn't been able to detect her magic through the Binding since the morning before, nor access or control his own.

"A small castle on the western coast was overrun with vines and trees. They say it was pulled down into the sea, and that Gerallt's body was washed away in the rubble."

"That sounds like Lira's magic," Aidryn murmured, his heart beginning to pound.

"She hasn't been seen since that night."

His mind raced—he couldn't *think* beyond all the horrible possibilities. What could have possessed her to leave Rodhlan Ridge like that? Why had Thorne split the army? Had she been buried under the weight of a collapsed castle, washed out to sea with her uncle?

The questions overpowered him and he hung his head, breathing hard. Thorne had separated him from Lira to keep her safe, and—like she was prone to do—Lira had taken it upon herself to decide what was best. And now, she was likely dead for doing so.

"Lira," he groaned. The ache in his chest was too much to bear—and far worse than the arrow that had pierced him.

"Untie him, Terovi, for Rhona's sake," he heard Eiren say.

After a moment of grumbling, Terovi cut away the ropes that bound Aidryn's wrists. Aidryn took a long moment to gather himself before he rose. His wrists ached, his hands pricking as the feeling slowly returned to them.

"You are free to go, Aidryn Tarlach," Eiren said. "The assembly has determined your innocence and your will to do no harm to Va'hesk. You will go in peace. My men have already saddled your horse; he is just outside the tent."

Relief flooded Aidryn at the thought of going free, but he hesitated. "Can I not persuade your clan to help us?"

The adviser smiled sadly. "No. Go now, or we shall be forced to rescind our mercy."

"Thank you," he said, stepping toward the tent's flap. "I won't forget your mercy, Adviser Eiren."

When he stepped outside the tent and laid eyes on Fannin, he began to tremble with anticipation. If they were free to ride, then Aidryn was free to search for Lira. He paused at Fannin's side, stroking the stallion's mane and closing his eyes with a sigh.

Aidryn had not attempted to tap into Lira's power again since the morning before, but he called on it now, desperate for some clue she was safe. This time, her magic *did* respond—and he breathed a shaky sigh of relief.

"Come on, Fannin," he said, leading the horse down the pathway toward the meadowlands. "Let's go find Lira."

They passed through row after row of tents—some standing, others half-dismantled—on their way out of the settlement. Aidryn had not managed to draw out where the assembly wanted the clan to go next, but they certainly weren't ready to move yet.

When he and Fannin reached the edge of the settlement, he mounted and eased the stallion into a steady gait. But the sound of screams in the distance made him pause. He turned back to see plumes of black smoke billowing up from the center of the settlement. Tents were on fire—and in the dry, windy climate, they were burning as rapidly as straw.

Turning Fannin around, he prepared to re-enter the settlement at a gallop. But before he did, movement caught his eye. From the far southern end of the settlement emerged two riders bearing blazing torches. They discarded them in the tall grass, catching the meadow ablaze, too.

The riders wore the garb of Clan Beran, though they rode horses outfitted for Iathium's sentries. Aidryn's stomach turned as he realized who they were: Gidri and Mjit, two of the Beran warriors from his traveling company. Rage rippled through him and for a moment, he considered riding after them at top speed and putting his broadsword—the blade Terovi hadn't managed to warp—to good use. But the shrieks coming from the settlement were enough to make him forego the idea entirely.

Aidryn and Fannin raced back toward Va'hesk and into the rapidly-spreading blaze.

CHAPTER 48

LIRA

Meadowlands

"You can't take our horses," Fiadh snapped.

Challenge flashed in Eremon's eyes. He pressed the sword's tip just enough to slice a shallow cut in Caitir's cheek. She yelped as a trickle of blood made its way down the blade.

"Dismount," he repeated.

"Do it, Fiadh," Caitir hissed.

"You stay put, my lady," Fiadh said, swinging her leg over Edan's side and hopping down into the soft grass. "I'll help you." With a hand on the pommel of her sword, Fiadh started toward Senga.

Eremon stopped her in her tracks with a glare. "She can get herself down."

Fiadh looked panicked as she glanced between Eremon and Caitir. "But—"

"Don't. Argue."

Caitir gripped Senga's saddle and dismounted slowly, grimacing as though in pain. When she'd planted both feet firmly on the ground, she pressed a hand to the cut on her cheek, looking stunned. Eremon backed Senga several paces away and handed her reins to Lira. He clicked his tongue and Edan approached him without hesitation.

"Call your brother," he told Lira, holding Faolan's blade steady as she took Edan's reins, too. "Send them ahead of us."

Talfryn emerged from his hiding place, then helped Oda to her feet. The two approached Lira warily, keeping their eyes on Caitir and Fiadh.

"Look at you, Talfryn." Caitir pursed her lips. "Between you and the mangled Beran pup, I'd say you make one complete person."

Lira sucked in a sharp breath.

"*Don't* respond," Eremon said sharply.

Talfryn ignored the slight. Lira held Senga steady and helped her brother boost Oda into the saddle. "I don't like this," he whispered to Lira. "I don't want to leave you alone with them."

"You don't have a choice, Tal." Lira patted Oda's knee gently. "Try to lie forward on her if you can. Riding is going to hurt, but Talfryn needs his hand to hold the reins. Just hang on, please."

Oda shimmied forward, grimacing. "I need you to take my sword. Take the whole bandolier. It's not like I—" She sucked in a sharp breath through her teeth. "I can't fight anyway."

Lira and Talfryn helped her remove her belt and bandolier, taking care to gingerly lift the weapons away from her body. Once that was done, Lira donned the blades herself.

Talfryn swung up into Senga's saddle and looked down at Lira, his brow creased. "Get yourself out of here quickly. Promise me."

"I promise." Lira patted Senga's hindquarters as they began to move.

Her brother cast one more wary glance before clicking his tongue to coax the chestnut mare into an easy trot. The mare turned in the direction of Clan Beran's territory. Lira wished she could watch until they disappeared from view.

"It's not hard to guess where they're going," Fiadh said, moving to stand between Eremon and Caitir. "Pity we can't set fire to Halgeir, too."

Lira stalked toward her, halting at Eremon's side. "What are you talking about?"

Suddenly, Caitir looked pale. A little smile ghosted across Fiadh's mouth for a brief moment before she glanced off toward the east. "You'll figure it out."

Instinctively, Lira turned her back on them. In the direction of Va'hesk, she could see a great, black plume of smoke. But before she could react, she felt someone shove her—hard. She stumbled several paces before whirling to see Eremon clash blades with Fiadh.

"What did you do?" Lira demanded, dropping Edan's reins and charging toward Fiadh with the axe.

Fiadh grinned gleefully, turning from Eremon to meet Lira's blade. "Isn't it obvious?"

Lira faltered, and Fiadh disarmed her easily, knocking the axe into the grass. Her mind raced. There was too much happening all at once. And Aidryn—*Aidryn* was out there at Va'hesk, and now the settlement was burning.

Fiadh seized Lira, holding her blade to her throat. Lira froze, panic swelling in her chest. "It wasn't hard to persuade a few of those dense warriors to take a little extra kindling with them," Fiadh said.

"And it wasn't hard to get my blade under your lady's chin," Eremon replied coolly.

Fiadh whirled, releasing Lira, who gave her a wide berth and turned toward Eremon's voice. Sure enough, Eremon had seized Caitir and was now holding Faolan's sword to her throat.

"You really should work on staying focused in a fight," he said.

"Let her go," Fiadh said, her voice low—yet desperate, somehow.

"What exactly are you protecting?" Eremon tightened his

grip on Caitir, and she cried out. "Not her, certainly—a sniveling little beast playing dress-up in my mother's silks."

"Fiadh," Caitir cried.

Her companion slowly moved closer. Eremon kept a steady gaze trained on her every move.

Lira hung back, recalling her last encounter with Caitir in the spring, when she and Thorne had rescued Aidryn. Caitir had used her dark magic with abandon. She calculated the months—it might have been weeks later, perhaps, when she'd stolen that power for Fiadh. But since then?

It wasn't unusual for Caitir to rely on others to perpetuate her own rottenness. Aila had always filled that role. But there was something more to this.

Caitir's eyes were wide with terror. As Eremon shifted his grip on her and re-angled his sword, she tensed and swallowed hard. Lira did not miss the way her hand drifted to her belly.

"Eremon, she's with child," Lira breathed.

A wild laugh broke from Caitir's lips, forcing Eremon to let up on the blade. He released her and took a step back, but she did not fight him. "Yes, I carry the late Rí's only heir, and I will secure the throne for him—you can be sure of that."

"Lofty goals from someone who couldn't wrangle herself a crown," Lira snapped.

She was tired of this sparring—this *waiting*. Aidryn was on the other side of the continent, likely in grave danger, yet she was forced to keep her thoughts here and now.

"What are *you* going to do about it, Silira, Heir of All Things?" Caitir mocked. "And you, Eremon—risen from the dead, yet with no throne at all."

"We're taking Eremon's throne back," Lira said. Eremon raised his eyebrows, though the gesture was almost imperceptible.

Caitir narrowed her eyes. "Are you, now? What do you think Iathium will have to say about an infinitely powerful immortal seizing its throne? A being who might never die, securing the city for all eternity? Sounds a bit suspect."

She maneuvered just enough to face Eremon, taking in his face, his form. "You're terrifyingly beautiful," she whispered, as though in awe. "The throne is unworthy of *you*."

"Then perhaps you should keep it for now," he said, peering down at her, "if it is so far beneath me."

Lira worked her jaw, unsure of how to respond. His silver gaze flicked to her; clearly, he knew he'd struck a nerve.

"My lady," Fiadh said tersely, sheathing her sword, "let's get you home." She stepped closer to link arms with Caitir, but froze, her gaze falling to the sword Eremon held, then flicking to the second blade sheathed on his back. "What are you doing with my brother's swords?"

Eremon looked at her steadily, but didn't answer. Immediately, Fiadh whirled on Lira again, though she did not draw her blade.

"Faolan was with you, wasn't he?" she demanded. "Where is he now? And why does this abomination have his *swords*?"

Lira couldn't mask the grief she felt at the mention of her friend's name. Fiadh recognized it immediately, for her expression crumpled for a split second before she schooled it into rage.

"He's dead, isn't he." It was more of a statement than a question. Fiadh began to nod, her movements erratic, uncontrolled. "He died protecting *you*."

"Fiadh..." Caitir warned.

But Fiadh had already lunged at Lira, knocking her onto the ground. Lira wasn't prepared for the blow; the impact knocked the wind from her. As she struggled to fill her lungs again, Fiadh managed to pin her, wrapping her hands around Lira's throat and pressing down.

Lira grasped the sleeves of Fiadh's black doublet, struggling to break the woman's grip. Her pulse was pounding so hard— so *slow*—in her head and eyes that she accomplished little. It was as though she'd entirely forgotten her training with Oda. Above her, Fiadh was screaming, but her voice grew farther and farther away.

A dark figure knocked Fiadh off balance, and Lira gasped and coughed as the world around her rushed back into stark relief, the sky above her so bright her eyes ached. She felt a pulling sensation around her neck. Fiadh's fingers were wrapped around Lira's pendant now, and she was tugging as though she intended to yank the necklace right off.

"No," Lira rasped, clamping her hand onto Fiadh's. The young woman's dark eyes went wide, and a surge of her dark magic poured first into the pendant, and then into Lira.

Fiadh's corrupted power tore through Lira's body. She had never felt such a terrible, burning pain—had only felt a ghost of it when she'd witnessed it in her visions. Its sheer wrath ripped a tattered scream from Lira's throat and she convulsed on the ground as it dissipated, wholly out of control of her own body.

When it was over, the meadow around her was quiet. Her ears rang, overpowering the sounds of nature she might otherwise be able to hear. She felt strangely disconnected from her body, as though she were hovering somewhere above it.

A gentle touch pulled her back down, and she worked her jaw as if to speak. But there was a voice...

"*Lira—Lira. The words—you have to wake up so you can tell them to me!*"

The voice wouldn't let her get a word in edgewise, and besides, she couldn't remember what she'd wanted to say. So she closed her mouth again, and closed her eyes.

CHAPTER 49

AIDRYN

Va'hesk

Within an hour, Va'hesk was reduced to charred remains. Aidryn had doubled back, helping to usher settlers out of the blaze as quickly as possible. When he was satisfied they'd cleared the camp of people, he had called on his magic to direct their horses out of the pasture and away from the fire. Now, families were painstakingly accounting for spouses, children, grandparents, and grandchildren a safe distance from the flames.

He sat alone beside Fannin on a bare patch of dry, sandy ground, his body covered in soot, the reek of smoke clinging to his nostrils. Wildfire still burned in the grasses surrounding the settlement. The wind was blowing the fire eastward, toward the coast. Aidryn prayed it would not shift back into the meadowlands. Gazing off toward Rodhlan Ridge, he thought of Lira, hoping she had returned to her grandmother's valley.

Terovi, Eiren, and the rest of the assembly were huddled together not far from where he sat with Fannin. Though Terovi had mentioned plans to move the settlement, it was clear they hadn't yet been ready. And Aidryn happened to know of a once-populated clan territory in need of families.

With a nervous breath, he rose, leading Fannin to where the assembly stood with their own mounts. They all acknowledged him as he approached, and Eiren inclined her head.

"You returned to help us when you were free to take your leave," the adviser said. "Thanks to you, we lost none of our settlers or the Seanlaoch. For that, you have our gratitude."

"I accept your gratitude," Aidryn replied, "but there's one more thing I need to ask you for."

Eiren peered at him curiously, stepping nearer to him. "And what is that?"

Aidryn opened his palm and closed his eyes, seeking his magic. It surged to life within him, as warm and familiar as ever, and he had to fight to suppress the joyful grin that nearly spread across his face. His thoughts snagged on the image of an ornate, golden key, and a moment later, it appeared in his hand.

"Your trust," he finally answered, opening his eyes to find every member of the assembly gaping at him. The wind ruffled Fannin's mane, and the afternoon sun warmed Aidryn's skin. He had dearly missed spending so much time beneath the open sky.

Terovi locked eyes with Aidryn immediately. "You *are* the Key Keeper."

"I am," Aidryn said, running his thumb over the key. Its weight, its sheer power, felt wonderful in his hand—as though it was always meant to be his.

Eiren reached out to brush her fingers reverently over the golden key, then raised her face to Aidryn. Her demeanor suddenly seemed more like that of an acolyte than an elder of the clan.

"And this," she breathed, "is Iuchair."

The full weight of the word—its *implications*—pummeled Aidryn, and he sank to his knees, stunned.

CHAPTER 50

EREMON OF IATHIUM

Meadowlands

"Lira." Eremon crawled to her side and grasped her shoulders, shaking her. "Lira, can you hear me?"

She was pale and limp, eyes open but unseeing—and still breathing. Purple bruises were already forming around her throat, and her face was mottled with tiny, red-black markings the size of pinpricks where blood had risen to the surface of her skin. The wound on the side of her head had finally clotted, and her dark curls were matted with dried blood.

Fiadh had snatched the pendant from around Lira's neck, and Caitir had used it to *turas*. She'd pulled a pin from her hair and pressed it to the bronze tree, meeting Eremon's dark stare one last time before the spell swallowed them up. The thought of her eerie, pale blue eyes made him shudder—even more than the look of contempt on her unnervingly beautiful face.

He shook off the memory and nudged Lira again, calling her name. Why hadn't his ring protected her from that surge of dark magic? He grasped her hand, scrutinizing the ancient ring, and his heart sank. At some point, its stone had cracked down the middle.

"Why didn't you show this to me?" Eremon demanded. Lira blinked, as though struggling to understand his words. "I could have helped you. Nami's rotting *bones*, fixing this stupid ring is one of the only things I know how to do properly."

Lira would have perceived the ring's damage as some personal slight on her part—as though, by breaking it, she had failed him in some way. But he had cracked the stone more than once himself, trying to imbue it with protective magic for her. And each time, he had managed to repair it.

He closed his eyes and sent a bright flare of cobalt power into the stone, sealing the crack and filling it with magic once again. But his power met resistance when he tried to extend the protection beyond her, back through the Binding to Aidryn. Perhaps Fiadh's surge of power *had* broken the ring beyond his ability to repair it completely.

Lira still didn't answer, even through the flare of magic and the frustrated string of curses he uttered as he worked on the ring. If he'd known how to use his new power properly, he would undoubtedly have been able to heal her himself. As it was, there was no one to teach him how it worked. It was all trial and error, and so far, he was barely scraping by with what he'd been able to figure out on his own.

Eremon pulled Lira's head into his lap and pressed his hand to her cheek. She blinked rapidly, but never focused her gaze on him.

"We have an Itelorian stallion, Lira," he said, patting her. Still, no response. "Aren't there magical words to make Fannin run like the wind? I don't know them! But if you have Aidryn's magic, then *you* do."

He felt the side of her throat for a pulse. It was there, but faint.

"Lira—*Lira*," he pleaded, shaking her gently. "The words—

you have to wake up so you can tell them to me—so we can get you help. Please, Lira."

She opened her mouth as if to answer, then shut it. Her eyelids fluttered closed, her long lashes fanning over her pale cheeks.

"Lira!" Eremon shook her again, harder this time. "Don't do this—wake up."

She didn't stir.

Help. Help!

With a sinking feeling, Eremon realized he didn't know where to take her, or which direction to ride. He'd gleaned that Lira's allies were scattered and displaced, which meant his old allies were, too.

Caitir's words had shaken him to the core, though he'd tried his best to mask how profoundly they had affected him.

What do you think Iathium will have to say about an infinitely powerful immortal seizing its throne? A being who might never die, securing the city for all eternity?

The meadowlands warped around him as the word finally found its mark.

Immortal.

There was no time to square with exactly what that meant, or what he had become by transcending death. He did not belong on the mortal throne, but Lira had brought him back to take it.

She'd had no other reason to come back for him.

Now, she could be dying. The realization sent a cold dread through him, and he brushed his fingertips over her cheek.

"Sweet Lira," he groaned, smoothing her hair back from her face. "I need you to wake so we can argue about this stupid throne."

Eremon was dismayed to realize that immortality did nothing to soothe the feeling of panic that tore through him. The helplessness. What good was his seemingly bottomless well of power if he couldn't use it to fix this?

Carefully, he lay Lira's head in the soft grass and clicked his tongue for Edan. The stallion approached, halting beside them. Eremon gathered Lira into his arms and hefted her up and over the massive horse's back. He climbed up behind her, shifting her limp form until she was astride the stallion, too, her head lolling against his chest. Until she awakened, they would have to ride slowly—but at least they could begin.

Eremon skimmed the horizon, his gaze landing on the great plume of smoke in the east. He looped an arm around Lira's middle and nudged Edan into an easy trot. Va'hesk was where Aidryn was supposed to be—assuming he was still alive in the aftermath of the blaze. If Lira would wake for anyone, she would wake for him.

~

THE END

Notes & Acknowledgements

What an adventure! *Keeper of Keys* was an absolute joy to write. This story has my whole heart... especially Aidryn and Lira's romance. (Of course, if you spend any time talking to me about these characters, you'll also know that Eremon is currently shouting at me and vying for his own moment in the spotlight.)

It was difficult to keep Eremon's return secret through the many months I spent writing this installment in the series. (Well—I'm not going to pretend I didn't spill the beans a few times.) I fell in love with him when I first wrote him into *Defender of Histories*, and it was profoundly sad to say goodbye, even for a little while. I'm so excited to tell more of his story in book 3.

I cannot adequately express the gratitude I have for my family, friends, editors, artists, and readers who have come alongside me on this journey.

To Grant - thank you for supporting and encouraging me when I need to hunch over my desk for long hours to meet deadlines.

To Ellery - thank you for the contagious excitement and enthusiasm you have for these books. I promise, you can read them when you're a little older. :)

To Allie & Jo - thank you for helping me make this story the absolute best it could be. Your guidance has been infinitely valuable in developing these characters and their stories.

To Elisabeth - thank you for the in-depth, all-hours chats about characters, plot points, themes, and nuances. You were instrumental in helping me shape the final draft of this story.

To Elisabeth & Tim - thank you for beta-reading the second draft chapter-by-chapter, keeping me on my toes, and calling me out when you spotted mistakes in the writing.

To Christa & Mika - thank you for being my cheerleaders, enablers, and enthusiastic readers of rough-draft scenes. You've been a constant source of encouragement and inspiration. (Mika, I will forever think of you when I re-read the scene where Aidryn walks in on Lira.)

To Micheline - thank you for the beautiful interpretation of Lira's gown in your art. Your open-shoulder design inspired quite a few humorous and romantic scenes throughout this story that wouldn't exist without you.

To my readers and reviewers who have been part of my ARC team and online community, THANK YOU for your excitement and support for these stories. I can't wait to share the next installment with you!

- Haley

THE SAGA CONTINUES IN
VOW OF MAGIC...

HALEY WALDEN

VOW OF MAGIC

THE WITNESS TREE
CHRONICLES

VOW OF MAGIC
THE WITNESS TREE CHRONICLES, BOOK 3

When the saviors fear themselves, hope loses its spark.

Tense, enthralling, and laced with intrigue, readers love this epic fantasy tale of deception, redemption, and a forbidden romance that could topple a kingdom.

The world has transformed since Lira saved Eremon. Terrified of his own vast power, he resists his friends' urging to take his kingdom back from the tyrants who conquered it.

Instead, Eremon sets out to spy on Caitir, the woman who covets his crown, intent on gathering allies and sabotaging her efforts. But their undeniable attraction to one another entangles them in a scheme that could forever destroy his right to the throne.

Meanwhile, Lira is fighting a secret battle against dark magic that's slowly tearing her from those she loves most. Isolated, frightened, and desperate for Eremon to save the throne, she spirals down a destructive path that could spell doom for them all.

Relationships unravel, loyalties splinter, and the stakes are higher than ever. And with an enemy kingdom setting its sights on the continent, time is quickly running out.

Will Lira, Eremon, and their friends find the courage to conquer their inner darkness, reunite, and forge new bonds before their world is destroyed?

Vow of Magic is the mesmerizing, multi-POV third installment of *The Witness Tree Chronicles*.

~

Find *Vow of Magic* (*The Witness Tree Chronicles, Book 3*) at your favorite online book retailer.

Learn more:
authorhaleywalden.com

ABOUT THE AUTHOR

Haley Walden writes fast-paced, character-driven epic fantasy with magical adventures, spellbinding love stories, and unforgettable friendships. As a multi-passionate geek she has many obsessions, including music, martial arts, history, pop culture, and musical theatre. She lives in Alabama with her husband and children.

www.authorhaleywalden.com

THANK YOU!

Enjoyed what you read? Please leave a review on Goodreads or the retailer of your choice.

Reviews help readers like you discover new stories, characters, and worlds they'll love.

(Eremon would appreciate *heavy hinting* about the status of everyone's favorite monarch. This request is part of my penance for *Defender* chapter 15. You know the one—and he does, too.)